MW01168607

This Is a work of fiction. The characters represented in this book are entirely fictional. Any resemblance to actual persons living or dead is entirely coincidental, apart from those who gave prior permission to use their likeness.

First Paperback edition February 2023

Book Design by L. Douglas Hogan

THE COMPOUND:
A POSTAPOCALYPTIC TALE OF URBAN SURVIVAL

BY: B.J. GARCIA

Intro:

Kankakee, Illinois
70 miles south of Chicago –
April 10th–2025

In every possible way, Police Officer First Class John "Johnny" Gonzalez was average. Not "average," like normal; just slightly above-average, non-fancy generic white bread. He was good at a lot of things but never exactly amazing at any one thing. He was well aware of what he thought was his own mediocrity. John was always halfway decent at some things, but never enough to be the best. It was how he had lived his life. He was an extremely intelligent kid growing up, but not enough to graduate Valedictorian of his high school, instead finishing in the top ten. He was a talented athlete, but not enough to stand out to the college scouts. He always seemed to find himself the "B-Team All-Star." He was aware that he wasn't exactly normal, but never enough to be great. He thought this would change when he joined the Army National Guard at age eighteen during the waning years of America's long overdrawn "Global War on Terror" that had spanned nearly three decades. As an Infantryman, he learned a lot but never seemed to make a great soldier, instead watching his friends and peers get promoted ahead of him. After a short and boring career with no real combat or deployments, he got out of the military. He joined the Kankakee City Police Department, hoping to make a difference in his hometown. He found a real passion for law enforcement, despite his complex Libertarian political beliefs. John enjoyed the idea of strong men protecting weaker people from getting taken advantage of or hurt. He even enjoyed following in the footsteps of his father, a local police legend, who had spent nearly half a century as a police officer. John's father often told him growing up that "God made strong men to protect those who are not as fortunate."

Now here John was, almost ten years later. This was the time when most people had gotten promoted or sent to specialty assignments. John started out a hard-charger, making detective after only five years. After a few years with the sex crimes unit, he found himself getting burned out, as most do, and elected to go back to patrol, hoping to reinvigorate his love for the job. That shit wasn't all "Law and Order: SVU" he used to tell friends who asked him about work.

He'd had an uneventful day on this overtime shift so far, which he was thankful for as he walked a brief foot patrol. Police work had been changing rapidly in recent years to combat the uptick in violent crime, which was directly correlated to the current economic uncertainty that had been plaguing the country. John was almost glad that police work had shifted from enforcing what he saw as "dumb" drug laws and traffic enforcement toward responding to the monumental increase of homicides, robberies, and rape. He always thought that was more important than the "proactive policing" methods of strict drug enforcement and traffic stops.

John was thankful that his job paid well enough to maintain a good lifestyle; it also allowed him to set aside extra money for any uncertain times. Recently, the city had been steadily increasing its budget, officer salaries, and overtime availability. John had been taking full advantage of overtime. He had always been a workaholic, taking on multiple overtime shifts, side jobs, and contracts for security companies as allowed by his department. In ten years, his hard work ethic had paid off, putting John in very fortunate financial circumstances, much more so than most single men in their early thirties.

His mind wandered as he thought about the most recent shipment of silver bullion, ammunition, and freeze-dried survival food that had arrived at his house a few days prior. He had ordered a lot extra this paycheck because of another steady decline in the stock market that had him more worried than usual. A few podcasts he listened to had also been mentioning much higher inflation rate than the mainstream media had been reporting. The Eight percent they had been talking about was suspected to be almost double that number. He'd been wise enough to prepare in case of anything thrown his way. A hazard of his profession was paranoia, hypervigilance, and constant situational awareness of his environment. Most people just thought of it as pure paranoia. When talking to friends, John would casually speak of many "What if?" scenarios. Although he was careful to mask the most extreme of his worries, he was still often chastised by casual acquaintances for being a "total Debbie downer." John hadn't fully embraced the label of "Prepper," although he was fully aware that he was one. His "hobbies"—shooting and collecting guns and ammo and saving precious metals and long-term storage food—were as important to him as those directly involving his career.

John's mind shifted back to work. He had been trying to walk more foot patrol, as he had been gaining way too much weight lately and he was beginning to realize that his thirties were not going to be kind to a former athlete who didn't enjoy working out.

He finished his walk around the downtown block and paused to look up at the sun shining off the tall public library Highrise through his Oakley sunglasses. "Well shit, it's still beautiful after all these years," he exclaimed out loud. It stood out like a beacon of light in a town that had taken its hard knocks during the ups and downs of this recent economic roller coaster the United States had been subjected to over the past two decades. He took a deep breath and got back into his squad car, deciding to grab another coffee from the Dunkin Donuts at the gas station a couple blocks down. The sun would go down soon, and nightfall was when the city would start to get popping with shootings, robberies, and domestic violence calls. He listened to a podcast in his squad car as he drove a couple blocks. Joe Rogan was interviewing a financial venture capitalist named Peter Schiff, one of John's favorite financial gurus because of his love for precious metals for stability during financial instability in stock markets.

John pulled in through the back way and parked his squad car in the large Gas N Wash station's side lot. He stepped out, hardly paying attention as he walked to the corner of the building. He was looking down at his cell phone when he heard the words squawk from his radio that would forever change his life: "ALL CITY UNITS, SHOTS FIRED. POSSIBLE ROBBERY IN PROGRESS—GAS AND WASH, SUSPECT OFFENDER TWO BLACK MALES WEARING ALL BLACK—"

John looked up at the doors just as the two described subjects came out holding their Hi-point pistols. They immediately turned and looked at him, raising their guns and cracking off rounds at him. As quickly as he could, while caught off guard, he dropped his cell phone and thumbed off the thumb break safety on his Safariland level III duty holster, which held his Springfield 1911. He was able to "clear leather" as the first shots from the Hi-Points zipped past him. He let off a few rounds from the hip before finally getting a good sight picture on one of the subjects. Everything felt like slow motion as he lined up the tritium night sights on the first man's chest and let a pair of rounds loose. He could see the .45 ACP hollow-point rounds tear a hole through the man's chest. He was attempting to get his sights on the next man as he felt the hot burning sensation in the left side of his neck. It threw his next two shots off as the slide locked back. It was then that a stray round hit his head, and the world went black...

CHAPTER 1: THE RECKONING

In The Hospital—Approximately Six Weeks Later.

John awoke to tremendous pain. Everything felt fuzzy. As his senses slowly came back to him, he heard a quiet newscast on what appeared to be a report on the economy. He normally would have rolled his eyes at the idea of listening to any one of the shitty news channels as the reporters droned on about the awful things in the world. He didn't like it, seeing as how he saw the most negative side of the world on a daily basis. However, as he became more alert, he noticed the newscaster's words: "Inflation has risen to substantial levels...As the unemployment levels continue to rise...Stock markets in danger of crashing...UN and EU advisors being called upon by Congress...The President has come under fire by Democratic congressmen and women again..."

John snapped back to reality as the TV was shut off. His blurry eyes attempted to focus on the blurrier figure who had stepped into the room.

The nurse cleared her throat and said, "Well, now...look who's awake. Let me go see if I can find the doctor."

A short time later, a different nurse returned, looking tired and haggard as she came close. The faint smell of cigarettes rose from her when she leaned in toward John's face. She peered closely into his eyes, looking at the bandages on the side of his neck. "Six weeks, Doctor. Not too bad for this kind of trauma. We all knew he was a fighter," she said to the older man who had quietly but quickly shuffled in behind her.

He gave a slight smile and said, "Let's make sure he takes it slow, Helen. Get me vitals and a report later. I'll look over his charts when I get a chance. Too many damn patients here. You'd think it would have gotten better with so many insurance companies going under...But people don't stop getting sick no matter if the money runs out...." The doctor trailed off and wandered towards the door, still muttering to himself.

A page come over the intercom: "Doctor Harrison to Emergency Room for another Trauma. Third doctor call. Third doctor call."

"Dammit," he said. "Another gunshot wound. There's three doctors down there already. I'm not a goddamn trauma surgeon..." he complained again, taking off at a slow jog toward the elevators.

"How long have I been out?" John weakly asked the nurse. "The last thing I remember is..." he trailed off, groaned from the pain, and raised his hand to clutch his head as the sharp pain returned.

"Take it easy now, son," the nurse said, intercepting his hand before he reached his bandaged head. "You were unconscious for over six weeks. They brought you in, and you were already unconscious when they rushed you to surgery. You damn near died, kid. I suppose I should contact someone from your department and let them know you're awake. They'll want to talk to you. Get some rest; you've done too much already today."

He had no problem drifting back into a deep sleep. Whatever drugs they were giving him were sure as hell working well.

When he woke up again, it appeared to be early in the morning. He didn't know how long he had been out. He reached up to rub his eyes when he heard, "About fucking time, Gonzalez. I've been up here for a couple hours every day since they told me you'd woken up. You're one lucky bitch."

"Big Sarge? Hey man. What are you doing here?" John asked slowly as he looked up at the fifty-something heavily overweight sergeant from the detective bureau

Sergeant Simmons grinned down at him. "What the fuck do you think, man? You got into a shooting, John. I've been trying to get your statement. But lucky for you, your punkass was out for so long, Internal Affairs, the State Police Shooting Integrity unit, and the judge already ruled on it. You've been cleared of any wrongdoing. You don't even need to talk to a Union Rep, you lucky bitch! One of those mope fucks died on site. The other is still in the wind, though. Sorry to tell ya."

"I don't remember shit, Sarge. Everything is still fuzzy."

The sergeant adjusted his belt under his large belly and said, "It's okay, buddy. I went through this shit when I had only two years on in '93. It was just as bad back then as it is now. Except now, you tack on this shit economy. At least back then, we could blame Clinton. We get a few Republicans in office to give us hope, and they still manage to fuck things up...Anyways, you just heal up. Take your time, kid. Don't try and rush back to work. Shit's getting messy out there. The economy is only getting worse, and this town is a ticking time bomb. We got a hold of your parents when this happened. They were out West with your older brother. They're probably at your house now, though. At least your old man had enough sense to retire at the right time. I got one more month 'til I turn in my retirement papers myself. But anyways, I'll give your family a call and let them know you're awake...and still fucking retarded...." He clapped John on the shoulder gently before turning around and waddling out of the room.

It wasn't long before Helen the old nurse came back in, looking more haggard than before. She gave him a weak smile and said, "You're looking more spry than ever. You even have a little more color in your face." She slowly changed the dressing on his neck. "Your neck is looking good. It was a bit more shallow a wound than we thought. Nicked the artery but didn't bleed much. They got to you pretty fast, from what I hear. Now this one, on the other hand," she said, motioning to the side of his head, "the bullet ricocheted off the side of your skull. It looked way worse than it was, bleeding all over the place. Took a small chunk off of your skull too. That is what I suspect rendered you unconscious for so long. Put you in a coma. It's healing up nicely, though. I think we can have you up and out of this bed in another month, probably less. The city's insurance company isn't exactly happy paying for all this. Now, if you'll excuse me, we're packed to the gills with patients and short-staffed. I've got fourteen other patients I need to see to on this wing alone...With the insurance companies withholding payments, the hospital has been laying off nurses and CNAs. Two nurses on our floor took early retirement, and I've got two months left until I can do the same..."

A short time later, he heard the footsteps in the hall and the click of the cane on the tile floor. He knew who was coming, and it put a smile on his face. A minute or two later, his father stood in the doorway with a big smile on his face. The once-over-300-pound bear of a man looked weathered and weakening but still held that piercing smile and kindness in his eyes that everyone knew was sincere. He limped over to his son and put his weathered old paw on his shoulder. "I'm glad you're alive, son. Your Mom and I were so damn worried about you. In case I never told you, I'm proud of you. Your mom is parking the car; she'll be up in a minute. I was supposed to wait for her, but you know I couldn't. Sergeant Simmons called me and told me you were awake...He said something about brain damage, but we all know that was from before." He cracked a smirk at his son and continued: "Oh, and don't worry, we've been taking care of your house and your affairs while you've been laid up. Your mother still loves your dog more than me."

As if on cue, John heard the elevator doors open with a little ding. He heard the slow steps down the hall until his mother's short frame appeared in the doorway. The warm smile that glowed with the brightness of the sun broke over her face. "My baby boy!" she exclaimed as she slowly shuffled over to him. She threw her arms around him and began to sob lightly. "Jesus Christ, we were so worried about you! That was the worst phone call we could have ever gotten. We hustled out from Oregon back here. You were still unconscious when we got here. I'm just go glad you're alive! Anyways, I'll go see if I can get you some coffee and food." She pinched her husband's cheek and shuffled off again.

His father groaned as he lowered himself into the chair next to John's bed. Looking up at the muted news on the TV, he said, "It's getting pretty bad out there, son."
"How bad, Dad? How bad is it getting?"

"Well, kid, you know I never sugar-coated things to you. You're too smart for that. It's getting really damn bad. I think the economy is going to crash soon. Even the mainstream news started using the big bad 'R' word...I started to pay attention when I heard the word Recession. I think all hell is gonna break loose. I figured it would when I sold our house here two years ago and put the money into our camper and rig. I convinced your mom to stay out in Oregon with your brother. I always knew you were better prepared if shit went sideways. I figured we could stay close to your brother and ride it out with him. Don't tell your mother, though. I don't want her to worry about things any more than she already does."

His father sighed again, looking away toward the TV, then continued, "I took the liberty of looking over your house. I paid your bills a little ahead from some of our savings. The money is starting to not be worth as much anymore. I cashed your last few month's paychecks and put them into a bunch of that silver you like and ammo for all your guns. A little went to food and some batteries and supplies. The truth is: You need to get back up and running. I'm going to liquidate most of our savings to put into our own equipment. But the way things are, we need to get back to your brother in Oregon. He and his wife need us more. They've got the little baby twins to think about now, and you can handle yourself. We will stick around long enough to get you on your feet, but we need to get out before things get any worse and we can't travel. I know that's a lot to put on you, given what you've been through, but it's just the way things have to be."

John was still trying to process everything that was going on. His head hurt, but if things were getting as bad as everybody made them sound, he still had a lot of work to do. He looked around and saw his cell phone on a table beside him. He reached over and picked it up, turning the phone on. It started buzzing and dinging with notifications. John answered and sent some texts, instead focusing on logging on to some of his favorite websites and ordering supplies furiously. He checked his bank account and ordered more food, ammo, and supplies. He noticed warnings on all the sites advising of "inventory shortages" and "lengthened shipping times." John paid extra for expedited shipping fees regardless. He realized he had been intently working on his phone and not paying attention to his dad. He set the phone down and returned to the conversation.

"The doctor says I'm making pretty good progress. I think I can be out of here in a few weeks. I'm just going to be dealing with the balance issues and migraines that probably won't ever go away. I think I can push it, and I need to get things into gear around here. There's work to be done."

His dad said, "At least they didn't pressure you to retire. Those fucking crooks in City Hall. Too busy embezzling grant money and gambling away our pensions to give a damn about us...Remember eight years ago when I got stabbed in the side, and the insurance said they were paying too much for me to continue the rehab? They pushed me to have that emergency surgery to be a quicker fix than all the rehab. All I got out of that crock of shit was this cane and never walking the same again." He motioned to his cane.

John said, "At least it finally forced you to retire, old man. When your youngest son is working in the department with you, it's time to get out of there before you become a dinosaur. You were already older than the whole day shift patrol. Only Old Sarge Wayne had you beat with time in service."

His dad said, "Yes, it was the right time, but I just wanted to go out on my own terms."

John's dad, Richard 'Rich' Gonzalez, had been one of the oldest police officers in the department ten years ago when John was hired as a rookie. "El Oso Viejo," as many of the city's Hispanic citizens called him, was the very first Hispanic police officer ever hired back in the early 1970s. He had spent over twenty years as a homicide detective until a new chief had pushed him back out onto patrol to pressure him into retiring. Rich went back to day shift patrol without complaint for two years, while his son was on the midnight shift, having just started with the department. Eight years ago, he got stabbed in the side near his spine by a felon during an altercation at a domestic violence call and was forced to medically retire by the City Administration.

      The next few weeks were a blur for John. Physical therapy and endless medicines, but progress was made nonetheless. Things were getting worse on the outside, which made his situation more pressing. The coming weeks would prove to be a crucial time. He was more and more worried as the hospital's care visibly declined. He could only imagine how much worse it was on the outside. The physical therapy sessions were packed full of patients there for different reasons, with fewer staff therapists monitoring their progress. John was often left alone to do his therapy while the physical therapists and assistants were pulled away to assist other patients. John had regained his balance and was able to walk unassisted and move around without the fear of falling down. The hospital laid off several assistants, and the doctors and therapists were also getting laid off. Many times, John would take himself to the physical therapy areas and walk a couple of miles on the treadmill or lift light weights and do yoga stretching without any interaction with someone from the PT department.

      John worked harder and harder, pushing his body to the limits during physical therapy, and after five grueling weeks he was released to go home. Both the nurse and physical therapist told him they thought it was too soon, but that the city's insurance had pressed the doctor into clearing him because they wouldn't pay anymore. The doctor told him that he was to stay on "bed rest," an order which John secretly laughed at.

      While he was still in tremendous pain and the migraines kept coming and going, he was still able to get up and walk around for a few hours every day. He even began to walk a couple of miles a day with his mom or dad's assistance. As he got stronger, he still struggled with the psychological trauma that he had experienced. He carried the weight of the shooting. It was different than the others he had been involved with before. The other on-duty shootings had been with multiple officers, and one of the times, he hadn't even hit any of the assailants. This one was much different; it had been up close and personal. He still had nightmares where he saw the eyes of the two men at which he had shot. On many nights, he awoke in a cold sweat, hyperventilating, and his heart beating quickly. The episodes lasted only a short time but were terrible for him. He felt helpless and weak. He only hoped the episodes would pass. The nightmares paled in comparison to the panic attacks and sleepless nights. He didn't tell anybody about the panic attacks and nightmares, not even his parents. He remembered having a drunken conversation with one of his college roommates, Mike, about PTSD and all the psychological trauma soldiers had to deal with when coming home from war. Mike had told him that he was never quite sure if he had what constituted PTSD, or whatever it was with all those messed up emotions he had about combat. John just wanted his life to get back to some small sense of normalcy as quick as possible, and he didn't need to be bogged down with friends and family pulling at him to go get therapy or talk to some shrink. He had enough things on his mind. He decided to keep his mouth shut and focus on what he could do: get home and prepare for what was coming.

CHAPTER 2: THE PREPARATION

June 23rd – Kankakee, IL

When he pulled up to the large two-story brick house in the subdivision on the west edge of town, it was a welcome sight. He smiled as he saw his faithful German Shepherd staring out the window. The dog barked loudly as the car pulled into the driveway, wagging his tail and yipping with joy. John would have run up the front steps if he were able. Instead, he decided on taking the smart approach, taking his time. As he opened the front door, he was immediately met by his wiry ninety-pound twelve-year-old German Shepherd. The dog jumped up into his arms and nearly knocked him off his feet, greeting him with doggy kisses. Jax had been a present to himself; he'd adopted him from a local rescue after graduating from police academy.

His house was what he and a few friends often jokingly referred to as "the Compound." It was a former two-story 5,000-plus-square-foot warehouse-type brick building on the far edge of town; built in the 1920s as a speakeasy club during Prohibition, it had been rumored that Al Capone had used it as a stash house at the height of organized crime in Chicagoland. John loved the building for its history.

Because it had been abandoned for several years, he purchased the building and adjoined empty double lots for only $100,000. His father had pulled a few favors with a friend on the city council to get the building re-zoned to be a residential home. John began renovations immediately. He loved the building's structure, as the outer walls were a solid layer of brick and concrete, and there were multiple hidden rooms and stairways and even a hidden cellar entrance aside from the basement. The upper story windows had heavy wooden shutters. He spent nearly another $80,000 to add stairways and modern amenities and divided the upstairs into multiple bedrooms. Each floor had a whopping layout of almost 2,900 square feet. The downstairs was divided into the kitchen, the large dining room/bar area, two living rooms, two guest rooms, and an office. The large basement and hidden cellar were divided into storage areas, with heavy-duty shelving already built from the Prohibition era and many new shelves John had built. All the external doors were replaced with heavy blast-resistant armored doors with reinforced lock systems that rested on ball bearing hinges. He had an intricate security system with external and internal cameras and motion sensors and lights; he added a three-car garage onto the side of the house as well. He had also spent the money on an in-ground pool in the backyard and added to the large lower deck. Although everything was very pricey, John was always a workaholic, working as much overtime, extra shifts, and side jobs as he could manage to afford the expenses.

The Compound was built like a fortress, a modern-day castle. To add to the castle-style look, John added a tall brick wall around the lot and painted it to match the building itself. The Compound had a certain appeal and draw to the eye of those fond of history. John made money renting rooms to friends or new unmarried guys on the department for years on and off and even rented rooms through Air BNB. The full bar downstairs was a big draw, and he got a decent supplemental income from the various rentals before the economy began to plunge in recent years. His mother still often frowned at his house, calling it "ugly" and "not homely enough" to be a place where he would hopefully raise her future grandchildren.

The Compound was only accessible from a cul-de-sac at the end of the subdivision on the city's west edge. The newer subdivision had been built around the old speakeasy, which had once sat alone outside the city limits. To the rear of the Compound was a cornfield marking the modern city-proper limits. That cornfield only extended a few acres until it hit a larger patch of trees, making a small forest.

Life could have almost returned to normal if things weren't getting increasingly shitty. John was still on medical leave from work indefinitely, which was okay with him. He did not envy his brothers and sisters in blue, as he lay awake many nights, hearing more and more gunshots through his open windows. Gunshots were nothing new in a decent-sized city like Kankakee, even ten years ago, but they became more and more common, and (scarily enough) sounded closer and closer to his neighborhood. He even heard what sounded like larger caliber weapons. John would have worried more if he hadn't remembered that his father was sleeping downstairs in the front room with his Mossberg 500 tactical shotgun at his side. Even though pushing seventy, the old man was more than capable of protecting them. As a police officer in this very city for over forty years, he had been in three shootings in his long and highly decorated career.

Most nights, John's sleep was still fitful and not long enough. He often got some sleep during the day, taking short naps throughout the daylight hours when he started to get too exhausted to function.

During the day, most of John's time was spent in a flurry of activity. He knew things were only going to get worse. Other than his own recovery and trips to outpatient physical therapy, he spent a lot of time taking inventory of his stock of food, supplies, ammo, and weapons. John had been preparing for something like this for years, mostly in secret. Very few of his friends and co-workers knew John was what most people considered a "Prepper." His years of military and law enforcement had shown him the worst of humanity. He knew the government could not be relied upon if things collapsed on any large scale. He had spent the last ten years gathering supplies, building skills, and compiling a network of allies just in case something like this might happen. He sent messages to check in with several friends who also saw the writing on the walls. The economy was declining, and law and order was beginning to break. He was still in contact with a few friends from the police department, where he was told that shootings involving officers were happening multiple times a week. Officers on patrol were now required to carry long guns, shotguns, and AR's with them at all times. Many people had begun wearing plate armor and helmets, equipped like the troops overseas. Another police officer in a county to the north had also been shot a week ago and was in critical condition. The rumor was that he wasn't expected to live much longer.

One morning, John was relaxing on the couch watching TV with his parents and sipping coffee. The news wasn't good, but he was glad to still enjoy the modern comforts of civilized society while they still could. All of the news channels were filled with stories of the stock market numbers dropping on a slow, steady decline. In the last thirty-six hours, the market had lost nearly 8,000 points. Publicly traded companies in corporate America had already begun to panic, attempting to move assets and companies overseas. It was the beginning of a widespread panic. Larger corporate companies had been laying off workers in droves. Mass layoffs were looming, and facilities were being closed down. Civil unrest, protests, and even smaller-scale riots had begun in larger metropolitan areas and cities. There were not enough police and emergency services to prevent the incidents, and the riots were slowly getting out of hand. He got nervous, especially seeing how out of hand Chicago was getting, less than seventy miles to his north. The big city was crumbling, and the chaos that was erupting was sure to spill out and reach them soon. Kankakee was one of the largest metropolitan centers south of the City and suburbs of Chicago. It was getting bad in Chicago and was only going to get worse, both there and here.

John knew things were slowly getting worse, but he hadn't really started to experience the effects firsthand. Then, one morning, he and his father decided to take a trip downtown to the large bank in the town square complex. He wanted to pull out cash as his most recent paycheck had direct deposited into his checking account, and his father wanted to do the same with his retirement check.

As they drove up to the bank, they could see the parking lot full of cars and a line nearly out of the door full of desperate people. The ATMs outside were offline.

As the crowd slowly moved inside to the large lobby, John noticed the many security guards, wearing matching uniforms of the bank, but carrying a mismatch of weapons. Some only had pistols in leather holsters on their hips, while a few had shotguns slung on their back or cradled in their hands. "Amateur hour," he whispered in his father's ear. Dad cracked a small smile with a chuckle. Both men carried concealed pistols under their jackets.

The people waiting at the tellers' counters were barely kept organized, making a loose gaggle. It made John nervous. The lobby looked like a mosh pit. Over the loud conversations of the people in line, he heard a large, fat woman in a faded pink shirt screaming at the man behind the counter: "WHAT THE FUCK DO YOU MEAN THERE'S A WITHDRAWAL LIMIT? IT'S MY FUCKING MONEY!"

The teller's response was lost in the roar of several other people in the crowd yelling in agreement. The teller made a pointing motion, and two security guards walked over, one pointing a bright yellow Taser at the woman. She quickly gave up and was escorted out of the bank by the two security guards. The crowd quieted down, but there were still several grumbling complaints from people in line.

A large bearded man wearing a local plumber's union shirt turned back to John and his father and remarked, "Let's hope we can speed this up so we can get out of here before there's a riot. Am I right?"

John cracked a slight smile. "No shit. I'd rather just get whatever money I can and get out of here without getting shot."

The tall plumber gave a smirk and said, "You mean shot *again*, right? Aren't you that cop that got shot a few months ago? Glad to see that you're still alive, man."

They shook hands and exchanged pleasantries for a moment, and he said, "The name's Mitch. Nice to meet you."

"I know you. You bought me a drink at the bar on the river one time," John said.

Mitch stroked his chin. "Hmmm...I must have been pretty fucked up since I can't remember it. Sure wish I had gotten to know you better sooner than now, buddy. These are some weird times. You take care of yourselves, gentlemen."

The line had dwindled by that point, and Mitch nodded slightly and took his turn with the teller, leaving shortly after with a disappointed look on his face. He wished John a quiet "Good luck, buddy," on his way out.

John walked up to the teller when it was his turn and gave the teller his bank account info. He asked to withdraw his entire check, and the teller said with the tone of practiced repetition: "Sorry, sir, there is a $500 cash withdrawal limit." As agitated as John was, he said calmly, "That will be fine."

The tired and agitated teller slowly counted out the cash and handed it to John. He moved aside, and his father quickly went through the same routine. They got out of the bank as quickly as they could.

"Let's try and hit a few ATMs on the way home. Maybe old Bud's gun shop is still taking debit cards. Plus, it would be nice to see the old man again while I'm still in town," said his father.

They drove a few blocks, attempting to use a few of the different ATMs at various businesses. They were successful at a few, but they could only get a few hundred dollars more out of their bank accounts. They even got creative and went to a local currency exchange to purchase different denominations in Mexican pesos, Canadian dollars, and Euros using their debit cards. It seemed as though every retail store, bank, or money lending business they passed had one or several armed security guards at the counters or entrances. Most of the ATMs that were still working already had crowds of desperate-looking people hanging around them. Those they avoided, instead choosing the smaller grocery stores and shops further away from downtown. They even hit up gas stations where they could select "cash back" with purchases. They bought energy drinks, beer, and snacks to avoid too much suspicion. They even purchased a gas can and filled it at the pump to use cash-back at another station.

The last stop they made was the small gun shop on the northwest side of town. Bud was an old retired Marine gunnery sergeant who ran his business out of an old machine shop's garage. He used his retirement money to fund the hobby of reloading and selling ammo. Bud had been a good friend of Rich for several years. Both father and son often went to spend time with the old man. He was lonely after his wife's death several years prior but kept himself busy with his shop. John and his father often brought their spent brass from the shooting range and gave it to Bud to reload into new bullets. They usually split it half and half: They paid Bud for the price of his materials, and Bud gave them half of the reloads he made and sold the other half in his store.

Today, when they drove up to the shop, the doors were closed and shuttered. They exchanged looks but decided to step out of their vehicle anyway. After a few loud raps on the door and on the metal overhead garage door, they shouted Bud's name. It was quiet for a little bit, but they heard a shotgun rack after a few moments of silence.

The old man yelled, "Go away! I don't have any cash, and I ain't got shit left in stock! Go away unless you want to die!"

They both stepped back from the door and John yelled, "Woah, take it easy, old man. It's your friends! Just checking in on you!"

His father added, "You wouldn't shoot a fellow senior citizen, would you, Old Man?"

Bud said quietly through the door, "Gonzalez? You two alone?"

"Yes, sir. Just father and son. No worries, Bud. Just wanted to check in and see how you're holding up."

After a few moments of suspenseful silence, they heard the deadbolt click on the door to the shop, and the door was thrown open. The weathered old man was wearing his usual suspenders and his bright red Marine veteran ball cap. He smiled over the old wood-stock Remington pump-action shotgun cradled in his arms. He set it next to the open door and motioned them in. "Hurry inside, boys, come on in."

Rich remote-locked his pickup truck, and they both looked back over their shoulders before hurrying inside.

Bud closed the door and locked it behind them. "Sorry, boyos, been a little tense here lately. I'm getting old, and it's just me in here."

They stood in silence for a moment, then his father spoke. "Are you in trouble, Bud? Have people been threatening you or trying to get to you? You know we're always here to help in any way that we can."

The old man looked at them and quickly said, "Oh no, no, I'm fine here...." He trailed off.

Both visitors looked around. The shop was messy and in disrepair. The glass cabinets and shelves were dirty and covered in dust. The lights weren't very bright, and many bulbs were out. Most of the shelves were empty. There were only a few guns left in the glass cases, and even less ammunition boxes stacked on the shelves.

Old Bud saw them looking around and said, "It's not as bad as it looks, I promise, boys. When things started getting bad with the stock market, I made better sales numbers than I have even when we got Democrats in office. Guns and ammo were flying off my shelves. I can only imagine how good the big box stores were doing."

Rich asked Bud, "So you were doing well at first. How have things been recently? Because I have to be honest here, my friend...you aren't looking so good."

The old man smiled and replied, "I'll be honest, my friends. I don't have much left here in stock. I got cleared out with the panic rush once the economy started to go bad. I only kept a few guns for my personal stash. I thought it would be great, but then the inflation hit, and almost all of my suppliers dried up. The rest of them drove up their prices so high, I couldn't afford to restock fully." After a short pause, he took a deep breath, then said, "I won't lie to you boys...I'm flush on cash...but I don't see much of a future here. I don't have any resupply plan. All of my good suppliers have dried up, and I can't get any new product shipped in. So, I had to close shop. No new guns or ammo at all." The old man in the Marine cap sat down on a stool behind the counter and began to hand-roll a small cigarette. He licked the rolling paper closed and twisted the end before continuing, "All I have left is some odds and ends for reloading, some brass and powder, a few cases of primers. It's not much, but whatever you need that I have is yours." Bud lit his cigarette, took a puff, and then flipped on a light switch. The dark room brightened instantly.

Rich said, "Look, my old friend. We will buy whatever you have left, but my son is healing up, and I need to get back to my other son in Oregon. You look like you could use somebody to look after you."

Bud cut him off, "Stop it, you old brute. I'm old but not helpless here. I still have my apartment above the shop, and a stack of cash now. I'll be fine. I'm not going anywhere."

John didn't want to get in the middle of his father and Bud getting into an old-man fight, but he still decided to cut in: "Are you still taking credit cards?" He knew it was a dumb question, but he wanted to direct the conversation in their favor. Bud shifted over to look at him and said, "No, I'm not. Either cash, coins, or I could use food so I can hole up here for a while."

"I can get you whatever you need. I'll pay half in cash and the other in food and whatever supplies you need. And you know there is always a standing offer to stay with me at the Compound. Just say the word, and I'll come get you. My dog could use the company."

The old Marine smiled and said, "I'll stay here for now. I'll be fine. Take what you need from the shop and just bring me the supplies. If I ever need anything else, I'll be in contact. It's getting dark; you boys should go."

They stood up and shook hands. He put all of the remaining ammunition and reloading materials into a cart and wheeled it out to their vehicle. John handed Bud a stack of about $400 in cash and a few silver coins from his pocket. He also quickly ran out to the truck to grab some of the food and snacks they'd purchased on their journey back from the bank. They shared a brief handshake, and Bud said, "Just bring that food and stuff over in a day or so. Now get home

John handed Bud a small handheld HAM radio and told him, "If you need to get a hold of me and the phones go out, use this. It's on the right channel already. You're close enough to my house that it should reach if you're upstairs in the apartment and near a window."

The Marine nodded and accepted the small radio with no more words as he watched the old and young cops both limp over to the vehicle and speed away.

On the way back home, they decided to try one last stop at an ATM. Down the street from Bud's shop was a small outdoor strip mall with a long-since-closed Ultra Foods, a few small stores, and a barbershop. These stores were all closed, locked, or boarded up. Around the corner was a Walgreen's Pharmacy, which still appeared to be open for business. On the side of the building near the drive-thru, an ATM was still lit up. It was starting to get dark. They decided to make a quick pit stop at the ATM and try to make a few purchases at the pharmacy afterwards. They parked their truck at the end of the alley and walked over to the ATM. They were both able to withdraw $200 each and attempted multiple transactions from different accounts. They were successful for a few different transactions on different cards, until the ATM changed, and the screen read "Out of Service."

They began walking around toward the entrance to the pharmacy when they heard a woman scream from the direction of their parked truck. John took off at a jog toward the end of the alley, and his father limped off quickly after him. Their pace quickened when the woman began screaming louder: "SOMEBODY HELP ME!!!!!" John and his father both drew their pistols from underneath their shirts. John rounded the corner and saw two scruffy-looking men attempting to drag a woman into one of the boarded-up stores. The woman's dress was ripped open, and her panties were around her ankles. Both men were punching and kicking the woman as they climbed into the store through a broken front window. John yelled, "POLICE!" and raised his 1911 as he rounded the corner.

The group had disappeared into the building in the nick of time. "Shit!" John said aloud, painfully running to move into the dark storefront. He flicked on the weapon-mounted flashlight on his 1911 and stooped into the dark storefront, his eyes straining to adjust to the light as he began to sweep the room.

John followed the screams of the woman further into the back rooms of the small store. As he slowly crept into a back room, one of the men turned the corner, screaming and barreling down on him with a knife. The dirty, scruffy man collided with him, winning with the element of surprise. John managed to keep his pistol in between them as they collided, both falling to the ground. He was able to deflect the blade coming down on him with his left elbow above his head while thumbing off the safety of the pistol in his right hand. He pushed the 1911 into the man's chest and pulled the trigger. The man went limp after the loud boom echoed through the dark room and a hollow-point .45 ACP round tore through the man's chest. He pushed the man's limp body off of him and attempted to sit up. The other man had been attempting to rape the poor woman over in the corner while John struggled with the first man. The man turned at the sound of the shot and managed to pull his pants back up and clamber to his feet. The woman lay still, sobbing on the ground. The rapist started to move toward John.

CRRRACK! A loud, bone-crushing sound filled the air as a long wooden cocobolo nightstick connected with the rapist's skull. John's father had quickly moved into the room and swung the small oak tree of a nightstick that he had so infamously wielded in his nearly five decades as a police officer. The crack of the man's skull was a gruesome sound. John was almost certain that the impact on the rapist's skull had killed the man instantly, but the man moaned slightly after hitting the floor. Another loud CRACK! sounded as John's father swung another devastating blow into the man's right knee, almost assuredly shattering the kneecap and any other essential parts for walking. The man groaned again as Rich put the full weight of his body onto the man's scrotum with his right boot. He switched the nightstick out of his right hand and began to move his free hand to draw his pistol, saying, "Pigs like you who rape women don't deserve to live. John, you're my witness, this shitbag tried to pull a pistol on us…" As Rich began to draw his pistol, another gunshot rang out. The woman had gotten up, grabbed a small revolver that one of the men had dropped, and stepped around the old man. After firing the first shot, she fired the remaining four shots into the man's body wildly, still pulling the trigger after it had gone empty. The revolver continued clicking as she sobbed loudly.

John moved and attempted to comfort the woman, trying to get her to loosen the grip on the revolver. "You're safe now, lady. We're both police officers. Let us bring you to the hospital or somewhere safe...."

The woman didn't even acknowledge his words and took off at a full sprint out of the store, still barefoot and almost completely naked. She ran down the street, still holding the revolver in her hand. Both the men started after her, but she was gone in an instant.

Rich shrugged his shoulders and said, "Well, we better call this in...we've got two dead shitheads and gunshots. Better get out ahead of this. Take pictures with your phone before crime scene techs get in here and fuck up the scene." He pulled his cell phone out of his jeans pocket and dialed the number for the dispatch center. The dispatcher answered quickly and asked for the emergency. Rich identified himself and asked for an officer and detective to meet them at their location. The dispatcher told them to hold and said she would pass along their message to the shift commander.

"That's not very standard..." Rich said as the dispatcher hung up on them. "They sounded busy as hell...The call center sounded like chaos in the background." They gathered their items and collected their wits.

As they walked back to the truck, Rich's phone rang, and he answered quickly. The patrol lieutenant who called him said, "Mr. Gonzalez, I don't have the guys to send, and it's getting dark. If it happened like you said it did, then we'll send a detective out in the morning to check on it and follow up. Right now, Kankakee is not the place to be after dark, so get your asses back to safety before the sun goes down." He hung up.

"Jesus…That's for damn sure not following standard protocol," Rich said to John.

"Looks like the days for protocol are over. There's barely even any law and order anymore. I think we did society a favor wasting those two shitbags over there. Now let's get home. It sounds like we don't want to be out anywhere at night…" John said to his father as they both climbed into the truck and took off.

After their quick ride home, John decided that he needed to batten down the hatches, and it was time to take his action. It was obvious that the situation wasn't getting any better. Crime was going unchecked, the police were losing any grip on law and order in the city, and the danger was creeping closer and closer to the safety of his home. Criminals were going unchecked, and it looked like his parents wouldn't be able to travel safely for much longer.

The next morning, finally, three months after his shooting, John turned in his papers to take indefinite medical leave from the police department. A detective also came to his house to get statements from John and Rich about the shooting from the night before. At first, John was nervous, but when the detective came, the first thing he said was, "We went to the shooting scene. Just two bodies of some shithead bums nobody will miss, and no rape victim to witness. State's attorney isn't going to waste time on any investigations or charges. There's nothing we can do. Your two short statements will suffice for an open and shut case. We're all stretched thin as it is. Unless you want to un-retire and come back, and Junior wants to come off medical leave and help us out, I'm done with ya both." The detective shook both their hands and turned around and left, walking down the front steps back to the parked squad car where a patrol officer was waiting.

"Well, If that's any sign as to how the world is going to hell…Then I think it's about time your mother and I get back to Oregon," Rich said. John shook his head solemnly in agreement.

Over the next few days, John cashed out his remaining time off and took part of the money to bulk order another 10,000 rounds of .223 ammo for his ARs, .308 for long rifles, .22LR and 5,000 rounds of various 9mm, .38spc, .357 magnum, .40, and .45 pistol ammo online from various websites and paid a hefty extra fee for expedited shipping. He called in favors from friends that owned local gun shops, and even paid extra to have them deliver the ammo to his house. He was unable to withdraw much more in cash, so he ordered all of these things online using debit and credit cards. He spared no expense paying extra for the next-day and overnight deliveries. He also spent a large portion of the money remaining in his bank accounts on batteries, canned food, military MREs, freeze-dried camping meals, and other long-term survival food. The rest went to silver and gold coins and rounds, and a small amount of cash to keep on hand and in his safe. It was a gamble to see if postal and delivery services would even still make the deliveries in time before the rest of the world went to hell, but John figured it was worth the risk. The dwindling money in his bank accounts didn't seem like it was going to be worth much of anything anymore.

While the cell phone networks were still up and running, he reached out to all of his fellow prepper contacts, offering a shelter in place at his house. It was an open offer amongst those he trusted, but he wanted it known for when things got worse.

He had also attempted to contact his oldest brother Nick, but could not reach him, which wasn't uncommon. Nick was a genius, a tech researcher for a corporation in Champaign, the college town a few hours south of them. Nick also made extra money contracting for the federal government. He often was put on top-secret research contracts because of his security clearance through the company. It wasn't uncommon before everything changed for him to not have any outside contact outside of his roommate for a month straight. John sent texts, made calls and sent emails to both Nick and his girlfriend offering for them to come stay with him if things got bad. None were returned. This was still fairly normal, so John tried not to worry.

John also decided it that it was definitely time for his parents to leave. He wanted to see them off while the highways were still remotely safe to travel. They would not be for too much longer, he surmised. Very early on a warm, muggy Illinois summer morning, he said goodbye to his parents. He knew they would be safer out west with his brother, but that didn't make things any easier.

He loaded spare supplies and some ammo into his parents' large fifth-wheel camper. Last, he handed his mother a scrap of paper with all the HAM radio frequencies he used. The night prior, he and his dad had wired in a mobile HAM radio under the dash of truck, like a typical CB but with much greater range. In an emergency, or if the cell service went down, he wanted to know where they were, or if they'd made it safely out to Oregon. He hoped they could use the large CB/HAM radio antennas on top of the truck cab to its best capabilities. He hugged his mother tightly, hoping this wasn't the last time they would see each other. He shook his father's hand quickly before asking him, "What route are you taking?"

"I'm going to take I-80 west as far as we can. It swings farther south after Chicago. Iowa, Nebraska, and Wyoming should be fine, other than being a little close to Denver when we skim the Colorado state line. If all else fails, I have the maps to take some state highways and side roads. The great plains are more sparsely populated. I don't suspect much trouble on the interstate once we get clear of Chicago. I give it a few weeks journey taking it slow. I'll text you updates along the way, and we'll make contact as soon as we stop every night at 9 P.M., and every morning when we start again."

John gave one last final hug to his dad and walked them over to their custom Dodge Dually Pickup. The large pickup had been highly customized by his father with his retirement money to pull their large fifth-wheel camper. It had been upgraded with ramming bars on the front, a steel-reinforced skid plate attached all the way up to the bumper, and Kevlar puncture-resistant tires. The shocks and air bag suspension were upgraded to handle the heavy load of the camper and its contents. The heavy tires hurt the gas mileage, but to counteract that, the bed held two large external gas tanks inside the bed underneath the fifth-wheel attachment, reinforced by steel sheeting. The interior of the vehicle held several hidden compartments with pistols and even an overhead compartment holding a short riot shotgun. John admired his father's paranoia and practicality. He knew where he got his own from.

John opened the passenger door for his mother, helping her make the high step up inside. She was still surprisingly spry for a nearly seventy-year-old woman; those aqua aerobics classes had paid off since she retired, he thought.

He went over and opened the driver's side door for his father. He was wearing his old duty weapon, a Glock 21 in .45ACP with a large Streamlight TLR2 light and laser combo mounted on it. He carried it on his hip in an old beat-up Kydex holster. Rich was even carrying a few spare magazines on his belt. Next to his gun on his right side was his gold detective badge that read "Retired" on the top.

His father handed him his other beat-up old detective star that he'd worn for almost twenty-five years. "In case we never get to see each other again, this is for you. I'm so proud of you. You're a leader, John, but you don't recognize it. You're stronger and smarter than everyone out there. Like I told you when you first became a cop, go out there and make a difference. Protect the weak. Be the sheepdog."

John returned his dad's embrace and said, "Come on, old man. I hate the stupid 'Sheepdog' phrase more than I hate goodbyes. Just get there safe. Love you both."

And with those words, his parents departed, speeding out of town toward Interstate 57 that would take them north to I-80 West. His German Shepherd whimpered quietly as John waved goodbye.

John went back inside to do an inventory of his gear. He was a little anxious about being home alone now as things spiraled out of control. He was worried about the loss of law and order that he was sure would be continuing. He prayed that his brothers and sisters in blue would not be harmed in the weeks to come.

He went to the fake bookshelf that hid his gear room. He slid the hidden compartment open to access the doorway to the 10-by-15-foot room which held his gun cabinets, safes, shelves, and most of his ammo storage. He went over to a shelf and picked up his TYR multicam plate carrier, a set of Multicam fatigues, combat shirt, his "battle belt," and his high-cut ballistic helmet. He brought it all out into the living room, feeling a sense of relief at having his full kit out and available. He loaded spare magazines for his pistols and rifles, checking and double-checking his equipment.

After about an hour, John got a text message from his father's phone that read, "On I-80 in the Burbs. All good so far. About to clear the big cities. So far so good. -Mom." He smiled, thinking it probably took his mom ten minutes to type that short message.

As the hours of the day went on, John decided to make a few more phone calls. The first was to his closest prepper buddy, Andrew. He had met Andrew over ten years ago when they worked as corrections officers at the county jail. They had quickly bonded over their military backgrounds and their shared interests in prepping and survivalist practices. They were total opposites in some ways. John was a tall, overweight Army veteran, and Andrew a short, skinny Marine veteran. They often joked that they were like the movie "Twins" with Arnold and Danny DeVito. They were both outspoken and political, something that drew them together, and they were often labeled as "assholes" by the others on the department. Even though they hadn't worked together in years, they were still very close friends, often hanging out on days off and training, shooting, and prepping together. They also kept in touch via HAM radio portables they had been training on for the last few years. He considered Andrew one of his closest confidants in sharing the prepping lifestyle, and they had been preparing together for the worst for years. He knew Andrew had a significant amount of supplies and ammo, but he also had his two young children to take care of. He had a larger house than Andrew, so he reached out to him.

He dialed his number on his iPhone, and in only a few rings, his buddy answered. "What's up, you fat fuck?" were Andrew's first words.

"It's getting bad, little buddy," John replied, shaking his head slightly suppressing a chuckle.

"How bad? You think it's gotten ALAMO level yet, big man?" Andrew asked.

"I think it's getting pretty damn critical, man. You interested in bugging out to my place? You know I got the room. It would be good to set up a more centralized base of operations for when shit gets worse."

Andrew was silent for a minute, then said, "Yeah, man, if you can get your truck and trailer over to Bradley and help me move all this shit over and bring the kids, let's do it. I don't think I'm going back to work since this thing seems to keep getting worse."

It was decided that they would meet up the next morning and conduct the move from Bradley, the next town over.

John's next call was to another single friend he knew might be interested. He called his buddy Theo, a young Chicago cop that he had known for nearly five years. They had met online through a shooting group and became good friends. Theo was twenty-five years old and had been a cop for Chicago PD for the past three years in the toughest neighborhoods on Chicago's South Side. He was a tall, slender, light-skinned black man who was soft-spoken, with a mild country twang in his voice. He enjoyed fine cigars and any whiskey he could get his hands on. He was a goofy young kid but very athletic and exceptionally talented at Brazilian Jiu Jitsu and had a mildly successful amateur MMA career before joining the CPD.

When he answered the phone, he asked, "Hey Theo, how is shit up by you?"

"This city was always shitty, bro; it's hard to tell the difference."

John laughed. "But seriously, man, how are you? Is shit getting bad up there? We need you down here."

Theo paused for a minute and replied, "CPD is hurting, Johnny boy. It's always been bad up here, but the city ran out of money. They started laying us off in crazy amounts. My last day is tomorrow, then I'm out of work and SOL. I don't know what to do. I don't have any family here since my OG died last year. But hey, enough about me, how are things by you?"

He thought for a moment, then said, "Theo, you know I'm always here for you, brother. Before shit gets worse, we're gonna call an ALAMO. Get all your shit and move down here to me."

Theo replied, "Thanks for the offer, bro, it means a lot to me. I don't have many other options. I'm gonna pack up my stuff and ALAMO to you. I don't have anything keeping me here anymore. Let's ride this shit out. I'll see you tomorrow or the day after if I can get all my shit packed up and moved." He then hung up.

ALAMO was the code word amongst John's prepper friends that things were bad enough to completely pull the plug on everything else in life and batten down the hatches, shelter in place. If he was the one calling the code red, it was agreed upon that it was an open invite to host all other friends and family at his location. He only hoped that those he trusted would make their way safely to him.

His next call was to an old Army buddy he called Tango. Tango was an older friend that he had been shooting and training with for years. Tango was a highly skilled firearms instructor who had been a security supervisor at a nuclear plant for years. He was also a highly skilled long-range shooter and had been teaching his skills for years. Tango lived about twenty miles away near the nuclear plant in Braidwood. He picked up after the second call.

"Yo, Greybush, am I not important enough to answer the phone for?"

"Fuck off, Fatty!" Tango replied.

"Hey bro. I know shit is getting bad. If it gets really bad by you, wanted to let you know that ALAMO is in effect down in Kankakee at my place."

Tango replied, "Good to know. The nuke plant is keeping us working no matter what. Power has to stay on, but I got my kids at my place. I got Will the Ginger at my place for now. If shit gets worse here, I'll hit you up and—."

In that moment, the cell phone line went dead. John started at his phone for a minute in disbelief, checking his iPhone over and over. There was no service even after restarting his phone several times. A text came in warning of "Intermittent service outages. Matter will be resolved promptly." Then he realized…It had begun. He went back inside and turned on his TV to the closest news network.

CHAPTER 3: PULLING THE PLUG

July 1st – Kankakee IL

John watched the news channels, flipping through several. It didn't matter what network, liberal or right-wing news, it was all bad news. STOCK MARKET CRASH and RUN ON BANKS loaded the headlines. INTERMITTENT POWER OUTAGES, CIVIL DISORDER, RIOTS IN CHICAGO, LOS ANGELES, DENVER, AND NEW YORK began to take to the screens. Newscasters began talking about hyperinflation and government safeguards against economic depression. A national banking holiday and stock market trading moratorium was declared by the Federal Trade Commission. Thankfully, John had pulled most of his financial assets out of the stock market and other volatile markets weeks ago, but it still concerned him, nonetheless. The government had suddenly stopped all economic stimulus assistance payments and all welfare payments. All ATMs from most major banks were immediately closed and taken offline. The news made it sound like it would only be for a day or a few days, but John knew it would be much longer. The media was already using the "Big D" word. Once the media began stirring the pot and fanning the flames of unrest, John knew it was over. The mass panic would soon explode and take over now that it had reached the masses.

He watched the screens, his anxiety spiking during the multiple news clips of buildings burning, mass rioting, and looting in Chicago. Riot police were pushed further and further back, retreating and withdrawing from certain neighborhoods altogether. There were multiple reports of police shooting civilians and looters, with many videos from camera crews in the middle of the mess and various home-recorded videos obtained from social media. Many areas in Chicago had descended into utter chaos. It looked more like Mogadishu than one of the largest cities in America. In some of the worst areas, police had withdrawn from entire neighborhoods and precincts, giving the rioters and looters free reign to burn and destroy. The Mayor of Chicago declared a state of emergency, and the Governor called in the National Guard to attempt to keep some areas under control. The Guard had very little response, as most members did not report to their units. Others showed up and went AWOL after picking up their equipment. The city was quickly descending into lawlessness in many parts occupied by masses of rioters.

John waited the remainder of the day out and made contact with Andrew by HAM radio. Andrew told him that he was nearly finished packing all of his supplies and ready for his exfil in the morning. It was too dangerous to travel by night but still relatively civilized during the daylight.

The next morning, John got ready. He dressed in slightly more incognito clothing that would attract less attention. He donned a khaki pair of 5.11 tactical pants, as he usually would, along with his green Salomon low-top hiking boots and a thin, long-sleeved shirt over his soft body armor. He loaded his 1911 in a Kydex holster at his side, along with multiple spare mags. His Colt MK18 clone short-barreled rifle sat in the seat next to him. His Tahoe was mostly empty, with the exception of his spare ammo and assault pack in the passenger seat. He wanted the maximum amount of free space in his vehicle to carry all of Andrew's gear. He knew the ride to Andrew's place would be short, and taking main roads, he wasn't expecting much trouble, but he still couldn't shake the feeling of uneasiness that sat in the pit of his stomach.

After hitching up his trailer, he took a deep breath and pulled out of his driveway, making the short trip north into Bradley. Along the way, he took note of the large number of homeless people out walking, collecting cans and scrap, rummaging through garbage, or begging for money. It seemed that most businesses were closed, especially the smaller non-chain businesses. Even one of the local supermarkets had been boarded up. He passed gas stations where the gas prices had nearly tripled since he got shot. John was glad his father had thought to order a refill of gasoline in the large 1000-

gallon farm gas tank in the lot by his house, another gracious gift from his parents' savings account. This was one of the few times John had been out of his house since getting out of the hospital, and he was saddened to see the state of affairs since. The few banks that were still open had more armed guards outside of them than usual, with signs showing even smaller limits on withdrawals. He was glad he had attended to most of his banking before his parents left.

He continued driving, taking it slowly since he was pulling his enclosed trailer behind his SUV. He let his thoughts drift to his brother out west and wondered how his parents were faring on the first days of their journey. He was spacing out, driving north on a main road near the Walgreen's Pharmacy and McDonald's, when suddenly a lone shot rang out. He snapped back to reality as the round struck the Tahoe's passenger side. He swerved, nearly losing control of his vehicle. He expected more rounds to start coming, so he righted his direction and punched the accelerator, ignoring all traffic signals. A burst of rounds began popping off from different directions, but none hit anything crucial. He cruised into the edge of Bradley, doing nearly sixty miles per hour. He encountered no other resistance beyond the initial foray. He rolled up to Andrew's place, only a few blocks into Bradley, and screeched to a halt.

Andrew was outside loading equipment into his small SUV; he was wearing his Glock 19 on his hip on his full duty belt, with an AR-15 slung on his back. "About goddamn time, Fatboy! Help me get loaded up; we're burning daylight here!" Andrew exclaimed, walking up to his car.

As Andrew noticed the bullets in the side and rear of the Tahoe, he said, "Holy shit, man. You alright?"

"Yeah, took a couple of rounds on the way. I didn't stop to fight or survey it. Might want to take a different route back. Anyways, let's get your shit loaded. You think we've got enough space for all of your stuff?"

"I think so, except maybe my motorcycle. Might have to leave that behind," Andrew said.

John answered, "I know how much that old piece of junk means to you, bro. If we have to strap it to the roof, we will make room."

They spend the next several hours loading all of Andrew's gear, equipment, and food into the SUV and trailer with the help of Andrew's kids. Tuff boxes and gear lockers were loaded and stacked as high as they could fit in the trailer. Boxes of MREs and canned foods, and even Andrew's gun safes were piled into the small enclosed trailer, straining the shocks. As promised, even the motorcycle was shoved into the trailer, barely allowing its doors to close. Every nook and cranny of both of their SUVs were also stuffed full of all of the extras, clothes, electronics, radios, and valuables.

Once the kids were seated in Andrew's car, John turned to him and said, "I'm the bigger target. I think I should go first. I don't want you and your kids getting shot at, bro."

"Of course you're the bigger target, Fatboy! What are you, about 315, 325 now?" Andrew quipped with a smile.

"Fuck off, midget!" John retorted.

"You get in contact with any of the other guys?" Andrew asked.

"Yeah, Theo is bugging out; hopefully he'll be here in a day or so. Will and Tango are still working, so I don't think they're coming. I'd like to have a few more people at the house. It would definitely help with security. So, let's hurry back to my place; we can brainstorm it more when we're safer. I want to start unpacking before it gets dark. Kankakee after dark isn't exactly Wrigley Field on a Saturday day game."

Andrew said, "Yeah, I'm not overly enthused about leaving home and holing up in Kankakee. Kind of jumping from the pan into the fire if you ask me."

John looked around and motioned to Andrew's street, where several homes had boarded-up windows and trash was blowing down the street. "This place ain't exactly Mayberry either. Now let's get moving." After a last glance and a sigh, the last thing they did was screw plywood boards over the doors and ground level windows of his house, in the hopes that it would deter looters.

They mounted up and pulled back south into Kankakee, trying to take side roads as long as they could. They couldn't avoid the main roads for long, and soon found themselves cruising along the large main road along the river. John's heartbeat began to increase as he neared the place where he had taken fire on his way up. He began to pick up speed, blowing through the intersection. Thankfully there weren't too many cars on the road anymore. He cleared the block without problem and peered through his rearview mirror, making sure that Andrew did too. They were a few blocks down when they heard a few shots ring out, but none seemed to be in their direction. Just a few anxiety-filled minutes later, they pulled safely onto his block on the west edge of the city.

John backed in the trailer and opened the garage. It would be a quick alternative to stash most of the big stuff in his garage and do the moving tomorrow in the daylight. The sun was already starting to set, with the sun barely touching the top of the tree line. They worked quickly, pulling the large tough boxes and cabinets into the garage. The children even helped carry bags, clothes, and smaller boxes inside. He got them settled into the largest guest room downstairs. He had built bunk beds into some of the rooms to save space for additional shelving in the closets. Once all of the large equipment was unloaded, he pulled both vehicles into the empty half lot next to his property, pulling the wooden gate closed around the property. He had purchased the lot next to his property and built a tall wooden privacy fence around it. He used the lot as both vehicle storage and had planted a large garden two years ago. The last thing John did was walk around the perimeter of his property, pulling the storm shutters closed over the outside windows and checking to make sure all gates were padlocked. He checked all the outside security cameras and made sure they were on and functioning, then came back inside and deadbolted his front door closed. The sun was already gone, and it was nearly completely dark. He could faintly hear the sound of multiple gunshots going off in the distance toward the center of town to the east. What disturbed him more than the sound of gunshots was the lack of emergency vehicle sirens.

It was a little past 10 P.M. once he had finished pacing around. He checked on Andrew, who was tucking his kids into bed.

Andrew stepped out of the room and told him, "You look exhausted, man. This place is buttoned up tight, and we're all here and good. Go get some sleep. We will figure this shit out tomorrow. It's gonna be another long day."

With that, John decided that Andrew was right. It had been a long day, and he felt like shit. He grabbed a beer from the fridge and walked upstairs to his room with his faithful Shepherd following at his heels. He sipped on his beer and took off his gear and pistol, setting it in a loose pile on the couch next to his bed. He kicked off his shoes and laid down on his large king-size bed, his dog curling up at his feet. Even with the distant gunfire, he was able to quickly drift off to sleep.

CHAPTER 4: REGROUP AND RE-ARM

JULY 2ND – Kankakee IL

John awoke at around 7:30 A.M. with birds chirping and a still silence in the air. The sun had just begun to rise. It might have been a beautiful day, all things considered. He instinctively checked his cell phone, at first forgetting that cell service had been completely disrupted yesterday. Unsurprisingly, it was still down; he figured it would be on a more permanent basis. He was happy that the power was still on at all, although he worried it wouldn't be for much longer. He figured that today would be another long day of preparation. He felt groggy, but knew he needed to get up and start his day.

John got up, slipped on a pair of sandals, and walked downstairs. He made a pot of coffee, although quietly, because Andrew and the kids still were asleep. He stepped out onto his back deck and lit his large flat top grill. He prepared a large meal of eggs and bacon from his refrigerator. He figured it would be nice to treat themselves while things were still okay. He saw no point in saving too many things, when you could die any day. It went against a lot of his beliefs as a prepper, but he often had a hard time saving things for the long term. He was lost in his own thoughts as he began to cook the large spread of bacon and eggs for breakfast. Walking back and forth between the back deck and the kitchen to refill his coffee mug, he tried to not make too much noise.

Andrew emerged from his room, walked out onto the deck and stretched his arms. "Mornin'," he said mid-yawn.

John laughed at Andrew, who was wearing shorts, a T-shirt, slippers, and his Glock in an old leather shoulder holster. Andrew rubbed his eyes and said, "Always prepared, right? I bet you cooked breakfast with a gun long before this ever happened."

John answered, "Damn right. Never know when you'll get ambushed on your back porch. They had too many questions the last time I killed a guy with a pair of grilling tongs." And both friends shared a laugh.

Andrew grabbed a coffee and sat down at the patio table. "What are the plans for the day? I need to figure out what to keep the kids busy with."

John replied, "First, breakfast. We can still relax for a little bit. Let you guys get settled in. Let's get your stuff moved, let you guys get comfortable. Make this house a home. I think that'll be important for the kids. Then later, we can work on a few projects around the house. Just a few things to work on that I couldn't do by myself."

"Speaking of all alone," Andrew interjected. "We need to get more people here. You have the room, but this place could get overrun in a heartbeat with any halfway decent-sized force, and we would be totally fucked. Just you and me can't defend this place by ourselves. I'm going to get critical here, like I usually do, Johnny: We have plenty of food and supplies; we need friends. We have no lookout post, no advance warning if people decide to run up on us. Your gate might keep a few people out, but it won't stop a vehicle. I don't know how much longer I can sleep peacefully here without figuring this shit out."

"You're right as usual, buddy. You always seem to catch the things I didn't think of. After sending my parents away, I never really thought ahead about being alone. We need friends. Theo is on his way; I'd assume he will be alone If he makes it from Chicago. Three of us still isn't shit. Do you have anybody we might be able to reach on the HAM radio? Maybe friends from the jail or any of the deputies?"

"Fuck, man. This was something we should have planned out long ago. This lone wolf Rambo type shit isn't gonna cut it... I guess we could try and reach out to some of the Militia groups out West and down South. I don't know if I really trust some of those three percenters though. They were a little extreme before shit got bad, even for me. The jail is probably in lockdown. I haven't been back to work in a couple weeks. I dropped all my vacation time when shit really started to get bad. The people who weren't prepared probably stayed behind because of the food stores and generators there. God knows where the deputies are. Probably dead or in the wind for all we know. You've seen how bad the city ended up. How many of those cops stuck around to work?"

They continued brainstorming until Andrew's children came out to the smell of breakfast. They decided to spare the kids from the doom and gloom talk and instead helped the children to the hearty spread of bacon and eggs. The conversation shifted back to things around the house they wanted to get done.

Andrew told his daughter, "Hey, maybe we can put you to good use here, and you can decorate the house. This bachelor pad could use a woman's touch, so it's not so ugly and gloomy." She smiled and nodded, continuing her breakfast. "No hanging up boy band posters everywhere though" That's where I draw the line!" John joked.

After breakfast, they set out to move all the items that were in the garage into the house. The personal items and clothing were brought to their room by the kids. He and Andrew dragged in all of the heavy tough boxes and gear into the basement, where it was transferred into the storage lockers lining the wall in the basement which were labeled with his name. His large gun safe was kept on the first floor just outside his room, mostly because it was too heavy to try and move down the stairs. Even though the house had a small freight elevator that led into the basement, it still made for hard work. Andrew and the kids moved in all his long-term survival food storages and MREs into the various storage areas in the house, deciding on lumping all their stores together. Andrew tasked his daughter with re-organizing the food storage shelves by expiration date, keeping the soonest to expire up at the front to be used first. His daughter also moved in all the fresh food into the pantry and kitchen and garage refrigerators, using the same method.

Both John and Andrew had attempted to store at least two to three years of food per person. Andrew did his best preparing for all three of them, and John just tried to store as much long-term food as possible. John and Andrew took to filling and checking all the water storage containers that he had. He had a rainwater catch system attached to his gutters and at other rain barrels around his property and ensured they were properly functioning. John kicked himself for relying on the city for all his water and not having thought of trying to have a well dug somewhere on his property.

They spent the morning setting up all his spare solar panels throughout the backyard and fenced-in lot. They also charged all of the batteries from the electric outlets in the house. John wanted to take full advantage of the local power grid while they still had it. He checked the solar panels on his roof, which would be enough to power his home if the grid went down. He had spent a large amount of his savings nearly five years ago investing in a fully off-grid home battery bank and solar system from Tesla. His house gathered solar energy from the multiple 200w panels on all different angles on his roof, which could both be transferred back into the power grid, where the power company would pay him for the electricity generated. The power could also be stored in the 48v battery banks, keeping him off the grid entirely. It was well worth the $20,000 he had invested, and at five years, the system had nearly paid for itself already. John suspected it would soon become invaluable.

After a few hours of working and inspecting the house, John went back inside to grab a drink of water. He was passing his office when he heard his basecamp HAM radio quietly squawking. In his rush of working throughout the day, he had left it on to scan one of his channels that his and fellow prepper friends used to communicate. Sometimes he would leave it running to other prepper channels, listening to HAM operators having conversations with contacts throughout the country. Lately the conversations had changed to talking about how now was "the time" they had been preparing for, and how things were crashing all throughout the country.

Interlude One- Family Ties

John had been happy to keep up with a few operators that were preppers or members of local militias near Bend, Oregon, where his older brother lived. While his brother was not necessarily a prepper, he was familiar with a few of his contacts. He hoped to stay in contact with his family through these contacts. He had often bribed his prepper contacts near his family, mailing them small gifts and supplies in the hopes that they would remember him and look out for his family if things ever got bad. He didn't tell his family he had a safety net set up near them, but he suspected that they knew. He had met some of his favorite contacts while out visiting his brother several years ago; they were an older couple in their seventies named Bill and Susan Kirkpatrick. Bill was a Vietnam veteran who became a prepper after his son had died fighting in Afghanistan during the twenty-year Global War on Terror. He had taken the loss of his only son hard, having always hoped that he could rely on his son to take over the family ranch and land they owned in the foothills around Bend.

They'd met at a shooting range. He had always enjoyed shooting with his older brother, who was a hell of a shot with a long-scoped rifle. This was something that John had never been good at, as much as he had tried. While they were shooting, Bill Kirkpatrick was sitting next to them on the 500-yard range. He walked over and made casual conversation, noticing his assault pack with various police patches and Infrared flag from his old military uniforms. Bill admired their rifles and made small talk with John and his brother, Luke. After a short amount of small talk, he found out that his ranch adjoined the small plot of land that Luke had just purchased. They nearly shared a driveway. They laughed at what they thought could have been divine providence. Bill remarked how similar Luke looked to his son, only ten years older. He and Luke bonded over long range shooting and deer hunting. Bill and his wife Susan had picked up "homesteading" to keep them busy around their ranch and keep their thoughts away from the loss of their son. Bill and Susan had become avid canners and gardeners and raised a small herd of cattle and horses. They both had gotten into HAM radio, since it reminded Bill of his days as a radio operator in Vietnam. Even through the technology had greatly changed since the 1970s, Bill picked it up easily, and Susan had proven adept at it as well. Bill exchanged information with John, and they kept in contact regularly for years. He told Bill not to tell his brother that he was keeping an eye on him, and they shared a laugh and agreed to keep each other's secrets.

After John departed for home those years ago, he was glad to know that his family was watched over. He was also a little jealous that his family would be safe at a larger and better stocked survival retreat at the Kirkpatrick ranch than he would be at his home back in Kankakee. He was happy though, at the prospect of the strong bond that was forged between Bill Kirkpatrick and his brother. Luke filled the void that had been left by the loss of Bill's son. They became as close as father and son, shooting and hunting together. Luke spent much of his time off work helping out at the ranch, doing most of the manual labor.

Over the years, Bill kept in constant contact with John over the HAM radio waves, assuring him that as things got worse, he would take care of his brother. Recently, just before the cell service had gone out, Bill told John that Luke had been laid off from his job with the Federal government. The Feds had deemed the wildland firefighters a "non-essential government employee group" and terminated them en masse as the economy began to slip into freefall. Bill told John that he had moved Luke and his wife into the spare rooms of the ranch house to be closer together. They kept Luke's cabin as a fallback point and a stash house for spare gear and supplies. Bill was unaware that John and Luke's parents were heading back home to stay in Oregon with them.

"Well shit, Johnny boy, I hear the interstates are getting pretty hairy. Things aren't too bad here locally, other than everybody feeling the effects of the economy. Everybody is losing jobs. I suspect it won't stay stable for much longer. Have you been in contact with your parents? I don't know how long it will take for them to get here."

John started to get worried. It had been nearly three days since his parents left, and he had been so busy that he hadn't remembered to get in contact with his parents to check on their progress. He had given his father a spare HAM radio but wasn't sure it was going to reach. He also hadn't had the time to show his parents how to use it, other than the basics of turning it on, charging it, and monitoring the air. He hadn't expected the cell service to go down so quickly. He told Bill to hold on and changed the HAM radio station over to the emergency frequency that he had set on the small radio he'd given to his parents. He made a few short transmissions attempting to make contact. After five minutes with no reply, he made a few short transmissions, telling them to make contact as soon as possible and try to make contact with Bill. He switched over and gave Bill the frequency he had left his parents' radio on and asked him to monitor it for him. Bill had more spare time than he did and thankfully obliged. "You know I'd do anything for you guys. You helped raise my second son. I'll get them here safely, boy. I'll make a regular status check-in with you every night at 9 P.M. your time. KP Out."

CHAPTER 4.5 - REGROUP (CONTINUED)

July 2nd – 4:00 P.M. CST, Kankakee IL

John was sitting at his desk in the office, absorbed in thinking about his parents. He was in a daydream when he heard one of the radio frequencies that he scanned begin to pick up chatter. He snapped back to reality and checked the small screen on the base radio. It was a frequency he had saved that he used to keep in contact with his prepping friends and militia north in the Chicago area and further north in Wisconsin and Minnesota. He turned down the other channels he was scanning and tuned in to the Chicago channel. He soon realized that he recognized the voice on the other end. It sounded like Theo, which he soon confirmed with the coded call signs coming out.

"District 5 George to K21, emergency traffic, over! Come in K21."

He knew that was for him. K21 was the police radio call sign for the beat that he lived on in Kankakee. And he knew that Theo was assigned to Chicago PD District 5 currently. He quickly picked up the mic and answered. "5 George, go ahead for K21."

Theo finally answered. "Shit, finally, man! Been trying to reach you for twenty minutes. I think we just got in range of this hand radio. I-57 is bad; had to get off and take Route 45 down. We took heavy fire. We're rolling in on flats and rims. Should be there in about twenty minutes. I think we've got a tail. We're gonna be coming in hot. White Explorer, Alamo plus one. Over."

"Roger 5 George, we'll be waiting with open arms in the endzone for the Hail Mary." He wondered who the plus one would be. But he figured they must be important if Theo had let them in on it.

John had to hurry up. Worried about the chance of a tail following Theo, he wanted to be ready. He alerted Andrew and told him to get ready. He then went and grabbed his kit. He threw on his duty belt with the drop leg Safariland holster, his TYR multicam plate carrier, and grabbed his AR.

Andrew climbed up John's radio tower onto the roof to get a good vantage point. He took one of his long-range battle rifles and spotting scopes to get a good view of the area. John heard a round being chambered on the AR10 sniper rifle, a clone of the US Army's M110, as Andrew called out, "I'm set. Not much moving that I can see. I'll keep an eye out towards the main roads in."

With Andrew on overwatch, John went out to the gate and opened it up, pulling the padlock off and pushing the wooden gates open. He was checking his rifle and pistol when he heard Andrew yell from the rooftop, "Incoming! I see Theo's white Explorer coming in hard, throwing sparks everywhere. He's got two vehicles flowing and shooting at him. Coming down Curtis Street now! Get ready for a fight!"

He heard a shot ring out from Andrew's AR-10, then a few more, as he emptied his mag. Andrew began reloading, and John could hear tires screeching and metal rims scraping as the vehicles rounded the corner. Theo's Explorer was pulling a small, enclosed trailer and took the last corner so hard he almost rolled. The Explorer was riding on rims with sparks flying. He pulled up onto the sidewalk, clearing a line of sight on the trailing vehicles which were still shooting at him. John raised his rifle and opened fire on the first vehicle, dumping a full magazine into the windshield. The older Buick swerved and jumped the curb, crashing into a tree. The second car, a red Pontiac Grand Prix, swerved to avoid the accident and kept coming. Andrew fired four well-placed shots from the AR10 into the Pontiac's driver until it slowed, then rolled to a stop in the middle of the street. Two men attempted to get out of the old Buick but were shot down by Andrew. Theo rolled his vehicle into the lot and hopped out with his AR at the ready, taking up a fighting position behind the cover of the brick wall around the compound.

John and Theo cleared the wreckage of the cars, finding all four occupants of the two vehicles to be dead. They quickly pulled gear off the dead men and dragged it all into the perimeter of the fence. John noticed that none of his neighbors came out to check out the commotion. He suspected that many of them had either fled or bugged out by now. He'd seen a few of the houses' occupants loading trucks or vans in the last few weeks but hadn't spoken to any of them. He hadn't seen a single one of the neighbors on his block in almost a week. He made a mental note to speak to the guys about going to check the houses for any useful supplies in the next few days.

John turned to Theo finally and shook his hand. "So your trip down looked eventful. We can talk about that later. Who did you bring with?"

Theo replied, "Sorry, bro, I grabbed a hose jockey, but it's one we like." He motioned to the car and out stepped their friend, Big Rob. Rob was a 6-foot-3-inch 300-pound black man who wore big-framed glasses but had the strong frame of a former football lineman. He was a Chicago firefighter, whom John had met a few years ago through Theo. They'd gone shooting together from time. Rob was also a paramedic and helped teach tactical medicine to John, Theo, and several other friends.

Big Rob smiled big as he limped away from the car. He had his bandaged arm in a sling. From the blood on the bandage, it appeared that he was still bleeding. He was was a welcome sight, and John walked up to him and gave him a big hug. Rob said, "I brought as many first aid supplies as I could spare and stole a bunch from the ambo on my way out." He winced as they hugged and added, "There's a story behind this... oh and, I'm sorry... I brought another guest."

The back door of the Explorer came open and out stepped a petite light-skinned black woman wearing hospital scrubs. She looked to be in her late twenties, with glowing brown eyes. She sheepishly said, "Uhh… hi. My name is Shonna." She extended her hand out to shake John's.

"This is my girlfriend, Johnny," Rob interrupted. "She's a nurse at the Children's Hospital. I'm so sorry, brother, but we didn't have any better option. Theo came through and saved us as we were trying to make our way to his place to get out of Dodge. Then shit got crazy. We wanted to hit you up to ask first, but it got bad before we could make contact. We grabbed our medics bags and my bug-out bag and a duffel bag with some spare supplies. Sorry, but all I got is my Glock 19 on me for weapons."

John answered him quickly: "Relax, man, you're all welcome here. The more the merrier. We've got you covered on anything you guys need. Now let's get you guys inside and all settled in."

He led Big Rob and Shonna into one of the spare bedrooms. He conveniently picked the one that he kept the medical supplies in. "Take your time getting settled in. Get cleaned up and get some rest. I'll make some food in a little bit once we get the supplies moved in." He then went back outside to Theo, who was pouring water on what remained of the smoking, shredded tires on his car.

Theo turned to him with a big shit-eating grin on his face and pointed to the trailer. "The car's taking a shit, but I came bearing gifts, brother. As much as I could fit in my trailer on short notice."

John was happy to see that Theo had already closed and locked the gates to the lot. Theo knew his way around his place well and came down to visit often on his days off. Aside from Andrew, Theo knew best most of the intimate details of his prepping and supplies. He was glad to see that Theo had made it safely.

He looked Theo up and down. Theo was wearing a green pair of 5.11 tactical pants with his work duty belt that held his long slide Glock 34 in 9mm with a red dot on it. He had on a black T-shirt under his work tactical bullet proof vest emblazoned with his Chicago PD star and his last name on it with "District 5 Tactical Unit" above his nametag. Other than looking exhausted, he didn't look to be in too bad of shape.

Theo walked over and opened his trailer. John was glad to see that Theo had it stacked nearly to the ceiling with ammo crates and tough boxes. He had even brought two large portable generators and a few larger solar panels. He saw several gas cans stored near the front securely tied together. John was happy to see that bullets had not damaged anything critical, striking only a few duffel bags stuffed full of clothing near the top of the load.

They took turns carrying items into the house and storage shed. Andrew came down a short time later, shaking Theo's hand and saying, "Sorry I took so long; had to let the kids get acquainted with Big Rob and Shonna. I think they've made friends. My daughter is pretty stoked there's another woman around. Let's get your gear inside, Theo. You still have a spare gear locker down in the basement."

They began dragging Theo's gear down to the basement, where they had kept a majority of the equipment. John had been able to take several old large gear lockers from the police department when they remodeled the locker rooms. He got his pick of the ten best lockers and brought them home, where he lined the basement with them. He'd offered the space to friends that wanted to store gear in his house. Theo already had a small amount of gear and ammo in one of the lockers. He took the small bedroom in the basement nearest to the gear storage room.

They carried Big Rob's bags and the few bags and boxes full of medical supplies and trauma kits into the house. He was happy to see that Big Rob had brought several high-quality trauma kits and military grade combat lifesaver bags. He left their personal duffel bags outside of the other main floor guest room, where they were already fast asleep. He figured they could use the rest. He told Theo to go get some sleep once his gear was moved in. It was already dark, and he could tell that Theo was exhausted. Theo retreated downstairs into the bedroom in the basement, dropped his gear, and knocked out.

John and Andrew walked the perimeter of the fence line and made sure all of the doors and windows were secured, smoked cigarettes and took a moment to chat.

"I'm feeling a lot better about things now that we have this motley crew here. I think we are doing well. At least a lot better than before."

Andrew replied, "Yeah man, I'm feeling a lot better. Might even have time to post up an LP/OP and guard around the clock, or at least when it's dark."

"Yeah, you're right, Andrew," John said. "What do you think about putting up some sandbags up on the roof and a camouflage net up? Your position seemed like a really good spot today. You did some damn good shooting up there today. I felt glad you had my back while I was stuck on the ground."

Andrew thought for a minute and said, "Yeah, honestly it was a great spot. Your house sits a little higher than most of the others in the neighborhood. I had a good view and pretty clear line of sight in almost every direction. The roof isn't on that hard of a slope, so I think it would work well. Let's make that the project for tomorrow." John checked his watch, seeing that it was already past midnight. They went back inside and parted ways, heading to sleep. He slept soundly, knowing he was amongst friends, and in good company.

CHAPTER 5: CIRCLING THE WAGONS

July 3rd – Kankakee IL

John woke up the next morning later than he'd hoped. It was already past 8:00 A.M. and the day had long since begun. He walked down the stairs and was glad to see that nobody else was up yet. After yesterday's event-filled day for everyone else, he was glad that they all could sleep in and get much needed rest. He went to the kitchen and made a large pot of coffee, as was his morning ritual. He decided to cook a large breakfast for everyone. He stepped out onto his back porch and lit the large flat top propane grill and began preparing a hearty breakfast. A short time later, Big Rob and Theo stepped out onto the porch with him, holding coffee mugs that he'd left out on the counter for everyone to serve themselves. They passed out a few large cigars that one produced from a small portable humidor. The three enjoyed a very nice cigar with their coffee as the breakfast was being heated on the griddle. He knew that Theo and Big Rob had very good taste in fine tobacco and cigars. John often laughed to himself when he wondered how large a portion of their budgets went toward cigars, but he couldn't comment as he also had a large 300-cigar humidor in his den.

The others in the household smelled the food and began to filter out onto the large back porch. Everyone served themselves and helped themselves to a large spread of eggs, bacon, breakfast sausage, and fried potatoes. He enjoyed making a large heavy meal for breakfast; it helped carry people through the day in his personal experience. He thought it was also a great way to start the day on a positive note. Plus, you never knew if you would have the time or means to have another meal later in the day.

After eating, John, Theo, Andrew, and Big Rob sat in chairs around the patio table puffing on their cigars. Theo began to tell his story of how his journey down happened:

"After you contacted me, things all fell into place. We got notifications at work that we were being laid off indefinitely in two days. Barely any notice, and it's even against our union contract. Can you believe that shit? The third largest city in the United States, and they just said, 'fuck it' and gave up. They basically started disbanding the whole police department. Guys had been going AWOL left and right. I knew I had to get out of the city, or I would be dead. I went ahead and left work and told them I wouldn't be coming back for the last day. I knew I had work to do, and I was playing major catch up. I went to the bank and tried to close my accounts, withdrawing all the cash they would let me. The only reason they let me do anything this late was because I was still wearing my work uniform. Then I went straight to the grocery store and loaded up on all the batteries and canned goods I could buy. I was pretty well stocked already, but I wanted to grab as much extra as I could. I then went and filled up as much gasoline as I could. I filled up all ten gas cans I had for gasoline, and the other five that I had for diesel for my second generator. I booked it home and started packing. My neighborhood isn't bad, but it was getting worse in a hurry for sure. I backed my trailer up right into my backyard to unload my gear. Luckily, I had most of my stuff in the house consolidated and packed up for easy transport. I made the call to Rob to tell him to get ready, and I was going to come pick him up. We had talked about it on and off for weeks in case things got any worse. After that, things got bad. I was alone, trying to unload everything from my house into the trailer. I was dragging some boxes out of my house when I caught a few gangbangers trying to steal some of my shit. I dropped the box, turned and drew down on one. One of the idiots tried to pull out a gun on me, so I shot both of them. I was sure there was going to be more gangbangers out pillaging the neighborhood, so I had to step it up. I hurried up and finished as quickly as I could, buckled up the car and trailer, locked up my doors, and took off. As I was leaving the alley, I ran into

more bangers. I figured they were coming to meet up with the other looters. They shot at me a little, but I took off and hauled ass over the few blocks to Big Rob's place. When I got to his place, he was still trying to pull together some of his gear. He hadn't been as prepared to go mobile as I was. I figured the gangbangers would soon discover that I had killed their guys and would be coming after me. We grabbed as much of his gear as we could grab by hand and just piled it in the back of the Explorer. Rob had to leave a lot of stuff behind, but we managed to get a good amount of his kit, tactical gear, a few guns and some ammo, and his medic's packs. We got most of his medical supplies too. We didn't have much time to grab anything else, because the bangers showed up. I know they were looking for my vehicle, so it was only a matter of time until they found me so close to my house. We piled into my car and took off as fast as we could. I was going to start heading down the interstate, but Big Rob was adamant that we had to go get his girlfriend at the hospital. I didn't want to go back into the city, but I wasn't going to let our boy Rob down. We took off into the Southside toward the hospital. The bangers kept on our tail all the way to the hospital. I couldn't drive well enough to lose them because I was pulling the trailer. We rolled up to the hospital, and Shonna jumped right in. Luckily, we didn't have to stop and find her; she was waiting right in the front. When we showed up, the two cars of gangbangers started opening up at us. I think they thought we were going to bail or something at the hospital. We took off down I-57 as hard as we could. I was hoping that they would give up when we got out of the city, but I guess killing one of their gang members was unforgiveable in their eyes. They weren't going to stop until we were dead. They chased us all the way down I-57. We ran into roadblocks and were shot at by others on the interstate several times. We finally got off around Matteson and just took Route 45 down to Kankakee. It was a bumpy ride, but I'm glad we made it. I can't think of any other place I'd rather be when the shit hits the fan."

When Theo wrapped up his story, Andrew shared his plans for the LP/OP lookout on the roof that he wanted to get built. It would be a great addition to the security of the house. He pulled out a sketch he had made overnight and a list of needed equipment. They spent the remainder of the morning filling sandbags up and hauling everything up to the roof and stacking them among the other needed supplies. Andrew, having the most experience with long range shooting, took the lead with the planning.

John already had most of the supplies, tools, and some lumber on hand. His house had a perfect spot below the crest of the roof, where the slant was on a very shallow angle. After a brief discussion, the consensus was that the roof needed to be reinforced to support the weight that they planned on adding to create the LP/OP. They didn't have quite enough solid material to reinforce the roof and also complete the structure on top, so Andrew suggested that they go salvage supplies from the old K-Mart warehouse east of town. As exciting as that may have sounded, he was very against going too far from the compound. Things were too uncertain to travel all the way across town. He instead suggested going just west of town to the old Roper/Sears warehouse ruins looking for building materials. On Court Street just west of the city limits was the old crumbling warehouse that the city had neglected to tear down. Instead, the city fenced off the area, which stretched from Main Street all the way out of town to the land that the railroad company owned west of the city limits. They agreed on the safer trip west of town and came up with a quick impromptu plan. They loaded up their gear, hitched one of the trailers to John's Tahoe, geared up and headed out to the west.

It was a short journey to the edge of town, only a few blocks from the compound. They cleared the neighborhood with no resistance and made it to the chain-linked fences of the factory. They all jumped out, cut a section out of the fence with tin snips and looked around for the building materials they needed. They scavenged wood and metal beams that they found lying around. The warehouse was in ruins but appeared clear. The guys were quickly dragging the building materials into the trailer, sacrificing security for speed. This ended up being a mistake. A voice suddenly chimed out, "WE DON'T APRECIATE YOU TAKING OUR SHIT." Suddenly a young man stepped out of the shadows. He appeared to be in his late teens or early twenties. He was dressed in dirty, baggy sports clothes that resembled gang clothing. He was carrying a Glock in his right hand, but it wasn't raised.

John was the only one carrying his rifle and immediately raised His MK18 at the gang banger. He broke the silence first: "What do you mean, 'we'? How many of you are there?"

Theo and Rob scanned the rest of the immediate area.

The gang banger cracked a smile and said, "You're outgunned, bitch." And three more teenagers stepped out into the open, standing in a line facing the group. They held an assortment of weapons; one had a sawed-off shotgun, another a Hi-point pistol, and one (alarmingly enough) cradled what looked to be a Mac-10 sub machine gun. The teenagers looked barely older than sixteen. They all held their weapons low, not pointing them at the group.

It was a show of force, and John knew that none of those kids were killers, or even seasoned gang members for that matter. Most of them still had a look of youthful innocence. It was a bluff on their part, and he knew it. He didn't want to call their bluff, but it seemed to be their only option. He shot a sideways glance at Andrew, who he knew was also thinking along the same lines. "Now, let's all remain calm here..." he started slowly. "Nobody needs to die today... We got what we came for. No harm, no foul."

As he spoke, Theo picked up on his cue and backed away, closing the trailer slowly and quietly.

"Here's how this is going to work: We're going to leave, and everybody lives to see another day."

With the group's calm and confidence, the gang bangers began to show uncertainty in their actions. That uncertainty slowly turned to fear. The group could all sense it. The teen gangbanger who had been doing the speaking spoke again. This time his voice was shaking. "Yo. Yo... shut the f-fuck up! We ain't tryin' to hear your bullshit. We... we want your shit, now don't make us take it."

John cracked a smile and decided to try to channel his best Clint Eastwood vibe: "Do you wanna die here, boy? You ever killed a man? Because I have. Most of us here have. We've all seen death, and we aren't afraid of it. Truth is, you're all too scared to shoot, but any one of my group would drop you like a fat chick on ice skates and sleep like a baby at night."

The gang banger began to shake, and the other three slowly started lowering their guns ever so slightly. The window of opportunity was open, and John, Theo, Andrew, and Rob all drew their pistols from their belts with lightning speed, the result of years of practice. In an instant, the tides had turned, and the gang bangers were caught off guard with their weapons lowered, staring down the barrels of the four men across from them holding pistols centered on their chests. Two of the younger gang members suddenly dropped their guns and put their hands up in the air.

"You pieces of shit!" yelled the banger that had been doing the talking. He and the other man that hadn't dropped their guns still held them low in their arms, their body language showing signs of defeat, even if his words hadn't admitted it.

"Now who's out gunned? **Bitch,**" John said, mocking the first words of the gang bangers. "Now drop those guns before we have to kill you. Nobody needs to die here. Set your guns down, and step back. If you do everything we say, you get to live to see another day."

The gang banger slowly lowered his Mac-10 to the ground, setting it at his feet. They all stepped back from their weapons, tears showing in the eyes of the two younger ones.

Rob slowly moved forward and collected the weapons from the ground and put them in the truck. They all slowly backed away, jumped in their car, and sped away.

Rob spoke up from the back seat first. "You bullshitting ass motherfucker! I'm glad we got out of there okay, because I'm not cool with shooting fucking kids, man!"

Everyone else was silent for a moment until Theo finally spoke up, "This is the world we live in now, guys. No more bullshitting; we almost had to kill those shitbags, and I'm okay with it. I think it's a reality that we all have to come to terms with."

Andrew just leaned back in his seat, unusually silent with a quizzical look of introspection on his face. He knew that of this four, only John and Theo had been involved in shootings at work. Prior to this new change in the world, it was the closest thing to actual combat that Americans would see stateside. And even those two were still dealing with the psychological trauma that came with it. All four had seen their share of death and faced their own different psychological trauma more than the average American would in their lifetime, given their choices in occupation.

The rest of the short ride back to the compound was completely quiet. They soon pulled back into the gates of the compound and began unloading the materials from the trailer. John was glad that they could focus their uneasy minds on a specific task. It would help keep their minds off the previous events. Once they all got to work, everyone quickly pushed the feelings to the back of their minds and the collective moods improved.

The only thing said was when Andrew caught John in passing. "You know, we need to start thinking a little harder about taking trips outside the wire now, Johnny. Need to think if it's worth the risk or not. That could have been a lot worse, and we need to start thinking about that. That's all I'm going to say about it. I know you're thinking the same."

John just nodded to his friend rather than adding unnecessary words. They were both thinking along the same lines. They needed to focus on the building of the LP/OP structure.

They first reinforced the roof below where the LP/OP was planned, adding wood and some metal beams underneath the roof in the attic. They then stacked sandbags into a fighting position about four feet tall and nearly twelve feet long in a "U" shape. They put up a wooden frame to keep the sandbags in place. They decided on building up beams to enclose the LP/OP and give it a plywood roof. They shingled the plywood with the same shingles of the roof in an attempt to keep the LP/OP hidden from a distance. They attached camouflage netting to the sides of the post. Once the frame was in place around the sandbags, everything appeared to be finished with the frame. They spraypainted the wood dark brown to match the roof around it. The structure was built a little down from the peak of the roof, called the "military crest" so that from a distance the structure wouldn't silhouette. The person sitting in the LP/OP would still be able to see for a few feet gap in the rear as well, and the rear of the structure was lined with sandbags.

While this was going on, Andrew had the double duty of both overseeing the construction to the best specifications and keeping a lookout with his scoped AR-10. He would spend part of his time scanning the surrounding area, and the other part barking orders and making corrections. He was a bit of an asshole sometimes, but it was best to defer to his expertise in this matter.

Once the structure was finished, they began to move in gear and equipment. They built a small, shelfed desk inside the walls, and small cabinets and cubby holes to store gear. They moved in a short lawn chair and a shop stool with wheels on the bottom to allow freedom to move around. They also moved up one of the spotting scopes set on the tripod. They left an ammo box with a rangefinder and a military surplus PVS-14 Night vision optic and spare batteries. They left spare ammunition and magazines in the cubbies. A spare handheld two-way radio and HAM radio was also set up. They set up a CB radio and police scanner and power outlet strip, which was all wired to a solar panel on the roof. It was a very nice set-up and had a great view of the surrounding neighborhood.

As they worked, they took turns standing watch for security. While John took his turn and stood security on the roof, he couldn't help but notice how quiet the streets were in his subdivision. No cars or people were out, even during the middle of the afternoon. He scanned the streets watching cats and stray dogs running around, digging through trash. He could faintly see smoke farther east into the city but could not see where it was coming from. He figured that this was the calm before the storm, and his prediction came true; as the sun started to get low, he noticed the sporadic gunfire around town start to pick up. And at about 8:00 P.M., the lights started to flicker, and the power went out.

It was only a matter of time. This is it, when it all starts to go downhill, he thought. The solar battery banks were working, and the power to his compound went back on after a couple minutes when John turned off the main power breaker, then turning on the transfer switch box for the battery bank. Everyone went around and unplugged and turned off all non-essential electronics and lights. They all walked the perimeter and pulled the shades on the inside and closed the heavy shutters to all the second story windows to ensure that no light got out. The whole company shared a silent dinner together and went their separate ways. He figured tonight would be a good first night to have a standing guard in the LP/OP. Being a natural night owl, he volunteered to take the overnight watch. He grabbed his kit, an assault pack with spare ammunition, a few snacks and an MRE. He last grabbed his AR and his long rifle, a Springfield M1-A with a 1-8X magnified scope. He slung the M4 on his pack and carried his M1A. As was becoming the new nightly ritual, he and Andrew walked the perimeter and fence line, now checking harder for any light escaping from the house. After the perimeter was secured, and the gates were secured and checked, Andrew went inside to sleep.

John climbed up onto the roof and sat down on the chair of the LP/OP. He was amazed by how dark everything was. The stars seemed so bright, and the moon's natural light illuminated the streets. It was bright enough that he only used the NVGs sparingly to scan the shadows once every hour or so. He had agreed to take the whole overnight watch, and in exchange, he would sleep away the morning when the sun rose. He didn't mind, as he wasn't a big morning person, and since the group had started to come into place, he felt safer about sleeping and letting the others carry some weight.

It was a boring few hours early in the night. He even turned on the radio quietly to scan and see if any FM radio channels were still on the air. After wasting an hour or so and finding nothing, he finally got bored of hearing the static and a few channels with only emergency messages on loops. As the night went on, the worst parts of the city woke up. The sporadic gunfire picked up further into the city. Scarily enough, he even heard what sounded like spurts of automatic gunfire. During the various volleys of gunfire, he winced, remembering his own shooting. He half hoped that none of his brothers and sisters on the police force were still out there trying to work. The streets had been getting worse and worse during the slow recession leading up to the market crash, and he knew the results of it more than most.

Hours passed with no major occurrences close enough to cause major concern. He wrapped himself in his woodland camo poncho liner which was commonly referred to as a "woobie" by most members of the military. Boredom set in, but he tried to maintain his focus. He kept his mind sharp by naming the streets in his neighborhood and planning routes of ingress and egress to his subdivision. He munched on an apple and some trail mix. He jotted down some notes in his "write in the rain" field notebook about long-term concerns, security concerns, and brainstorming locations and stores for supply runs. He kept himself occupied, and the nighttime hours passed gruelingly slow. Finally, after what seemed like an eternity, the dawn began to break. The gunfire had long passed hours ago, and he was enjoying the near absolute silence.

He scanned the neighborhood, adjusting to the light beginning to break on the horizon. He checked his watch. It was just before 5:30 A.M. He was relieved that his shift was soon over. He began to gather his personal items and tidy up the LP/OP. He packed his assault pack and set it near the rear of the structure. He sat back down and began recording in the watch log book, a large leather-bound notebook that a friend had previously "requisitioned" from the county jail years ago. He jotted the date, hours worked, his name, and a few notes:

> –Sporadic gunfire throughout night
> -Possible automatic weapons?
> -no major movements on west side of city
> -stray dogs/animals
> -fire/smoke far east (fire not visible)
> -No movement in immediate area (possibly already abandoned subdivision?)

He figured he would discuss a few of these things with Andrew when he came up for his guard shift. He sat for a few minutes with his thoughts, when he heard Andrew climbing the radio tower to the roof. A short time later, his short little Marine buddy appeared, lugging his AR-10 and assault pack on his back. Andrew dropped his gear down next to the entrance to the LP/OP and scooted in, sitting down on the chair next to him.

"How ya feelin', big man? Long night? Anything good to pass on?" Andrew asked him.

They discussed the notes in the field notebook. "Well, we know how bad Kankakee was getting before all this shit went down. You of all people, you big dumb bullet magnet. There were a lot of guns out there, and now… well, it's open season out there, Johnny…" Andrew said. "Now… automatic weapons… that's a scary thought, man…We have a good amount of firepower here…" he said, patting his trusty scoped AR10 long rifle, "but if someone or a group hits us with automatic fire, it could really put us in a tight spot… putting it lightly, we'd be fucked." Andrew drifted off for a moment, staring off into the distance. "Shit, man, I wish it were legal to own one before all this… I'd have dumped some fun money into a good belt-fed light machine gun." Andrew had a large grin on his face.

John looked back at Andrew's beaming smile and said, "I'd kill for one. Brings back good memories for me… I was a machine gunner for a few years in the Guard… there's nothing like a good rip from a belt-fed LMG to get your blood flowing."

Andrew chuckled and said, "Maybe write that down for the long-term goals. Never know what we could find out there when we have to start venturing out to scavenge for supplies."

They chatted back and forth for another twenty minutes until John yawned loudly in mid-conversation. He decided to check out and head to bed. "I'm going to knock out for the morning. I think Theo knows to come up and relieve you in eight hours. When I wake up, I'm going to get working on making sure all our new guests are properly equipped and taken care of. I'll see you in eight or so."

He grabbed his gear and climbed down off the roof. He went to straight to his bed, opting to skip breakfast. By approximately 6:45 A.M., he was in bed and fast asleep.

John slept hard until a little past noon. He wanted to sleep in longer but knew that there was still plenty work that needed to be done. He got up, threw on some clothes, strapped on his 1911, and walked downstairs. He met a few of the group down in the kitchen. Shonna was helping the kids prepare some lunch for everyone. They were cutting up fresh greens from his garden and preparing sandwiches. He greeted the kids warmly with a hug and gave Shonna a big smile. He grabbed a sandwich for himself and grabbed a couple to run up to Andrew in the tower, since he still had a few hours left of his shift.

After he delivered food up to Andrew, he came back into the house. He ran into Theo and Big Rob sitting at the island in his kitchen enjoying their food. He sat down and spoke to them. "Look guys, I know you didn't come here with as much gear as you probably ideally would have wanted. I want to let you know, as you already *should* know, that *mi casa es su casa*. You guys are family now. Everything I have available to spare is for you guys to use. You're my friends, and now, all we have is each other. I want to make sure that you are fully outfitted for a combat load and also any comfort items that you need. What can you think of that you need?"

Theo said, "I was able to get almost all of my stuff out, man. I was a little short on my water, but that's harder to move safely. I didn't get nearly as much food and clothing as I wanted, but I'm pretty set as far as combat gear. I figure the comfort items, food, and hygiene stuff we can go out and scavenge from all these abandoned houses in the neighborhood here soon."

Big Rob spread his big hands. "Look Johnny, I'm sorry Shonna and I didn't come here with shit. I don't want to feel like a freeloader here; we will earn our keep, brother…"

John cut Rob off: "Bro, you guys have more than earned your keep here. You brought a lot of good medical and surgical supplies and tons of experience that we desperately needed. You and Shonna add a world of medical knowledge that I'm going to be needing a lot of. You two are a valuable asset to all of us. You're fucking family. Don't forget that."

They shared a quick one-armed hug, and Shonna peeked her head out of the pantry. Upon seeing them, she quipped, "Okay you two! You gonna kiss now? Should I start looking for another man?" She shared a big toothy smile, her beautiful light brown eyes beaming.

As they all shared a good laugh, John noticed that she wiped a tear from her eye. She said, "I just need to thank you so much for taking us in. You didn't know me at all, and you had no obligation to let me stay. I owe you so much."

He said, "It's really no problem at all. I want to get you guys outfitted with a full combat load. At some point, we are all going to need to go 'outside the wire', so to speak. Outside of the safety of this compound, I want all of us to have a full kit. I have extra gear for all of you. Shonna, do you have any tactical or shooting experience?"

Shonna looked at him sheepishly. "I grew up black in Chicago. I grew up in neighborhoods where people were getting shot every day. Does that count?"

He didn't know how to respond and started to stutter, "Uhhh... well..."

She interrupted him with a chuckle. "I'm just fucking with you, man. My parents were both college professors at UIC. I grew up near the Loop. But my dad was a big follower of Malcom X. He was a gun enthusiast who believed in raising a strong black girl. He said I needed to know how to defend myself. My parents made me take Krav Maga and I learned how to shoot. I used to carry a little .38 revolver in my purse to and from the hospital. I had a little experience shooting an AK with Rob too."

After lunch, John led them downstairs where he kept the spare gear, as well as the gear and guns that they had confiscated from the dead. He got Rob fitted into some tactical pants and multicam fatigues that he had in his size (thankfully, he was a bit "fluffy" with a similar build to Big Rob). He had a battle belt with attached pistol and rifle mag pouches and a drop-leg Safariland duty holster for the Glock 19 that Rob had brought. He dug out a Streamlight weapon light for his pistol as well. He fashioned a drop leg attachment on the opposite leg for a small medic's thigh-rig medic pouch. He had previously invested in several sets of the medic's thigh rigs and was a big fan of them. John carried one on his personal kit and liked having the medic's gear readily available, especially in the capable hands of an experienced tactical medic like Big Rob.

He gave Big Rob ten spare magazines for his Glock 19. He grabbed a black plate carrier, which was conveniently labeled with large "MEDIC" markings on both sides. For Rob's battle rifle, he grabbed an AK-47 that they had taken from one of the gang members that had attacked them on the way down. It had an underfold stock, making it fairly compact, which would help Rob act in his role as a medic. He had a few spare magazines and pouches for his carrier. They had also discovered that the gangbanger had an illegally modified weapon that made the AK fully automatic. They mounted a spare red-dot optic that he had on hand, and added a foregrip and picatinny rails to it to mount a weapon light and Infrared laser. Luckily, he had stocked a spare AK and magazines, and a decent amount of 7.62 ammo for the AK, since it was a very common weapon. He also gave Rob the spare full-sized AK and all the accessories, cleaning kit, and ammo he'd need. Rob had been a big AK fanatic as long as he had known him. All of the other guys gave him constant shit for his refusal to use the AR-15 platform like most of their other shooter friends.

John next helped outfit Shonna. As apprehensive as he was to have someone with her valuable medical skillset outside of the wire in danger, he knew that it was a necessary evil that would have to happen from time to time and wanted her equipped as best as he could. He first gave her a spare set of soft body armor and an old bulletproof vest of his from work. It was going to be plenty big on her, but it still fit comfortably. He had a custom-sewn outer vest carrier with MOLLE loops sewn on, where he had attached magazine holders, a flashlight holster, multiple tourniquet holsters and a small tactical individual first aid kit (IFAK) attached to the front. He gave her a black battle belt with more magazine pouches, and one of the drop-leg medic bags. He dug up a spare black ballistic helmet, which had Velcro patches with the red cross that said "MEDIC" across them. He hooked her up with a few assault packs for her to configure on her own to make a medical bag. Since Shonna had come with no weapons whatsoever, he gave her one of his spare pistols, a subcompact Glock 26 in 9mm, since it used the same 9mm magazines as most of the others at the compound. He pulled out a few holsters for her to wear around the house, and a sturdier duty holster to wear on her battle belt. He also gave her a small Smith and Wesson model 642 "Airweight" .38 revolver with pink grips. It was like the revolver that she had described as carrying in her purse, and he knew that she was familiar with it. For a battle rifle, she received an AR-pattern 9mm carbine with a folding brace. It was compact enough to allow her to work, but powerful enough to be a formidable personal defense weapon if things went bad. It took thirty-round Glock 9mm mags and would also take the 9mm magazines from their Glock pistols, allowing her to carry only one type of magazines, lightening her weight load.

After ensuring that both of their combat kits were all loaded up and well-stocked, he asked them both, "Now, are there any personal items, clothing, or any other items you might need? I tried to think of everything when stocking up this place, but I know I missed some things."

They came up with a few items like rain gear, ponchos, spare shoes, assault packs, and extra blankets for their beds. When asking about personal items, such as hygiene items, Shonna shyly asked,

"Umm... I know I'm the only adult female here... so I hesitate to ask about... you know... woman things..." She trailed off, looking a bit worried.

John said, "I thought of that too. I have a small supply of feminine hygiene products, but those are definitely going to be high on our priority list of items to scavenge or acquire. Oh, and sorry, but you'll have to settle on using men's shampoo and soap for showers for a while." He grinned.

Once they were done, John headed back upstairs to make sure that Theo had gone to relieve Andrew on time for his guard shift. Big Rob and Shonna went back to their room to stage and organize their gear to their own personal standards and comfort. He was happy to know that Shonna had also seemed to have taken on the role of "mother hen" as the only adult female in the house. She had taken over watching Andrew's two children, keeping them organized with tasks around the house like cleaning, cooking, and tending to the garden. Shonna had also showed her knack for organization. Her mild OCD had come in handy, as she was very good at organizing food in the pantry, supplies and gear in the arms storage room downstairs, and the abundance of medical supplies in their room. She started an inventory log of all their gear, supplies, food stocks, weapons, and ammo in a notebook, which helped piggyback from what John had started before the compound had taken on multiple residents. It was a relief that not only had everybody started to settle into their new lives, but also that everyone had seemed to find their sense of purpose.

Later that afternoon, John stepped outside. The day had begun to get a bit warm, and he put on his Multicam boonie hat and rolled up his sleeves. He checked the fence line and checked his water collection barrels that were attached to the downspouts for the gutter system on his house. He stood in the shadows on the side of his house near the open lot, lit a cigarette, and leaned against the house. He didn't smoke often or have a preferred brand, but he kept a few packs in his cigar humidor for when he had a few too many drinks. He tried to relax with the cigarette but couldn't help feeling a bit apprehensive about not having a rifle with him. He ducked inside and grabbed his M1A, which was closest to the front room, along with a few spare magazines which he stuffed in his cargo pockets and stepped back outside to continue enjoying his cigarette. He took out his field notebook and began jotting down some notes.

He was lost in his own thoughts when he heard the CB radio squelch and Theo yelling from the top of the roof, "We have incoming about ten blocks out! Black police vehicle being followed by multiple vehicles. Shots being fired. Need all hands on deck! We're gonna get hit hard!"

John raced back into the house to throw on his full kit and belt. He grabbed his ballistic helmet and Oakley sunglasses, ensured that a round was chambered in his M1A, and ran back out to the front yard.

CHAPTER 6: BORN IN THE U-S-A

July 4th – Kankakee IL

John clicked on the radio on his kit and asked for a SITREP from Theo up on the roof. He could hear the police sirens and gunfire approaching their location. He knew the next words out of Theo's voice on the radio, "They're definitely heading our way. Contact imminent. Three blocks out!"

He opened up the gates to the lot and took up a fighting position out on the sidewalk behind one of the wrecked vehicles from the day before.

Getting set, he heard Big Rob and Andrew running out and glanced over to see them in their full kits. Rob took up position behind the next car and Andrew scampered up to the roof to lay down behind his rifle.

Theo chirped up on the radio and yelled, "Turning the corner now! Contact!" He saw the black Police Tahoe turn the corner at nearly forty mph, lights and sirens rocking and tires screeching. It picked up speed on the straightaway towards the house, bullets ricocheting off it as multiple vehicles turned the corner, hot on the heels of the Tahoe. The Tahoe pulled just short of the entrance to the compound, clearing the line of sight to the vehicles in pursuit. He saw multiple people hanging out of the windows of the vehicles in pursuit, firing various small arms in their direction. He and Big Rob opened up from their positions, dumping full magazines into the vehicles.

Andrew and Theo were on the edge of the roof, firing multiple shots down onto the street. After nearly five minutes of a sustained firefight, the fire from the marauders' vehicles began to subside.

John and Rob moved up to the next cover closer to the enemy vehicles with Andrew and Theo covering from the roof. They cleared the enemy position. Only one marauder was found still breathing and barely clinging to life.

Rob turned to ask what they should do with him, when John unholstered his 1911 and executed the man with a single shot to the head. They cleared the remaining carnage and the bullet-ridden vehicles, finding no others alive. They separated weapons from the corpses and headed back to the large black police Tahoe.

John walked up to the driver's side door and it opened. Out stumbled a short Hispanic female in dark fatigues and police uniform. He knew her! Dezeray Ruiz took a few steps and stumbled into his arms. She was bleeding lightly from a cut on her head. She looked up at him, gasping for air, and said, "Sarge… got hit… He's bad… Couldn't think of anywhere else in the city to bring him… on short notice… Hospitals got overrun…"

Rob ran over to the passenger door and pulled it open, finding an unconscious grey-haired police sergeant in the side seat. He was bleeding heavily from a sucking chest wound. Rob quickly pulled him out of the car, threw him over his shoulder, and screamed for Shonna, "SHONNA!!! ONE URGENT SURGICAL MALE COMING IN!" Big Rob sprinted like the former star football player he was in his youth, closing the 200-meter gap from the Tahoe and through the open gates to the house in what seemed like seconds. Shonna threw the door open and they disappeared inside.

John sized up Dezeray and said, "Dez! Are you okay? Is anyone else following you? Should we be expecting another attack?"

She caught her breath and said, "I… I'm fine. I don't think so. Those were all the cars following us. I'm sorry, I didn't know where else to go. We're losing the grip on the city. It's open season out there! I… we need your help… I'm so sorry." She began sobbing, burying her face in his chest.

John held her tightly. "Let's get you together and all your stuff inside the compound. Can you still drive?" She stood back, wiped her tears, and nodded her head. "Good," he said. "Pull the squad inside the fence line; we're going to grab the guns out here and push the cars out of the street."

Dezeray hopped in the car and did as he said.

Theo came running out and said, "What else do you need, Johnny?"

"Let's push these cars in a staggered formation in and around the roadway. It will form a sort of barrier in the street. Then let's move these bodies into one of these yards and collect whatever useful gear we can find."

The two went to work pushing the cars into a loose, staggered formation blocking most of the street leading up the compound. Next they dragged the bullet-riddled bodies into one of the open yards down the road and threw them into a loose pile. He noticed that they were all young males who were heavily tattooed with gang symbols and wore various gang colors. He didn't recognize any of them personally but wasn't paying any particular attention. There were approximately ten bodies, a substantial force. He was happy that the four of them had managed to repel such a large force without sustaining any casualties. Once the bodies were piled up, they poured gasoline on the bodies and lit them on fire in an ungraceful funeral pyre.

They carried the gear back into the fence line. They didn't find much useful, beyond some AK-47s, a few AR-15s, and many various Hi-Point and other cheap pistols and revolvers. There were small amounts of various ammunition in boxes in some of the vehicles, along with a few water bottles, sports drinks, and some unopened beer cans and liquor bottles, which were also carried inside. They closed the fence again and went back inside the house.

John could hear the screams of the old sergeant. Shonna and Rob had already gone to work in an attempt to save the life of the police veteran. He and Theo walked into the dining room, where Shonna had set up heavy plastic sheeting over the table and floors as an impromptu operating room. They asked how they could help. Shonna was fast at work with trauma shears removing his clothing.

Rob, who was assisting, asked John to bring in as much spare medical gear from the cabinets in the guest room as they could. He told Theo to go to the kitchen and start boiling as many large pots of water as he could.

Big Rob hooked Sarge up to an IV bag and monitored his vital signs. Shonna wiped the blood off and applied an occlusive dressing to his chest. The old sergeant was breathing with great difficulty, with his chest rising and falling unevenly.

"His right lung is collapsed, Shonna. Tension Pneumothorax is setting in. We're gonna need to get a chest decompression needle in on my side," Rob said. He pulled a sterile needle out of one of the trauma kits, felt for the third intercostal space between the ribs on the sergeant's side, and inserted the needle in between the ribs.

You could hear the whoosh of air, as the pressure buildup in the lungs was relieved. Rob taped the needle in place and cleaned the area around the wound. Shonna was busy scrubbing the area around the chest wound, making sure that the entire entry wound was covered. Sarge's breathing slowed down to a controlled rate, and he drifted back into an unconscious but stable state.

John went to check on their other new guest, He didn't have to go far; he found Dezeray sitting down against the wall outside, crying. She still held her pistol in her hand and was covered in blood and dirt. He grabbed the Glock 19 from her hand and put it back into her holster on her duty belt. He kneeled down next to her and grabbed her by her shoulders, giving her a light squeeze. "Hey, it's going to be alright. You got him to the right place at the right time. I'm glad you thought to bring him here. Are you hurt or hit anywhere? We should check you out; I'm sure the adrenaline is starting to wear off."

He helped her stand up and gave her a quick look over. Dezeray Ruiz was still new to the department, and he didn't know her well. The twenty-six-year-old Hispanic girl was a firecracker. She was a tough little Latina at five-foot-two who had just joined the department before his shooting had taken him out of work. He had only met her a handful of times. He knew that she had just come out of the active-duty Army, where she had just finished up her second contract, having two different combat deployments overseas. She was a tough girl, and it was hard to see her broken down like this.

Her uniform and clothes were torn, and she was bleeding from a few minor cuts and scrapes and a small bleed on her forehead, but he found nothing major. He felt a little embarrassed checking her up and down, because by all means, Dez was a total fox. She was an absolutely gorgeous young woman, with dark brown hair, beautiful brown eyes, a darker complexion, and a very nice set of legs. Her tight athletic figure could be noticed even through her work pants, even though he tried not to pay notice to such things. John always tried to think of his sisters in blue as more than physical objects to look at, and he was often appreciated at work for treating them as fairly as he did his male coworkers on the force.

Dez stopped crying and began to chuckle; she noticed he was flustered and was blushing a little. She was still covered in Sarge's blood, and John was wiping it off with his hands to make sure none of it was hers. He was clearly trying to avoid touching her ass.

"You're such a gentleman. What, you never touched a girl's ass before? You're never gonna get a second date if this is your idea of foreplay."

John smiled, still somewhat embarrassed, and said, "Let's get your vest and outer layers off. You can take a hot shower upstairs and get all this blood off you."

She looked surprised and said, "Wait. You still have power AND hot water? Damn, the rumors about you at work were true, Gonzalez. I took a chance coming here because some of the guys on the force said that when shit got bad, you'd still be here fighting it out. Even in this shit city... I remembered your address. When I was training with Sarge around the time of your shooting, I remember him coming by the neighborhood to show me where you lived. He said it was important to remember where other cops lived, and you're one of the few that stuck it out and stayed in the city... I like your house by the way... I always thought it was cool... And way too big for a single guy like you... I mean, uhhh... not that it matters that you're single or whatever..." She trailed off.

He snapped out of his embarrassment and began to laugh. "It's okay, it's okay. I'm glad you thought of me. I have more than enough resources to help. Shonna in there was an ER nurse, and Big Rob was a Chicago Fire Department Paramedic. He's taken care of more trauma injuries and gunshot wounds than some combat medics overseas. Sarge is in good hands, I promise you. Last I saw, he was getting stabilized. They got the holes plugged and the bleeding under control. I'm going to go check on him, then let's get you upstairs so you can get cleaned up and get some rest."

John went and checked on the group in the improvised trauma center. Shonna was washing blood off her hands, and Big Rob was throwing bloody gloves, bandages, and clothes into a plastic trash bag that Theo was holding for them.

Shonna began pushing fluids and medicine through the IV drip. "I managed to steal some meds from the hospital on my way out. He's on some pain relievers and mild sedatives, and this IV push of Propofol will keep him unconscious in the short term. It's not much, but I think we can keep him under while the worst of the pain subsides and let his body start healing now that the bleeding has stopped. He's going to need blood soon too. His tag on his vest says B Negative, so if anybody is B-neg, or O negative, I'll need them to give some blood later for a transfusion. He lost a good amount of blood, and IVs are only going to do so much. We'll get this place cleaned up and worry about that later. For now, he's stable and asleep."

Theo pulled the bag closed and said, "Yo, Johnny, I'm going to check out that squad they came in. I think it might have a few useful surprises that may come in handy for us. Then I need to get back up and relieve Andrew on guard duty. I'm going to cover the rest of the afternoon for him until you come back on, since he's been stuck up there."

As Theo departed to check on the vehicle, John went over to Dez; she was sitting on a chair near the stairway. She had shed her vest and outer layer and was holding both in her hands. Her uniform shirt was shredded, and her vest hadn't fared much better.

"C'mon, you can use my room to get washed up. I already slept this morning, so you can get some rest in my bed afterwards. You're in a safe place now, Dez."

He led her up the stairs to the master bedroom and showed her to the bathroom. He gathered a spare t-shirt, towels, and a bath robe for her. When he came back to knock on the bathroom door that was ajar, he was surprised when she answered the door in only her work pants and sports bra. She had taken off her boots, duty belt, and undershirt and thrown them down against the wall.

She had her hair down and smiled at him. "Relax, I'm not naked yet." She accepted the clothes and items from him and laid them on the counter. As John turned to depart, she grabbed him by the shoulder and turned him around. She closed the gap between them quickly and pulled him into a passionate kiss. He was taken off guard, and she pushed him against the wall. John had always been incredibly attracted to Dez since she started at the police department, but he was always professional, so he'd never pursued her, especially since most of the other guys on the department were already trying.

After a few minutes held together in a passionate embrace, she finally pulled away and said, "Well... now that that's out of the way... I owe you my life... and Sarge's life too. I always liked you, Johnny. Even when I started and all the other horndogs on the department started trying to chase my tail (even the married ones), you were always so genuinely nice and professional to me. All the other younger girls said you were always like an older brother and protective of them when they started. It's hard to believe that you were single. A lot of the girls had a crush on you, even though I think you're a total dork. Some of the girls almost thought you were gay, except we've heard some stories of your escapades with the ladies back when you were a rookie." She smiled, still in his arms. "Sarge was my first Field Training Officer. I owe him my life multiple times over. He taught me everything he knows. He spoke so highly of you, John. He said that you were a damn good cop, and a great detective, even if you didn't always show it. Working night shift these last few months, it was hard taking your spot while you were gone, but Sarge always offered to partner up with me and helped me get home safely every night.

"He told me you had been smart and saved away a bunch of money from investments or something over the years, and that you would be fine if things got bad. I couldn't think of anywhere better to take Sarge after he got hit, since the hospitals shut down."

John said, "Relax Dez, you guys are more than welcome here. You have a new home now. We're gonna ride this out here together... Oh, and in case you think I'm rich or something shallow like that, I'm not. All of this; the house, the guns, the supplies... those were all the 'investments' I made over the years with all the returns from some of my wise monetary investments in stocks and bonds plus a shit ton of overtime. I'm that crazy prepper guy that you don't know about. I'm sure people had their suspicions, thus all the talk at work, but they really had no idea. I've been preparing for something like this for over ten years. Getting shot almost took me off track, but thankfully I was pretty much healed up and back on track when this shit hit the fan."

Dez ran her hands up and down his back and said, "Are you all healed up, big guy? Care to join me in the shower and help me get all cleaned up?" Her hand slid around, grabbing his crotch.

He felt his blood flowing and a fire in his gut. "I shouldn't... You're still all riled up from all this. I have so much to do... but..."

Dez shushed him with a finger to his lips and led him by the hand over to the large shower. She turned on the water and while she waited for it to get warm, she slowly kicked off her pants and pulled off her bra.

"Am I going to have to undress you too? Or are you just gonna stand there like you're getting a free show?" She kicked off her underwear at him and stepped into the shower.

He quickly shed all his clothes and followed her in. He helped her rinse off in the nearly scalding hot water and ran his hands all over her exceptional figure. She turned around to face him, and he pulled her into his arms. They chuckled together and made passionate love for what seemed like an hour, until the water started to get lukewarm.

They eventually got out of the shower and dried themselves off. John noticed that (aside from her exceptional naked figure) she was even more gorgeous once she was not in a uniform. He also observed that she looked absolutely exhausted, even though she appeared to be refreshed from the warm shower. He let her get bundled up in her fresh oversized clothing and bathrobe and made her get into bed.

Dez said sleepily, "You know, a lot of the guys on the department think you're an asshole. You're quiet, keep to yourself, and don't really hang out with anybody outside of work. You work all that overtime but aren't really close to anybody. I think this is the most we've ever spoken since I started. The other girls on the department say you're nice and treat them with more respect than all the other guys, but you aren't really friends with anybody. What's up with that?"

John chuckled and said, "What, are you surprised that I'm somewhat normal now that you talk to me outside of work? I don't know... I never had any close friends on the department after my old man retired. I guess I was just worried that I didn't measure up to him. Old Sarge is about the only one who treated me like my own person, not just 'Old Man Gonzalez's kid'. It probably doesn't help that I've been in three shootings in ten years, when most people go an entire career without ever firing their weapon in the line of duty. I'm bad luck, Dez. I can't help if it fucked me up a little."

Dez let out a loud yawn. John covered her up and drew the blackout shades closed.

"What, not going to join me and try for round two, tiger?" she said softly.

"I'd love to, but you need to get some rest."

She quietly added, "Hey, I have some spare clothes and gear in a duffel in the back of the squad if you can grab that all for me..." She closed her eyes and started drifting off to sleep.

John turned off the lights, shut the door, and went back downstairs.

He ran into Theo outside, who had the police SUV up on a jack and was changing one of the tires that was going flat. "Yo, Johnny, this is one fine piece of machinery here, bro."

"It sure is", John thought. Dez and Sarge had picked one of the nicest vehicles in the police fleet to grab. The 2024 Chevy Tahoe Police Interceptor had an XLT full upgrade package. It was fully armor-plated, evidenced by the fact that despite dings and chinks to the paint job, there were no penetrations by bullets into the vehicle. The windows were all bullet resistant and could withstand blasts and up to medium-caliber rifle rounds. The vehicle was dark matte black, with ghost lettering decals with "Kankakee City Police Department" on the side that were only visible from very close up, and reflective with direct light onto them. The Tahoe had thick bullet-resistant tires, like those used on military Humvees overseas. It had a full grille guard cage covering the front end. This upgraded model had a gun hatch that could open in the rear seat that would pop up into a makeshift machine gun turret. It had the mount for any large weapon, but unfortunately did not come with one mounted. The other side of the back seat was a half cage for transporting prisoners. It was much larger in size than the civilian commercial Tahoe's and had a large bed of storage in the back, with an integrated gun and storage locker in the back hatch. The Tahoe had been purchased by the city last year in response to the recent uptick in violent crime across the country and in the city itself. Even though many critics had called it another consequence of the *"Militarization of the Police"* decried by Progressives and cop-haters, the city council had a hard time not buying upgrades after several other squads had been shot at and struck by gunfire in the last few years and amidst pressure from the police union.

Theo was spray-painting the bullet holes with a dark matte black rattle can in order to keep the vehicle dark. They popped open the rear hatch to take inventory of the equipment inside. This vehicle had been originally purchased for special SWAT tactics and usage only and was referred to as "the Tank" by most on the department. However, due to the uptick in violence, the vehicle was put into usage on regular patrol to give additional protection to officers. The vehicle was still fully stocked as it had been for SWAT operations. They sorted through the bags and cases strewn about in the rear compartment. There was a full trauma kit and first aid bag, spare body armors, a full riot armor suit, and two government spec M-4 Carbine rifles on a rack along the window. It was similar to his and Theo's rifles, except these rifles were fully suppressed and had the option for three-shot bursts.

"I'm stealing this shit," Theo said, grabbing one of the rifles. "Sorry, not sorry, bro. We can give my main rifle to someone else as a spare. This shit is too good to pass up."

John had no complaints about Theo upgrading his rifle. The city of Chicago still had strict gun laws, making it hard for Theo to upgrade his ARs; even his registered work rifle was not allowed the upgraded additions like shortened "SBR" length and a suppressor. John found Dez's duffel bag with her spare clothing. He also grabbed her rifle bag and assault pack. He separated them on the ground so that he could carry the gear up to her later.

Theo popped open the hidden floor equipment locker with the keys and exclaimed, "Holy fucking shit! It's like Christmas in this bitch!" He lifted out a military model M249 paratrooper model Squad Automatic Weapon. The M249 SAW was a belt-fed compact automatic weapon used in the military that was banned for civilian ownership. He also found multiple spare drum magazines and three metal ammo cans with spare belts of 556 NATO cartridges. Theo slung it on across his front and said, "Yeah... I'm taking this shit too. Go ahead and make a joke about the black guy looting the police car, and I'll shoot you in the foot." They shared a laugh, and Theo consolidated his newly acquired equipment and said, "I need to go relieve Andrew up on the roof. I'll catch you later when you come to relieve me." He grabbed his equipment, including the SAW, and climbed the radio tower up to the roof, although with a bit more difficulty carrying so much weight.

John went back to examining the contents of the Tank's locker. He discovered twenty flash bang grenades and six sets of military smoke grenades in various colors. There were a few spare magazines, and a few boxes of 9mm, .40, .45 ACP, and .223/556 ammunition. Beyond that, there wasn't much more exciting in the cabinet.

Andrew walked up behind him and said, "Am I seeing shit, or is Theo carrying a fucking SAW?"

John turned around to face his good friend, who laughed and said, "I'm just kidding, he told me. That's awesome. Kid can't shoot for shit anyways. It'll be good to have a heavy gunner."

They shared a laugh as Andrew leaned to look in the vehicle. "Ooh hell yes!" he exclaimed, grabbing a flash bang and two of the smoke grenades, clipping them to his plate carrier. He also snagged a gas mask that was clipped to the side cages.

John said, "Jesus, man, what am I running, a soup kitchen out here? Between you and Theo, I can't even keep this stuff long enough to take inventory of what we've got."

They shared a few jabs and insults back and forth while they carried the spare equipment back into the house and lugged them downstairs, locking it in some empty gear lockers. They labelled the locker with a strip of duct tape "Tank Supplies", which Andrew crossed out with a single line and wrote "Soup Kitchen" on it.

"We're going to have to explain that one to the others." They laughed. On their last trip to the truck, they pulled out the duffel bag that belonged to Old Sarge. His duty bag contained a bunch of spare magazines for his Colt 1911, a few smaller back-up pistols, a small pocket revolver, and an assortment of boxes of ammo. His duffel contained a few sets of spare clothing, a few spare uniforms, several more boxes of ammo, and a pair of combat boots. He had a small box of personal items: a picture of his deceased wife, Lily, his son's military photo, a small box containing a large wad of rolled-up cash, a few rolls of silver coins, and the folded-up American flag they'd given him when his son was killed overseas in Iran nearly three years before. The flag also had his son's purple heart and bronze star medals neatly stored next to them. They took especially good care of Sarge's personal effects and set them outside the dining room, where he was still lying unconscious on the table, now with a few pillows underneath him. It was a hard sight to see, but if anybody was tough enough to pull through, it was Old Sarge.

INTERLUDE TWO: "THE SALTY OLD DOG STILL BITES"

John had met Sarge when he first came on the force over ten years ago. Even then, he seemed old. He was old but not frail, by any means. He was called "Old Sarge" as a term of endearment by the guys. His real name was Sergeant Wayne Callahan. He told everyone that he was named after John Wayne but was no relation to "Dirty Harry" Callahan, because he said detectives were pussies, and even in the 1980s, a real man would have carried "God's gun," a Colt 1911. Old Sarge had been a member of the police department for a remarkable forty-two years at the time when the SHTF. He was already past the mandatory retirement age of sixty-five, but the city council made an exception, using a loophole that stated that his four years of military service allowed him to stay on an additional four years due to his later eligibility to join the force. The real truth was that Old Sarge had nowhere else to go. He was getting ready to retire after thirty-eight years on the job, at age sixty-two, when his wife died suddenly of pneumonia from a complication from a heart surgery. His son had been killed overseas fighting in Iran with the Marine Special Forces a few years prior. With his wife and his only son gone, he had nothing to look forward to, to keep himself occupied. After his wife's funeral, and when his leave for grievance was over, he came in and asked the Chief to cancel his retirement and kept working.

Old Sarge had served for four years in the Marines as a force recon grunt. He saw brief combat action in Grenada in 1983 and got out of the Corps shortly after. He joined the Kankakee Police Department in the fall of 1984. He served on patrol the entirety of his career. He was promoted to sergeant after ten years and was on the SWAT team and served as one of the department's master firearms instructors. As he got older, he was offered easier desk jobs and lateral promotions and specialty assignments within the department to jobs that would be easier on him, but he turned them all down. He often requested more strenuous jobs, offering to go to midnight and night power shift hours, and volunteering for the gang and tac units. Even though he was ages older than most on these squads, he was rarely denied, as the old, wiry Marine was in great shape. Even in his early sixties he still ran, swam, and lifted weights nearly every day. His latest project in his later years had been as a Field Training Instructor to the new hires. He found it a fun new challenge for him. He told the bosses that it "kept him young at heart" and helped him connect with the newer generation of police officers. For the past eight years, he had been training the new recruits. He was tough as nails and very old school, still wearing a classic uniform with his tie and long sleeves bearing his sergeant stripes and multiple service stripes on his sleeve. He still wore a dress cap on patrol, with aviator sunglasses during the day. He was made fun of for still wearing full leather basketweave duty belt and equipment, along with his Colt 1911, which was still kept in a leather holster. The joking was kept to a minimum though, as he kept his appearance immaculate, his gear and boots freshly shined, and was a crack shot with his old 1911 railgun. He enjoyed training new recruits, and he was loved by most of his rookies. He had lots of spare time to devote to their training, and even spent lots of time with his guys and girls outside of work. He would often take his trainees out for lunch or dinner on their days off to get to know them better personally. He said that he learned just as much from his new generation of cops, as he had to teach them. He learned how to better use computers, and had even adopted a newer smartphone recently, an upgrade from his antique flip phone.

His most recent trainee, Dezeray Ruiz, was one of his favorites. He liked her military background, something he said most often made a very good basis for becoming a great cop. Besides her small stature, she was tough as nails, and didn't take shit from anyone. He helped to teach her more patience. Even after her field training had ended, he would offer to partner up with her for some shifts. They had lunch together often, and he joked that if his son were still alive, he hoped that she would have married him. Old Sarge cared for Ruiz like a daughter. She came to him for advice, both personal and professional. He steered her away from the other young guys on the force that were always chasing her, trying to date or hook up with her. They would have to get through him, he always said. Not too many of the young men had enough courage to go through Old Sarge to try to get involved with her. He steered her in the right direction, and she looked up to him like a father.

He was loved and respected by most everyone on the department and even on the streets. Even the gangbangers were known to nod their heads in respect as Sergeant Callahan drove by. As he described it, "This is the third generation of criminal and lowlifes I've arrested. I dealt with their fathers and mothers, and their grandmothers and grandfathers before them." He attributed the respect to the grandparents often raising the youngest generation of kids as their parents were often locked up in jail or prison. Even the old-time gang bangers had taught the new school of gang bangers to respect the salty "Old Sarge." It was a nickname that one of the older local gang leaders had given to Sergeant Callahan, and it stuck. They hated the tough as nails old white cop, but everyone had grown up hearing his stories. He got to know the community and its members. He treated everyone with respect, even the young bucks that hadn't learned to give respect yet. They had heard the old war stories about the times he had been shot in gunfights and survived, the people he had shot and killed in other gunfights, and even the times he had run into burning buildings to save little Black and Latino babies from the burning projects. He was a tough old bastard, and even in the Hood, he was looked at as nearly untouchable. Old Sarge had been in six fatal shootings in his long career, a number which was up in the highest number of police shootings in the country. He was rough but fair. And he was always justified when he had to use deadly force.

Sarge often walked foot patrol, even in the worst neighborhoods in the city, and would walk up to greet the old-timers sitting on their porches. He remembered most of their names and details about their families. He would take off his hat when speaking to the women, and firmly shake the men's hands. He would say, "Even some shitbag criminals grow old. And they usually grow out of being shitbags themselves, even if they still raise them." He would hand out treats and snacks to the little children, and it was a common sight for him to give out diapers and baby formula that he had purchased with his own money to young teen moms with little babies. He often prevented violent gang turf wars, going to the leaders of the gangs himself to mediate deals and broker peace. He was seen as a legend by both police and criminals alike.

After being transferred to night shift patrol, John became very close to Old Sarge. They bonded over their mutual interest in shooting, and the fact that he was the only other person on the department that still carried a 1911. Sarge made fun of him for carrying "a tricked-out fancy 1911," because his Springfield Operator had tritium night sights and an attached Surefire weapon light. They often volunteered to ride together when Sarge wasn't the acting shift commander. They shared many long nights and good conversations in the squad car. Sarge thought of him as another son. They also often had lunch and dinner together and hung out off-duty. Many evenings, he and the old Sarge sat watching football or baseball games and sat together in Sarge's house drinking beers or glasses of fine bourbon and smoking cigars. He suspected that he had taken on the role that was left behind when Sarge lost his son years back. Maybe that's why he planted the seed to Dez about finding John in the collapse.

The man was indeed a legend.

Chapter 6.5 – IT'S NOT ALL FIREWORKS, SPARKLERS, AND BARBEQUES ON THE 4TH

July 4th – Kankakee IL – Afternoon

Shonna and Rob looked after Sarge while he recovered. They were able to start giving him blood, as John was also B Negative, the same blood type as Old Sarge, and Theo and Andrew were both O negative, universal donors. They each gave a pint of blood, which Shonna stored in some spare blood bags from the hospital and stocked the remainder of them in the garage refrigerator. She changed his bandages and dressings and gave him a pint of whole blood. After finishing and discarding her gloves, she came out of the room to speak to John.

"It was a through and through shot with a large caliber rifle round, most likely an AK round. It was shooting fast enough to rip right through his soft vest. Luckily enough, it went straight through his chest and didn't tumble. Mostly soft tissue damage, and it knocked his lung, but I was able to sew that up. I'm leaving the entry would open to allow it to heal on its own for a little bit. We will need to keep the room as clean and sterile as possible, so I'll need as much bleach as you can give me."

John said, "Thank you, Shonna. We owe you a ton. That man means a lot to me, and I appreciate all your efforts to keep him alive. If there is anything you need, supplies or medical instruments that you can think of, we will go get it for you. I was told that the hospitals shut down after the power went out, so we should be able to make a quick run and swipe some from the closest emergency room. We may even be able to raid the pharmacy, if you can write down a list of medicines that we may need."

"I wish you didn't have to take the risk... but since you're going to go anyways... bring a trailer, because I want you to grab as much shit as you can carry. We're going to need a trauma center here in the future, and I could use as much of the equipment available in an ER as you can get me. It will all come in handy; a hospital bed or two, an EKG, a defibrillator, an IV drip machine, vital monitors, fresh sheets, blood bags, IV tube lines, catheters, bandages, splints, slings, syringes, medicines. Get it all. I'll start writing down all the medicines I want you to get. I'm sure all the narcotics have long since been raided, but I'm willing to bet that whoever went in for the happy pills was too stupid to know anything about antibiotics. Those are what we will need the most. Just take the whole storage refrigerator if you can handle it." She turned to let him leave, then sheepishly started again. "Oh, and maybe I should ask Dez too... but in case you boys find it... Don't forget the feminine products. As many as you can get your hands on. We do have three ladies here now. Just let Dez know to keep an eye out."

John retreated to his office to do some planning, and more importantly, some alone time to think. He pulled out his field notebook and began jotting notes. He pulled out maps of the area and began studying routes to both hospitals in town. He worked up an impromptu operations order and finalized the plans. He got on the two-way radio and called for a muster of all available adults in the house for a briefing in five minutes. He went and woke up Dez, who was still hard asleep in his bed. Andrew's daughter and son went up to the roof with binoculars to keep watch temporarily. His daughter was eleven and responsible enough to keep watch and man a radio.

By the time five minutes had elapsed, everyone was in the kitchen. John began by telling everyone:

"Okay guys... The time has come where we need to leave the safety of the compound to get items we desperately need. It's going to be all hands on deck for this one, for personnel: I'm taking lead, Andrew will be on long range/overwatch, Theo's heavy gunner, and

Dez on radio. On the ground strike team is me, Theo, Big Rob, and Dez. Staying in the rear will be Shonna and the kids. Shonna will button up the perimeter once we head out, make sure Old Sarge is stable, then she and the kids will sit overwatch in the tower while we are out.

"Next is Equipment Loadout: We go full combat kit, plate carriers or soft armor. Other than that, we go as light as we can. At least six rifle mags on everyone, plus a few extras for the sidearm. Assault packs with extra ammo if you want but keep room to carry anything extra you have room for. Also bring along empty duffel bags, rucksacks, and satchels. For transport, we're taking the tank. It'll fit all of us, but we're going empty, no extra supplies in it, and pulling an empty trailer. We will go as light and as fast as we can.

"For Execution: timeline is as follows: We step off in exactly one hour, no exceptions, so get packed and back together ASAP. We're taking the back roads through the neighborhoods to St. Mary's Hospital ER. It's off the main roads, and there are more back roads leading there. We need to hit it as quickly as we can. We will run side streets to a block south of the hospital, where we will drop Andrew at the church. Andrew will climb to the bell tower and set up overwatch, then we go in. We'll park the tank to block the ER ramp, then hit it as fast as we can. Our best guess is that the hospital has already been hit by looters, so it should be abandoned. No power or lights, and it should be dark by the time we get there, so I don't suspect any armed resistance, possibly only squatters or scavengers. Once we get on site, I want in and out as quickly as possible. As soon as we hit the ER entrance, clear the area and be in and out in less than thirty minutes. Return home by 21:15. The time is now 19:08, we'll step off at 20:00. Everybody get geared up and meet back here ASAP."

After a short amount of time, everyone had collected themselves and their necessary equipment, and mustered back together in the courtyard. John checked everyone up and down and started double checking their gear and weapons. They all piled in the blacked-out police SUV and rolled out of the gate. Shonna quickly closed the gate behind them.

It had been a tiring few days, and John looked around the car, noticing how weary everyone looked. Dez was yawning and rubbing her eyes. He felt guilty about having to make her go back out into the shitstorm so soon, considering that she had just narrowly escaped it. He knew they needed all the shooters they could get, however, and Dez was one hell of a shooter.

They sped along, taking side streets as quickly as they could. It was the first time John was going so far from the safety of his home since he had come home from the hospital, and the first time leaving the confines of neighborhood since the shit hit the fan. He was a little nervous but felt the need to get a good look at how bad things were getting out there so close to his safety area. He noticed that his immediate subdivision appeared nearly abandoned; he saw no people out or signs of houses being inhabited. It was a good buffer zone. He'd never very close to his neighbors, but he still felt a little sad nonetheless. He hoped that they'd made it out safely.

As they left the immediate area near his subdivision, things got progressively worse as they got closer to downtown. People were out wandering the streets, scavenging through trash cans. It was like a sight from a Mad Max movie. Multiple homes had been completely burned down; some were partially burned, and even a few were still on fire. John quickly figured out why, as he saw many people standing around burn barrels and trash piles on fire. He noticed that a few people were armed and had shotguns or rifles slung, and a few had pistols in holsters. He kept the speed of the vehicle as fast as it would handle. He wished that they could have left earlier, as he was worried that it was going to be completely dark by the time they started getting everything loaded up.

After what felt like an eternity but was more like a ten-minute drive zigzagging along small side roads, they pulled into the large church parking lot just south of the hospital. Andrew hopped out and jogged up the stairs. After ensuring he got in the building easily enough, they waited a few minutes for Andrew to make the long run up the stairs into the bell tower. A click came over the radio, and Andrew keyed up, "All set. Eyes on the hospital. All dark, a few stragglers out and about, but no major arms or equipment that I can see. Just a few people rummaging through some cars in the parking lot. ER ramp looks empty. I've got you covered; clear for approach."

And with that, John hit the accelerator and gunned the big SUV and trailer around the corner and pulled up the back way to the emergency room ramp. He parked directly in front of the large entrance doors, and everybody hopped out. He told Big Rob to stay posted near the vehicle. "While you're out here, check the ambulances for supplies. Anything you can grab that isn't bolted down, take it! Open up the doors and be ready for us to bring out as much shit as we can carry."

John, Theo, and Dez raised their weapons and pulled open the glass sliding doors. It was dark, with only the fading evening sun lighting the hallways. They all turned on their weapon-mounted flashlights and lit up the empty corridor leading to the ER. It seemed empty. The hospital smelled worse than usual; there were pools and streaks of blood on the floors and walls. They pushed open the doors leading to the ER and made entry, keeping the doors propped open. They cleared the large thirty-bed emergency room and found nothing other than a few bodies left to rot. The smell was putrid in those rooms, so they closed the doors and drew the curtains in those areas. Once the immediate area was cleared, they went to the closest empty room and went to work. Dez picked the cleanest-looking gurney and unplugged all the wires. She piled all the equipment in the nearby rooms onto the bed. John did the same in the next room, stacking every piece of medical equipment on his gurney.

Theo jumped the counter to the nurses' desk and went back to the medical supplies closet. He threw open the doors, opened his duffel bag, and began throwing in emergency supplies. Surprisingly, the supplies weren't very scarce in the closet; the only items missing seemed to be needles. Theo piled in bandages, slings, wraps, sheets, towels, disinfectant, and bottles of rubbing alcohol until his duffel was full. He tossed it over the desk and began loading the next duffel bag full of the remaining supplies and other random boxes and pill bottles laying around. He grabbed the duffels, jumped back over the counter, and threw them on Dez's hospital bed.

"We'll be right back! Let's hurry this up and we might be able to push a little farther to see if they have any food stored in the cafeteria," Theo called back to John. He helped Dez push the loaded bed out into the hallway and back out to the truck.

While they were gone, John went back behind the desk and over to the storage room where the medicines and antibiotics were kept in a large stand-up cooler. It was much larger than he thought it would be, taller than him, and he struggled to move it at first. He dragged the cooler out of the room, trying to navigate the objects behind the nurse's desk. He cursed aloud several times. He was making little to no progress and it was taking forever. By slowly pushing and pulling the large cooler, he managed to move it towards the hospital bed he had waiting. He paused to take a short breather, hoping that Theo and Dez would soon be back to help him lift it onto the rolling bed. He leaned against the counter of the nurse's desk, listening to the quiet, still sounds of the hospital. Suddenly, the quiet was broken by a loud rip from a belt-fed weapon. After a few bursts of automatic gunfire, he realized that the closer gunfire was Theo shooting his SAW and big Rob shooting full auto bursts from his AK. He was still in a bit of shock when Dez burst in the ER, yelling, "Johnny, let's get the fuck out of here! We're engaged. About five to ten armed tangos. Small arms. They hit us from the Court Street side." She helped him pull the large cooler on top of the hospital bed gurney and quickly pushed the heavy burden out of the ER onto the exit ramp.

As they emerged into the moonlight, gunshots and bullets began snapping in their direction. A bullet struck the cooler next to John's hand just before he reached the safety of the trailer behind the bullet-resistant police SUV. They pushed the bed on the trailer and stuffed it in next to the other items. The trailer was surprisingly full, given the short amount of time they had spent. He was buckling up the back door of the trailer as Andrew came running up the opposite side of the ER ramp.

"I was worried you fuckers were going to forget me. Let's get the fuck out of here!" Andrew yelled, almost out of breath from his two-block sprint from the bell tower. Theo was up top on the gunner's turret ripping cyclic rates on the SAW. Big Rob was already in the driver's seat, and Dez was leaning out of the passenger window emptying magazines at the small blockade of vehicles. Andrew pulled open the door to the back seat and motioned John in.

John climbed in, and as Andrew was jumping in, a round struck him in the top of the back-armor plate, and another tore into his shoulder, spinning him around. He stumbled into the doorway, and John pulled him inside the vehicle. Big Rob tore off down the ER ramp, heading straight at the group shooting at them; they were taking cover behind old cars blocking the Court Side entrance to the hospital. Big Rob didn't slow down as he rammed through the vehicles and raiders.

Rob turned west onto the main highway that cut through the middle of town. He floored the accelerator and they pulled away from the area as quickly as they could. Dez yelled "Careful, don't forget all the important shit we're pulling back there!"

Andrew was lying across the back seat in John's lap; he was bleeding heavily from the shoulder wound. John grabbed a pressure bandage from Andrew's kit and wrapped it around the wound. "It doesn't look too bad, little buddy. Looks like a small round that nicked your shoulder; a glancing blow. Once we get the bleeding stopped, you should be fine." He turned his attention to their driver. "Rob, looks like we're nearly out of the woods. Slow it down a little, and let's get off this main road onto some side streets. First beer is on me when we get home, boys and girls."

Rob turned south on the first available side street once they got over the bridge across the Kankakee River. They zig-zagged off the side streets into the smaller neighborhoods, making their way west as quickly and discreetly as they could. A few stray bullets were fired at them from random directions, but they all glanced off the Tahoe's bullet-resistant armor paneling. Rob blacked out the lights of their vehicle and slowed down to a crawl as he turned into the subdivision. After a short halt and look around, they determined that nobody appeared to be following them, and they pulled on down the block toward the compound.

Dez radioed Shonna to let her know they were coming in the wire, all bodies up, one gunshot wound, non-ambulatory, not critical.

They rolled up to the gate and it slid open. Shonna and Andrew's daughter pulled open the gate just wide enough for the tank and trailer to squeeze through. Rob turned the vehicle around and backed the trailer up close to the house. Everyone jumped out. Dez helped the girls close and lock the gate, while Rob and Theo helped grab Andrew's gear. Andrew was able to walk himself out, although he was in great pain. His daughter ran up to him and started crying when she saw the blood on his equipment.

"It's okay, baby. Dad is gonna be just fine." She grabbed his hand, still crying, and walked him into the house. Shonna rushed in behind them to get washed up to take care of his wounds.

John told Rob, "Go ahead, Rob. She's gonna need the help. Theo, Dez, and I will get all this equipment pulled inside."

Rob grabbed the rest of his gear and rushed inside to assist in the cleaning of the medical room. Theo and Dez pulled open the trailer, and all three of them pulled out the bags and hospital beds. John told Dez, "Go roll your bed straight into the medical room and help Rob get it disinfected so it can get set up for use. Theo and I are going to get these medicines moved in and get the cooler plugged in."

As Dez wheeled her hospital bed away, he and Theo muscled out the bed carrying the large cooler full of medicines. He hoped most of the glass vials hadn't been broken during the drive. They slowly and carefully rolled the bed up to the house, lifted it carefully across the doorway, and wheeled everything into the former dining room that had become the new medical center.

They got the cooler pulled down and plugged in and left the rest of the supplies near the shelves set up in the room. The "medical center" was getting crowded enough with all of the other people attending to Andrew and Old Sarge. Andrew was sitting up in a chair, getting his wound cleaned and wrapped back up. Shonna said it wasn't bad at all, and he would be fine in a week or so, if it stayed clean.

John went upstairs to take off his dirty clothes and get changed. Theo offered to take the beginning of the night's watch at the LP/OP, and Dez chimed in to say she'd take over in a few hours. John realized, that in all the confusion of the last several days, he hadn't checked in on his parents. He hurried into his office and turned up the volume to his base station of HAM radios.

INTERLUDE THREE: A POST-APOCALYPTIC ROAD TRIP

On the Road- unknown location

The first part of the journey had been luckily uneventful for John's mom and dad. After riding up I-57 those few days ago, they got to I-80 just south of the outskirts of Chicago suburbs and turned west with no resistance. There were less cars on the road than what would be normal. It was early, but there didn't appear to be any cars making a commute up to the city as there normally would be that early in the morning. As he drove, Richard was also thankful that there were almost no cars coming south out of the city. He suspected in the next few days and weeks there would be a great exodus out of the big city, and Kankakee was directly in the path of the great horde.

Interstate 80 was fairly clear as well as they turned to head west. Richard noticed other people pulling campers, and RVs also heading westbound that had the same idea. He only hoped that those other poor people had a safe place to go to weather this storm.

They listened to the radio. The news was still as ominous as it had been for the last few weeks. The market and economy had begun its slow free-fall months ago. They wouldn't have even come back to Illinois if their son hadn't been shot. Thankfully, he was back on his feet and in good health. He had made a miraculously fast recovery, and just in time. Richard knew that they needed to get out of Kankakee and get back to Oregon as quickly as possible. Society was already starting to crumble, and law and order would soon fall apart. Luckily there was still the ability to travel safely, but it would get worse when the panic started to set in for the general, unprepared masses. The radio news anchor spoke about the stock market and the possibility of a looming "depression."

There it was—that was the word that would set off the mass panic. With the media beginning to freely throw around those words, Richard knew that things would get worse in a hurry. He made the decision to drive through the first night, while travel was easy and they were making good progress. At dinnertime, they stopped briefly at a large truck stop near Council Bluffs, Iowa. Richard was very tired, but he wanted to continue the quick progress they were making. They decided to take a short break and enjoy a cooked meal at the diner. Richard filled the gas tank. He cringed as he paid nearly eight dollars per gallon. He paid using his credit card, opting to save his stash of cash. Denise and Richard then went and bought a few food items from the truck stop's market. They opted for canned foods and easily stored meals that didn't need to be refrigerated. They also decided to splurge on some comfort foods and road snacks. "No need to suffer while we can still attempt to enjoy life," Denise said to Richard. They enjoyed a good dinner at the diner, keeping the camper and truck in view of their window seats. The bill came, and the waitress told them, "Sorry, cash only now. New policy." Richard cringed, as the bill had been marked up over double what was printed on the menu. It cost nearly $25 for each meal and the bill was nearly $50. Richard asked the waitress to fill his large travel mug with coffee, handed her $80, and told her to keep the change. She smiled and told them, "Stay safe on the road now. Lots more shady characters passing through lately."

Those remarks made them uneasy. Denise and Richard quickly walked back to their truck. As they got closer, two dirty-looking men came out from behind the truck, almost appearing out of thin air in the darkness. The two white men looked like meth addicts. They were both skinny and had soiled clothing that was already torn and nasty. The first one spoke, revealing his disgusting teeth: "Can you two spare some cash? My brother and I need some gas to get to the next town. Just a little, please?"

Richard stepped in front of Denise and replied, "No, sorry, son, no cash to spare. We need to get on our way, please."

The body language of the first man started to change, and he said, "We know you have cash! We saw you come from the diner. Don't lie to me!" He started to square up his body threateningly toward Richard, closing the gap between them slowly.

Richard was still a very large and imposing man, standing nearly six-foot-three even in his older age. As the meth addict came within arms reach, he began to reach into his pocket, saying, "Well, it's a shame that we're gonna have to take…" and a knife was coming out of his pocket. He was stopped in his tracks as Richard threw a haymaker punch with his right arm, knocking the first addict onto his ass. He lay there dazed, blood pouring out of a broken nose. The second bum was reaching in his waistband, still in shock, when Richard dropped his cane from his left hand and drew the Glock 21 that was holstered under his outer shirt and pointed it with the laser centered on the second bum's chest.

"Do you want to die today?" were the only words out of Richard's mouth. His voice showed no hesitation, and his eyes were fixed on both would-be muggers. After no response, and the first bum blubbering and still bleeding on the ground, Richard said, "You have two choices: Leave now, or die today. Both of you: Right here, right now. Is that how you want to go out?"

The first man got quietly to his feet and then both of the meth addicts slowly backed away, the first one quietly crying, "He broke my fucking nose, man…" Their nerve quickly broke, and they turned and fled.

When the two addicts had disappeared from sight, Denise and Richard quickly got into the large truck, started it up, and got back on the road.

"Well…I'm glad that we decided not to stay here tonight," Richard said as Denise held his hand. They pulled back on the interstate. It was nearly empty as the night had set in. Thankfully the power and lights along the interstate were still on. They made good time on their journey, as there was no traffic to battle during the night. In all the excitement, they both completely forgot to use their cell phones to make a call, or even use their radio to check in with their son.

They continued driving as far and as fast as they could for another several hours. They made good time from the edge of Iowa through the entire state until midway through the state of Nebraska until Richard was just too tired to continue. They stopped in a small town off the interstate calked Gothenburg. They pulled into a very small truck stop. It was quiet, and Richard got gas for not too much over the current market value. The lot was very quiet and well lit, so they decided to spend the night there. Before going to bed for the night, Richard made sure that everything was locked up, and they finally called it a night at close to 4 A.M. Richard kept his Glock 21 on the headboard next to his pillow. The doors on their camper had been replaced with a stronger metal reinforced security door with multiple locks. They were both physically and mentally exhausted and fell asleep as soon as their heads hit their pillows.

CHAPTER 7: FROM GOOD TO BAD

July 14ᵗʰ – Kankakee IL – About one week later

Andrew's wound healed rather quickly. He was still able to shoot his rifle, and after a few days resumed his guard duty shifts. He was in pain, but Shonna was able to control it with small amounts of some of the pain medicines that they had recovered. After a few days of small doses, Andrew said that he was feeling better, so he opted to save the precious medicines. After a good amount of rest, he was able to resume his normal activities. Andrew said that he would rather that Shonna be able to spend more of her focus on getting Old Sarge healed. He still hadn't gained consciousness, but the addition of the hospital bed and medical equipment (most of which was in good working order) helped keep him stable. Shonna said that he still had a long road to recovery. She gave him the remaining two units of whole blood that the guys had donated and continued pushing IV bags to help with the loss of all the blood. The hope was that he would possibly regain consciousness in the next few days; then he would be able to eat solid foods. This would help him gain weight back and speed up his recovery time.

Meanwhile, everyone else was beginning to settle into their roles and found jobs at the compound to keep busy and stave away the boredom and monotony. Andrew's kids settled into cooking and cleaning around the house. His daughter already had a knack for cooking and had learned the art of cooking for large groups. In their spare time, they took to reading, as John's house was always well stocked with books, and he had even squirrelled away some history and English textbooks which the kids used to continue some schooling in their spare time.

In addition to tending to Old Sarge's injuries and her medical duties, Shonna set up the smaller former dining room into an infirmary by moving the table out and moving in both of the requisitioned hospital beds. She also moved all the shelving and cabinets containing all of the compound's medical supplies including all of the supplies requisitioned from the hospital run. Shonna had quite the knack for management and logistics and organization, so she also took to inventorying all the food stocks and other essential supplies. She reorganized and resupplied the pantry of food and rotated in some of the supplies from the long-term storage buckets in the basement.

Dez had rested up and recovered from the trauma of her trip in. She also settled in to sleeping in John's room. He welcomed the company and enjoyed the pleasures that came along with her companionship. For the first time in months, John had mostly peaceful sleep without many nightmares when he had Dez cuddled up next to him. He made sure that she was resupplied with full tactical gear and ammo that she hadn't had on her arrival, but unfortunately, she and Shonna were still short clothing, as John had never really any reason to stock women's clothing. They both made sacrifices and wore spare clothing from the men. Both women were able to fit into Andrew's spare pants, as he was the smallest in stature of the men.

John, Andrew, Theo, and Rob shared guard duty and took to walking foot patrols in a several blocks' radius around the compound. They didn't make contact with anybody, as the neighborhoods appeared to be fairly well evacuated. They took turns dressing in regular clothes, only carrying concealed pistols, and walked the neighborhoods, knocking on doors and attempting to make contact with any remaining survivors while someone covered them on overwatch from the tower. Andrew had taken to making notes about the various houses and what possible resources were there based on what was in plain view. He continued to jot down locations and addresses by taking notes and drawing crude maps in his notebook. They were still doing okay, and John was very opposed to what he equated to "looting" his neighbors, even though the others were in favor of taking the needed supplies. That all changed one day when Shonna took him aside after dinner and told him, "Look, John, you were very well stocked and prepared, but I don't think you prepared to stock enough food for the nine of us here. I did the rough math, and we only have enough food to last us five to six more months. It won't last us through the winter. We can start gardening but will only have enough for one crop of vegetables until fall sets in and it's too cold for much more harvesting. I'm going to start planting in the backyard tomorrow. But we are going to need more long-term food and canned goods to help get us through the winter. Maybe some more blankets and clothes for us girls. I think we need to start looking into going through all of the abandoned houses and see what your neighbors left behind. I know you don't feel right about this, but we are going to be in bad shape if we don't start doing this now."

John thought for a moment. "I guess you're right; I just don't feel right stealing from our neighbors. Even if they aren't here...I just feel like there's still a chance that they might come back, and it isn't right...but I suppose you're right...We need to find a way to survive the winter." He needed to think on this for a little bit. John excused himself and went to his office. He turned down the radios that they were constantly scanning and sat in silence for a few minutes, until Andrew came in and sat down in a chair across the desk from him.

"I know, bro...It sucks to have morals sometimes. But we really do need this stuff, and I'll be damned if I'm going to let my kids starve this winter. It's better that we have this stuff and not some looters, ya know? Plus, I've been taking notes and collecting intel, and I think some of your neighbors have some decent stuff based on what you told me about them. A block down, the local artist—he was an alcoholic. I'm sure that he has plenty of booze in his bar; the local mechanic another block down will have plenty of tools and motor oil, maybe gasoline too. In the other direction, we have the country club cook; he will have plenty of food; we will have to see what is still fresh and what was stored. I think we can collect propane tanks from all of the backyard grills, plus the charcoal, and siphon gasoline from the cars to store and stabilize for this winter. We need all of these things; it's not like we are going to steal their jewelry and flatscreen TVs, man. And we can leave notes, like receipts."

John lifted his head from his deck and finally broke his silence. "Okay. Let's do it. I don't feel good about this at all though, for the record."

John, Andrew, Theo, Dez, and Rob rolled out, pulling wagons behind them. They started with the closest neighbors. They knocked on doors and cleared the houses first to ensure nobody was left inside. They collected any useful items that they could find. Any canned goods in the kitchen were piled into one of the carts. They also found dog food for John's dog and clothing for the women in their sizes. Dez piled several different outfits and shoes into her cart and smiled. They found a few small pistols and some boxes of ammo but not many other useful items. They moved on to the next house, locating similar items, and filled their carts. Once a cart was filled, they returned it to the compound and emptied out its contents in the living room, where Shonna and the kids took inventory and stocked the items in the appropriate place.

A few houses down, where John's neighbor was known to be an avid hunter, they located a crossbow and a compound bow, along with several arrows and crossbow bolts. They found a large amount of venison, which was still good because his freezer was connected to a solar battery like John's. They located some long-rifle ammo, but no rifles. They suspected this hunter had bugged out to his cabin in the woods but had left in quite a hurry. They also found several bags of his homemade jerky, and canning supplies, which they gladly appropriated. His gun cabinet was left open, but empty, another indicator that he had left in a hurry.

They spent the remainder of the daylight going from house to house. John's neighbors had not been as well prepared as he was, and he could tell by the various states that he found their residences in. Some houses had been abandoned in a hurry, while others had not. They were still able to scrounge canned goods from these houses, but many of them nearly vomited when opening the refrigerators that had been without power for weeks, letting the foods spoil. Those sights and smells were nothing in comparison to the bodies they discovered in many of the other houses. In one particular house, which had been owned by a wealthy banker, they discovered a gruesome suicide scene where the banker had shot his wife and then killed himself shortly after. John read the suicide note that read:

> *"To whom it may concern,*
> *I was a rich, powerful man, but none of that mattered in the end. I amassed wealth that did not translate to the end of the world. Stock markets did not mean anything in comparison to solid and tangible items of wealth. If you are reading this, I am dead, and my fortune has been for nothing. I lived with no regrets but died with many."*

Within his room, they found a small wall safe hidden behind a painting, which they pried open with a crowbar. The safe contained several gold and silver coins, a large stack of paper cash, and even a few small gold and silver bars. Normally, John would have been opposed to taking such nonessential items, but, as he had previously said to Andrew, "The guy was a total dick, remember? Plus, the bastard shot his own wife before he offed himself. What a chickenshit way to go out..." They gave the couple a quick burial in their backyard, digging shallow graves and placing small wooden crosses on top of their resting places. Rob said a few words of comfort, and a quick prayer for their eternal souls, and they decided to wrap up their scavenging for the evening. It had already been a tough day, both physically and mentally for all of those involved. They brought their spoils home, and each went their separate ways.

John retreated upstairs to his room. Dez found him there, silently reading his Bible, lost in his own thoughts, his head bowed in prayer. She slowly approached him and put her hand on his shoulder. Only then did she realize that he was in tears. She told him, "I never knew you to be a religious man. Are you okay, John?"

He replied, still weeping, "You're right. I never really was one, but all that I've seen, all that I've been though, just makes me...angry. If there is a God, He needs to look after us...so that we never become evil like that bastard there..." He broke down into tears again, and she came closer to him and held him in an embrace. She said, "As long as good men like you keep standing tall, evil and other assholes like that will never prosper. Come here, baby, let's get some sleep tonight. We can move forward in the morning." She undressed him and pulled off her clothes, and they got into bed and held each other. They enjoyed each other's company and fell asleep in each other's arms.

They awoke early the next morning, got dressed, and went downstairs together. The sunlight had barely risen above the horizon, but Shonna and Andrew's daughter Megan were already preparing breakfast. John smiled as he smelled another hearty meal of eggs and ham. He was very happy to smell one of his favorite meals, but sad, knowing that such meals would soon be in short supply. He thought that there was a need to start finding farm animals to raise in their yard, or possibly on the closest neighbor's property. He would discuss the matter with Andrew later, but for now, he enjoyed his breakfast and coffee, all while holding hands with Dezeray. He smiled as his eyes met hers. He wondered if she really loved him, as he believed that he had come to love her. He thought of the possibility of their future together, if maybe someday all this mess would be over with, and they could build a life together. John had never seriously given thought of his future with a woman, but even now, he knew that if he lived through these hard times, he wanted to make a future with Dezeray. He only hoped that she would feel the same way. In this moment, he supposed that he would stop worrying and just enjoy the good times while they still had them. They enjoyed their coffee and food in silence together until Andrew walked in.

He smiled with a signature shit-eating grin and said, "Hey you two lovebirds, I remember when a woman looked at me like that; then a few years later we had two kids together, I get locked in, and she leaves my ass with these two." He chuckled. "I mean, the kids are the best thing that's ever happened to me, so I can't really complain." He took a seat in the kitchen near them and ate his food.

A short time later, Theo came in. "Yo, Johnny, I was listening to the radios and there's a guy asking for you, bro. Said it was Bill KP, if that means anything to you. He said he needed to talk to you."

John stood up from the table abruptly. "Yes, that's my brother's neighbor out in Oregon. He was supposed to be looking after my family. I hope it's good news." He hastened to his office to get on his radio.

"Hey buddy, you with me?" Bill's voice came from the hand mic.

John picked up the microphone and answered his old friend, "I'm here, old man. Sorry I haven't been able to reach you. How is everything by you?"

Bill answered immediately, "Thank God, I was worried that you were dead. Everything is still okay here, but things are getting pretty rough elsewhere. We found that out when it took so long to get your folks here. I've been trying to reach you for a few days. They finally made it here safely, although not without missing a little skin off the top of their nose."

John let out a sigh of relief, then asked Bill, "It's been over a week since they left. What happened? And are they both okay?"

Bill stopped him. "Calm down now, son. They're both okay. The truck is a little shot up, but the bullets missed your parents, so don't worry. Your old man is a tough old guy. I think he had to shoot his way out of a few bad situations, and they got turned from the main roads out here. The highways are full of roadblocks and looters now. They left early enough to make good time for the first part of their journey out of Illinois though. I'd let you talk to your family, but Luke is out hunting, and your mother and father are resting up from their long journey. They only got in a little bit ago and it's been a while since they could both sleep in a safe place without having to watch their backs. I'll contact you again soon when they wake up. How is everything by you? I bet it's getting shitty up there so close to Chicago."

John hung his head. "It's getting pretty bad by us, Bill. I was pretty well set up before all this hit. I still have power and a good amount of food and supplies, but now we have a substantial and growing force here, which is both a good and bad thing. We need more people to defend my house, and the conflicts are getting worse every time we go out for supplies. We've taken several hits, and I don't think we can ride this out without a larger force and more supplies. The city is bad, and getting worse, and it's not going to get much better when the hordes come down the interstate fleeing the big city. I'm sorry I haven't been able to keep in contact with you, but it's been a whirlwind since this all started."

With that, Bill told him, "That's okay, Johnny, I'll make contact in about three hours and let you talk to your family. You go about your business. You sound like you've got plenty to do."

John sat for a moment and though about his business. What he had told Bill about needing a larger force rang true in his head. He also thought about the needing of a large force and the much-needed supplies. He began to consult some of his maps and notes on the area and came up with an impromptu plan. He decided to run it past Andrew, who was nearby in the living room, laying on the couch. He and Andrew went into the office and sat down at the desk, and he went over his plans. "Okay man, tell me if I'm wrong here, but what we desperately need is both food and numbers for a substantial force. I'm putting out another call to Tango and Will. At this point, we need the numbers. We also need to start thinking about raiding a large supply of food and expanding our reach of the base. I want to raid the warehouse south of town and steal a semi-truck full of food. I also want to expand our base to the house next door. We have extra solar panels, so we can start wiring in that house to our grid. I want to get it set up as an additional stash house for supplies, and additional beds for our expanding force. I want us to go out and start expanding our numbers. What do you think?"

After absorbing the information, Andrew thought, scratched his chin, and finally said, "Have you thought about trying to reach out to our contacts in the local police departments, other militia groups, and the National Guard? The Armory is just south of town, and we both have contacts there. We should see who is holed up there, and how many troops they were able to muster."

"I agree. Let's go for the supplies and see what happens with that first, then we can work on expanding our numbers. It's gonna take some time to plan and recon." They decided to get to work on a plan for getting the truck full of supplies on their raid on the warehouse.

INTERLUDE FOUR: CITIZEN SOLDIER
Early-Mid June.

Major Michael Lyon could see the writing on the walls. Since he worked for the government, it wasn't hard to see the writing on the wall for months. Michael was a major in the Illinois Army National Guard assigned to full-time staff position in Springfield, Illinois for the past four years. He had been promoted to major five years ago after leaving his first command of the Infantry Support Company in Joliet. Commissioned as an Ordinance Officer, he had made captain very quickly, assuming command of his first Company within only three years after commissioning. He was an exemplary soldier and an even better leader. The men and NCOs under his command all liked and respected him. His promotion to major had been what he thought was his career move; however, his last several years of boring staff positions had been excruciating. He felt like the years lasted forever and he was anxiously awaiting his chance to be promoted to Lieutenant Colonel to be able to take command of a Battalion. Over the last few years, it became evident that the state and federal government was unprepared for an event of this magnitude. As the economy began its slow freefall, the state was slow to react, but it began delaying paydays and direct deposits into their bank accounts. Michael started to see the effects. Many lower-level staff members and civilian employees began turning in their resignations or requesting transfers to different units closer to home. Michael felt their pain. He commuted nearly three hours a day, driving from his house in Bradley. He had already begun withdrawing portions of his paychecks and keeping the cash or buying more ammo for his gun collection. He and his wife began to get worried, especially since the paychecks had been getting delayed more and more as the state ran behind in paying salaries. Michael volunteered to do his staff duties from the nearby Kankakee National Guard Armory to save on gas, and his request was approved. He moved into sharing an office with a recruiter. He cringed a bit at being the highest-ranking officer in the building during the weekdays, but he enjoyed having a ten-minute drive to work instead of a few hours. He had his equipment and rifle moved to the Kankakee Armory as well, telling the Springfield command that he would be doing weekend drills with the local unit instead of with the Springfield units.

Although the move closer to home was a small comfort, things were getting worse and worse as the state and national economy began to slowly collapse. He was disturbed at how bad violent crime had risen in the area after hearing that one of his college roommates who was a Kankakee police officer had been shot in the head. He allowed all staff members at the Kankakee Guard Armory to carry their firearms on their persons in the Armory while in uniform. He secretly began meeting with the senior NCOs in the Armory, asking their opinions on a tentative plan for what they could do if the economy did collapse and how to combat the most likely scenarios. The first problem would be if the state called for an emergency muster of the troops; many would not show up. He figured that most of the Guardsmen would stay home and attend to their families. He advised the NCOs to secretly reach out to those married soldiers who lived within fifty miles of the Armory that if things got worse and the guard unit was activated, they would allow their families to stay at the Armory. It wasn't an officially authorized order, but he decided that once things got worse, he would need as many men and women to command as possible in order to be combat and mission effective. Michael also set off on a mission to strengthen the infrastructure of the Armory. It had recently been expanded to the nearby airfield, allowing the Aviation helicopter unit to move into their facility. Kankakee was one of the largest National Guard Armories south of Chicago between the big city and the state capitol in Springfield. It held four Companies: The Infantry Company, a Military Police Company, the new addition of the Blackhawk Helicopter Aviation Company, and an Army Reserve Support Company and Engineer Platoon. He immediately requested work orders to expand the fencing around the entire facility and to secure the gates. Because the Armory was a mile or two south of the Kankakee City limits, and it hadn't been seen as a great security threat, Major Lyon was able to get the emergency work order pushed through in a rush because of the "volatile situation in the area and being able to secure the valuable assets within the Armory" as he put it to the general in Springfield. The order was approved, partly in thanks to his friendship with this general, and the work on the fencing and gates began less than a week after the order was approved. Major Lyon also flexed a bit of his rank and authority over the Armory by having the generators for the facility inspected, cleaned, and repaired, and also ordering a large amount of extra supplies to stock the Armory and facility. He was able to slip by unnoticed when he ordered nearly triple the usual monthly supply of everyday items such as cleaning supplies, toilet paper, bedding, and food stocks for the cafeteria, as these items were rarely looked over with as much scrutiny as the arms and essential military items in supply requests. He then submitted a large order for extra MREs field supplies and arms for the arms room. This order was a much harder request to get approved. He submitted orders for double the normal amount of small arms ammunition and included rockets, machine gun ammo, and mortar rounds. He argued that the requests usually took a very long time, and the Units within the Armory had their summer annual training two-week field exercises coming up and were in dire need of the ammunition for live fire exercises. He was able to secure a few more armored Humvees, two MRAPs, and two more "deuce and a half" supply transportation trucks.

Major Lyon instructed the supply sergeant to begin falsifying their official supply log books to show that the Armory had much less supplies than they actually had. While it was a common practice on a smaller scale, this was a very serious charge at a larger magnitude, so Major Lyon wrote a handwritten note taking the blame for this order and ordered the supply sergeant to keep it on his person in case this was ever discovered; the major told him that he would take the blame and punishment if it ever came to that. With that insurance, the supply guys happily cooked their books.

The situation on the outside slowly became worse. Major Lyon took a day off work to get a few personal affairs in order. He and his wife decided to liquidate most of their savings and put that into buying food stocks in bulk for the Armory; they also decided that before inflation and interest rates got any worse, they would pay off their home mortgage and vehicle loans and insurance in large lump sums. He had his wife pack up most of their important items and prepare to make the move to the Armory in case that was needed (which he suspected it soon would be). Major Lyon then went and visited his old college roommate in the hospital. His old roommate had been one of his closest friends as an adult; their friendship had begun in college when they were nearly inseparable living together with a few other ROTC classmates. His roommate had never commissioned as an officer, instead staying to finish his enlisted contract. He'd elected not to re-enlist, becoming a police officer instead. They had grown apart a little in the last few years, both becoming busy in their personal and professional lives, but they still kept in touch. Major Lyon knew that his old friend was a prepper, and he was eager to rekindle their close friendship, knowing that they could both be of great mutual support to each other when things got worse.

His friend was barely conscious when Michael went to see him in the hospital, so he mostly spoke to his parents. He asked his dad how long it was expected to take for him to recover. John's dad told him, "Mike, it wasn't good, and I know you know that this is bad timing. He should be allowed to go home in a few more days though. He's been making a quicker recovery than the doctors first thought. We don't want to rush him out, but if we can get him home in the next few days to recover, he will be okay on his own. We need to get back to our other son in Oregon. Things are getting bad out here, but we will be safer out in Oregon. John will be able to take care of himself once he gets up on his feet."

Mike told Richard, "You guys should get out as soon as you can..." He waited a moment for the nurse to leave the room and lowered his voice a bit. "The writing is on the wall here Mr. Gonzalez. I can see it. The federal government is being held together by Band-Aids, and the state isn't much better. I think the economy is going to come collapsing down in the next month or so, and the state won't be able to hold things together without the federal support."

With that, his old friend in the hospital bed began to stir. John woke up and rubbed his eyes, then looked at his old friend standing there in his military uniform. "Well shit, if it isn't my old friend Mikey."

Mike turned and walked over to the hospital bed and wrapped his old friend in a big hug. When he eased up, he said, "I'm sorry I didn't come to see you earlier, John. I've been dealing with a ton of work issues with all this shit going on."

He replied, "It's okay, brother. Working for the government, I get it."

They both laughed and Mike said, "I hear you're out of here in a few days. You going to be okay on your own after your parents leave?"

His friend sat up in his hospital bed and said, "Yeah, Mike. You know me; I'm prepared for stuff like this. This whole getting shot thing is just a little setback. I'm almost all healed up. When I get back home, I'm putting out word to a few friends to come hole up at my place before things get worse. What about you and your wife? You got a place to stay?"

Mike told him, "Well, I got myself transferred to the Armory in Kankakee to be closer to home. I'm the highest-ranking officer here, so I'm the de-facto commander of the whole installation for now. When things get worse, I'll order a full muster call and see who shows up. I guess we will just go from there, but we'll have to cross that bridge when it comes to it. What about you, man? Are all of your uhh… 'preparations' in place? You're going to be okay?"

"Yeah, man. My house in on lockdown, and I've got the right network of people to support. If things get bad, I should be well stocked, and I'll hopefully have a sizeable group to keep control of my area. Speaking of, are you going to loop in the rest of the wolfpack?"

Mike straightened up and said, "Bro, I'll be honest with you. I've been so busy looking over things at the Armory, I almost forgot to prepare in that aspect. Nick is still with the Kankakee Unit, so I expect him to show up if I ask him. Frazier is still in command out in the Indiana National Guard, so I doubt he will be able to make it up out here. But I'm going to try and contact him. You get a hold of me if you need anything, John, I've got to get running." He shook his friend's hand, then Richard's, and hugged Denise. He told them to have a safe journey home and quickly departed, checking his phone.

Mike was not happy at seeing the texts from his wife telling him to check the news about the stock market.

As the weeks passed, and the economic situation became worse, he began receiving notice that many of his younger junior enlisted troops were calling in, asking to come in for active orders, as they had lost their jobs or been laid off. Many of the young men and women were single and had no other support structure outside of their civilian jobs. Some even showed up to the Armory without asking for orders and just offered to help clean or do other tasks so that they could have a place to stay. Since the stock market had collapsed, nearly thirty to forty junior enlisted troops from the various companies stationed at the unit had showed up.

Major Lyon put in a call to his command in Springfield and asked to have these young privates on active orders, requesting funding for "area peacekeeping" missions. His request was surprisingly approved; however, all junior enlisted soldiers were only granted half pay due to "budget restrictions." It wasn't much, but Major Lyon was happy to be able to provide his troops some temporary relief where they could have a place to stay and eat for free. He only required the troops to be in uniform on weekdays excluding "casual Fridays," and he sent out large groups to go and pick up the soldiers and collect their essential belongings and bring them to the Armory. His only requirement was that these soldiers bring any food items, military clothing and equipment, and he allowed them to bring any and all personal weapons and ammunition with them. Most of his junior enlisted were college students or young single soldiers with little to no family ties, so their moves were easy and quick. He selected one of the E-5 sergeants who was a recruiter stationed at the Kankakee Armory to oversee the moves and to keep the junior enlisted soldiers "in line."

Major Lyon had still not heard from the captain who was the Company commander of the Kankakee Infantry Unit, which was concerning. He was the owner of a large security company in the Chicago suburbs. He had also attempted to contact the Company's first sergeant, who was a Chicago Police sergeant. His calls, voicemails, and texts had not been returned, which made him very worried. The news was not good coming out of Chicago and the suburbs. He finally remembered to call his old friend and member of the "wolfpack" which was he and his friend's nickname for their tight-knit group that had begun in college when they attended ROTC together.

After college, the four friends had kept close, all being groomsmen or best man in each other's weddings. Mike and Nick Frazier had both gone on to commission as officers, Frazier going on to the Indiana National Guard, where he was currently a major in the Logistics and Support Brigade Staff. Nick Holden had not commissioned as an officer, instead remaining enlisted in the Illinois National Guard. He reached the rank of E-7 Sergeant First Class and was currently serving as the Weapons Platoon Sergeant of the Second Platoon of the Infantry Company at Kankakee.

Major Lyon called his friend Holden, who had been the best man at his wedding, and he picked up on the first ring.

"Hey Mikey, what's up, brother?"

"Nick, things are getting bad. Are you able to get up to Kankakee and stay at the Armory? Everything is going to shit, and I've gotten a bunch of the junior enlisted to come stay here on orders, but I have almost no NCOs to command the troops. I'm the only officer here. I keep trying to contact the state to put out an emergency deployment order to muster the companies out here, but they keep denying me. Are you able to get out of work and move up here to help ride things out?"

Holden replied, "Is this an order, Sir? Hahaha, just kidding, man. My wife was down in Mexico when this started to get bad, so I told her to stay down there with her family where she will be safe. I'm down in the middle of nowhere out here south of Springfield, but I heard it's getting bad, and the steel mill is starting layoffs. I'll go ahead and put in for military leave and move as much as I can to you."

"Thanks, brother, I could really use you here. Get up here as fast as you can." With that, Major Lyon hung up. He had recently moved into the Company commander's office in the headquarters section of the Infantry Unit. He heard a knock on his open door and looked up to see the staff sergeant who was one of the full-time staff at the Armory complex.

"Sir, turn on the news now! It's not good." The staff sergeant turned on the closest television to Fox News, which was usually on the TVs around the Armory. The news anchors were speaking with loud, frantic voices, and flashing headlines read, "STOCK MARKET COLLAPSE. FEDERAL GOVERNMENT THREATENS SHUTDOWN. RIOTS AND FIRES RAGE OUT OF CONTROL IN MAJOR CITIES ACROSS THE COUNTRY. BANK CLOSURES AND TRADING HOLIDAYS DECLARED. IS FEDERAL STATE OF EMERGENCY DECLAREMENT NEXT?"

"What do we do now, Sir? Should we contact higher command for orders?"

"Sergeant, I don't think there is going to be a 'higher command' for much longer. We are going to take matters into our own hands. Start out a phone tree call to muster all of the available troops to the Armory, all four Companies. Get me the Company commanders and first sergeants of the Infantry Company, Support Company, MP Company, and the Aviation Company on the phone with me ASAP. If you can't get a hold of them, work your way down the line. The highest-ranking person you get on the line first starts the phone call tree for muster orders. Get all your troops as fast as you can to report to the Armory for orders. Same as before: Families are permitted to stay in quarters at the barracks as long as they bring as many essential supplies as they can. I'm typing up the orders now. Also, reach out into the records and check with any current Guard soldiers from other units that live in this county, and tell them to come in if they have nowhere else to go. Make it snappy Sergeant!"

The staff sergeant gave a quick salute and replied, "Yes Sir, time now!" and ran out of the room to his office, where he began making frantic calls to the various Company commanders and senior staff.

Major Lyon called the other NCOs including the three recruiters into his office and gave them the same orders. All needed to start reaching out to as many soldiers as they could, as fast as they could. He even allowed the recruiters to call any other soldiers that the recruiters could muster, both active and recently separated to be invited to the Armory, under the same conditions. They all got to work as quickly as possible.

Major Lyon called his wife, all while still typing up the orders. His wife answered and quickly said, "I know, I heard the news on the radio. I'm headed to the Armory as quickly as I can. Just resigned from work and grabbed our last bags from the house. I'll be there in half an hour. Love you." She hung up, and the major stood up from his desk, still in a bit of a panic. He paced around the office to calm his nerves a bit.

He was snapped out of his daydream by a phone call coming through the desk. He answered, and it was a general from the Staff in Springfield. His voice boomed through the speaker: "Major Lyon, your orders' activation without my authorization is both ballsy and a direct violation of the chain of command. You're way over your head on this one. Luckily, I think it's the right move. State and the Feds aren't answering calls. I can't get the governor to answer me to authorize state-wide authorization for activation orders. For now, you're on your own, and you have my blessing. You're the highest-ranking officer that I've been in contact with south of Chicago. I hope your supply has some insignia and extra uniforms in stock. Consider yourself a Full Bird as of right now. Official promotion papers are in an email on its way to you now. Congratulations, Colonel Lyon. You're on your own as of right now, and you won't have any more support coming from Springfield. I've got nothing to offer…Best of luck. Call me if you still can when you get your muster organized so we can—."

And with that, the phone lines went dead. Lyon heard the groans from soldiers within the halls as they all realized that their cell phones no longer had service either. The staff sergeant stepped into his office without a knock and said, "I overheard the conversation. Congratulations, Colonel Lyon. I'll run over to supply and let him know of the battlefield promotion. I'll be your witness on the orders, Sir."

Lyon looked up at the staff sergeant, and said, "Thank you, Sergeant, but you have plenty of work to do already. I'll start pulling my own weight now. Even Officers work too sometimes."

Thankfully, most of the office phones were hard-wired land lines and still worked. Lyon leaned out of his office and told the rest of the NCOs to continue trying to make contact with as many soldiers on their muster list as possible. They were also making contingent plans to go out in groups and make contact with local soldiers in person. Now-Colonel Lyon stepped out of the office and went over to the supply office with a big grin on his face.

CHAPTER 8: FROM BAD TO WORSE
August 1ˢᵗ

They had spent the last few days carefully planning the raid on the warehouse. On two separate occasions, they sent out small groups of two or three to conduct quick recons of the area. The first was just a quick drive by of the area by three of them in Theo's Ford Explorer, outfitted with new tires, courtesy of John's neighbor's garage. They made a quick drive of their planned route, taking side streets until they reached Schuyler Avenue, which turned into State Route 45 out of town, which led to the warehouse. They encountered little resistance and were able to drive down to the warehouse easily. Once in the area, they did a quick drive by of the warehouse complex on South Tech Drive, which appeared abandoned. They did a drive around the building, taking notes of entries, exits, and the semi-trucks and trailers parked around the dock areas. They did not see any people out around the factories, and the area looked abandoned.

For the second reconnaissance, Theo drove John and Andrew out to the area and dropped them off on foot. They climbed onto the roof of a neighboring abandoned factory to conduct recon on the warehouse for twenty-four hours. They took turns on the rifle and spotting scope, while taking notes of the movement around the area. Other than a few scruffy-looking bums in and around the warehouse, it didn't look like there was any significant amount of people in the warehouse. There were no other vehicles or significant movement during the day.

He and Andrew both quickly got bored. They took turns on the spotting scope, and the other would nap, smoke cigars, or read a book they'd taken along.

"I know we need to monitor this place for a full twenty-four to make sure nothing changes, bro, but this shit is killing me…" Andrew told him, while laying back, his head resting on his pack as he puffed on his cigar.

John replied, "I don't know, man. Maybe things will get exciting tonight. Who knows?"

The morning faded, and the afternoon also slowly dragged on. They took to monitoring the area they could see beyond their target. There was a small amount of foot traffic along State Route 45 to their east. They saw destitute travelers walking and carrying or pulling their belongings in wagons. John assumed it was because their cars had run out of gas. A few carried handguns and had hunting rifles or shotguns slung across on their backs, and some carried more than just what they had on their backs. It was a sad sight. It was concerning to see refugees coming from the south. The area south of the Kankakee Metropolitan area was pretty much small farm towns and villages all the way until the larger college town of Champaign. John had not expected many refugees to leave the rural areas and head north into Kankakee, unless they were coming to meet family. It worried him that refugees would soon begin to flood the Kankakee area from the south as well as from the city of Chicago and its suburbs. He knew it might soon be happening en masse.

He was scanning through the scope of his rifle when Andrew tapped his shoulder. "Look to the southeast, man, past the I-57 interchange. Down Route 45, past the jail. There's smoke and dust kicking up from the area of the National Guard Armory. What do you think, Johnny? That looks like a lot of activity out there. Lots of bodies, lots of movement. We need to get in contact with our people out there. I think there's a sizeable force out there that we need to ally ourselves with...or at least figure out who they are."

John nodded and silently agreed. He thought of the irony of the fact that after the collapse of the economy, and the subsequent breakdown of life as they knew it, they had possibly regressed back into individual tribes, groups, and nation-states, all vying for power. He shared this thought with Andrew, who was more of an intellectual than himself usually.

Andrew said, "Hmm...I guess I agree with you, man. I'm a bit surprised that your dumbass thought of something so intellectually stimulating before I did. But it's probably true. Maybe we ought to read up on our medieval history when we get back home."

John just replied with, "Fuck you, dude, I have smart ideas most of the time. But I'm the looks of this operation, we all know this. Since you're short and ugly, I let you have the smart ideas."

They chuckled together, and Andrew said, "I love you too, fucker." They sat in silence for a few minutes, until Andrew said, "Wait...I have an idea." He went over to his small handheld HAM radio. Andrew closed his eyes for a few moments in thought, then began to flip around frequencies until he stopped at a certain number. He muttered to himself, "I hope this is still right..." and said, "What was your unit's call sign back when you were in that National Guard unit?"

John replied, still catching up with Andrew's train of thought, "Uhh...The commander was Comanche Six."

Andrew stopped and said, "Okay...now what is something I could say so the commander knows it's you, and you personally speaking?"

John thought for a minute until he remembered that his old roommates Mike Lyon might be commanding the unit, and his good friend Holden would be there as well. He told Andrew, "Okay, use the call sign 'Wolfpack Seven.' The commander should know it is me, or at least it should ring a bell."

Andrew keyed up on the radio, transmitting loudly, "Comanche Six, Comanche Six, this is Wolfpack Seven Romeo. Calling any station this net. Any station this net, please transmit to Comanche Six. Blue, Blue, Blue. Friendlies attempting to make contact." The line was silent for a few moments, and Andrew repeated his transmission.

John frowned and said, "Dude, what the hell are you trying to do? What channel are you on? You know that isn't secure comms—" when the line was suddenly alive with an unknown voice: "Go for Comanche Six Romeo. Identify yourself, Wolfpack." John was incredibly surprised but then snatched the hand radio from Andrew, keyed up and said, "Comanche Six Romeo, I need to get in contact with Major Michael Lyon ASAP. I don't know or care who you are, but I need to speak to either Major Lyon or Sergeant First Class Holden TIME NOW. This is imperative. Wolfpack, Over."

The line was silent for a moment, but after a few moments, the unfamiliar voice spoke up, "Which member of the Wolfpack drinks Jack Honey, and which one drinks Jameson?"

John smiled, knowing he had finally gotten through to one of the men over at the National Guard Armory he needed to speak to. This was a passcode to ensure that the person they were speaking to knew the intimate details of their friendship. John keyed up the radio and said, "Frazier was all about the Jack Honey even before it came out. My boy Mikey loved the Jameson, and Holden and I would drink anything that had alcohol in it, but considering we were all around twenty-one, we would drink anything. I hope Mikey's tastes haven't changed too much in the last few years. He's one of my best friends, and It would be cool if we could ride out the end of the world together."

There was silence for nearly a full minute, until the familiar voice of one of his dearest friends came over the radio, "Wolfpack for life, my brother. I'm so glad to hear your voice. Are you doing okay,

Johnny? The commo guys said you have to be pretty close to have a signal this clear. Where are you?"

John beamed and said, "Mike? Thank fucking God, man. I'm glad to hear your voice. I'm about three miles or so from your location; I'm working a stakeout for a personal necessity for my group. Are you doing okay?"

Mike answered, "Yeah man, I'm doing just fine. I have a decent-sized group here. How about you? Do you need anything?"

He replied, "No, Mike, I just needed to know that you were out there. We should meet up if you are able to travel. Do you think you could come make it to my place tomorrow?"

Lyon replied, "I haven't been outside the wire since this all started, and apparently you have. Do you think that the route is safe enough for me to travel there?"

John said, "Bring a little bit of security, and you should be okay. Say my place, noon tomorrow?"

"Works for me, brother. Look forward to seeing you. Comanche Six, Out."

John gave a toothy smile to Andrew, who returned it and said, "You're welcome, dickhead. Not only do you get reunited with your boyfriend, but now we got the government about to breathe down our necks."

John retorted, "Oh shut it, man. Don't get jealous now. Getting all Libertarian on me over there. Plus, this could be the alliance we need to take the city back. Now let's get back to watching this warehouse. One task at a time. We scope out this warehouse, then hit it in the morning, and we're back home in time to meet Lyon and his forces, if everything goes right."

The rest of the night passed uneventfully, and they both were able to get a few hours of sleep. They called the others on the radio at about 7 A.M., giving the all clear to proceed to their location and start hitting the warehouse building to begin their raid.

At around 8:30 A.M., they received radio traffic from Theo, advising that they were in the area and ready to begin the assault on the warehouse. Andrew stayed on top of the neighboring factory to provide sniper cover and overwatch, while John descended the ladder. He quickly but quietly made his way across the road to the edge of the warehouse facility, where he hid behind the abandoned guard shack until he heard the low rumble of the Tank's powerful engine in the distance and the tires squeal as Theo turned the corner hard in the large armored vehicle. He watched as the Tank regained speed and rammed through the fences of the warehouse. Theo ground to a halt near one of the side doors, and the team all got out.

John came running from the fence line to regroup with them at the vehicle. No words were exchanged, as they all knew the immediate task at hand, following their plan. They all immediately continued in a loose file to the closest door. Theo used a battering ram to blow the heavy security door off its hinges. They filed into the warehouse, meeting little resistance. It was dark and smelled of stagnant air and mild body odor. They turned on their weapon-mounted flashlights and spread out in pairs to explore the warehouse. Once they found the large pallets of canned foods, they located the overhead doors leading to the outside ramps. They opened the overhead door that had one of the semi- trailers backed up to it.

Theo ran outside to check that the semi still would start; finding that it did, he started it and began warming up the engine.

Big Rob hopped on the nearest forklift and began loading pallets of canned food into the trailer. They were nearly done filling the trailers when Andrew's voice crackled over the radio. He was yelling, "Large force incoming! You've got at least ten to fifteen vehicles heading your way now. Prepare for contact!"

The line was still open when they heard his rifle rounds begin to ring out above them. Rounds began striking the ground outside the warehouse. They next heard Theo letting loose short bursts from his SAW. Everyone except Big Rob ran outside to engage the oncoming threat. Rob continued to load the last few pallets onto the trailer as quickly as he could.

The group was met by automatic gunfire. "GET COVERRR!" yelled Theo as he engaged the oncoming hostiles from behind a metal dumpster. The rest of them dove behind crates and concrete barriers, then returned fire at the oncoming force. The firefight lasted for nearly half an hour, until they were all nearly empty on ammo. As their supply dwindled, and the sounds of the battle began to die down, a Hispanic voice yelled out from behind the large group of cars, "Ayyy, Holmes, give up the shit over here and we won't kill all you bitches. Just give it up now and we won't kill you. We got thirty homies out here ready to kill you all in the name of the almighty LKA."

John said to himself, "Fucking gang bangers? Really? It's the end of the world, and we're out here getting shot at by the Latin Kings?" He then yelled back to the Latino gang member, "Fuck you, we'll go down fighting. I'm ready to die here today. I've killed more Kings than any Blood or Crip out there on the streets, and I'll keep stacking your useless shithead bodies until my last dying breath, homeboy!"

The Latin King replied, "That can be fuckin' arranged, punk ass bitch!" And both sides began firing again, their barrages of automatic gunfire chipping away at each others' cover. They were returning fire and screaming insults back and forth. The situation began to look more and more hopeless, as their ammo supply became seriously low. The barrage began to slow down as the gang members also seemingly began to run out of ammunition. The gunfire became more and more sporadic, but they continued to yell at each other from behind cover.

John was loading one of his last pistol magazines into his 1911. Suddenly, they heard a loud barrage from a large belt-fed heavy machine gun. He heard multiple .50 caliber machine guns opening up and the sound of large rounds striking the metal vehicles of the gang bangers' vehicles. He heard the screams of the gang bangers, and then it began to quiet down. There were a few moments of silence before his radio chirped up, and his old friend Michael Lyon's voice came over the net: "Lucky I was headed out to our meeting early; I was nearby to come save your ass! Come on out, man. The coast is clear."

John and the others slowly stepped out from their covered positions and faced their saviors. He looked out and saw three tan military Humvees with soldiers manning the turrets at the top and the mounted .50 caliber machine guns still smoking.

Mike Lyon stepped out of the rear of the middle vehicle, dressed in his military fatigues and carrying a pistol on his hip. "I figured I'd travel light. I thought we would encounter little to no resistance, according to you. We heard the firefight begin when we headed out. We may not have stopped, but your guy Andrew contacted me on the radio, saying you were in contact and needed our help. We were luckily close and got here just in time to help you out." Lyon walked over and embraced his old friend. "I'm glad we made it in time. And I'm glad you're okay, brother. Now let's get you loaded and move out back to your place. Take what you can carry now; I'm going to send some of my troopers and engineers to remove the rest of what we can from this warehouse to bring it all back to my Armory. We have nearly five hundred mouths to feed, and we're in dire need of this food to keep our people fed."

They moved back inside and set to work. Big Rob was still hard at working loading pallets of different types of foods and canned goods onto the truck until it was nearly full. A couple also moved over to the dead gangbangers who were torn to shreds from the .50 cal to see what weapons they could scavenge from their remains. They found a couple AK-47s still intact, but little ammo left. Their vehicles held a few packs of bottled water, and some food, which they loaded into the cab of the semi-truck they'd requisitioned.

After almost another hour, when the semi was full, they sealed up the truck and closed the door to the trailer. Theo and Big Rob hopped in the semi and pulled away from the loading dock. More of Lyon's troops arrived at the warehouse with more loading equipment and trucks. They took their place as the rest of the original group pulled away from the warehouse. One armored Humvee took the lead, with John and the rest of his group piled in the Tank. Theo and Rob were in the semi in the middle, and the last two Humvees brought up the rear. They sped along back into town towards the compound. As usual, they met little in the way of armed resistance, although a few pot shots pinged off the armor of their vehicles. This didn't bother them much, as it had become more and more common recently. As they continued their ride northbound, they were mostly distracted, and they hardly noticed the two motorcycles that had pulled off of a side street and began following the caravan at a distance. They drew closer and closer toward the compound, in a daze, until someone finally spotted the tail. "Looks like we picked up a shadow. Two motorcycles have made every turn we have for the last few miles," Andrew yelled from the passenger seat over the sound of the loud engines and wind rushing through the open windows.

John looked back and saw the motorcycles, which were ridden by two large men wearing leather biker jackets. They were clearly attempting to keep their distance but were making every turn they did as they headed back into town. "Shit!" he said. "Let's try to shake them; we can't let them follow us back to the compound."

Andrew, who was already having another conversation on his handheld radio with Theo and Rob in the semi at this point, said,

"Fuck. Nobody had the foresight to get comms link up with the Army guys on our six? We can't exactly stop and have a friendly chat with our allies and let the bikers catch up. There's bound to be more of them out there."

John answered, "We can't take that chance; we have to shake them. Or take them out. And I really don't want any more bloodshed today."

As John said his piece and they all began to brainstorm ideas of what to do, the bikers quickly closed the gap between them and the column of vehicles; they sped up and came up on the rear vehicle. Both bikers pulled put submachine guns and began to fire the automatic bursts into the Humvee.

"It looks like we aren't going to have a chance soon," John said to Andrew. From their rearview mirrors, they could see one of the bursts strike the gunner in the Humvee's turret, and the vehicle swerved off the road, nearly crashing into a telephone pole. The next Humvee sped up alongside the semi, and the soldier driving motioned to the west.

"I think he wants to pull over in the high school parking lot. There we can get rid of these bikers," Theo's voice came over the radio.

"Okay, let's do it," Andrew said.

The convoy sped up until they reached the Kankakee High School parking lot where they circled around quickly and took up defensive positions around the semi-trailer. The two bikers sped by, keeping straight on Jeffery Street and disappearing on the other side of the high school. They all breathed a sigh of relief for a moment. One of the National Guard soldiers, a Sergeant named Millon, and Big Rob were tending to the wounds of the soldier who had been shot. The radio operator had taken a knee next to the open door of one of the Humvees and was calling in a situation report to Colonel Lyon, who was still back at the warehouse with the remainder of his men.

The silence was broken by the sound of motorcycle engines in the distance. "Shit, they must be coming back," Theo said.

As the noise became a dull roar, it became evident that there were more than just two motorcycle engines. John cursed as fifty or more bikers came into view, all wearing leather jackets with a flaming skull emblem. He recognized them as the Outlaws biker gang. He had seen them before but never in this great of a number.

The bikers entered the parking lot and began to ride in circles around the convoy. The National Guard sergeant was already calling for reinforcements on the radio, while the others were taking up defensive position behind their vehicles and readying their weapons.

The bikers finally pulled their bikes into several long rows in a semi-circle around the stopped convoy. The leader of the group of bikers was a large bearded and tattooed biker who looked like a Viking. He stepped off his motorcycle and stood there sizing up John and his team. He had his sleeves rolled up, revealing large swastikas and Neo-Nazi Aryan Brotherhood tattoos. The patch sewn on the chest of his vest read "Vice President." He walked toward the group and said in a loud, booming voice, "Nobody needs to die here today. We just want that truck full of food that you took from our wetback gang brothers...Give us that, and I won't kill every one of you. You're hopelessly outnumbered. I have ten times the men you do here and now. All I want is the food, and you can walk away. Now what do you say?"

John crouched behind the front end of the Tank as he listened to the biker leader. He looked over at Sergeant Millon, who was still furiously speaking on the radio handset to the rest of the Army unit. Millon made eye contact with him, cracked a smile and held a thumbs up. Then he held up three fingers and mouthed the words "Hold on" to John.

John set his rife on the hood of the Tank and stepped out into the open. He held his hands up and walked closer to the biker gang leader. "If we give you what we have… what's to stop you from just taking it and killing us? I'm gonna need some kind of guarantee that lets me and my men walk out of here."

The biker smiled and said, "You're right. There's nothing guaranteeing that I let you leave here alive." He raised up his pistol and said, "You die first."

Just as the biker said those words, the loud whir of helicopter blades began to fill the air. The thunderous noise grew louder and louder until several large Blackhawk helicopters broke over the treeline. They flew low and hovered over the group. One of the Blackhawks turned sideways, showing a crew chief with a minigun pointed right at the bikers. Over the loudspeakers, a voice boomed out, "Stand down, by order of the United States Army. Stand down and drop your weapons or you will be fired upon."

The bikers began to panic, most jumping back on their bikes and starting the engines. More panic ensued as a group of military vehicles came charging down the road and blocked the bikers inside the parking lot. The gang was now outnumbered by dozens of soldiers pointing mounted automatic weapons at them. Most of the bikers put their hands up, knowing they were outgunned.

Out of one of the lead vehicles stepped Colonel Lyon. He walked towards the biker leader until they were only an arm's length apart and stared him down. "I am Colonel Lyon, United States Army…And you are?"

"I am the vice president of the Outlaws of Illinois, and I'm not telling you my fucking name, GI Joe."

Lyon shook his head and chuckled. "And why are the Outlaws suddenly so interested in Kankakee? You had what, maybe five, ten members here in the Kankakee chapter before all this shit went down? Why are all of you here?"

"Fuck off, Army man. I don't answer to no man, especially not no Government man."

Without missing a beat, Lyon calmly answered, "You sure do answer to somebody. You scumbag white trash bikers are too dumb to organize on this level. Most of you are usually too busy selling meth out of trailers down in Iroquois County to do any real crime. What changed? Who do you answer to? Why are you suddenly working with gangs of all different colors?"

The biker laughed and said, "Like I said, I ain't telling you shit. You're a slave to a government that ain't even around to hold your leash no more."

With that, Lyon had had enough. He swiftly kicked the biker in the stomach. The man yelled out in pain and dropped to the ground. After catching his breath and climbing to his feet, he said, "You stupid son of a...You can't stop it...You can kill us...but we're only the muscle. They're going to come for you. All of you...And you can't stop it!"

CHAPTER 9: A FIGHTING CHANCE

Lyon towered over the biker leader, who was visibly shaking at this point. "I said WHO, YOU FUCKING SCUM!" Lyon yelled and back-handed the biker across the face. "Who are you so afraid of? Nobody in your punk ass little biker crew. Now who is pulling enough muscle that's got you scared?"

The large biker wiped the back of his hand over his bleeding mouth and said, "They'll kill you all, man...It doesn't matter how many big guns you got. Their reach is too long and too powerful. It's join or die."

Lyon said, "It doesn't matter. Who is it? Who is coming for us?"

The biker chewed on his thoughts for a moment and finally said, "The Mexicans...Not just the Kings, not just the Chicago Gangs. The whole fucking deal, man. The Cartel. The Sinaloa Cartel. They're coming down from Chicago to expand their reach. They're gonna set up shop here and in Joliet. Then they'll have a foothold on the whole northern part of the state. They're paying us to secure their travel routes, then they start bringing down their local gangs of Latin Kings to control the area. Any major resistance and they bring out their big guns. The Cartel did it in Chicago. Killed most of the police and National Guard that were resisting up there. If you resist it, you're dead...You're all fucking dead."

"Yeah, I bet asshole. Tell the Cartel we'll be waiting. They can't have our town. We'll kill every single one they send." He drew his service pistol from his holster, clicked off the safety, and shot the biker leader in the head. As his body collapsed, Colonel Lyon told the rest of the bikers, "One of you deliver that message to your masters. Now all of you get the hell out of here. The next time we see any of you near us or our people, you're dead. And take his body with you. I won't stand to see this scumbag bleed out in a school parking lot."

Some of the bikers jumped on their motorcycles and sped out of the parking lot, heading back toward the south of town. Most of the small cluster of cowards had no care for the fates of their fellow men, more interested in tearing out of danger. The majority of the group was still standing with their hands up uncertainly.

"I have a feeling we shouldn't have let them go. We killed one and got our intel. We just let them leave to run back and regroup, bro? Bad choice, man," John told Lyon, who was re-holstering his pistol, his hands beginning to shake.

The colonel wiped sweat from his brow. "We don't even know the intel he gave is solid. We couldn't risk a massacre in the streets at the hands of the U.S. government...Or whatever is left of it...." The colonel trailed off. He turned to his old friend, grabbed him by the shirt, and pulled him away from the group for a private conversation.

In low, grumbled tones, he told the colonel, "What the FUCK, man? We just going to be judge and jury out here now? What was all that about?"

Lyon finally stopped shaking and replied, "Stop it, Johnny. We both need to be strong for our men. We need to think this out. What if what he said was real? I mean REALLY real. If this is really the Cartel, we're in over our heads here. Shit is gonna get bad real soon. But If he was bluffing, and we're only working against the local bangers and bikers, we'll be up for a decent fight, but not outgunned...But if what he said was true...we are royally screwed. I had to throw my own bluff to look strong to those shitheads. I wanted them to go back with their tails between their legs. If they go back to their supposed Cartel bosses and we look like a force to be reckoned with, they may not have the balls to touch us. It was a gamble I'm willing to take."

John shook his head. "Either way...we have work to do. We need more men, and we need that fast. We need to take control of as much real estate as we can manage. We have to work together and strengthen our defenses here. We have to take this city back. As much as we can. The more bodies we keep safe, the better."

The Colonel nodded. "You need to understand one thing though; not everyone can be saved. You can't be some kind of messiah. We will work hard to save only the people that can serve a purpose, and those who can fight. If the government ever recovers, that is something I can swing to them. You have to understand the reality of the situation. We can't save everybody, Johnny."

"I get it. Just understand that we work together on this. You do things your way, and I'll do mine my way."

They shook hands and walked back to the group. The bikers that still remained were now loading their dead brother and had already tossed their weapons into a pile in the parking lot. Pistols, submachine guns, and shotguns were piled onto each other, all while the soldiers held them at gunpoint. One by one, the few bikers dropped their weapons and were patted down and stripped of any other weapons, food, ammunition, or other supplies. Near the end of the line, one of the other bikers, another large bald man with dozens of tattoos started to argue with the soldiers monitoring the line of detained bikers.

The biker was yelling, "You really think we're just going to roll over and take this? We're gonna come back with ten times as many and kill you all!" He stepped out of line and lunged at one of the soldiers and had to be tackled by a few more of the soldiers before he could be subdued. The remainder of the bikers were still kept under control. While the rowdy biker continued to struggle, two soldiers attempted to put him in flexicuffs. The biker was still spitting and cursing when they finally got him under control.

Colonel Lyon started toward them, but John put a hand on his friend's arm and said, "You've done enough today, my friend." He stepped over to the big biker and punched him in the stomach, hard.

The biker doubled over in pain, then coughed and spit in his face. "Who the fuck are you? You aren't in charge like the Army man over there. I only deal with the important people. We own this town, and you ain't shit!"

John drew his pistol and pistol-whipped the man across the temple. The biker began spitting blood, eyes crossed and a dazed look on his face. John raised his 1911 to the man's forehead and said, "Who am I? I own this town now. Go ahead and call me the new fucking mayor of Kankakee." John pulled the trigger and shot the biker in the head.

The two soldiers yelped in surprise and dropped the biker's body. John turned to the remaining bikers who were still being held at gunpoint by the soldiers. Hiding his racing heartbeat but gaining confidence, he yelled, "Anybody else want to try next? Any of you fuckers want to try to be a big badass anymore? WE own this city now, not you. If you have any brains, you'll get out and never come back. If it were up to me, you'd all be dead. Now get out of here now before I waste any more ammo on planting them in your skulls trying to get my point across."

John walked over and cut the leather vest off of the two dead bikers, a tremendous sign of disrespect to biker gangs. He held the vice president's vest in his hand and said, "We will be keeping these just in case you need a reminder of who is in charge here."

The bikers were allowed to get back on their bikes, after a few picked up the dead bodies of their executed members. They rode out silently in a loose formation, heading up toward Court Street. A few Army Humvees were tasked with following them to ensure they got out of town.

The rest of the group waited around anxiously for nearly ten minutes before Colonel Lyon's radio operator (RTO) came up and tapped him on the shoulder. "Sir, scouts confirmed: The main group got on I-57 and headed northbound to Chicago. A couple split off and went south out of town." Lyon nodded, and a sigh of relief swept through the leaders huddled around under the shade of a large tree along the school parking lot.

"Well, now that we went full cowboy and off the rails, I think it's safe to say that there are no longer any rules out there. Anybody who is not allied with us is now a threat that needs to be eliminated. How are we going to move forward with this?" The Colonel surveyed the crowd.

John scratched his chin for a moment and said, "Well, Mike, my little band of merry men is well armed, equipped and capable, but we're just that; we're too small an element to be combat-effective outside of small engagements and skirmishes without your support. We need to link up with any surviving police, first responders, and resistance groups, and any leaders from the government that might be left. If I can gain enough men to have a sizeable group, we can operate and eliminate the threats from within the city. But I need you and your guys, Mike. More than you know."

The truth was that he had a group of hardened warriors, but even those warriors had limits. They were fighters but not practiced killers. The real combat had begun to take a toll on the members of the group mentally. It was more and more common to walk in on a member of the compound alone in a dark room crying or staring off into nothing. It was a dangerous gamble, and he knew it. After every armed skirmish, firefight, and battle, the wear and battle fatigue became more evident. Most of the group had little real-life experience with taking lives. Theo had been in shootings on duty but hardly anything as hot and heavy as what they were going through.

The only ones in the Compound with any combat experience were Andrew and Sarge.

Lyon answered: "Ok. Where do we start? Truth is, I need you and your guys to be able to operate independently of my guys. Our mission right now is to support local recovery, not force it. The last contact I had with my superiors at state level wasn't very clear, but mission parameters were to secure the entry and exit of the limits of our metropolitan area and let local levels recover on their own. We're just here to guard from outside threats. Everything within city limits is up to you. We can get the ball rolling, but we can't do everything for you. They can't have what is left of the United States government by killing U.S. citizens in the streets. Now what do you need?"

"Well. We could use an escort further into downtown. We've encountered pretty heavy resistance when we tried before. Get me to the City Hall and police station to check for survivors. If there are any people out there still holing up, it should be enough to pad our numbers a little. From there, we can regroup survivors in my neighborhood. Start pushing out from there and clearing little by little. How long do you think I've got to secure the city before the outside problems start hitting you guys?"

The Colonel said, "Things seem to have slowed long-distance travel down for the moment. I'd estimate that you have a month or two to get the city under control before we start having the refugee survivors and hordes of people up to no good coming down from Chicago." After a moment of silence to let that sink in, he continued, "There is some good news though: The Armory is just down the road from the County Jail. When I began to circle the wagons and secure our installation, I sent men to the sheriff's complex to see if there were any survivors. From what we gathered, the sheriff never made it to the complex and we can assume he's dead. The highest-ranking officer is one of the Detective Bureau lieutenants and there are a few patrol sergeants left. They called a muster for all of the remaining deputies to take their families and retreat into the complex. They have twenty deputies along with their families, and about twenty Corrections Officers and their families. I went ahead and secured their facility, meaning that I ordered all violent felony inmates to be immediately executed. All misdemeanor detainees awaiting trial were released. I had to make the tough call. None of their leaders were willing to do it. The good news is you will now have forty men at arms under your command. I'll have the lieutenant and sergeants report to you immediately. We will help to secure the houses in your neighborhood to accommodate them and their families, and then they are all yours. I think they will agree to be under your command, as long as I tell them to. Quite frankly, they're scared shitless of me after seeing me order the inmates executed."

Andrew, who had been silent up to this point, leaned into John's ear and whispered, "This is good news, man. Better than we could have hoped before. We're gonna need gear to equip them. I doubt many of the Corrections guys have anything other than their duty pistols. Most of them don't even have vests."

Lyon, overhearing their conversation, said, "Take all of the guns and equipment we seized from the bikers, and I'll take the ammo. With no resupply option, my force is going to be needing it. Beyond that, that's the extent of what I can offer. Any organized civilian groups of use that hit our perimeter will be vetted and sent your way. Now let's say we call it a day. I'll come stay at the compound tonight to get a look at what we'll be working with in your area so we can plan further."

They shook hands and went separately to their respective groups to update their men. Lyon sent his troops and helicopters back to the National Guard installation with the captain that was his next highest-ranking officer. Lyon took his command vehicle and one more escort Humvee to come with him to the compound.

Once everybody was briefed in John's group, they mounted their vehicles and headed north up Curtis Avenue. Fortunately, the high school was near the edge of town and just down the street from the entrance to his subdivision. It was a short and quiet drive.

As they pulled into the compound, the sun was already low on the horizon. After all the vehicles, the stolen semi-truck, and the two Humvees were inside the lot, John and Andrew hopped out to secure the perimeter per the nightly routine. Theo, Dez, Big Rob, and the children took to offloading the seized equipment from the police Tahoe. After that was done, they opened the semi-trailer and began to pull out all the seized canned food from the warehouse using the forklift they'd taken from the warehouse, and a few pallet jacks John owned.

By the time a large portion of the pallets of food were offloaded, it was getting dark. John told everyone to close the truck and head inside to wash up, eat dinner, and get some rest.

After everyone had showered and changed clothes, most of the group met back out on the porch. Theo brought out cold beers from the fridge in the garage and passed them out to everybody, while Shonna came out with a large roast she had prepared for dinner while they were gone. She set it down on the table and kissed Rob. "I'm glad you guys are all okay and made it back in one piece. Quite frankly, I'm already tired of patching up bullet wounds. Oh, and speaking of: Sergeant Callahan woke up this afternoon for a little bit! We spoke for a few minutes, and he was able to eat some solid food. He's back asleep now, but in the morning I think he may be ready to try to get out of that bed."

"That's great news!" Dez exclaimed. They all raised their beers in cheers of joy and Rob crossed himself in silent prayer. They ate their food and made small talk. The mood was still light and cheerful, even given the rough day. After dinner was finished, a few of the group went their separate ways. Dez went up to the roof to take her turn in the LP/OP tower; Big Rob and Shonna took the kids inside and put them to bed and then went on to bed themselves. Lyon's men went inside to sleep on the various couches and cots set up in the living room.

Remaining outside, John, Lyon, Theo, and Andrew stayed outside to hash out the fine print for the plan moving forward. Theo passed out cigars, and they sat around the table discussing the details and drank more beer.

"Starting tomorrow, I'll have some of my guys transport all the remaining sheriff's department guys and families here to the neighborhood. I'll have my engineers clear all the closest houses and get them set up with defenses and power."

Andrew spoke up. "That would be good, Mike. We can spare some solar panels. Between what Theo and I brought in, we've got maybe ten large panels. Maybe enough to power two or three houses if we stretch it. If your engineers have the heavy equipment, you think you could hook us up with some HESCO barriers for around this group of houses and fill them with dirt? If we can manage it, that would put a decent bullet-resistant barrier around the neighborhood. Would really protect our little homefront here."

Lyon replied, "I think it's doable. We can outfit maybe four or five more houses for living with some of our solar panels and generators. We can build barriers as far as we can manage and fencing around what we can't cover around your street. If we can fit four or five families per house, and outfit one of the houses like a barracks for all the single officers, we can make it work. It's gonna be a tight fit, but that is going to be all we can spare. As for the rest, you'll be on your own, so make it work, or find a place to squeeze it in."

Theo also brought up a good point. "We've got about forty or fifty new bodies coming in, and probably more if we get the city's first responders. We're going to need someone to manage all of these guys. Sort out who does what, and how we keep this place sustainable. It's a big chore."

"We'll make it work. One of the sheriff's guys will have to take care of their own," John told his friends.

After the meeting was concluded, John checked the notebook he kept in his pocket and realized that Dez was actually covering for his shift of guard duty. He felt guilty and immediately gathered some items to get ready to go relieve her from the LP/OP. She must have volunteered to go up so that he could have his meeting with the others. He grabbed his assault pack and M1-A long rifle, along with a bag of snacks and food for the long night. He also secretly grabbed a few bottles of beer, a bottle of whiskey, and a few cigars. He wanted to still enjoy a few modern comforts while he could, and since he was the de-facto rule-maker, he hadn't made a rule against drinking or smoking on guard shifts. John never was one to take life too seriously, and he wasn't about to start now. Plus, after this world had gone to shit, you never knew if today would be your last. No use in going out miserable, he thought.

After getting his items together, John climbed up to the roof and made his way to the LP/OP. He relieved Dez, who tried to pretend that she didn't realize that she was covering his shift. She gave him a quick hug and a kiss on the cheek and gave him an update on the situation (nothing out of the ordinary to report) and departed quickly to get some sleep. After that quick kiss, he would have given anything to spend the night with Dez in his bed. He was beginning to feel more and more lonely. The compounding interest had begun to weight more and more on his soul. Above-average stress was nothing new to him, and normally he thrived on it given his choice of career, but this situation had gotten more and more hopeless. The stress and depression had begun to take hold in his mind and hadn't retreated behind his usual wall of sarcasm and coping positivity. The darkness was all around now. As hard as he tried to stay positive, it was harder and harder to portray the facade of a strong leader to the men and women that had fallen under his command and control.

John took his place in the lookout tower and read over the notes in the pass-on notebook. Nothing out of the ordinary. Gunshots and even more sustained bursts of gunfire had become more and more common at night as observed by the men and women on watch in the LP/OP. It should worry him, but he had begun to get dull to the harsh reality of this new world. All that mattered was the short-term survival of those he cared about. After reading the book, he scanned the area with the night-vision goggles to ensure that the compound's perimeter and their immediate area of control was quiet and secure. Next, he opened the small cooler bag he'd brought up, cracked a beer and lit a cigar. He relaxed back in the chair inside the sandbag bunker, eventually cracking his second and third beer. John got lost in his own thoughts. He recalled the shooting he'd been involved in while still on the job. He slowed down the whole incident in his mind and replayed it in slow motion...getting the broadcast over the radio, looking up, dropping his phone. Reaching for his gun as he met the armed robbers exiting the store, clearing his holster, and drawing his 1911 on the criminals. Something came back to him...He'd drawn down on the first robber exiting the store. He remembered setting the sights of his 1911 on the man's chest. His eyes had locked with the criminal's. In that split second, his mind froze. He remembered staring into the man's soul. The eyes he'd peered into were not those of a hardened criminal, but the scared eyes of a young man, a boy even. Before these thoughts were processed by his brain, John had pulled the trigger, bullets flying and tearing into the robber's body. In that split second, he'd wondered if he had killed the wrong one. Some scumbag had recruited his younger sibling, or some newbie trying to get initiated into a gang by committing his first major crime.

The thoughts weighed on him. He suddenly couldn't forget those young, innocent eyes staring back at him. He had taken a life. It wasn't the first time...but it was the closest he had really been to death, and it seemed like the one that would continue to haunt him.

It wasn't his last, and sadly there would be many more. He woke up from his daydream and realized he was out of beer. He hid the bottles, relit his cigar, and pulled out the bottle of whiskey. He took a pull from the bottle and a tear emerged from his eyes. He tried to stifle the sobs as they arose in his throat, but it was too much to push back down. He began to sob quietly. His only luck was that it had happened while he was alone. He could allow himself to break down; it was healthy, but he knew he couldn't afford to do it in front of all those that looked to him for direction. John couldn't afford to look weak to those he was trying to lead. He knew he should talk about it with someone he trusted. Maybe he could talk about it with Lyon, or maybe Andrew, but too many of the others were barely holding it together themselves. He couldn't afford to fall apart in front of the others who were barely hanging on themselves. He had to be strong for his men. He tried to gather his mental strength and instead think of how they were going to survive this new world. It was growing harder and harder, considering he had made the mistake of drinking himself into a haze. He spent the rest of the night trying to gather his thoughts and make plans for the future, but it was difficult, both because of his drunken haze and the dark veil of thoughts that had settled upon his conscience.

The hours passed, and John bided his time in the LP/OP as the sun began to rise. He tried hard not to nod off as the sun began to rise and the light emerged over the post-apocalyptic landscape that had once been his beautiful city. He was doing his final sweep over the immediate area with his rifle scope when he heard the sound of another person climbing the commo tower up to the roof. He began to pack up his trash and gear into his bags as Theo popped up above the roof's horizon. It was around 6 A.M., and early as fuck. He didn't envy the people that had to work guard duty in the day that had to get up early as hell to be there on time.

Theo tossed his pack up onto the roof and dragged his bag over. He was carrying a large travel mug of coffee and smiled at his friend. "Hey brother, I took the liberty of making your morning pot of coffee extra strong." As he came closer, Theo winced and said, "Smells like you could really use it, bro. You okay? You smell like booze...a lot of booze. If I were you, I'd skip breakfast and get some sleep...." He stopped and sat down on the lip of the dugout. "But for real, man...Are you doing okay? I know you think you have the whole weight of the world on your shoulders, but maybe you could just relax for a little bit. Let's put all the grand plans on hold for today. Maybe just enjoy one more peaceful day. Seems like you could use it. And I know we all could..."

John looked his friend in the eyes and put his hand on his shoulder. With a smile he said, "I couldn't do this without you, man. All of you...just...thanks. I need to get some sleep."

Theo put his hand on John's shoulder and gave him a squeeze and a smile back.

With those last few words and a kind but reassuring look from Theo, John gathered his things and descended the tower down to the ground. He shouldered his bag and gear and made his way back into the house. He was happy that he didn't have to run into anybody else on his way back to his room as he didn't think he could bear the shame of having to be seen in this state by anybody else. He made his way back up the stairs into the master bedroom, closed the door behind him, and quietly set his gear down next to the closet. He shed his clothing and went to the bathroom to rinse his mouth out in the sink before making his way back over to the bed. He slowly climbed into bed and squirmed his way in next to Dez, who was still fast asleep. She stirred slightly, cracked open an eye and kissed his cheek, adjusting herself to wrap her arms around him and snuggle up next to him. She softly mumbled, "You smell like booze and cigarettes, Johnny...remind me to start visiting you on your guard shifts. Smells like you're having fun..." Dez quickly drifted back to sleep, her head on his chest. In that moment, he started to relax and feel better. These beautiful moments should be enjoyed. The peace and harmony wouldn't last like this much longer.

INTERLUDE FOUR:
POSTAPOCALYPTIC ROAD TRIP
(continued)
On the road—Central Nebraska—unknown date

Richard awoke early, as was his habit, despite the late night. At 7:38 A.M., he rolled over and rubbed his eyes, then put his glasses on. He took a quick shower, then changed clothes, still opting for cargo shorts and a T-shirt for a tourist look. He still wore his trusty Glock 21 in his holster, but the open carry of his pistol on his hip drew fewer odd looks this far west as it would have closer to home in Illinois. The small truck stop did not have a diner, so they settled for purchasing a few nonperishable items from the small shop that was only accepting cash and decided on a home-cooked breakfast in their camper. Denise was puzzled when Richard bought a carton of cigarettes and a few packs of lighters, considering he did not smoke. He told her, "They had a sign that said, 'tax free for cash' and the prices were as cheap as they were before the economic collapse. Can't turn that down, it could be useful." They chose meat from the freezer, cooking breakfast sausage and toast. After eating breakfast, they returned to the shopette and both re-filled their travel mugs of coffee while paying for gas. The kind older man at the counter said, "Take the coffee on the house, young man. Least I can do for buying a hundred dollars' worth of gas. Where you two lovebirds headed?"

"Oregon, to stay with our son," Denise replied, while Richard cracked a small smile and nodded in agreement and went outside to pump gas. "Maybe another day and a half of hard driving, and you'll make it 'long as the roads stay clear," the attendant said. With a smile, he patted Denise on the hand and said, "Glad you've still got family to find in all this mess. Godspeed. I hope y'all make it there quickly. I'll be praying for you." She thanked him, shook his hand, and went outside to meet with her husband, who was nearly done pumping the gas into their pickup truck.

They got back on the road. Even in the more sparsely populated states, there was more traffic on the interstate. It wasn't anything too unusual, but the hair stood up on the back of Richard's neck for sure. He had hoped to make good time and drive as far as possible today. He found himself slowing down their progress, driving slower and braking harder when driving by the abandoned vehicles pulled off to the side of the roadway. Richard remembered the lessons his son had taught him about vehicle borne IEDs and ambushes along the roadways, and it made him both nervous and paranoid. He wished he could relax and drive faster, but the years of being a detective made for keen eyes and a very analytical mind. It was both a gift and a curse. He was constantly scanning for threats, and the highway consistently gave more things to scan. He also noticed many more destitute travelers abandoning their vehicles and walking on foot after running out of gas. He had enough of his own problems to worry about. Denise would have normally complained about not stopping to help the desperate people along the roadway, but she had begun to realize that even her compassion had its limits. Their safety and getting to their family were absolutely the priorities, and everything else was in her way. A devout Christian, she often closed her eyes and prayed for the men, women, and children they saw. The first few times broke her heart, and she nearly argued with her husband, but she knew that her compassion could be a weakness, and survival was more important. She learned to control her compassion so that it didn't become weakness. Her husband was loving and compassionate, but not if the situation didn't call for it. During nearly half a century as a cop, he had learned when to be callous and stoic, covering up his emotions and learning to be calm in tough times. Denise knew that these events were just as hard on him, but together they remained strong. Their only goal was getting to their son. The foot traffic and packed interstates cleared out as they passed through the area closest to the Wyoming/Colorado state line where Interstate 80 came closest to Denver, Colorado.

A few times, when the highways appeared mostly clear of vehicles and foot traffic, they pulled over and checked cars for supplies or to siphon whatever gasoline might be still in the tanks. They rarely found much of anything that could be of use. Occasionally, they managed to scrounge a gallon or more of gas, although most of the abandoned vehicles had run out. Finally, they both came to the consensus that it was too large a risk to keep stopping along the roadway and risk getting into any engagements.

They were wasting far too much time. Richard filled the pickup truck from the gas can with the recently siphoned gas and decided that it was time to keep making progress and put more miles on their drive.

Richard no longer cared that he was speeding excessively, pushing the large pickup towing the camper to the limits of its maneuverability. He cruised at speeds close to eighty miles per hour. The highway was still mostly clear of obstructions, which helped them cover lots of ground very quickly. Richard wanted to get past the next large metropolitan area north of Salt Lake City, Utah before they ran out of daylight. They both knew it was not a good idea to bed down for the night near highly populated cities. As they exited Interstate 80 onto Interstate 84, the sun was getting low. Richard remarked, "Probably less than an hour left of daylight, but we need to get clear of the Salt Lake area. We can't get stuck in this highly populated area." Denise agreed and pulled out the map to look for camp grounds or small towns along their route. As she was shuffling through the bag at her feet, she came across the small handheld mic for the HAM radio that their son had given them. Despite the hours of driving, both of them had been preoccupied and had completely forgotten to turn on the radio to try and make contact with their sons. Neither she nor her husband were exceptionally tech savvy, and embarrassingly enough, neither of them had paid much attention to their son's instructions on how to work the radio before they left. She picked it up and showed it to her husband with a soft exclamation before turning it on. After hearing a soft "beep," Denise turned up the volume knob, screwed in the longer antennae, and set it in the cup holder. At first, they only heard static. For nearly twenty minutes, they drove in silence, listening to the static of the empty channel. After that, Denise finally spoke up. "Do you think maybe we are on the wrong channel or something…?" Just as she finished her sentence, the radio squawked and they heard a faint, static-filled voice: "Mom and Pop Caravan, come in, over. Mom and Pop Caravan, if you can hear me…this is Bill Kirkpatrick. I hope you can get this. If you can't reply, I am monitoring this channel 24/7. Just keep driving until you can reach me. Luke is safe with me." Denise breathed a heavy sigh of relief and turned toward her husband, who was smiling but still focused on driving. They'd both recognized the voice of Bill, their son's neighbor, and knew the message was for them.

"Should I answer it?" Denise said. She already knew the answer and picked up the radio even before her husband grunted in agreement. Her first few attempts to transmit were unsuccessful as she pressed the button and began to talk. She decided to wait another fifteen to twenty minutes as they passed through more open terrain and headed further north of the Salt Lake City proper.

After waiting a grueling twenty minutes, Denise picked up the radio and pressed the talk button. She made a short transmission and hoped it went through. She didn't know any proper radio etiquette, but that wasn't going to stop her. "Bill, if you're there, we can hear you. Please, for the love of God, I hope you can hear this." After waiting through some static, she repeated her message again and again.

After a few minutes, a garbled transmission finally came through. "I can hear you, Mama! I can hear you…Loud but not so clear. Where are you? Over."

Denise beamed and tapped Richard's arm in excitement. "We're uhhh…a little north of Salt Lake right now," she said, trying to look for road signs along the interstate and consult her map at the same time. "We're running out of daylight. We can't make it to you tonight. We're gonna need to stop somewhere soon."

Bill replied, "OK. Let me think for a second…Have you guys passed Brigham City yet?"

Denise consulted her map and replied, "No, we're still about thirty miles south of there."

Bill told her, "Give me ten minutes. I have a friend out there that runs a little truck stop off the interstate that would be perfect for you. Just keep driving, and plan on getting off the interstate at the Brigham City exit. Look for the smaller truck stop painted red. I'll get in contact with them to make sure it's safe and let them know to expect you."

They continued driving as the sun sank lower on the horizon. Denise spied a sign that said ten miles to the Brigham city exit. She looked over to her husband who was starting to show fatigue. He was visibly restraining himself from nodding off, and his eyes were red. After about five minutes, they spotted the exit and pulled off the interstate. To their south, they saw a dimly lit truck stop about a half mile down the road and turned toward it. As they reached the stop, they saw that a chain-link fence had been erected around the perimeter, along with makeshift barriers of plywood and abandoned vehicles. Richard slowed the truck down and approached the entrance. They saw a man on horseback with a rifle slung on his back. A young boy pulled open the makeshift gate. The man on horseback rode up to the driver's side window and said, "I take it you're the Mom and Pop Caravan I'm supposed to be expecting?"

Denise leaned over and said, "Yes sir, thank you so much. Bill Kirkpatrick told us this was a safe place to stay the night."

The man said, "You're in the right place." He leaned down and extended his hand to shake Richard's and tipped his cowboy hat to Denise. "My name is David Montgomery, and I own this place. Bill is a good friend of mine from the war. Since you're friends of his, you can stay the night here. I only ask that you pay something that is a fair price for sleeping in safety tonight. We can talk about that in the morning. I'm sure you're tired. Are you set for grub?"

Richard nodded. "Yes sir, we are. Thank you! You name the price, and it's yours. As long as we can get some sleep and get on along to our son tomorrow."

They pulled into a spot in the lot close to the little shopette, locked up the truck, and got into their trailer and went to bed for the night. Feeling safe as they could in these strange surroundings, they both fell asleep very quickly.

Nearly ten hours later, Richard was awake, sipping coffee in the front kitchenette area of the large camper as the sun came up. Looking out the window, he surveyed the area. The small truck stop had the usual gas pumps and gas station/shopette, which was attached to a slightly larger general store and supermarket. Around the parking lot, there was also an auto shop, a semi-truck repair shop and car wash, and a small bait and outdoors shop. The truck stop, although very close to the main highway, was in a fairly defensible area, as it was surrounded by steep hills on three sides and only open to the area facing the highway, which as he knew from the night before was already fenced and blocked in. In his opinion, they appeared to be very well off in this little settlement, although he wasn't sure how many people were living there. The open lot of the truck stop had a small assortment of cars, pickup trucks, a few semi-trucks with trailers, and multiple campers and RVs. He did not see any people out and about yet, so it was difficult to determine what was occupied.

David Montgomery came out from the shopette carrying a large travel coffee pot and headed towards Richard's trailer. He was wearing jeans, a black and red flannel shirt, and a pair of moccasins. He'd appeared friendly enough, but he was still unfamiliar, therefore he wasn't a friend. He was openly carrying a semiautomatic pistol in a leather holster on his hip, so Richard took a small revolver from a nearby cabinet and set it in a hidden holster taped to the bottom of the kitchenette table just as Montgomery knocked lightly on the door.

"Come on in," Richard replied. The door opened and the older man climbed up the steps into the large camper.

Montgomery shook Richard's hand and started, "I figured I'd bring some coffee. It's been a little while since I've been able to have a friendly conversation with someone that I haven't had to turn away from the shop under the threat of shooting them." He had a kind and sincere smile, and Richard detected truth in his statement. He scanned the old timer's face and body language as the man sat down in the chair across from him. He appeared very weary and tired in his movements. His voice had stress in it, and the confident man seemed to drop his guard once out of the sight of others. He poured coffee into a tin cup that he had brought with him and leaned back in his chair.

"Bill Kirkpatrick speaks very highly of you and your family. He told me all about your sons and what you've gone through since this all started. I'm glad to see you've made it this far. Chicago is a loooong drive from here. You were smart enough to leave early. You and your family were some of the few that were smart enough to see this all coming. But that being said, I know how hard it must have been to leave your other son behind." Montgomery paused and looked over at Richard, who was nursing his cup of lukewarm coffee.

Richard finally reached over and poured fresh coffee from the pot Montgomery had brought. He took a sip of the strong, hot coffee, and replied, "Seems like you and Bill are close. I take it you talk often?"

Montgomery sensed the apprehension in Richard's voice and said, "Sorry, I know I seem to know a bit too much about your family's personal business, but Bill and I ARE close. He saved my life in 'Nam. And it's the nature of the beast. He knows that I'm not very trusting of strangers. I've turned away hundreds of people from my gates in the last week alone. Bill figured if he didn't fill me in all about you, I wouldn't let you in, and you'd be forced to stay somewhere unsafe. You guys mean a lot to him, and he made sure that was very clear to me." He let out a soft chuckle and continued. "Bill isn't just a stubborn old mule; he's fiercely loyal. He loves the people and things he cares about with all his soul. I saw that firsthand when he dragged me out of that ambush in the jungle. If I hadn't agreed to take you in, he was likely to have driven here and shot me himself. Joking, of course." He laughed at Richard's confused look.

Richard asked, "What can we offer you for allowing us to stay here last night? I don't know that we have too much to offer in the way of money, but we can find something that you could use."

Montgomery replied, "I wouldn't dream of charging you for my hospitality. My conscious wouldn't allow it. What I can do is offer you a service. I'll help you map out the safest route to get you to Bill's place. I know the state of the local area a lot better than you could guess on a map. In exchange for that, we could really use some food or guns. The people I have here didn't have much, and unfortunately, I've had to front most of my goods to keep us afloat. We've tried trading with the Mormons down the highway, but it's been a dangerous road. I have plenty of coins and cash from the people that have paid to stay here, but not enough food to keep us prepared for much longer, and I could use guns and ammo to protect us better. Here's my proposal: Along with helping you map out your best route to Bill and your son, I'd like to buy as much of the pre-packaged food and extra weapons you have to spare. I can pay in a mixture of cash and silver. That's the best I have to offer. I'll buy whatever you don't need to finish your trip to get to Bend today. Bill assured me that once you get to him, you won't need to worry about what you've brought."

Richard wondered if Montgomery intended on sounding as legitimately desperate as he did just now. But his words were sincere. He was just an old man who was trying to stay strong as a leader and survive. Richard said, "Ok. I'll grab whatever I can give to you, and we can haggle out a price. Let me wake up my wife and she will help me sort everything. If you could cook us some breakfast and come back with a few helping hands to move everything in about an hour, you have a deal."

The two men shook hands and Montgomery poured the rest of his pot of coffee into Richard's mug and said, "I'll be right back with all that. I'll have my wife rustle us up some breakfast and be back in the shake of a tail." With that, Montgomery departed.

Richard first got on the HAM radio and spoke to his son. Luke told him, "Dad, I talked to Bill. His friend is legit. It seems like they really need what you can give them. Don't give away too much but put on a good enough show that Montgomery will be happy. We have a good amount of food and stuff stored here at Bill's ranch. Just don't give away too much ammo, 'cause I don't keep mountains of ammo like my little brother does. Unless he sent you with a ton, just give them what little extra you can spare. It should only be about half a day's drive to Bend from where you guys are. I'll talk to you when you get back on the road."

Richard went to fill in Denise, who was already up and about in the bedroom. They both got dressed into better travel clothing to start the day. She had heard the last part of the conversation and began to pull out their food stores. They had packed the bottom storage of the camper with several freeze-dried food buckets, along with a few cases of military MREs that their son had given them. Richard suggested giving Montgomery most of the food items with shorter shelf-lives, including their canned goods and the MREs. They took out about ten buckets of the freeze-dried foods from their storage and kept the rest. The amount of food they had to offer Montgomery was still sizeable. They piled it up along the outside of the trailer.

Next, Richard opened up the gun safe. He took out two long hunting shotguns that he was willing to part with, along with two buckets of shells. He grabbed one of the extra Glock pistols and two ammo cans of bullets for it. He placed a .38 revolver alongside those and a few boxes of shells. He carried them all out to the kitchen table, then came back to stare at the gun safe. Richard figured that they had plenty of hunting rifles, but he wasn't sure how prepared Montgomery's people had been with battle rifles. After a few minutes of indecision, he caved and grabbed one of his bare-bones M16-style AR rifles and a small ammo can with around five hundred rounds of .223 ammunition with a couple of thirty-round magazines. Checking his watch, he realized that the hour had nearly passed. He went to the door of the trailer and saw Montgomery heading towards them, along with two teenage boys pulling hand carts and wagons. Montgomery was riding his horse and pulling a makeshift buggy-type trailer behind it.

Montgomery motioned to the boys. "These are two of my grandsons, James and Billy." The two boys shook Richard's hand and stood back from the two men. Montgomery stepped down from his horse and surveyed the food that was laid down next to the trailer.

Richard told him, "Ten buckets of freeze-dried food, eight full cases of military MREs, and these two boxes of canned foods. This is what we have to spare for food."

Montgomery nodded and said, "That is plenty fine, my friend. And what can you offer for guns? I have a few men who aren't very well armed."

Richard stepped back up into the trailer and brought out the two 12-gauge shotguns and the buckets of shells. He set them on top of the stacks of food. He then brought out the two pistols and the ammo.

Montgomery surveyed the large pile of goods and whistled. "Well now. You sure have a lot to offer." He lifted up a satchel from one of the hand carts, opened it, and handed Richard a large chunk of cash. Richard figured it was roughly over a thousand dollars.

"That's about fifteen hundred dollars. I know the cash isn't worth nearly that anymore, so there's more." Montgomery handed over a small stack of about five, ten-ounce silver bars and a small canvas bag of assorted silver coins.

With all of the goods on the table, both men took stock of what each was offering, doing a rough mental tally. The goods that Denise and Richard were giving up were far more valuable than the monetary value of what they were receiving, and both knew it, but it was an agreeable enough deal. Richard had purposefully withheld the M16 still sitting inside the camper for this reason. He and Montgomery shook hands and nodded, signaling that both halves had agreed upon the deal. The two teenagers began to load the supplies into the wagons.

Montgomery said, "My friend, I think this deal is very fair. But I could use a little more help if you can provide it…Let us make a new deal." Richard sensed a little uneasiness in the old man's voice. Montgomery continued, "It's my turn to ask a favor: we are desperately in need of more defense weapons. I'm sure that you have better weapons to offer, and I am very willing to pay whatever you think is fair for them. I need a few more of them assault rifles. Only a few of us have anything more than shotguns, pistols, and hunting rifles. If you have a few of them semiautomatic military-type rifles, I'll pay handsomely for them. You can have free pick of the supplies that we have left in the camping store. I'm begging you. Please, we need those weapons."

Sensing the desperation and knowing he had withheld more than what he was willing to give, Richard felt guilty and replied, "Ok, Mr. Montgomery. I can offer you two, maybe three semiautomatic rifles and a little bit of ammo for each. But that's all I have to offer." And with that, he went inside and grabbed the M16, another AR-15 from the gun locker, and a Ruger Mini-14 ranch rifle. All were chambered in .223/556, so he grabbed a thousand rounds of ammo and the proper magazines and cleaning kits and walked them out to Montgomery.

Montgomery's eyes gleamed at the sight of the three "military-style" weapons, and he reached back into the satchel. He handed Richard two large gold coins. One gold coin alone had a monetary value enough to buy the three rifles before the economic collapse. Richard examined the coins and slipped them in his pocket. He locked up the camper, and he and Denise headed in with Montgomery to have breakfast in the main building.

After the modest breakfast, Richard and Montgomery walked over to the camping store so Richard could look at the supplies. "Take your pick," Montgomery said. Richard spent a few minutes surveying the small shop and selected a few odds and ends—a few things he had not thought to store in his camper before the trip. He grabbed two fishing poles and a small set of lures and hooks. He also grabbed a few animal traps and bait. He also picked out a few large handsewn quilts from the guest shop that he thought his wife would like; he was sure they'd be useful, considering the cold winters in the Northwest.

Seeing not much else of use on the nearly empty shelves, they went back to the camper, where Denise was already working on packing up for the remainder of their trip. Montgomery offered to top off their gas tank on the truck for them and fill a few of their gas cans. For this, Richard gave him back a few of the silver coins. "A fair barter, like you said, Mr. Montgomery. Now, as much as I'd like to hang out, we need to get on the road so we can see our son."

Montgomery held up a large map he'd grabbed from the rack in the shop and laid it out on the kitchen table. He gave them directions, tracing the route with a highlighter. "Okay, right now, you are here." He pointed. "Keep on 84 as long as you can to the Idaho state line. The highways are safe enough if you drive fast and don't stop. Once you get to the start of the big national forests in Idaho, turn off onto State Route 78. It will take you a few hours out of the way of the most direct route, but you don't want to go through Boise. From what we've been hearing from the Mormon traders, the large cities are in complete disarray. Best to avoid the large city centers altogether. Idaho State Route 78 will skirt south around the national wildlife areas and you can get back onto interstate 84 somewhere closer to the state line with Oregon. It should be smooth sailing once you get into Oregon until you make it to Bend. Just stay on the main roads and drive as fast as you can. In about ten to twelve hours, you should make it to Bill's place."

Richard watched as he traced the route, marking different landmarks and the turn offs. When Montgomery was finished, they shook hands and parted ways. He and Denise got into the truck and pulled out of the gates of the truck stop, getting back on the interstate. They quickly climbed to a fast speed. The sun was already climbing. Richard checked his watch, seeing it was already nearly 8:30 A.M. They needed to make up ground to get to Bill's place before it was too dark to navigate the back roads to the ranch with their large camper. Denise grabbed his hand and said, "Home stretch, honey. We'll be with our son soon."

INTERLUDE FIVE: EL LEON DEL NORTE
Chicago, IL

Juan Luis Garcia was born for this. Despite all that God and others had tried to do to intervene in his life, he had been steered upon a path that nobody wanted for him, but he felt he was destined for. He was not like most of the young Latino children growing up in the Pilsen neighborhood in Chicago's near southwest side. The young boy was brilliant and booksmart from a young age, but also a talented athlete, running and playing fútbol and baseball in the streets with his friends. Like many minority kids of the tough inner-city Chicago neighborhoods, Juan Luis was drawn into the criminal underworld at a young age. By twelve years old, he was already selling drugs on the street corner. It all started with just selling small amounts of marijuana and cigarettes for extra money with his friends. Soon, after realizing how much money he was making selling bud to students at his school (and some teachers, too), he began to expand his business. He found the older brother of a friend, "Chicho," who was a new gang member for the local Latin Kings. Chicho helped him gain entry into their drug pipeline, providing him with a steady supply of crack, cocaine, and heroin. Once the Latin King gang leaders started noticing how much of their product this little kid was moving, he started gaining favor amongst the gang. By fourteen years old, Juan Luis was "jumped in" to the street gang. After the vicious beating he received from the gang (a long-standing tradition in street gangs known as "blood in-blood out"), he was accepted as the street gang's *"Hermanito"* or "Little Brother."

He didn't stay "Little Brother" for long, as he was soon moving so much product through the streets that he was the leading distributor of heroin and crack in the entire near west side of Chicago. At sixteen, Juan Luis dropped out of high school and instead completed his GED. Next, he enrolled in the

University of Illinois in Chicago, taking Business and Economic classes. He continued to move drugs throughout the entire neighborhood, even while living close to campus near Lake Shore Drive. After only three years, at the age of nineteen, Juan Luis graduated with honors from UIC with a major in Economics and a major in Business management. He ran his street crew like a business, meticulously and with every move heavily planned and scrutinized.

Juan Luis moved back to the Pilsen neighborhood and enrolled in a program for his Master's degree in Business. When word had spread through the Latin King's gang that he was growing soft, going through a swanky university instead of "running the streets like he should be," Juan Luis staged a brilliantly planned coup. He set a meeting with the gang boss, or "Jefe," at one of the warehouses his crew used for stashing contraband and money from their criminal exploits. The boss traveled with a large crew for protection, even for private meetings. When the boss arrived at the factory, Juan Luis let him in. They took a walk along with his protection to a room in the rear of the factory. Juan Luis opened the door and told him, "I know you think I've grown soft. I know what the word on the street is. I'm here to prove otherwise…." He ushered the boss in, where there was a pallet of cash stacked in the room. Easily over a million dollars. The gang boss gasped. "You've been hiding profits from the crew, Hermanito!"

Juan Luis simply answered, "No. I AM the crew now."

He whipped out a switchblade knife and stabbed the gang boss in the jugular. Blood gushed out of his neck like a geyser, spewing his lifeblood all over the room, Juan Luis, and the closest members of the protection detail. The men in the former boss's protection crew were caught off guard and had no time to react, as they were suddenly held at gunpoint by Juan Luis's men appearing from the shadows. Many of the protection detail dropped their guns, threw their hands up in defeat, and swore their allegiance to Juan Luis as the new Jefe. The ones that didn't were shot by his men, and their bodies disposed of in enemy gang territories. At twenty-two, Juan Luis had become the leader of the Latin Kings gang for the entire Pilsen and surrounding neighborhoods.

His quick rise to fame in the criminal underground attracted much attention, both by law enforcement and criminals alike. Juan Luis was flooded with requests from other gangs for alliances or mutual agreements for street business as well as increased scrutiny from the law. Juan Luis had appeared on the radar of the Chicago PD as well as the ATF, DEA, and FBI who were working to combat the increased crime in the second city. He was not a fan of the spotlight that had appeared on him but was still cunning enough to stay out of trouble while expanding his criminal domain. It was this spotlight on the law enforcement radar that got him noticed by even higher powers than the United States Government: the Sinaloa Cartel.

One cold Chicago winter day, while walking in the park with his mother, Juan Luis was suddenly surrounded by police lights from dark SUVs. They were not the white and blue checkered cars of the Chicago PD; they looked like federal vehicles. Out stepped a slim, black woman wearing a thick black peacoat and sunglasses. She walked straight up to him and said, "June Simmons, FBI. We need to have a talk. One that decides if you live or die today." She ushered him into the back seat of the blacked-out SUV where a Hispanic male in a very expensive Armani suit sat on the far end of the back seat. Juan Luis slid in and closed the door behind him. He said, "If you are going to kill me, you should know that I have powerful friends who will—."

"Cállete, niño. I am your powerful friend, if you shut your smart mouth for once. There are more powerful people out there than you, if you choose to believe it. If we wanted you and your little band of street thugs dead, we would have done it already." The man smiled grimly.

For the first time in a long time, Juan Luis was genuinely scared. "You aren't with the Feds, are you?"

"No, little boy, I am not," answered the man in heavily accented English. "This little dog and pony show here was to get your attention. To show you that even our errand boys are more powerful than you."

"Who the hell are you?" Juan Luis asked, trying to hide the obvious fear in his voice.

"I represent powerful interests like your little crew *outside* of the United States. We are interested in taking over you and your crew in Chicago. You have proven yourself to be a competent leader already, and my bosses wish to extend the invitation to join our organization."

"Wait…" Juan Luis paused. "You're with the Cartel, aren't you?"

The man in the suit smirked and handed him a black business card with only a phone number on it. "Call this number. They will get you straight. And por favor, do it soon. It would be a shame if I had to have you killed."

The door opened and Juan Luis slowly slid out of the car.

"Oh, and one last thing," the man in the suit said. "Buy yourself a suit. Those street rags don't flatter a man of your caliber at all."

Juan Luis walked straight home and called that number. As scared as he was, he knew this opportunity was not one to be passed on. With the Cartel, he would live to be a king.

In only eight years, he rose to the rank of top lieutenant in the Chicago area cartel. Known for his brilliant planning, logistics, and careful tactics, he nearly doubled the Cartel's net profits in the city. He had successfully evaded arrests and raids by the ATF, Chicago PD, DEA, and even an assassination attempt suspected to have been ordered by the CIA. He had an uncanny knack for resolving problems without direct violence. He rarely let situations escalate to outright armed conflicts. "Too loud is too dirty, Compás," he often told his underlings. He preferred to work by subterfuge, sabotage, and diplomacy. Everyone knew that he wasn't afraid to get dirty himself, but he preferred not to. Rumors and stories of when he was a Soldado, a street-level soldier of the Latin-American gangs, ran rampant. The current younger soldiers had heard many tales about his brutality and tenacity in fights.

The only prison time he ever served was when he was convicted of a federal weapons violation and sentenced to ten years. Juan Luis did five years, getting out early for "good behavior." His young soldiers spoke of his time in prison when he killed three men who attempted to jump him in the showers with nothing but a hand-made shank. The guards found him in the shower, washing the blood off his body while three large Aryan brotherhood muscleheads lay dead, each with their throats cut and multiple slashes and stab wounds. Somehow, through the aid of a high-priced gang lawyer, he was never brought to trial for murder.

Two years later, following the assassination of the area drug lord, "El Leon" Juan Luis became the drug lord of the entire Midwest, controlling the cartel's gangs and influence in Illinois, Indiana, Kentucky, Wisconsin, Minnesota, and Iowa. He became simply known as "El Leon del Norte" (The Lion of the North) because he was quiet, smart, and deliberate. He mostly let others strike for him, but when push came to shove, everybody knew who was in charge.

He had risen to high favor with the Cartel bosses in Mexico because of his gift for logistics, despite being born in the United States, which was unusual in the Cartel leaders on the U.S. side of the border. He was a genius with calculating the complicated process of moving contraband through the black-market pipeline safely and without interference from law enforcement. Chiefs on the U.S. side of the border often had great difficulty moving drugs, guns, and persons across the border and into their respective zones of control. The United States government had greatly increased border security in the past decade, making it more and more difficult on the Cartels and greatly hurting profits. Juan Luis had developed newer, more effective methods of transporting cargo across the border and all the way up to his hub in Chicago. Juan Luis had also been the one who had convinced the Cartels to start getting in the business of human trafficking. In the past ten years, Illegal immigration into the United States from Mexico had increased thirty percent, despite efforts by the U.S. Border Patrol. The Cartels had all begun competing for the new lucrative business of smuggling people across, and it had also broken into the international human trafficking business.

CHAPTER 10: THE MAYOR WITH AN OFFICE OUTSIDE CITY HALL

When John awoke, his room was still dark, but after looking at his watch on the nightstand, it was only 1 P.M. He pulled back the blackout curtains and let the sun shine in brightly. Peering outside, he saw a flurry of activity. Lyon had made good on his promises and there were several heavy machines, bulldozers, backhoes and trailers with equipment piled on them. Soldiers dressed in their uniforms were atop the machines in a frenzy of work.

Feeling guilty for sleeping the morning away, John shook off his weariness, put on pants and a shirt, put his gun on his belt, and went downstairs. He first stopped in the kitchen and grabbed a cup of coffee. Shonna and Andrew's daughter, Megan, were making sandwiches for lunch. He grabbed one off the tray, sipped on his coffee and stepped outside. The members of the compound were all scattered about doing various tasks. He spotted Big Rob sitting up on the top of the stone wall around the complex facing the neighborhood. Rob had a pair of binoculars up to his eyes and was scanning the landscape, a radio in his other hand. John walked over to Rob and climbed the ladder propped up on the wall next to him.

"What the hell are you doing, Rob?" he asked. Without setting down the binoculars, Rob replied, "When the engineers got here and went to work, we all offered to help, but Lyon said his men had it handled. The only way we could be of use was to just keep an eye on the surrounding area and watch their backs for them. Theo and Andrew are up on the roof with their long rifles on overwatch."

John thought for a minute and said, "Any problems yet?"

"Not really. A couple pot shots at the heavy equipment when they were convoying it in, but Andrew and Theo were both Johnny on the spot. They were both up on the roof watching the convoy and immediately started firing in the area of the shots. Once those high-caliber rifle rounds started coming back in their direction, nobody has popped out since."

John figured he would go pop up onto the roof and check in with the guys. He said goodbye to Rob and walked over toward the tower. As he got there, he heard Andrew's voice: "HEY FUCKFACE! WAY TO SLEEP THE DAY AWAY WHILE THE REST OF US ARE WORKING OUR ASSES OFF HERE!" He climbed up the tower and popped up onto the roof, coming face to face with Andrew. "Oh, shut your loud yap. Anything important going on up here?"

Andrew motioned out toward the neighborhood up the street and said, "Nope. The weekend warriors have been hard at work since about 8 A.M. They're making damn good progress. I told the lieutenant who was in charge to put up the defenses first. They're lining the perimeter of all of the closest houses in the neighborhood closest to the compound with Hesco barriers like we talked about. They even brought in the dirt from out of town by the Guard base. The entry to the street is going to be the gate, complete with an entry control point, barriers, and barbed wire. One way in, one way out. This whole block is going to be a Goddamn fortress. A few of them are out in the closest houses getting them wired up for the solar power and getting them back on the grid. They said all the deputies will be on their way out here sometime this afternoon and they'll start moving into the houses. I figure once they show up, we can go out and help move in our new neighbors."

John nodded silently, scanning the scene below them. He saw the soldiers putting up the barriers, and the back hoes dumping the dirt to fill the barriers. It was a surprisingly fast process, with a few solders following on top of the barriers to smooth out the dirt on the top of the wall of earth. Another group was setting up razor wire on the outer edge of the walls. He was surprised to see that the perimeter was over halfway completed around the neighborhood block. He observed that the soldiers had also built platforms along the end of the wall spaced out evenly for guard towers, all lined with sandbags. He was very pleased with the work. Lyon had once told him that the Engineer unit had spent a large portion of their most recent deployment in Iran building remote bases for outposts, also known as Combat Outposts or "COPs" as they were most commonly referred. This was nothing new for most of these soldiers, and at the rate they were going, they would be finished with plenty of time to spare before nightfall.

John turned to Andrew and said, "I think I'm going to go down and talk to the officer in charge of this group and see if they could use anything. Want to come with?"

Andrew glanced at his watch and said, "Sorry, man, it's about my turn to take over the LP/OP duty. I'll tell Theo in case he wants to follow you." And with that, he turned and walked over to the LP/OP.

John descended the tower and stopped back inside the house to grab his MK-18 rifle and slung it on his back before venturing out into the neighborhood. He stopped close to the wall where he found two soldiers hammering together a wooden platform for a guard tower. They looked up when John approached and gave him a polite head nod.

"Good afternoon, sir. How can we help you?" the taller one said.

He said, "I'm looking for your commander or the NCOIC. Whoever is in charge of the group here."

The soldier nodded and said, "I believe Lieutenant Beales is somewhere by the edge of the wall. He would be on the street side by the command Humvee working on the plans." The soldier pointed northward toward the end of the block.

John thanked the soldier and headed up the street until he found what he guessed was the command vehicle. He spotted the lieutenant speaking to a sergeant and a couple of other soldiers. They were all peering at a piece of paper and map laid out on the hood of the vehicle. The lieutenant was a tall, wiry, nerdy-looking man with a pencil-thin mustache and neatly groomed hair. He wore wire-rimmed glasses and a serious look.

As John approached, the lieutenant turned toward him and said, "Ahh yes, you must be Mr. Gonzalez. The colonel said I should be expecting you, sir. What can I do for you?"

He shook the lieutenant's hand and said, "Sir, I was just here to thank you and check in. Wanted to see if there was anything we could do for you?"

The lieutenant said, "Not much. As you can see, my boys are pretty good at this kind of thing. We should be able to have the barriers completed in another few hours. I suspect by mid-afternoon. The engineers I have wiring the houses to get power back on should be done around that time as well. If we are finished with time to spare before the light starts to dwindle, we can finish any small odds and ends you may have, like lighting, additional fighting positions, and fortifying the gate. Is there anything other than that you can think of, sir?"

John scratched his chin and said, "Well, first and foremost, I owe you an extreme debt of gratitude for doing all of this for us. This will really put us in a good position to start taking back control of this city. As long as you finish the perimeter walls before the deputies get here, that's the biggest concern. Everything they need in their accommodations is up to them beyond that. Once we finish the walls, I'd like to ensure that the front gate is as reinforced as possible. Barriers, car roadblocks, and a fighting position behind it on the road with a machinegun nest. If you guys can run commo cable wires from the front gate to all of the houses and to my compound and hook us up with some field telephones, that would be great."

The lieutenant was taking notes and nodding while listening. He said, "That can be done fairly quickly. We are also setting up a helicopter landing pad in the empty lot closest to your residence. For any emergencies, according to the colonel. In case he needs to evac you. Also, if we have time, we were instructed by the colonel to ensure that the barriers to your compound are secure. My men are prepared to extend your walls higher with our Hescos around your entire property. Colonel Lyon stressed that you and your group's personal safety was of the utmost importance."

John smiled at the lieutenant, and said, "All of that will be perfect. Thank you. If you would send a runner and let me know when the deputies begin to arrive so I can get them settled in?" They shook hands again, and John walked back to the compound to get some lunch. His watch read nearly 2 P.M., and he was hungry.

Around 5 P.M., the work had slowed down significantly. The wall was complete, and they had begun the finishing touches on the front gate and guard towers on either side. The bulldozers had come down in their direction to reinforce the wall around the compound. The Hesco barriers stood a few feet taller than the walls of the compound, so it made for a nice catwalk around the outer perimeter. The compound's members looked in amazement at their new defenses.

A soldier came running up and told John that the deputies were on their way and would be moving in all of their stuff in one move. They were to be on the lookout for a very large convoy of sheriff's squad cars and moving trucks and vehicles. They would be escorted by a small contingent of Cavalry Scout vehicles but would need to be given cover on their way in.

The engineers had begun to pack up the equipment they were no longer using; they were putting their heavy equipment back on the transport flatbed trailers and clearing the road of their vehicles. There was a lot of movement going on at once, and it worried John that the wannabe snipers from before might still be in the immediate area and up to no good. He didn't want to be caught off guard, so he directed Theo, Rob, and Shonna to come with him. As they walked, he explained that he wanted them to move along the wall up to the front gate so they could cover the entry of the incoming and outgoing convoys.

As they reached the front gate, the engineers filed up in a loose convoy, all loaded up and ready to go. A soldier slid the front gate open and shouted up to John's crew, "We're all out of here. The convoy is down the road. When they get here, the Cav Scouts are turning right around and escorting us all back to base. You're on your own from here."

John gave the soldier a thumbs up and watched him run forward and jump into one of the transport vehicles.

A short time later, they saw a long line of vehicles approaching on one of the roads. Two Armored Humvees were in the lead, with two in the rear. There was a long line of marked sheriff's department SUVs. There were also a few U-Haul moving trucks in the mix. Near the front of the convoy was also the large tan military MRAP (Mine-Resistant Ambush Protected vehicle) that had been given to the sheriff's department by the federal government many years ago. The military Humvees in the lead peeled off and pulled around to position themselves in the convoy of engineer vehicles, and they all headed off.

The convoy of sheriff's vehicles pulled through the gates into the safety of the newly built base camp. John ran over and closed the gate behind the long line of vehicles. Most had pulled onto the street and parked. Some of the people got out of their vehicles. John recognized most of the faces of the men and women. They were all wearing a random assortment of gear, most wearing their uniforms,

Kevlar vests, and police duty belts. Some wore plate armor and carried AR rifles slung on their fronts or backs.

John recognized the lieutenant. Bill Hunter was a tall, lanky white guy with short greying hair. He had previously been in charge of the detective bureau before the collapse. Hunter was a smart but quiet man. Very well organized. His planning and preparedness for investigations had made him a very effective detective for years. John walked over and shook Hunter's hand.

"Lieutenant Hunter. Glad you all could make it."

Hunter smiled wearily. "I'm glad you would have us. It looks like you're pretty well set up here. I might have preferred to stay at the sheriff's department complex, but after the fuel and generators ran low, we didn't have much more of a choice, and the National Guard made it pretty clear that they didn't have the room for our numbers there. I'll be honest here, son, I'm not too happy about moving my men and their families right into the city and putting the wives, husbands, and children in the middle of the hornets' nest out here. We've heard horror stories of how bad the city is right now. And I'm not sure that your Army-built dirt walls are going to stop the maelstrom out there."

John made note of the lieutenant's troubled tone and his body language which showed near disdain. He realized that Lyon hadn't given the deputies much of a choice in moving into the compound. The lieutenant clearly wanted to do things his way and wasn't happy that he had been forced into a situation where he wasn't in charge of his own people. John decided that he was going to go light on the niceties. The time for diplomacy had passed. People needed to realize that it was going to be life or death from here on out.

"Lieutenant Hunter, you are invited guests into our little base here. And If I had to guess, I'd say we're the safest place in the city right now. You and your people are more than welcome to leave if you don't like the arrangements, but I think that's a decision up to the men and women who are putting their families in danger if you leave. I'm not here to play diplomat. If you guys stay, you can be in charge of all of your people's personal affairs, but you are in MY house now. And you play by MY rules. I provide you a safe place to live and will help with supplies, and all that I ask is that you do your best to sustain yourselves and collect supplies to ensure survival and also that your men help man the gates and walls around the remainder of the block. You pull your weight, and we will do our best to help you in any way that we can. That's the bottom line, no bullshit. Deal?

The lieutenant looked defeated but mostly weary. He said, "For the record, I'm not happy about this, but if it gets the safety we need, then I'm sure we can make it work."

John replied, "Good. Now you and your men can move in to all of the houses on the west side of the street. I would suggest merging the families into some houses, and the house closest to the gate be made into a barracks for the single men. I'll leave the accommodations and personal arrangements up to you. If you need anything, let me know. My people will help to stock the towers and gates with some extra ammunition and essential items. Take the rest of the afternoon to get your people settled in. I think you've all had a rough day, so I want to have a little celebration tonight. How does a nice relaxing neighborhood barbeque and bonfire sound?"

The lieutenant said, "That would be great. I hope you have lots of beer." He dredged up a smile and held his hand out, which John shook. Both men departed to brief their respective groups.

Over the next few hours, the sheriff's department crew spent their time moving into their new accommodations. John's group watched from inside the compound walls as the families moved in. They had minimal personal effects. The U-Haul trucks were loaded with useful supplies, food, ammo boxes, weapons cases, and even a pair of the sheriff's department's ATVs. They appeared to be fairly well supplied, which eased the minds of the compound members, who had worried that they would come begging for supplies.

Theo stood next to John and said, "Gonna have a big welcome party tonight, huh? I hope they brought their own beer."

Rob had gone inside once John told everyone the plans. He was helping Shonna and the kids make burgers out of the frozen beef in one of the garage freezers—fortunately, John had purchased a beef cow from a distant cousin's farm earlier that year.

John told Theo, "The guy in charge wasn't too happy at feeling like he wasn't in control anymore. I told him that he could control his own people's affairs, as long as they stayed in their own lane...."

"That's gonna be a slap in the face when you tell them we're planning on using them to help us roll into downtown to check the City Hall for survivors. Hopefully the party tonight will soften the blow."

"You get it, bro...I just hope they do. Maybe we can sweeten the deal and offer to stop along the way to scavenge some buildings for any supplies they need. I'll take a look at the maps and see if there's any hot spots we had marked on our route to the City Hall."

"Food, water, guns, or booze bro. Stick to the basics," Theo said with a small smirk.

Dez stepped out of the house into the front yard where John and Theo were standing. John hadn't seen her since he went to bed that morning. She walked over with a cup of water in her hand, took a swig, and stood next to him. He shot her a sideways glance, but before he could speak, she said, "If either of you make a joke about why I'm not in the kitchen helping out, I'll shoot you in the foot. I can't cook for shit. Rob was the only smart one to get hitched to a domestic goddess."

Both he and Theo put their hands up in a "I give up" gesture. She kissed John on the cheek and said, "You've been busy all day. Making new friends I see. Hear it didn't go that well." Under her breath, she said, "I can't stand those snooty county fucks...Always acting like they're better than us city cops when we're the ones getting shot at every weekend. I can't wait 'til we go get some of our people, the real warriors."

John said, "Don't worry, they'll find their place here. They're powerful allies that we need. They'll serve their purpose in helping us get to whoever is surviving in the city. We can't rely on the National Guard for much longer. We're going to need the strong patriots to get the area under control as soon as possible."

Dez and Theo both thought over what he'd said. Theo finally said, "Forget all that shit for now. Let's get ready to party tonight!"

John said, "Not to be a party pooper, but remember, this welcome home party is really just a nice way to break it to the deputies that we're gonna be putting them to work and dragging them along to push into the city in the next few days and look for the city cops and other survivors that might be of use."

"Rent ain't free, bitch!" said Theo, laughing. "They're gonna learn that in a hurry."

A few hours later, everyone was enjoying the warm summer evening. The larger collective that now inhabited the fortified neighborhood around the compound had begun to gather around. The men of the compound had set up a large grill on the empty grass lot near the compound's walls. A bonfire was going as the daylight had begun to fade. They had dragged out containers with beer and filled with ice from the freezers. John decided to "spare no expense," so to speak. The waste of supplies and luxuries would make for a good welcome gesture to the county men, women, and their families.

It was important that they build trust and goodwill amongst the group. The last thing John wanted was for his new neighbors who were well-trained and relatively well-armed to get uneasy and jealous with the well-stocked and fortified compound next door. He wanted to put on a show for the newcomers. It served a dual purpose, as he wanted to both show goodwill and gratitude, but also to soften the blow when he informed the men that he needed to use them for the movement further into Kankakee. It was going to be dangerous and possibly cost lives, but the risk was worth the reward.

As the night settled in around them, the rest of the collective began to gather, drawn by the smells of burgers and meat on the grill and the joyous sounds of the crowd. They all stood in groups around the fire and grill drinking beer. Many of the new men and women knew some of the members of the compound, and old acquaintances were struck into renewed friendships.

After an hour or so while everyone enjoyed their drinks and food, the talk turned to business. The newcomers discussed their sleeping arrangements and schedules for guard shifts for manning the gate and towers.

John approached a group of the higher-ranking deputies who were already talking shop with Theo and Big Rob. Theo took the cue that the conversation was going to get more serious and began to pass out a few cigars from a small leather case he kept in his cargo pocket. They all lit their cigars and took puffs together. John took the opportunity of the break in conversation and started with a small salute with his cigar: "To our new friends. Cheers, boys." They all nodded in agreement and he continued, "Now that we are all settled in, I hate to make you guys all go back outside the wire so soon...But there's something you need to do for us. We're going back out there. We need a column of vehicles to push into the city, downtown. Check the police department for survivors. Get in, get out as fast as we can."

The county lieutenant interrupted him before he got the next thought out. "We just get here and now you wanna spring this bullshit on us that's gonna get my guys killed? Lure us into safety just to put us in even more danger than we were before! Look kid, I didn't bring my people to be your errand boys and lap dogs..."

John raised his voice and said, "Look. This is non-negotiable. We've got it on good intel that there's still some cops stuck out there and we HAVE to get those survivors."

At this point, they were nearly yelling at each other, and people began to take notice. A few of those in the circle were getting uncomfortable, when suddenly the attention was drawn elsewhere. The lieutenant noticed the hush that had come over the crowd and shut his mouth with a snap.

Old Sarge limped out into the lot on a pair of crutches, and all eyes were drawn to him. Most stared out of amazement at the old warrior, but the few that knew him well were mostly surprised to see a man they had thought of as infallible in such a weakened state. He hobbled along still heavily bandaged and leaning heavily on his crutches. It was a welcome sight to see him alive and well. Theo walked with him, carefully guiding the old cop every step of the way. They made their way over to John and he shook the hand of the old warrior. Old Sarge turned to Theo and said, "You think I'm healthy enough for a beer, son?"

With a big toothy smile, Theo replied, "I'll be right back, Sarge!" and ran off to fetch him a drink.

Sarge turned to John and said, "I like that kid. He's a good boy. You know, when old-timer cops like me and your dad were coming up, people were horrible; they used to say little black kids from the hood like him were animals and would never amount to anything. If those old racist fucks could only see us now, they'd shit a brick. I like that kid. Someone raised him right, and he's one hell of a man. And a cop too…That's hard for a young black fella in the big city." He smiled as Theo came jogging back with a couple beers in his hands and handed one off to Old Sarge. They said a cheers and clinked glasses with a smile. "I'm gonna adopt this fucking kid if he keeps this up."

Old Sarge turned to the lieutenant and said, "Bill, with all due respect, son. We've known each other a long time so I won't pussyfoot around this: Now that everyone heard your little dick-measuring contest with our host here. That's right, I said he's our *host*. Without Johnny here, we'd all be fucking dead. I know I would be. So, you can show a little bit of fucking gratitude, or you can see yourselves the fuck out!"

Everyone stood around dumbfounded by the strong words from the frail-looking old man.

Lieutenant Hunter started back. "Wayne, Wayne, calm down, old man. I just don't want to put my people on the line for less reward than it's worth."

Old Sarge cut him off, calmer this time. "What it's worth? It is worth us going and saving our people too. Our co-workers, your brothers and sisters in blue. Our job is to serve and protect, and now our mission is to go out there and save lives, as many as we can. We can't do that without you and your guys." Sarge took a long swig of his beer, then added, "Worst case scenario is we get the lay of the land and maybe get to raid the place for supplies. But it isn't gonna get to worst case scenario. We're gonna find all of our cops out there still fighting. I'll ride shotgun if I have to."

Lieutenant Hunter softly said, "Okay. We'll go. Just for you, Wayne. Although I don't think you need to go…"

Theo added, "And I doubt the doctor's gonna let you go. If I even ask, Shonna is gonna shit a brick. She's more likely to shoot one of us than let you go."

John quickly spoke, taking the chance to come out on top of the argument, "Tell your teams we'll need maybe five of your best vehicles full of men. About half your guys. We'll take whoever you pick or volunteers. My guys will lead out in the Tank, and a couple of yours can come up in the rear with the MRAP. We don't need a ton of time; I want to be in and out as fast as possible. Leave a little after noon tomorrow."

The lieutenant said, "Well...I'll go talk to my guys...At least it gives us time to recover from the party tonight..." and walked off towards a gathering of his people.

The rest of the evening was still enjoyed lightheartedly by most, who tried to forget the situation they were in, but John couldn't help but notice a few dirty looks from some of the sheriff's department employees for the reminder of the evening.

CHAPTER 11: ROAD LOADIN'...WITH MY BOYS

Mid-August

The next morning, most of the crew slept in a little later than usual. A couple were nursing some pretty hefty hangovers. Theo had brought out a few bottles of whiskey and convinced people to start doing shots last night, and that didn't end well for anyone. After a few large pots of coffee were made and the aroma drifted through the house, most of the members of the compound were awake by 10 A.M. and gathered around in the kitchen reminiscing about the party. Theo had still gotten up early and helped Old Sarge move into one of the rooms upstairs on the second floor. Theo also moved his own personal items into another one of the rooms next door to Sarge's new room. "It's lonely down in the basement bro!" he remarked to Andrew while passing him in the living room.

After a light breakfast/lunch meal, everyone took to getting their gear in order for the planned journey into the city. Again, Shonna was asked to stay behind with the kids, along with Old Sarge, who was still recovering and not very mobile yet.

"Goddamn it, I want to go!" he said, despite everyone's objections. He finally was calmed down and said, "Fine, but If I'm stuck in the rear with the gear, I'll stay on the radio and listen at least."

By 11:30, the members of the compound stood outside in the courtyard next to the Tank. Dez was topping off the gas tank and checking the engine while everyone else looked over each other's gear to make sure everything was good. Since they were going so far from the compound, everyone carried extra ammunition, and most had brought along assault packs or rucksacks with them.

Andrew said, "I'm bringing my small bug-out bag with me. Never know if any one of us might get separated from the whole group and have to hump it back on foot."

John gathered everyone around and gave a quick brief: "Okay guys, pretty straightforward plan; not too many details, and only our main objectives and contingency plans: Mission goals are to go straight to the Kankakee Police Station and check for survivors. If we take contact along the way, we will break contact and keep moving toward the objective. We'll blow right through roadblocks if we have to. Our route is straight east on Court Street to downtown. No more zig-zagging; I want in and out as quickly and directly as we can. If anyone is separated from the group and can't continue on to the police station, break contact on foot. Head south out of the danger area and make your way down to one of the bridges on the river. Either move south to the National Guard base or head back west to us from the south edge of town by the high school road. Secondary objectives when we get there are securing all useful supplies and equipment besides police personnel to include weapons, ammo, fuel, armored vehicles, and food stores. Also, we can be looking for other first responders, firefighters, nurses, EMTs, and city-elected officials, as long as it doesn't drag us down for time or affect the main objectives. Everybody understand?"

After receiving acknowledgments from the group, he hopped into the Tank. They drove out into the rest of the neighborhood to meet the county guys who had volunteered (or had been volun-told) to go. They took up their position at the front of the group nearest to the gate, and another five vehicles filed in behind them, including the large, armored MRAP in the rear. John got out and gave the same briefing to the rest of the group and added, "Let's watch each other's backs out there, and everybody makes it home safe today." With those words, they all saddled up and rolled out of the gate.

John was glad he was in front so that he could set the speed of the convoy. He sped through the side streets until they emerged onto the main road, Court Street, that would take them directly across the bridge into the downtown area. The convoy reached nearly sixty miles an hour, as they blew through intersections and didn't slow down for anything. The fast pace of the convoy helped pass by anyone who might be watching the road and attempt to send pot shots in their direction.

They quickly made it across the bridge and past the hospital. As they passed the emergency room ramp they'd left those many days before, a group of looters started shooting at the convoy. John sped back up, maneuvering around stalled and overturned cars obstructing the roadway. The sheriff's squad cars were not bullet-resistant like the Tank or the MRAP, so he made his way through the maze and gunned it through. They travelled the remaining several blocks as quickly as they could, knowing that they had now lost the element of surprise and the convoy of vehicles had attracted lots of attention. He gripped the steering wheel tightly as they neared the Gas N Wash gas station where he had been shot several months earlier.

Sensing the tension in him, Dez said, "Hey, I know a guy that got shot over there!" pointing to the gas station, which incited a laugh from everyone inside the vehicle. Theo leaned in from the gunner's turret and said, "I hope the fucking coffee was worth it."

The heckling eased John's nerves a little as they went over the rise in the road over the train tracks and the Amtrak train depot. Once they reached the intersection of Court and Schuyler, he slowed to turn north. As he rounded the corner, more shots began to ping on the ground from the taller office buildings around them. They rushed north and turned onto Oak Street. He could see the police department down the block and made his way toward it, bullets now pinging off the armored MRAP at the rear of the convoy. The onslaught began to subside as they covered the distance to the department.

John began to relax again as they neared the front of the building at the intersection of Oak Street and Indiana Avenue. He slowed as they rolled toward the public entrance, which was barricaded by a stack of wood, garbage cans, and even the park benches that had originally been on the sidewalk. John stopped the Tank near the edge of the intersection and slowly stepped out. Some of the others stepped out of their vehicles, all very apprehensively. He surveyed the large multiple-story brick building named after a former mayor. Nothing moved in the windows, and there weren't any lights showing throughout the building. He finally decided to give it a chance and yelled, "HELLOOOO!!! ANYBODY HOME?" while knocking on the wood covering the front doors.

"Where the fuck is everyone? There has to still be someone alive in here," Dez said, the hope in her voice fading.

John shrugged and turned around to face the others who were scanning the nearby buildings. Andrew and Rob were both standing at the hood of the Tank, pointing at the large old National Guard Armory diagonally across from the police department. The large stone and concrete building hadn't been an Armory since the 1960s and had only been used as a community center and gymnasium since then. The fenced-in lot was barricaded with metal sheets and wrecked cars. John saw some smoke rising from behind the fence just as Rob began to remark, "Hey you don't think they might be over—."

ZIIING!—

Just then, a bullet whizzed past their heads, coming from the direction of the old Armory. They all dove behind the cover of the Tank as they took incoming gunfire. Andrew was under the front fender of the Tank in an urban prone position, his scoped AR-10 focused at the building.

"I think it's coming from the second story of the old Armory," Andrew said, trying to line up a shot while bullets started bouncing around the vehicle. While the fire started to pick up in volume, it was still inaccurate, and the convoy was able to start shooting back in the direction of the old Armory. The incoming fire increased in volume until it was a dull roar. They heard bursts from what sounded like automatic weapons opening up on them until they couldn't move from behind the cover of the Tank's armor. Theo jumped down from the turret of the Tank after the rounds began pinging the roof much too close for comfort.

The convoy was pinned down. They all took cover behind their vehicles as the gunfire continued, wild shots spraying in their direction. John was wildly trying to figure out a plan, but the gunfire grew more and more rapid, bullets pinging off their vehicles and the ground around them. The convoy attempted to return fire, but most could barely get off a few shots before having to dive back behind the cover of their vehicle.

Several of the men and women were wounded or grazed by incoming fire. Theo, who had bounded down to the next vehicle in line, a police Tahoe, was over top of the hood sending near cyclic bursts from his SAW in the direction of the old Armory's tower. He was about the only one still out in the open returning fire.

Dez turned to John and yelled, "What the fuck are we going to do? If we stay here, we're gonna die!"

He felt overwhelmed, his mind overloaded with thoughts. The bullets impacting around him had his mind fuzzy and out of focus. John finally stuttered out the words, "Fuck, fuck, I don't know...I don't know!" He finished with a yell. People were looking to him for help, and he had no clue what to do. One of the county sergeants a vehicle over was bleeding from a shoulder wound while another was attempting to bandage him up. The sergeant was looking in John's direction and yelling to him, but the noise of all the chaos around him drowned out the voices.

The situation seemed hopeless until they heard a different sound rip from another automatic weapon. The men slowly peeked out from their vehicles as the rain of bullets coming down on them began to slow its pace. Just then, an old lifted Chevy Silverado screeched around the corner. What looked like an M60 belt-fed machine gun was mounted to the rear of the vehicle, and a familiar-looking man was unleashing long bursts of automatic gunfire from the M60 toward the second-story windows of the old Armory. "Cowboys from Hell" by Pantera was blasting through its loudspeakers over the loud exhaust coming from the vehicle. It careened down the street toward them. Another man leaned out of the passenger window with an M79 hand-held military grenade launcher and sent a round into one of the Armory's windows as they passed by. A large explosion rocked the second floor as the grenade hit, and fire blossomed from the windows.

The incoming gunfire died down and finally came to a halt as the building began to burn. They heard voices screaming in panic as the second floor was slowly enveloped in flames. The old Black Silverado pulled in front of the convoy on Oak Street and continued to fire on the building. The driver, who John now recognized as his good friend Steve, leaned out of his window and yelled, "We've got you covered. Get around the building to the north lot. We'll mop up this bullshit." Steve cracked a shit-eating grin and threw a half-full beer can at him.

John said, "Are you sure? Might be a lot of them in there."

Steve said, "Nahh, we're good. The bros have been road loading since Pontiac, and they're ready to kick some commie ass. These pussies don't stand a chance! The ones who aren't still in there turning into Luke Skywalker's aunt and uncle, at least..."

With that, the caravan loaded up and pulled around to the rear of the building, where they found the closest of the gated entrances to the police department's parking lot. As the vehicles rolled up, the gates were opened by two Kankakee City police officers, both wearing full tactical gear.

"Hurry up, before they start shooting again!" said one, as the convoy flooded into the gated north lot.

John parked the Tank near the few vehicles left in the parking lot. Many were missing tires or riddled with bullet holes. He stepped out and told the first cop who had spoken, "Gary, go get whoever is left in charge and make it fast. We're getting you all out of here to safety. And Jimmy, go alert everyone else. Have them start packing everything they can. Arms, ammo, food, supplies, fuel, and anything else important. As fast as they can, as much as they can. Go now."

The two men entered the police station and disappeared up the stairs. Just then, the Silverado swung around and backed into the lot, stopping to block the open gate. Out stepped the ragtag crew that inhabited the old pick-up truck.

John greeted his friend, Steve Regas. Steve was a shorter but well-built man with short hair and glasses. He still wore his short-sleeved Department of Corrections SORT (Special Operations Response Team) uniform shirt, a pair of khaki tac pants, and black and white Chuck Taylors. Over his uniform he wore a small black plate carrier which held spare magazines; and two Dunkin Donuts iced coffee bottles peered out of his pouches. A Beretta 9mm pistol was in the drop-leg holster on his belt, and he had an AR-10 slung on his back.

The man in the back manning the machine gun was another friend, Chuck. Chuck Findlay was a very tall and exceptionally handsome former Marine that John had met while working at the county jail; he had moved on to be a state trooper. Chuck was wearing a pair of dark tac pants and a cut-off shirt underneath his tan plate carrier, which was slung with spare bandoliers of ammunition for the machine gun. Chuck gave a nod and wave but stayed standing in the bed of the pickup truck to scan the roadway.

Next out of the truck stepped John's friend, Hoover. Hoover was a former Army Cavalry Scout. Hoover was one of his buddies who was a notorious "gun nut"—he had more than a few gun safes full of various guns and ammo and other exotic armaments. He wore a long sleeved multicam combat shirt and a large plate carrier loaded with rifle magazines. He had two exotic FN 5.7 pistols in drop-leg holsters on both legs attached to his battle belt and held the 40mm grenade launcher cradled in his arms. Hoover had a big smile and said, "Sorry, that building's on fire because of me, but you're welcome for saving your asses."

John told Hoover, "Hell no, you guys saved our asses. Now who else is still in that truck?"

Out stepped another one of his old friends, Kyle Puleo. Kyle was a muscle-bound man who until recently had been a police officer in the county to the south. He was originally from the East Coast and spoke with a heavy Boston accent. He wore dark duty tac pants and a sleeveless shirt under his black police plate carrier. His police duty belt held his Glock and spare magazines and he held an M249 SAW. He wore a Boston Red Sox baseball cap backwards, which was his usual signature look. He stretched, flexed his muscles, and sniffed the air, saying, "Smells just like a Patriots' game in November."

John greeted his good friends and asked, "Where the hell have you guys been? And how the hell did all you guys end up together?"

Steve replied, "Hell man, nothing can keep the bros separated. When this shit started to pop off, I was at work. The Pontiac prison went on a soft lockdown and we weren't allowed much movement in and out. I was able to get to my cell phone and send a message to Hoover. Hoover and Chuck met up at my place in Kankakee; they grabbed my truck and went down to Watseka to get Kyle. The three of them made their way to Pontiac and I was able to sneak out of the tower I was in and bail out. We stopped on our way out of Pontiac to hole up for the night at the National Guard Armory there. There's a Cav Scout unit stationed there, and thankfully Hoover and I have some friends there. They only had a small detachment of soldiers that made it there, but we were able to borrow some supplies. The armorer served active duty with Hoover, so he gave us this M-60 and a few more of these presents, and he even helped us weld the machine gun mount to the truck. We piled in as much ammo as we could fit in the truck, grabbed some booze for the road, and hauled ass back up here. There was a little bit of trouble on the way, a few half-ass road blocks, but we blew through them pretty easily with the machine gun. We were finally able to get to my house a few days ago. We were getting settled in when word came through on the radios that you boys needed help, so we figured we'd do what the bros do best: drink booze and wreak a little havoc."

John pointed to the grenade launcher in Hoover's hands and asked, "So your buddy straight up gave you a grenade launcher and live high explosive rounds? How'd you pry that away from the government?"

Hoover said, "Uhh...yeah...I totally didn't own this before...And I'm uncomfortable answering your questions in a police station parking lot..."

John gave his friends big hugs and introduced them to the other members of the compound. He grabbed Steve by the arm and said in a low voice, "By now, I think you've seen how bad shit has gotten out here. How about you and the boys move into the compound? We secured all the block around it for the rest of the cops and their families, but there's still plenty of room inside my place for you and the bros. Now, I'm asking...how soon can you get all of your guys' stuff moved into the compound?"

His friends looked at each other, and Hoover said, "We're gonna need some trailers, for my gun safes, oh, and stuff for our families too, I suppose..."

John smiled at them and said, "We've got plenty of room for you guys and your families. Go get your stuff packed and get over to the compound. We'll be back there as soon as we can get everyone over here packed up and moved. I'll radio ahead to our people and tell them to have the people manning the gate watch out for a Silverado hauling four drunks and a machine gun."

Steve gave him a nod and a fist bump, and they all jumped back into the Silverado. They cranked back up the Pantera, pulled out of the lot and sped off. Steve's house was only about a mile from John's, and he knew how to find the compound without directions.

The back door of the police department opened and out stepped a tall blonde woman wearing a police uniform. Sherry Morgan was a lieutenant in the patrol division and had been the afternoon shift commander for five years. She was around forty-five years old and kept in good shape, but the stress of the job showed in her face. She was like most cops; angry, divorced, and a borderline alcoholic, but she was known to be a firm and fair leader. She beelined straight for John, stopping inches from his face, and said in a raised voice, "Who the fuck do *you* think you are coming back from the dead and giving my men orders?"

John reeled back slightly and blinked a few times before finally answering, "Lieutenant Morgan, with all due respect, ma'am, but we just saved your asses. Whoever the fuck that was, they were pushed right up on top of you. It was only a matter of time 'til they moved in, kicked down the front doors, and overran you all in your sleep."

She rubbed her eyes, and looked as though she was preparing another retort, but thought against it. The stress showed on her face. She was skinnier than he had ever seen her, and a little frail. She said a little softer this time, "Look, Gonzalez, things are getting bad in the city. The gang bangers took over the projects and most of the east side of the city. The Outlaws biker gang moved in from the south and started taking over downtown and everything south of the city. We've lost ground and can't control much of anything outside of the station at this point. We haven't been able to even go out and patrol without getting shot at. The biker gangs have been raping and pillaging everything they come in contact with. We've heard reports of those sick bastards raping women and girls as young as ten. The people still left living down there have stuck with them because of their bullshit promises of protection. We can't get out to do anything to help. We just don't have the numbers. We've got barely thirty officers here, only small arms, and hardly anybody with combat experience. We can't make any difference anymore. We even tried to get in contact with the small militia groups we've heard about from around the area, but so far have had no luck. You guys are our first big break of luck. The truth is...we need you, Johnny. More than anybody has ever needed us. We need to take this city back."

John told her, "That's the mission, LT: We need to take the city back, and we have tremendous resources at our disposal, but we need your men. Here's my offer, and it is the ONLY offer to you and all your men and women under your command along with all the other families and other first responders. We have a very well-defended base of operations on the west side of town. If you agree to fight with us, then you and all of your people can move within our walls. We've got plenty of houses ready to move in that all still have power and running water. You guys get the same deal as the county guys."

She said, "Okay. It will be nice to sleep somewhere that feels safe again, but I don't like the idea of pulling out and giving these assholes the whole downtown. It doesn't feel like a win."

John said, "Don't worry; consider it a tactical withdrawal to gain a better position. We'll come take all this back soon. At least I hope so."

The next hour was spent loading equipment into their vehicles and the few vehicles that the city police had left. They were only able to get five patrol cars running, two of the armored SWAT BearCats, and one of the guy's large pick-up trucks to pull a trailer of gear.

John was happy to see the faces of nearly twenty-five of his co-workers from various shifts; there was a wide age range—most were younger and single, but several had managed to bring in their spouses and children along with. It added another fifteen bodies, but there were several very useful additions. Andrew's kids would be thrilled to have friends to play with, and many of the spouses would be very useful. Four of the spouses were City firefighters/paramedics and three were nurses.

"We're gonna need to throw another party," said Lieutenant Hunter to John. "Or is that just for bribery when you want us to do stuff for you?"

"Fuck off, Hunter." John said, walking away from him to check on the progress. His watch read 14:58. Nearly three o'clock. He went to find Lieutenant Morgan to try to speed the process. It was taking much longer than he had anticipated, and the firefight had delayed them greatly. He finally found Morgan helping load boxes on the trailer. She stopped to talk to him.

"The city purchased a bunch of freeze-dried food stores about six months ago and had it moved into the garage of the fire department building next door. We didn't know until one of the guys pointed it out to us. At least that bitch of a mayor did one thing right before it went completely to hell."

John was still fuming from the interaction with the county lieutenant and was only half listening. Morgan said, "That Hunter from county is kind of a cockbag, isn't he? How'd you guys get linked up with them?"

John said, "Long story. I'll tell you when we get back home safely. How long until we can roll out of here? We need to get the fuck out of here and get back behind the safety of our walls."

"That's the last of the important stuff. We're good to go now," Morgan said.

John motioned for everyone to load up. The vehicles all filed out, now forming a double wide column of vehicles with the Tank and the county MRAP in the lead. The men in the last vehicle out closed the gates and padlocked them.

John had given instructions for everyone to blow straight through any obstacles in their way and not to stop for anything. He turned off onto Court Street heading back west and gunned the accelerator. They made quick progress back toward the bridge over the river. As they came close to the hospital where the cars had formed the road obstructions on the way in, he took the lead and accelerated to crash his way through the cars in the road. Everyone in the Tank braced for impact as he hit the closest car at around forty mph. The flipped Subaru hatchback blew out of the way and cleared a small enough gap for the convoy to file through in a single column. They cleared the road obstruction quickly and with no resistance. They all breathed a sigh of relief when they crossed the bridge and shortly thereafter turned down Curtis Street heading toward the entrance to their subdivision.

When they finally pulled up to the gate of the neighborhood's walls, Andrew let out a whistle. "What a fucking day. If we hadn't drank so much last night, I'd say we need to get drunk tonight."

The gate opened and they pulled through. They stopped at the end of the road at the gate to the compound and hopped out to help direct the city cops to their new homes. The sergeant who'd been shot in the shoulder walked over to John and shook his hand. He said, "Glad we all got out of that okay, buddy. I know it was worth it, no matter what Hunter said," and walked off.

The rest of the compound crew walked over to direct the new guests to their new living arrangements. The city cops settled into the houses on the east side of the street. The families and spouses of the nurses and paramedics all settled into the house closest to the compound, the house they had decided to designate as the infirmary/field hospital. They also agreed that half of the medical supplies from inside the compound including half of the seized items from the raid on the emergency room would be stored there.

As it started to get dark, a runner from the first gate found John and said, "Your friends in the pick-up truck are here at the gate." He told the young corrections officer to go ahead and let them in and told him to direct them to the gate to the compound. The young officer ran back toward the gate, and John headed over to open up the gate to the open lot next to the compound's driveway.

A short time later, he heard the loud rumble of the truck as it came into view pulling a small trailer and pulled up next to the compound. The bros all hopped out, grabbing rucksacks and duffel bags full of equipment and personal effects. He directed them down to the basement to stow their extra gear, ammo, and supplies. He let the guys pick their own rooms, with the three single guys (Kyle, Steve, and Chuck) opting to share the rooms in the basement with the bunk beds, and Hoover and his wife and five-year-old son moving into one of the large bedrooms left upstairs.

After making sure that everyone was settled in, John went to grab his bag, M1A and other stuff to begin his overnight watch on the LP/OP. As her was gathering a few items and stuffing some snacks from the kitchen into his bag, Steve walked into the kitchen to grab a beer from the fridge. Steve stopped him and said, "Where are you headed?"

John answered, "Up to the roof for my guard shift. What are you up to?"

Steve said, "I haven't been able to sleep through the night in weeks. Want some company?"

He told Steve emphatically, "Hell yeah. Someone to talk to is gonna help pass the time."

Steve grabbed a few beers out of the fridge with a smile and said, "Lead the way. I'm gonna grab my rifle and follow you up."

John climbed up to the LP/OP to relieve Rob, who was on duty. Rob was yawning as he looked at his watch. "You're early, brother, but I'll take it. Had to come straight up after we got back from the mission. Haven't even gotten to hit the shower yet. Thankfully there's a couple more people around who can plug up bullet wounds now, so I'm not as needed anymore. It's kinda nice to just be able to hit the watch duty after leaving the wire instead of spending the rest of the night mopping up blood and patching gunshot wounds. I'm sure Shonna feels the same way now."

John slid down into the LP/OP and looked through the pass-on book.

"Nothing too much since I've been up here," Rob said, "but someone from the county crew called on the radio to notify that they're going to be sending out a small group tomorrow to go look through the neighborhood. One of the retired deputies lives a couple blocks away. They wanted to go look around, get a recon of the area, and see if the guy is still alive. Said they're going out at first light, so you might still be working."

John said, "Sounds good. Glad they're keeping busy. That should help them not stay so stir-crazy. Plus, I think there's some good benefits to starting to show a bigger presence around in the immediate area."

Rob nodded in agreement with another yawn and checked his watch again. John looked at his own watch, noting that it was just before 10 P.M. "Go ahead and get on out of here. Get some sleep, buddy," he told Rob, who quickly gathered his stuff and headed down to the tower/ladder. Rob passed Steve at the edge of the roof and they greeted each other as Rob went back down the ladder.

Steve walked over and shimmied into the LP/OP next to John. "I didn't know the Chicago Fire Department hired Bears Football linebackers. Dude is fucking huge! Where'd you find him?" John laughed and said, "Rob is a solid dude. Met him up in Chicago through Theo. We used to shoot together all the time." Steve sat down, examining the LP/OP structure and all of the items contained in it and said, "Nicely done. You've got a good setup out here. And a pretty good crew to boot."
"Better now with you and the boys here," John said. "Now tell me all about the prison and how you guys got together and made it here. We've got plenty of time to kill..."

INTERLUDE SIX: LIFE BEHIND BARS SUCKS JUST AS BAD WHEN THE WORLD'S ENDING

Steve cracked a beer, handed John one, and began his story:

Well man, things weren't too bad in the prison in all honesty. Even though the economy started tanking, we all still had to go to work. Gotta pay the bills, ya know? We can't all be lucky enough to get shot in the dome and sleep through the worst of the collapse of the United States (he said with a very obiou smirk). Well anyways, I had to keep going to work. I checked in on the guys as much as I could, but we're all stubborn. Hoover couldn't move his family, no matter how bad things got. He was blessed living so close to the river. Kyle had to keep going to work too, and Chuck? Who knows where he's off galivanting to most of the time.

So, I kept making the long drive to Pontiac every day. As things started getting worse and worse, I started staying down in Pontiac during my work week and just coming back on my days off. It limited my time to pull provisions together, but Amazon was still delivering as long as I was still paying. Plus, all the overtime we were getting forced to do really helped for a while. All that extra money helped soften the blow of the thousands of dollars a month I was spending on freeze-dried food and ammo. When things finally went totally south and the market officially crashed, prison guards and staff started going AWOL left and right. Couldn't keep enough people there. Everyone figured it was more important to take care of their own families. The prison really wasn't that bad. The warden put forth some emergency procedures in place and called a state of emergency. They put the prison on a soft lockdown. We weren't really allowed to leave, and they put us on two alternating twelve-hour shifts. They made room for an officer's barracks, and we slept and lived in there when we weren't on shift. The prison still had plenty of food, and a good stock of large number 10 tin cans full of food. Once we were allowed to have our cell phones in the barracks with us, I figured it was the right time to get back in contact with the boys. We weren't really getting any news from the outside world at this point, so I wanted to see how the guys were faring. I got a hold of Hoover first, and the news wasn't good. I got a little scared. If Hoover was saying things weren't good, then shit must have been really bad. I asked if he and the boys wanted to consolidate, and if they wanted to roll down to Pontiac to come get me. I knew the road would be dangerous, so there was no way I was going to leave the relative safety of the prison walls to venture out on my own. The only way I was leaving was if I knew the boys were all together and with me. Hoover said he'd get the crew together and they would make their way down to me. Shortly after that, the phones went down. It was almost a week of no contact and I started to get really worried that they weren't coming down, or something worse had happened.

As things got worse and worse outside, and supplies began to dwindle, the warden decided to start releasing inmates that had short time left on their sentences. The warden got in contact with the National Guard Unit stationed in Pontiac and enlisted their help to be extra security while they processed these inmates out. He released all short-timers, then a few days later started releasing all the non-violent drug offenders. He planned on releasing all the non-violent offenders altogether. This cut the prison occupancy in half, which helped with the reduced staffing levels and growing shortage of food. During this time, there was a lot of movement and confusion. I was able to slip out and talk to the National Guard unit guys. I knew a few of them, and thankfully a few of them knew Hoover. I had a few of them keep an eye out for the boys so they could get word to me if they showed up.

Like I said, after a grueling week or so wait, I heard that Hoover and the boys had showed up in town. I made up my mind to sneak off and get out of there to go back home with my boys. I wrote a letter to the warden resigning and letting him know I was leaving, gathered my stuff, and snuck out of my tower and tried to blend in with the crowd of soldiers releasing inmates. I hitched a ride out with the Guard over to the Armory, which was only a couple blocks away from the gates of the prison. I was a little worried someone might shoot me for deserting.

Back at the Armory, I met up with the guys. Hoover had gotten a hold of everybody to bang out a plan to get together and get to me. He went to my house, grabbed my truck and a little gear. He and Chuck rolled down to Watseka to pick up Kyle from work, and they all hauled it down to Pontiac to come get me. Once I got there, we decided to get ready for the trip back to Kankakee. The Guard unit told us that the roads and highways were starting to get rough for travel. Bands of criminals had begun to make roadblocks on the main roads and highways and were robbing people of their valuables as they passed. The police that remained in the area couldn't control anything outside of the main towns. The boys had brought just a little bit of food and a couple of their guns, but I had nothing. The armorer from the Cav unit knew me and had actually served active duty with Hoover, so we were able to finagle a deal with him. He gave us this super old M60 machine gun that they had in the arms room along with a bunch of boxes of ammo. We took anything they'd give us at this point. In return, the commander of the Cav unit put us to work. If we went out and cleared the main road leading in and out of town, they would give us as many supplies as they could spare. Apparently, a gang of recently released criminals hadn't left the area as they had arranged deal with the warden. They had gotten their hands on some guns and started robbing people and supply trucks a few miles out of town; they'd taken over a little farmhouse along the road. The police and National Guard troops already had their hands full maintaining order in town and working on the release of inmates. Unfortunately, this group of bandits was blocking new supplies from being trucked into town, and they were growing in numbers with every group of inmates that were released from the prison.

We were sent out with one objective: eliminate the group. We were allowed to take anything we looted from them once we cleared the way for the passage into town. We rolled out in my truck and rolled in right on top of them. They let us right up to their roadblock, thinking we were just some group of idiots they were going to rob. By the time they tried to jump out and surprise us, we were danger close and able to do what we do best: wreak absolute havoc. We opened up with the machine gun and were already inside their perimeter. Chuck hosed the house full of them, and the idiots just kept coming out trying to run right at us. It was like fish in a barrel. There was about fifteen to twenty of them there, and most of them fell pretty easily running straight into the machine gun fire. The rest of us mopped up pretty easily. When all of them were dead, we took all the guns, ammo, and equipment we could carry. Most of the guns we seized were an odd assortment of pistols, shotguns, and hunting rifles. Nothing we could really use. We brought it all back to the Cav unit and traded it all for the machine gun, a M249 SAW, and all the ammo we could carry for them in the truck. They helped us weld a mount onto the bed of the truck for the machine gun and welded some light armor panels on the truck. Luckily, that old beast has the shocks to handle the weight.

Once that was all settled, we headed home. The Interstate was the fastest travel option. There were still some roadblocks set up by other groups, but thanks to the upgrades and machine gun, we blew right through them without much trouble at all. Whatever stolen supplies we acquired from them, we would try and drop off at the closest towns in exchange for meals or a place to sleep. It was a pretty quick trip outside of stopping for the roadblocks and returning the plunder to the local towns. It was our good deed. The only scary thing was to see how fucked up the world has gotten in such a short time. Everyday people are so weak and unprepared for anything like this. Even the small towns we passed through were littered with homeless camps and tents of desperate-looking people. We usually dropped off any food we found into these camps. We would drop off the guns we took off the roadblocks to either the local police, militia, or whoever was in charge of the town. Most people were pretty amicable, especially once they got over that a bunch of dudes in an armored pickup truck with a machine gun were waltzing right into their town giving out free stuff. Most of this stuff was stolen from people in their towns or people trying to get there anyways. It was only right. Some of these towns tried to pay us or barter for the items, but as far as we were concerned, we weren't in it for the rewards. Like I said, we were just doing what was right. One of the little towns on the way, Reddick, tried to hire us to be their new town sheriffs. I guess they'd had a bunch of trouble with raiders coming over from Dwight off Interstate 55. We politely declined, as we all really needed to get home. From Reddick, it's a straight shot east on Route 17 to home. Only a couple of miles past nothing but cornfields. Some of the small towns in the county along Route 17 west of Kankakee appear to have organized themselves into militias and secured their towns. There were a few roadblocks set up on the side roads leading off of 17 to the towns, but they didn't bother us If we were just passing by and we didn't bother to stop and chat. In no time at all we were back in Kankakee. Even on our side of town, things looked desolate and nearly deserted already. We had to cut a beeline straight across town to get out to Momence to get Hoover's family and guns. Luckily, we had his wife to drive his truck and transport all the gear in a big trailer.

We spent a few nights out there and caught our breath a bit. The Momence area wasn't too bad at first, but we kept hearing reports of raiders going up and down the river hitting properties close to the riverbank. Rumor was that these groups were coming from over the Indiana State line, and the groups were growing larger and larger. We considered joining the "Bordertown Militia" that was being organized by the guy that owned the gun shop in town before it went to hell, but when we tried to make contact with them, they sounded a little too disorganized and vulnerable for our liking.

When word started reaching us of houses not too far from Hoover's getting raided, we decided it was time to move to my place in Kankakee. When we finally got our stuff ready to move out after a couple of days, things were noticeably worse in the area. When we rolled out of Hoover's place, we saw a few places on the river just down the road on fire already. We hoofed it back to Kankakee again. When we got to my house, it had been about a month since I had been there. My front door had been kicked in and the whole upstairs trashed and looted. Thankfully, I paid all that money to hide the entrance to the basement behind that *fake bookshelf, and all of my supplies were hidden safely behind the false wall in the basement.*

We spent another few weeks getting settled in. Didn't even leave the house for anything. I finally thought to get on the radios and start to see if I could reach anybody else out there. Tried the police scanner, and not surprisingly the air was completely dead. I spent a while trying to remember what frequencies you used to communicate. When I finally found a channel you were on, we heard you guys screaming about taking fire and where you were. The lads and I decided to suit up and get in the game, so we grabbed a couple six packs, started shotgunning brews, and set out to go save your sorry asses. And apparently not a second too soon, because we showed up right in time to save you from the royal buttfucking you guys were fixin' to take.

They shared a laugh and John told his old friend, "Well shit, man, I'm glad you guys were there. And I'm damn sure glad to have you here with us now. We can do a lot of good out there now."

Steve sat back, handed him one of the last beers from the bag, and said, "Well, you know how we do. Just point us in the right direction and let the dogs of war loose. We're here to fuck shit up and maybe help you take back this shithole town."

CHAPTER 12: KNIGHTS OF THE ROUND TABLE
Mid/Late August

As predicted, at first light, just before 6 A.M., they heard the noise of the main gates opening and watched two county vehicles filled with men roll out of the gate and take off into the surrounding area.

"Not a bad idea, man. Getting out into the surrounding area. Making our presence known. Surprised the county guys beat you to it," Steve told John.

John rubbed his eyes and said, "Everything has been happening so quickly; it's been hard to think ahead. And until this point, we haven't even had enough people to think about going outside the wire safely without great risk. Maybe it's time we start sending out regular patrols. Fall is going to be setting in soon, and it would be good to start expanding our area of influence before the cold weather settles in. I'll talk to everybody throughout the day and come to a decision."

"I'm down for that," said Theo, yawning, as he stepped from the tower ladder onto the roof and walked up to the LP/OP. "Caught the tail end of what you said, and I think it's a good idea. Gives us something to do when we're not up here being bored."

"What are you doing up here this early?" John asked Theo.

"Andrew and I switched guard shifts. He has some stuff he wanted to work on this morning, he said."

"Better be a new guard shift roster then..." John said with a laugh. "Okay, I'm going to bed. I'll figure stuff out later."

He and Steve gathered up their stuff and climbed down the tower. They headed back to the house and parted ways to get some sleep. He went upstairs to his room, took off his gear, kicked it off next to the bed and jumped in next to Dez, who was still fast asleep.

John slept until around 1 P.M., when he was slowly woken from his slumber by the normal sounds of the house. He stood up and stretched, got dressed, and went downstairs to begin his day. He first stopped in the kitchen and poured coffee into a thermos. Thankfully, just about everyone in the house shared John's addiction to coffee, and fresh pots were brewed and consumed throughout the day. A decent portion of his prepping budget for food also went to storing coffee and coffee beans in his basement. He went to find Andrew to go bounce some ideas off him. He found Andrew sitting down at his desk in the office.

Andrew was looking over a map of Kankakee, taking notes in a field notebook, and monitoring the HAM radio channels. He looked up and acknowledged John with a nod but continued his notes.

John sat down on the opposite side of the desk and said, "You're sure keeping busy."

Andrew said, "I have to, especially when you're not around, sleeping beauty. Otherwise, shit wouldn't get done around here!"

He answered, "Glad to know my second in command has everything on lockdown. And I'd like to bounce some ideas off you."

"I'm betting we're thinking along the same lines," said Andrew, "but go ahead. Fatboy."

He did not acknowledge his friend's insult and instead began: "First, we get the new crew settled in, add them to the LP/OP and guard roster schedules, and find everybody a job or project to do around the compound."

"Easy enough," replied Andrew.

"Next, we need to start preparing for winter. It may be a cold and snowy winter, which means a few months of being fucking miserable and doing absolutely nothing productive. We need to start preparing the guard towers and the LP/OP for cold weather; maybe insulation and blankets and heaters. Also, we should start stocking more firewood near all the houses."

Andrew said, "Sure. Easy enough. Gives us something productive to do for the next few weeks. We should also get some people on making sure we can get the next season of crops in before the winter, and how much we can preserve."

John continued, "On that note as well, I wanted to start reaching out to see who is still around in our area. Expanding our area of influence will help make some new friends. See how many people are still alive. I figured we could start sending out daily patrols once or twice a day. Rotating each group: Us, the county, and the city guys each take turns sending out patrols."

Andrew told him, "I like it, I do. But under one condition: We can't compromise the security of this compound. And we can't turn into a fucking Salvation Army for every charity case that shows up. It's only a matter of time once we put ourselves out there and make it known that we're sitting pretty up here well fed, armed, and fat and happy with power and running water, that people will show up at our gates with some sob story begging for shelter. We can't let anyone else in, or we risk ruining everything we have now. It's cold-hearted I know, but me and my kids staying alive is more important."

John thought for a moment, then said, "I agree. And it's a tough choice, but you're right. I figured once we figure out who is out there, we can start making these streets a little safer. Get someone we trust in power out there, give them some of our seized weapons and supplies, maybe set up a shelter in one of the churches or schools that can hold a bunch of people. We might even be able to start a barter market out in one of the parks to get a local economy going."

Andrew interjected, "Don't get ahead of yourself now. That's a lot of work for just three months tops of decent weather left. One step at a time, big guy."

He answered, "Well, man...We wouldn't be in this good of shape if I never thought way too far ahead, right?"

They agreed to start going out on patrols of the area daily. To recon the area, make contact with anyone still alive out there, gather supplies, and set up friendly alliances. Andrew headed up to his guard shift in the LP/OP.

John decided to take a walk to check on the gate. He wanted to see if the group from the county this morning had returned yet. On his way out of the front door, Dez caught him by the hand. "Where are you headed?" she asked. He told her his plans to walk to check on the gate and see about the patrol from this morning.

"Okay if I tag along? I could use something to do, and plus we haven't gotten to spend much time together lately. I...just want to spend as much time with you as I can in case...you know. We just never know what might be our last moment together."

He grabbed her hand, leaned in and kissed her on the cheek. Holding her for a moment, he said, "I know. It's tough, I'm sorry. Come spend some time with me." They walked out of the gates of the compound together and headed up the street to the main gate of the base. They spoke to the group guarding at the gate, a group of young corrections officers he did not know. Most were holding shotguns or scoped hunting rifles that had been seized or found.

John asked the oldest-looking kid, "That group that went out this morning; did they come back yet?"

The kid answered him, "Yes sir, they got back 'bout half an hour ago. Sergeant Littrell led them out; he should be down at the second house." The kid pointed over in the right direction.

John thanked him, and he and Dez walked over to the house. The man in question stepped out. Sergeant Littrell was a short man with a greying short buzzcut; he was very well-liked and respected. He stopped at the edge of the yard and shook their hands.

"Glad you came looking for me. I was hoping I wasn't going to have to come find you to fill you in. We left at first light. At first, we were just going to look around the neighborhood, maybe check on the old man Stu that lives a few blocks down. He and his wife have kept to themselves since he retired, but even before all this, I liked to check in on him. When we got to their house, it looked like they had left and hadn't been home in quite some time. We checked the house for supplies but didn't find much other than a few gas cans and some canned food and a little bit of ammo left near his gun safe. After that, we checked around the neighborhood. Talked to a few of the neighbors. Some houses still have power, and there's a few families all holed up together. We gave them the food and told them to come find us if there was any trouble."

John said, "Well, that's a good start. And some good news to start it off with. I'm glad to hear it all went well."

Littrell shifted his body slightly and changed the tone of his voice. "Well...It' s not all good news, Johnny. After not having much to show for supplies in that neighborhood, the guys wanted to head up to Bud's Ammo Shop to see if we could grab some ammo and maybe some guns for the corrections guys guarding the gate. As you can see, they're a bit under armed...anyways, well...when we got there...It wasn't good...He's dead, brother. His shop door was blown wide open, and everything was smashed apart. We found him upstairs in his apartment. It looks like someone made him open up the safe and then shot him in the chest with a shotgun...then they carved him up. It was some sick shit, man...Look, I'm sorry, I know you guys were close. The guys gave him a proper burial. I'm just glad you didn't have to see it."

John stood there in shock for a moment, at a loss for words. Dez squeezed his hand, hoping to help in some small way. He finally said quietly, "Dammit...If only he would have come with me when I offered...none of this would have happened...stubborn old asshole."

Littrell told him, "It wasn't a total loss. It looks like whoever did this was just in it for money and the guns. His safe and gun safes were the only things cleared out. We managed to take his reloading bench and presses and load it into one of the trucks. We should be able to start making our own ammo once it gets set up. The old man had quite a stash of brass, buckets of powder, and bullets. It will keep us busy for quite a while. I think the city guys plan on going out tomorrow. Besides looking deserted, the neighborhoods around here seem pretty quiet. All the people that are still alive seem to be holed up and afraid to come out of hiding. Hopefully we can start to change that. Together."

They shook hands and parted ways.

John and Dez took a long walk of the perimeter to give him time to think and cool down a bit. They stopped again to survey the towers overlooking the front gate, while John made notes about how to make it acceptable for a cold winter. They talked to the kids guarding the gate and asked what they could use or what they needed.

One said, "A machine gun would be cool. We know you've got some already."

John told the kid, "Well, next one we find can go right up here," with a bit of a chuckle.

They also took requests for other odd items, like, "Hey, if you find 'this brand' of dip or chewing tobacco/cigarettes, liquor/candy bars, etc." He and Dez shared a few laughs about the requests.

"Some people out there haven't eaten in days, and we've got guys asking for candy bars," Dez said. "Reminds me of being overseas. Some of the kids in these half-destroyed villages we'd patrol through. Their village is on fire and in ruins, and these kids ask for water bottles and candy. It was such a trip."

He answered, "I guess we all need something to distract us from the things that should be bothering us…"

They both took notes of needed and "wanted" items and observations about the gate *(-Reinforce gate with steel rebar?)*, guard towers (*-more sandbags??*) and other random items (*QRF roster?*) as they walked. After walking the perimeter of the whole base, they headed back to the compound.

INTERLUDE SEVEN: LAST LEG OF THE MARATHON

Unknown date- Near the Idaho/Oregon Border

Denise and Richard hugged the small Highway 95 along the border of Idaho. Unfortunately, it was not the quick home stretch to their son they had hoped for. Several times, they had to pull off the highway onto side roads and frontage roads to avoid roadblocks or vehicle pileups that looked too suspicious. The last time Richard stopped, they pulled off to the side of the road. Richard said his back was bothering him from sitting for so long. He stretched a bit, and he decided to let Denise drive so he could ride shotgun and watch the road with a pair of binoculars and scan ahead for the threats that kept popping up. Luckily, they still had plenty of daylight left. He checked his watch, and it was only 11 A.M. They ate a quick lunch on the side of the road and packed up. Richard pulled himself up into the passenger seat and cradled his shotgun in his lap, and they got on their way. As much as they had hoped to feel safer in the open country out in the West, the increasing number of roadblocks and checkpoints started to bother them. They continued along the highway slowly, not making the fast progress they had before on the wide-open interstates. The highway was narrower and more winding through the hills, making them have to slow their pace even where there were no roadway obstructions.

They continued up through the highway until they reached the river crossing that would take them over the Oregon border. They luckily found the smaller border town called Nyssa on the Oregon side, instead of having to continue north to the Interstate crossing in the larger towns of Fruitland and Ontario. They turned down the smaller highway to cross the Snake River over to the Oregon State side. The road appeared clear until they reached the bridge to cross the river. There was a sharp bend just before the bridge, and by the time they rounded the curve, it was too late –

they came face to face with a roadblock. A flatbed trailer piled with sandbags and metal blocked the road, and five or so men holding rifles blocked their passage. Denise slammed on the brakes, stopping only ten to fifteen feet from the makeshift barrier.

The man who appeared to be the leader held his hand out in a "Stop" motion. He slung his rifle, hopped down from the trailer, and walked slowly to the truck. Richard casually unholstered his pistol and held it close to the passenger door at his side. The man studied the truck's occupants from underneath the brim of his cowboy hat. He put his hands up in a non-threatening gesture as he approached the passenger side. The men on the barricade still held their rifles at the low ready pointed in their direction.

The man slowly shuffled over to Richard's side and up to the open window. "Where are you two old folks headed to? Coming from Boise?" he asked.

Richard was apprehensive as he answered, "No. Came from the east. Need to get to Bend." He tried to keep it vague.

The man, looking slightly puzzled, answered, "All the reports say the big cities are getting bad, and we're too close to Boise here to take any chances. We aren't taking any more guests or refugees in town."

Richard answered quickly, "Sir, you seem like a sensible fellow. We are just trying to get to our son's ranch over near Bend. We've come a long way and just need to pass through."

The man answered, "I'd like to believe you, but we can't be too careful now. Especially with you hauling that big camper. We can't allow you into town rolling what might fit twenty people inside to hop out and kill all of us in our sleep."

Richard was getting slightly agitated. "Look, sir, I'm too old to deal with stuff like that. I just need to get to the Kirkpatrick Ranch outside Bend. If you men will let us through, you can even escort us through your town, and we will be on our way and out of your hair."

The man said, "That sounds fair..." He scratched his chin "But not without taking a look through your camper. Make sure you have no surprises waiting on us in there."

Richard cut him off. "You're not searching our car." He slid his Glock slowly up the side of the door, still hidden from the sight of the man in the cowboy hat.

The man finally said, "Okay, okay, I can let you through, but not without a price... for sending one of our men to escort you. Its gonna cost you. Coins, bullets, or food."

Richard said, "Fine. We'll pay the toll, as long as it gets us out of town safely." He reached into the glovebox, pulled out a few silver coins, and handed them to the man.

The man examined the coins, nodded, and motioned to the trailer to move.

The truck was rolled out of the way to create a gap in the road big enough to fit the trailer through onto the bridge and Denise nudged the truck and camper through. Richard watched the rearview mirror as one of the men from the checkpoint hopped on a horse tethered to one of the poles and galloped to follow them. The kid on the horse had a shotgun slung on his back and a pistol on his hip. He passed in front of them and kept them at a slow pace as they came through town.

Denise sighed. "They seem friendly enough."

Richard grunted back, "Yeah. I figured we'd have to pay a toll to get across the river...but that was just too easy. The guy didn't even haggle with us when I handed him a few silver coins."

"How much did you give him?" Denise asked.

"Oh, just a little handful I grabbed. Probably not even five or six coins."

"About a hundred bucks isn't a small toll," she said.

"Yeah, but that isn't much nowadays," Richard said.

The town was small and lively. There were people walking the streets, and there was open fruit stands in an open-air market in the open square along the main route they drove. There didn't appear to be electricity, but it was hard to judge during daylight. Most of the townspeople didn't make eye contact with them as they slowly passed, but several did examine their truck and large camper. It was a large spectacle, but thankfully, no longer looked brand new and shiny due to the long journey which had caked mud, dirt, and grime on the sides of the camper.

Denise and Richard both noticed the people eying their rig. "I don't like us getting stared at like a meal ticket..." she said quietly. Richard just nodded and continued to keep an eye around them.

The town was still small; the population sign stated the population was approximately 3,300, but he figured it was probably a third of that now. In a few blocks, the main buildings of town got further in between, and they neared the edge of town. The kid on the horse guiding them pulled to the side and pointed down the road. He tipped his hat, turned his horse around, and galloped back into town quickly.

Denise picked up the pace toward the edge of town, nearing a small gas station at the town limits. Suddenly, they came upon another roadblock. This time a bunch of cars and trucks blocked the roadway. Another group of armed men stood guard here. A different man walked up to the passenger window and said, "We're gonna need something to convince me to let you through."

Denise told him, "We already paid the men at the bridge! Now let us through."

The man said, "You think a few pieces of silver is enough to get you by? That was barely enough to let you into town. Now you gotta really pay if you wanna leave here...alive." The man smiled, showing yellowing teeth. He stepped closer to Richard at the passenger side window. "Now, I think if you drop that big camper here...that should be enough to buy your freedom. The camper and everything in it, and you'll be on your way..."

Richard answered in a low tone, "So...our camper and everything in it? Now what guarantees we get out of here alive?" His voice got quieter and quieter, prompting the man to continue to inch in closer and closer. Richard, whose arm was now hanging out of the open window, leaned ever so slightly out of the window. The man, who was now close enough to smell the chewing tobacco on his breath, didn't realize his mistake until it was too late. Richard reached out with his right arm, wrapping the man into a headlock and pulling him up partly into the window. He left hand now held his Glock 21 to the man's temple. "GO!" he yelled to Denise, who was already on it. She kicked the big truck into gear and stepped on the gas. The truck went rearing forward, gaining speed and closing the twenty or thirty feet toward the closest car blocking the road out of town. The big truck had gained enough speed that when it collided with the car, the ramming bars pushed it out of the way, tearing it off to the side and nearly colliding with the men operating the roadblock. Still in shock, the men on the roadblock unholstered their weapons and raised their rifles and began shooting at them. Once the car had been cleared, the truck gained speed quickly and opened a wider gap, leaving the town in their dust. Richard still held the man in a headlock; he was attempting to struggle but was losing the battle, having been caught completely off guard. Richard's old man strength and big bear paws clutched him tightly. The man's kicking and flailing feet slowed down as he lost consciousness. Bullets were still flying at them from the blockade. No shots were very accurate, but several hit the back of the camper (the biggest target). A few stray shots came too close for comfort. One struck the rearview mirror on the driver's side, and another struck the now unconscious man still in Richard's chokehold. He finally let him go, and he toppled out of the window and off the side of the road. Richard didn't know if he was still alive, and truthfully, he didn't want to know.

They both let out a huge sigh of relief as they sped down the small highway away from town. A roadside sign told them, "BEND 270 MILES." Richard checked his watch; it was barely past noon, and there was no more need to stop or delay progress.

"Maybe five more hours' drive if we keep a good pace," he said, consulting his roadmaps. Denise picked up speed on the open highway to make up time. They still had to turn off onto side roads before they reached towns, villages, or any other larger population centers. The incident in Nyssa had increased their paranoia, despite being so close to their son. Luckily, Highway 20 passed through sparsely populated country, and they only passed by a few tiny villages in their next few hours of driving.

After about four hours, despite turning off onto side roads several times to avoid oncoming vehicles or what looked like ambushes or roadblocks, they were very close to Bend. The Kirkpatrick Ranch was near the edge of the Deschutes National Forest, in heavily wooded and hilly terrain. When they got close, Richard turned on the small radio and tried to make contact with Bill Kirkpatrick. After a few attempts on the radio, Bill's voice finally came through; it crackled, but there was still a strong signal. "You guys must be close, I hear you loud and clear on my end!" Bill sounded excited.

Richard answered him, "We're not far at all now. Maybe twenty miles or so. Can you meet us at the edge of your property? We always have a hard time finding the driveway."

Bill said, "I'd guess maybe half an hour, right? I'll be out waiting on my horse. Luke is out hunting. He should be back tonight. See you two old folks in a few. Out."

Denise looked over and said, "Thank God. It's good to hear a friendly voice again for a change."

In a little over half an hour, they pulled onto the small road that was closest to the Kirkpatrick Ranch. This country was hilly, with thick forests and narrow roads, which limited their mobility in the large pickup and oversized camper. They finally came upon the small clearing which led to the Kirkpatrick Ranch's driveway. Bill Kirkpatrick sat on his horse at the edge of the road and waved enthusiastically as they approached. He rode up alongside the car and leaned in and gave Denise a big hug. "So good to see you two alive and all in one piece!"

"Glad we called ahead; your sign is gone. We would have never remembered where to turn!" Denise said.

Bill explained that he had taken down the large wooden sign next to their mailbox that said the family name and ranch. "Yeah, didn't want to attract any more attention than needed, even though we're a bit off the beaten path. Now let's get you two old folks up the hill and into the house. You both look exhausted." Bill silently examined the state of the truck and camper as they passed him on the small driveway and headed up the hill. Bill noted the mud caked on the camper and truck, and also the fresh bullet holes and broken mirror. He even saw what he thought looked like blood smeared on the passenger side door.

Once Denise pulled up the hill through the thick stretch of woods, they emerged into a much larger and flatter clearing. Bill owned a fairly large ranch where he raised a small herd of cattle, horses, a few dairy and beef cows, and a few acres of crops. His ranch settled into a small valley clearing that had several streams running through it, and his property backed up to the large Deschutes National Forest.

Denise pulled up into the large gravel lot and parked the truck near the house. Bill stepped off his horse and again greeted them both with big hugs. "You both look terrible, to be honest. I'm glad you made it. Why don't you come on in, get washed up and have a bite to eat? Then you two can go get some sleep. You're safe now. When Luke gets back, we can unload the camper and take care of moving your stuff in."

Denise and Richard grabbed their small bags form the front of the truck and walked in the ranch house. They were greeted by a flurry of hugs and kisses from Susan Kirkpatrick, Luke's wife, Hannah, and the several dogs in the house. It was already close to 7 P.M., so they hurried and showered and changed clothes, and ate a quick dinner around the table with the family.

At around 8, Bill excused himself to go check the perimeter of the ranch and check on the livestock. Richard offered to go with him, but he said, "No my friend, you and Mama Bear are in *desperate need of some beauty rest. There will be plenty for you to help me with when you're rested. Get some sleep, and Luke will see you in the morning."*

Hannah offered to come with him instead. Bill put on his coat and cowboy hat and grabbed his rifle and headed out the door with Hannah following behind with her Mini-14 rifle slung on her back. Denise and Richard went to the guest room and laid down in bed and were both quickly asleep.

After finishing checking the perimeter of the ranch, Bill and Hannah checked on the livestock in the barns and horses in the stable. It was nearly completely dark as they finished feeding the horses. As they walked back to the house, they noticed that the light was on in the small workshop shed closest to the house. They figured that Luke must have finally returned from his hunting trip. They walked to the shed and knocked on the door. Luke answered back, "Come on in, working on skinning this big beast." Bill and Hannah stepped in and greeted Luke, who was wearing a pair of overalls with a butcher's apron to cover his clothes. Luke was skinning a large bull elk he had shot on his trip up into the mountains that day. It was an impressive 600-pound nearly mature male. They stopped and listened to him tell the tale of stalking the elk.

Luke said, "It's actually pretty tough to track and flush these guys out into the open by myself. I'm so used to going in groups. I picked up the trail in the late morning and tracked a small group into a valley a few miles over. I wanted to try to get around and start flushing them back toward where I had parked the truck, but while I was making my way around, they pulled out into a clearing by the river. I had a perfect shot lined up from only about 150 yards. I got a single shot through the big guy's lung. He stumbled toward me for about forty or fifty yards (which did help put him in the right direction) before he finally died. I got him rolled onto my tarp and dragged him to the sled until I could get him tied up into a tree near the closest trail. I had to hump back over the valley to get the truck, which took me a good hour or so. Then I had to find a trail wide enough to get the truck as close to the tree where I had him hanging as possible. I was able to get right up to it and drop him into the bed of the truck. After a long and winding drive back, I made it home just after dark."

Bill whistled, "That's a pretty darn good size there, boy. Any bigger, and you would have had to quarter him and miss out on this beautiful pelt. We'll see if the old lady wants to make a blanket. That should add a couple hundred pounds of good meat for the winter. Proud of you, boy."

Luke smiled, still working on butchering the elk.

"Oh, and your parents made it in tonight; forgot to tell you! Not sure if you saw the camper or not on your way in. They had a rough ride in. They're fast asleep in the guest room."

Luke said, "I noticed the camper on the way in. It's okay, I'll see them in the morning. My back is killing me from the dragging and lifting anyways. We should probably get a hold of my little brother though."

Bill replied, "I figured I'd do that when I got back inside. I'll leave you to finish up with all this." He left Hannah there and walked back to the house, where he got on the HAM radio to contact Luke's brother to give him the update that his parents had finally arrived safely.

"Thanks for the update Bill; I'm glad to know they made it there safely," John told him over the radio. "Sorry contact has been spotty. We've been a little busy out here. It's not exactly quiet. How are things out by you?"

Bill answered him, "Ohh, not too bad. I have minimal contact with the outside world, thankfully. I get updates from time to time when I check in on my neighbors. It's worse closer to the cities. Bend is falling apart like most bigger cities. Not enough to go around and too many mouths to feed. It's going to be bad when the harsh winters hit the hills. It hasn't been as bad as California. That whole communist state imploded when the government wasn't there to give handouts anymore. Utah you already saw. The Mormons own as much of that state as they can hold, but we've heard some rumors about big troubles in Salt

Lake City. Something about cartels and whatever people on the radio keep are calling a 'black autumn' or something like that."

*   "Stay safe and keep in touch, Bill," John finished. The line went silent after that.*

CHAPTER 13: THE NEW LORDS OF THE LAND
Late August/Early September

The next few weeks were a flurry of motion and activity. Patrols went out every day, sometimes multiple times a day. Each time, they began to venture out further and further. They made contact in the nearby neighborhoods with survivors holed up in their houses or makeshift shelters. They made maps of occupied settlements and abandoned houses. Some abandoned houses and businesses were raided (with much heated debate) for supplies. They argued that the good outweighed the bad, as most of these supplies went to the groups of survivors to help sustain themselves and gain favors with the smaller groups of survivors that had started to band together within neighborhoods. A few small gangs had also banded together, causing trouble for these other peaceful settlements, and small armed conflicts broke out.

One of the main goals once an area was pacified was to help set up infrastructure and install a small local barter economy. They assisted in setting up some small farmer's markets. They offered security for the events. Some members sold or bartered items at these markets, and some offered services, such as using solar panels to charge car batteries for power.

As much as they had good news, there was just as much bad news. There were more and more incidents of patrols being shot at, getting in heavier and more sustained firefights, and taking casualties. In the last two weeks of August, patrols had taken six minor casualties. Four men had been shot in extremities like legs or arms, and two had been hit in the chest, only stopped by their ballistic armor and bulletproof vests. Luckily, the patrols were able to break contact and get back to the compound in time for the men to get critical lifesaving care from the aid station. The standard operating procedure (SOP) had been for the patrols to break contact in these incidents when taking fire and retreat, unless the firefight was only a single shooter or small group that was manageable to fight by the size of the patrol. The patrol leaders would report back to the base and report the location of heavy or unmanageable contact marking on maps of all the respective groups (the Compound, Kankakee City, and County). Most of the heavier resistance occurred the further east they went. Patrols had mostly pacified the areas on the west and south sides of the city closest to the Compound. The areas up to the river and leading up to downtown had become the border of the pacified areas, or the "limit of advance" as most of the men with tactical or military experience called it.

After a few close calls with patrols being ambushed, the worst was finally realized. On the last day of August, a very small patrol of county deputies was ambushed. This was different than before: The vehicle wasn't across the pre-established limit of advance of the borders of the pacified areas. It happened a few blocks inside the pacified zone. The two-vehicle patrol was driving a load of seized food to a small shelter that had been set up in a fire station across from Jeffers' Park just off the river. The meeting was supposed to happen in the park. When the county vehicles pulled inside the fence line to the park, an unknown gang opened fire on the vehicles with automatic gunfire. The vehicles were getting shredded by large caliber rounds. The first vehicle took the brunt of the onslaught. Three of the four occupants of the front vehicle were killed almost instantly by the gunfire. In the rear vehicle, the driver and passenger were both struck and killed by gunfire. The front vehicle caught on fire, but the rear passenger, a young corrections officer named Blanchette, was severely wounded but was able to crawl out of the back seat and flop onto the ground behind the vehicle. He crawled over to the rear vehicle and pulled himself into the front passenger seat of the second vehicle, where he lost consciousness.

Blanchette later told them that he thought he heard voices yelling in Spanish over the gunfire. One of the other rear passengers of the rear vehicle who was not struck by gunfire, a middle-aged female corrections officer named Jeanne Dwyer, jumped into the driver's seat and tore out of the park, crashing through the fence in reverse and sped off back to the Compound. When they arrived at the gates of the Compound, only six minutes had elapsed since they had taken fire. The vehicle rolled into the Compound and the injured officers in the second vehicle were rushed out into the field hospital next to the inner walls of the Compound.

When word reached the Compound members of the ambushed vehicle that came through the gate with critical casualties and wounded, John, Andrew, Theo, Dez, and Big Rob rapidly geared up and hopped in the Tank and began to roll out.

John jumped out at the field hospital to get a quick report of the ambush location from those who came back in. Officer Dwyer was out front of the field hospital building throwing up; she was being held by one of the county deputies. She stopped vomiting long enough to tell him where the ambush occurred and said, "Blanchette...only one who made it back to us from the front vehicle...still out there...He said he heard Spanish...It all happened so fast..." He patted her on the shoulder and ran back to the Tank and slid back into the driver's seat. Steve's pickup rolled in next to him. Chuck was up in the bed, re-mounting the M60. The Bros were still pulling on their tactical gear and strapping on body armor. Hoover in the passenger seat was still attempting to pull on one of his boots.

"If you're rolling out there, you guys aren't going alone. We got your backs," Steve said.

John nodded to the truck and answered, "There's still a county squad out there, and three bodies unaccounted for. Let's go."

The Tank and Steve's truck with the Boys tore out of the still opened gate to the base and sped toward Jeffers Park. They didn't bother waiting for the inevitable rush of county deputies that would most likely be rushing to also come to the aid of their fallen comrades outside the wire.

The Tank and Silverado rolled into the park only a few minutes after clearing the front gate. The sheriff's squad car was still on fire. Steve pulled the truck in front to take up a blocking position, with Chuck scanning the area and rooftops with the machine gun. John, Andrew, Rob, and Dez jumped out to check the squad car for survivors while Theo stayed in the Tank's turret also scanning the area.

Rob doused the car with a small fire extinguisher to put out the fire and the others began checking the car. Sadly, all three of the men in the squad were dead, riddled with bullet holes. They had been stripped of their weapons and body armor, and their clothing was torn. The supply package in the rear of the SUV had been taken as well. There were footprints in the wet grass leading to the two-story Glade Plumbing building next to the park.

John, Andrew, Rob, Dez, Steve, Kyle, and Hoover ran up and cleared the building. Up on the roof, they located piles of spent brass casings.

"This is where they opened up from," Steve said.

Andrew picked up a casing and said, "It's all 7.62. Probably AKs. And with all this brass dumped, it was either thirty dudes up here, or we're dealing with some more full auto AKs..."

Kyle let out a loud "Faaackk me, dude..." and Rob blew out a long whistle. They all moved back down to the cars out in the park.

Four county squads rolled into the park. Lieutenant Hunter jumped out of the lead vehicle, looking very pissed off. He didn't say anything to the group at first, instead telling his men, "Get their bodies into the cars. And cover them up for fuck's sake." Surveying the damaged squad, he finally looked toward the group. "Well. What the fuck happened here, boss?"

John answered, "Bill, shots came from the roof of the Glade building. We found piles of spent casings. Could have been twenty or thirty people firing from up there. Hundreds and hundreds of casings. Maybe full auto AKs. Looks like a set up ambush to me."

Hunter, still looking pissed off, but also showing the mental anguish on his face, said, "Set up? How'd they know they would be here? Oh, fuck." Hunter turned to some of his men. "Go send a group to check the fire station across the street. FUCKING NOW!"

A group of ten deputies ran across the street to check the fire station. A short time later, one of the deputies came jogging back over; a middle-aged, overweight deputy named Dan Hill. "Ehh… It's not good, LT. Been doing this job fifteen years and that is just fucked up…They're all hacked to bits. Men, women, and children. It's a goddamn bloodbath in there…"

Hunter turned back to the group and said, "What the fuck is going here? Why is it that every fucking time we lose people, it's my fucking guys getting killed? Fucking figure it out!" Hunter stopped speaking abruptly and walked off toward the fire station still mumbling to himself. When he was out of earshot, Deputy Hill told the group, "You guys should head back home. We can take care of the clean-up from here. It might help the guys have some closure giving us something to do. Plus, when you're around, Hunter is more of an asshole than usual. A lot of the guys still don't like you for making us do that run downtown when we first got here. And this won't exactly help anything here." Hill cracked a weak half smile and patted John on the shoulder.

The group from the Compound loaded up silently and headed back home. They only stopped briefly to yell at the young Corrections guys keeping watch on the gate for leaving it wide open.

"Do your fucking job, asshole! You wouldn't leave the cell doors open at the jail, would ya?" Andrew yelled from the passenger window of the Tank.

They moved on to the Compound and parked the vehicles. Everyone went their separate ways, while John, Andrew and Rob walked to the aid building to check on everybody. The news was mostly good, and Blanchette was stable. Andrew was uncharacteristically emotional, having worked with Blanchette at the jail.

"He's a good kid...I hope he makes it."

This event caused the next week to be a rough time for everyone. Patrols didn't go out at all. People felt stir crazy, but it was agreed upon by the leaders of each group that everyone needed to recuperate from the trauma and refocus. After the funerals for the five killed in the ambush, the bodies were buried in the field outside of the base. Their graves were marked with wooden crosses with their names written in marker.

After everyone had settled for a few days longer, they all met to refocus on the tasks at hand. Some of the leaders of each of the respective groups had portrayed the opinion that they were very pleased that nearly half of the city had been calmed down or pacified in the month since they had begun their patrols, but John and the other members of the Compound weren't overly pleased with the half-measure. Although nearly half the city had been pacified of enemy groups, very little of the groups of civilians they had come across were able to sustain themselves. Only a couple of small groups within some neighborhoods had formed local defense forces or a neighborhood watch to protect themselves.

"Too many people out there weren't prepared for something like this," remarked Andrew in a private meeting of the members of the Compound one evening after returning from a patrol. "Winter is going to hit these people hard, and we can't keep raiding places, stores, and abandoned homes to give these people supplies. It's not a sustainable practice. These people are going to die over the winter if something doesn't change," Andrew continued.

Everyone else was silent, not having any good solutions to the problem. Finally, John spoke up to the group in response to Andrew: "I want to continue over the river and through downtown and continue the mission of getting the whole town under control, but it doesn't look like we can even control what we have now. We need to shift our focus to how we can help keep these people alive over the winter."

Andrew told him, "That's great and all, but the real question becomes: How do we do that without any more of our people dying?"

It was all quiet for a moment amongst the group. The losses sustained during the most recent ambush were still fresh. John broke the silence and said, "The biggest problem besides that: Who is out there with that amount of firepower? And who has the balls to ambush two marked police cars full of well-armed cops?"

Theo said, "Look Johnny, I'm all for going out there and hunting down the assholes who killed our people, but we can't fight an enemy we don't even know. We gotta figure out who the hell is out there dumping fully auto AKs at people."

Kyle added, "Whoever is doing it is pretty well organized. They knew where to hit, where to shoot from, and were well coordinated. They were in and out without a trail by the time we got there. All in what, ten minutes or less?"

The discussion was opened on the floor now. What to do with this new threat. The unknown enemy. Ideas were thrown around by everyone. Some suggested strengthening the borders of the "pacified" zones of the city, sending people to man roadblocks or chokepoints along the borders of the zones under their control.

Dez suggested paying the small local militias in these areas to man the roadblocks, but the idea was shot down in conversation by the others because it would be a logistical nightmare. The several small groups were all too loosely organized, and most were too weak or small in numbers to manage a roadblock along with the peacekeeping in their local neighborhoods. These were all costly decisions, and by the end of the meeting, nobody had any better solutions to the problems than they had come into the conversation with.

A few of the guys volunteered to go out into the areas across the river and scout out things on foot. A few times over the next week, a group took one of the more incognito vehicles to drop one of the guys dressed in plain clothes to walk around the streets of downtown. The goal was to see what buildings or businesses were occupied, and where any of the enemy gangs may be coming from. Theo and Rob volunteered to take the first walk.

John and Andrew went to the closest tall building they could reach and climbed up to the roof to get a good vantage point over the downtown area and provide sniper cover. The backup vehicle acting as their QRF (Quick Reaction Force) consisted of Steve, Hoover, Old Sarge, and Chuck manning the machine gun in Steve's truck. Old Sarge had practically begged to finally get out on a patrol, so he replaced Kyle in the front seat of the truck last minute. He was a good fit to match up with Steve's group they called "The Bros." They were all military veterans and had each done combat tours overseas like Old Sarge. The Bros had adopted Old Sarge as one of their own and took to calling him "Old Man," which he had accepted as their term of endearment.

This particular afternoon in the early September, they decided to move over the bridge past the hospital and climb the tall public library building overlooking the center of the downtown area. Once they made it up to the overwatch position and scouted the immediate area, finding the streets mostly clear and quiet, he radioed to the others letting them know that they were set in position.

The QRF truck slowly crept through side roads and disappeared into the covered underground parking garage of the PNC bank where the first vehicle was parked. Once they arrived in their position, Theo and Rob set out from there on the walk. They wore regular jeans and large old jackets covering their pistols. Rob also grabbed a shopping cart that had been abandoned in the parking lot nearby. At first glance they would look like a pair of homeless vagrants walking around looking for trash and scrap to pick up. It was a good enough cover for them to walk around unbothered. They didn't seem to have to worry though, as the downtown area appeared to be abandoned. There was absolutely nobody out in the square where the local farmers markets were held, or near the fountain next to the train depot where the music festivals were held years ago: All were abandoned and beginning to look run down.

John and Andrew scanned the area from the rooftop of the library with their rifle scopes. "The whole downtown is abandoned; that's crazy, man," John said to Andrew, who thought for a moment and answered, "I don't know...I guess there's just nothing down here worth looting anymore. And apparently none of these shops or storefronts were safe enough to take shelter in. Who knows?"

John said, "Well...maybe there's good news. If we need to shoot anybody, hopefully we can draw them down here into the square. It could reduce the possibility of collateral damage—less innocent civilians getting killed in an ambush than if we brought the fight in to those neighborhoods."

"Even though we don't want it to come to that, not a bad idea," Andrew answered.

After about two hours of Theo and Rob walking around on foot and looking through the storefronts in the downtown area south of Court Street and south down Schuyler Avenue, they had found little of use, and the consensus was that the downtown area and square had been mostly abandoned, except for a few homeless vagrants sleeping or wandering about looking for shelter and food. The banks south of the open square had been abandoned and long since looted. There were burn marks near the safes and the outside ATMs had been pulled out or pried open.

Theo radioed up to them, "This area is all pretty dead. I think we're wasting our time out here. We're gonna head back."

John answered, "Sounds good; head on back. Make sure you aren't being watched, and we'll load up and head back home."

Theo and Rob slowly made their way back up to the PNC Bank parking garage. They moved straight across the large open farmer's market parking loss to save time. Confident they weren't being followed, they opted to take the shortest and most direct route back to save time.

Rob said, "We can keep checking behind us; that way if someone pops out into this big open lot, we'll see them."

They made it back to the parking garage and greeted the guys in the QRF truck. They radioed back up to the two on the roof and waited for them to retreat back down from the roof next door. They talked with the guys in the truck to kill the time.

"Anything good out there?" asked Old Sarge.

"Nah. It's a ghost town out there. In two hours, we only saw a couple of people out; just bums looking for food or shelter to sleep. The storefronts and businesses are all looted and stripped up and down the whole main stretch. Nothing out there," Rob said.

Old Sarge said, "I hate to see it like this. You think all the people are dead, or what?"

Steve spoke up from the driver's seat and answered, "Well, I suppose there's almost no houses around. This area is mostly zoned for business, not residential. People are probably holed up in their houses, not wanting to leave their stuff. Other than the initial panic after the first few weeks of chaos where people went out and looted the stores for everything, I doubt too many people see the need to hang around here."

A short time later, John and Andrew arrived back in the parking garage. "Doesn't look like you guys were followed. It's dead out there. A little creepy quiet if you ask me," said Andrew to the group as they approached. "Let's get the fuck out of here...today's a wash. Nothing useful I guess."

They all loaded up in the two vehicles to head home. "Who wants to stop by the liquor store on the way home?" joked Steve, starting up the engine to the Old Silverado.

The two vehicles slowly rolled out of the parking garage and crept back to the main street. They decided to take a different road back than they had taken in to avoid being spotted again. Steve led them south down Schuyler down to the bridge on River Street. They crossed the bridge across the river quickly into the friendly territory and headed back west toward the Compound. They were completely unaware that they had been spotted crossing the bridge.

The large Hispanic gang leader was standing on the roof of a building at the southern edge of the downtown area—an old health department building on the 500-South block of Schuyler Avenue. He and his men had been watching across the river towards the area where they had last seen the well-armed white men with lots of guns. When the two large trucks sped past them on the main road, it had startled him. Once he realized that these two vehicles matched the rumors and reportings of the well-armed men's vehicles, he told some of his men, "Follow them. Rápido! And don't get spotted. Tail them back to wherever they are staying. Mark the location on the map and get back here. Don't let them see you. GO!"

INTERLUDE EIGHT: THE KING OF THE SECOND CITY

For many, the collapse of the country's economy was a pure nightmare. It was the Apocalypse that nobody truly thought was possible. For Juan Luis "El Leon" Garcia, this was the greatest time of his entire life. While the government and most of the municipal infrastructure was not able to sustain itself after the collapse of the economy, the criminal empire of the drug cartel was largely self-sustaining. The cartel and criminal underground world in Chicago and the other large metropolitan areas throughout the Midwest operated outside of the law, and further did not rely on the government.

When the city came toppling down into chaos, El Leon jumped at the chance to seize power in the city. The cartel controlled millions and millions of dollars in cash, liquid assets, narcotics, guns, and manpower. These items were now nearly invaluable during the chaos of a societal collapse. Juan Luis set plans into motion immediately, seizing power in the streets of Chicago. The cartel employed the local gangs as foot-soldiers to seize territory, food, water, and other valuable assets. The local gangs began taking over complete control of their neighborhoods. The police and fire departments were unable to maintain control of the neighborhoods and were all quickly either killed or driven out of the area completely. With government assets dwindling, police and fire assets were almost completely disbanded.

With almost no resistance to the expansion of his criminal empire, El Leon seized power throughout the entire south and west side of Chicago. Rival street gangs were either employed as soldiers or destroyed. The cartel had access to a large illegal firearms trade, and now without government interference, they had full access to fully automatic weapons, military firearms, heavy machine guns, grenade launchers, and rockets. With weapons fit for an army, the cartel and allied gangs began a crusade of epic proportions across the city of Chicago. Large roving bands of gang members were sent to rape and pillage neighborhoods that were not under the control of the cartel. Within two months of the collapse, the cartel completely controlled over half of the city of Chicago and all of the south suburbs. El Leon had also sent his men to raid the rich neighborhoods in the north end of the city and along Lake Shore Drive and the Loop. The richer neighborhoods had extensive resources and wealth for raiding, but many of these rich people had purchased protection from the local militia groups that had arisen, along with the remainders of the police and government officials. These had been a trouble for the cartel, despite their superior numbers and weaponry.

In a meeting with his inner circle one evening in late July, El Leon talked strategy with his most trusted advisors. "Don Jefe, señor," began one of his most trusted lieutenants from the Latin Kings street gang. He was known as "Flaco."

"The north has been giving us trouble, and we have lost many men fighting with the militias there. We have started to pay los pandillas negros to die there instead of our men."

El Leon said, "Keep working, hermano. Those rich gringos won't hold for long. Keep throwing everything you can at them. Their riches will be worth the sacrifices in the end." He turned to another one of his lieutenants, a tall skinny Latino gang banger that his men knew as "El Jefe," who controlled the Latin Kings gangs in the south suburbs before the collapse. "Jefito, I need you to take your men and start moving out of the city. The larger towns are also rich with supplies and money."

EL Leon pointed to the map on the table in front of them. "Joliet. It is large, but very rich. There are also many Latinos that will be sympathetic to our cause. They will fall into place very quickly. There is also the state prison, 'El Statesville' over there, where you can recruit more soldiers. Go liberate the men from the prison and make them fight or be killed. Our people will control the whole state soon, and eventually we will take the whole country from the gringos."

El Jefe tried not to show the offence he felt by being called "Jefito," but he dared not object. Among his gang, he was the leader; however, the cartel boss was the supreme leader of the Latino criminal underworld. Any hint of insubordination or disrespect toward EL Leon, and he would be beheaded in front of all his men. He studied the map, averting his gaze from El Leon. He pointed to another spot on the map and said, "Con permiso, pero what about here, Padron? **Kankakee**. It is the next largest city beyond Joliet, and straight down I-57 from the suburbs."

El Leon looked and said "Hmmm…I don't know anything about that city. We have some stash houses in the woods east of that city toward the State Line, but I do not have any dealings there. I suppose it is worth a look while you are liberating Joliet. Go ahead and send your people there as well, compa." El Jefe smiled and nodded, happy that his idea was accepted by EL Leon, whom he both greatly respected and feared.

"Si Padron. Gracias." Jefe took his leave from the group and jumped into the large SUV where one of his men was waiting to drive him back to his territory and brief his men.

It was a short drive to his headquarters in Harvey, a small but impoverished south suburb of Chicago. The streets were mostly cleared of vehicles and people traveling other than the vehicles owned by the gangs who controlled the area. His large SUV pulled into the hospital that his gang had taken over to be his headquarters after the collapse. The hospital had many rooms, supplies, and generators still providing power and hot water, making it a post-apocalyptic paradise. El Jefe had kept many of the employees of the hospital alive to provide services to his men. He had even kept the gringo and black doctors alive, contrary to El Leon's dreams of Latino racial superiority. He knew these doctors and nurses were all still very valuable. El Jefe briefed his most trusted leaders of the orders to take control of Joliet and Kankakee. His men were eager. They enjoyed the raping and pillaging as they entered new areas. His men did not enjoy the occupation of areas after the initial excitement of killing the men and raping the women and children. His men were practiced killers, and Jefe too enjoyed letting them off the leash. Many of his men had been broken out of the jails and prisons throughout the Chicagoland area and returned home to their previous gangs. Along with sympathetic Latino boys and families, their numbers had greatly expanded to the size of a small army.

He ordered his main force to mobilize down Interstate 80 toward Joliet, while he sent a smaller group with one of his gang leaders. "EL Toro" was a huge man who had just gotten out of prison. He'd gained fame in prisons as a vicious fistfighter. He was in the middle of serving a twenty-year sentence for rape and aggravated battery on a police officer when he was broken out. El Toro was not particularly smart, but he was fiercely loyal to his gang, and he had killed men before to prove his loyalty. He could be trusted with the task, or at least as much as any of his men, Jefe thought.

One of El Toro's men told them, "I got a cousin down in Kankakee; we can reach out to him. We can recruit all of our gente down there and raise our own army once we get there, eh?"

Jefe told the man and El Toro, "Do it if you can, amigos, but if you cannot, just scout the area out and report back to me. Once we are done with Joliet, we will come to you."

El Toro's man said, "It will be no problem, Jefe. Kankakee is nothing but poor morenos and dumb rich gringos by the river. We can probably buy los negros gangs' loyalty to fight for us."

Jefe nodded to the man and turned to El Toro. "Do what you have to do."

El Jefe took his large group down Interstate 80 and began his raids on the city of Joliet. His men killed, raped and pillaged everything they could.

El Toro's man said, "I spoke to my cousin before the cell phones went down, Toro. He said the gringo biker gangs down there, the 'Outlaws,' control a lot of the city. But they are only loyal to one color: Green. If we bring the cash, we can bribe them to help us.

Toro said, "I was in prison with a Nazi gringo who was a biker down there. We will see if we can find him when we get there."

Toro loaded up his vehicles with supplies and guns and took his small expeditionary force of twenty men with him. They set off down Interstate 57 south toward Kankakee. They bypassed several small towns on their way. El Toro, sitting in the front seat of the lead vehicle, took notes in a notebook of the names and views of the towns from the Interstate. After about an hour of driving, the small caravan of vehicles entered Kankakee from the interstate exit on the east side of town. The men stopped at a Shell gas station to check for gas. His men jumped out and looted the gas station for whatever food and alcohol was left. The city's main streets appeared empty, with garbage strewn about. Stray dogs roamed the streets.

After the men siphoned some gas from the underground tanks, El Toro turned to his man. "Where does this cousin of yours live?"

"He lives in this neighborhood they call 'the junction,' Toro. It's a little hood north of here."

The men mounted back up into their vehicles and took off on the main street called Court Street. They drove into the middle of the city, until they turned onto Greenwood Avenue. They again drove through neighborhoods that looked rundown and consisted mainly of poor housing projects. It reminded them of Harvey and the rest of the poorer south suburbs of Chicago.

"I almost feel home," El Toro remarked out loud to no one in particular. They continued up to where the street ended near a large graveyard and turned into a small neighborhood across from some railroad tracks. The small neighborhood was a square of four streets separated from the main road, with only one route in and out. The neighborhood had several large brick housing projects, one of which El Toro's man pointed to.

"That's it. My cousin Manny lives in that building."

The men stepped out of their cars. Nobody in the neighborhood rushed out to confront the group of Hispanic men carrying AK-47s. They entered the apartment building and were led to the upstairs apartment. Toro's man knocked on the door and loudly called out for Manuel. A short time later, a short pudgy Mexican man in a white T-shirt opened the door to the apartment. Manuel greeted his cousin with a hug and shook hands with El Toro. "I figured you would be down sometime soon, Primo. Come in!" He ushered in all of the men, who packed into the small apartment.

Manuel poured out shots of some cheap tequila from a bottle for some of them and sat down at the kitchen table. "Kankakee is ripe for the taking, Primo! The blacks have been beating up the police so bad that they have given up on this whole side of town. The gringo Nazi bikers have been taking everything they can downtown and south of town. They say that the police aren't even out anymore. There aren't many of them left." Manny took a shot of tequila and poured another for himself. "So, when are all of La Raza coming down to take the city over?"

Toro answered him, "We are it for now. We need to get in contact with the blacks and the bikers. We are going to bribe them to keep things under control until our boss can bring more men down."

Manny nodded as he took another shot. Then he said, "I must warn you, señor, there are some rumors of a group in the west. Gringos with big guns and lots of people somewhere on the west side of town."

Toro replied, "The boss will deal with that when he comes. It won't be a problem."

Manny added, "Also, there are rumors of Army men being seen in town, and helicopters and tanks. But I haven't seen them."

Toro stopped and scratched his chin. He pulled a satellite phone from his pocket that El Jefe had given to him. He stepped back into a bedroom to call El Jefe to notify him of the situation. The news of Army tanks and helicopters was concerning, and way above El Toro's level of competence. Toro was a fighter, not a general, like El Jefe, or the cartel bosses he answered to.

El Jefe finally answered the phone call after several attempts. Toro heard rapid gunfire and explosions in the background as Jefe spoke over the garbled phone line. "I'm a little busy out here, Toro, this better be fuckin' important!"

Toro yelled over the phone line, "Jefe, this city looks quiet at first look when we got here, but our boy's cousin says there are rumors of a well-armed militia that controls one whole side of town. He says that there have also been rumors of Army men being seen in town. Tanks and Helicopters and shit, hermano. This is above my head, Jefe. I need someone smarter than I am to plan for this shit."

Jefe cut him off. Gunshots and explosions could still be heard in the background, louder than before, "Toro, I chose you for this mission because you are a man of action. You get shit done. You don't need brains, I need shit done. I don't believe fucking rumors. Go find out for yourself and fucking handle it. This is no different than killing morenos on the streets of the hood back home."

The line went dead, and Toro hung the phone up, a little upset that Jefe hadn't given him any advice. He thought to himself for a moment, then took Jefe's words to heart. It was time to get shit done. In this new world, only the strong would survive. And Toro was very strong. He stepped out back into the living room and addressed him men, who were drinking tequila with their host Manny.

"Listen up pendejos!" he said in a raised voice, "Manny, I need you to help meet up with all of the gangs around here. At least our people first. We need information, and more people. Then, we are goin' to go out and find these gringos with the guns, and we are goin' to fucking kill them and rape their girls. We gonna kill everyone in our way, eh amigos?" The men all let out a loud cheer and continued toasting with their tequila.

The next day, Manny introduced EL Toro to one of the local Mexican street gang leaders, a fat Mexican who was nicknamed "Kool Aid." Kool Aid ran a small crew that was mostly young wannabe gang bangers that sold drugs and did small robberies for cash. Kool Aid told Toro, "If you want to be anybody out here, you better get friendly with the blacks out here, amigo. There's a lot more of them than there are of us. And they run the dope game out here. They the ones who ran out all the cops from this side of town when shit went crazy."

Toro told Kool Aid, "When my boss gets here, we won't have to worry about the blacks. For now, I just need them to not kill us while we are out moving around. Our main concern is the gringos on the other side of town."

Kool Aid replied quickly, "The white boys with all the guns and tanks and helicopters and shit? I don't know where the Army dudes are coming from, Ese. Probably the airport. But the other white boys with guns…Word on the streets is they was all pigs. Got the 5-0 squads and everything."

Toro smirked. "Good. That makes things easier. I love killing cops. Now where can I find them?"

Kool-Aid said, "I don't know. Somewhere on the west side of town. None of the bangers go that way. They say you don't pass the river wearing gang colors, or all them crazy ass white people with guns will shoot at you."

"Anywhere across the river then?" Toro said. "Where is a good place to cross? Somewhere we might find a few of the puercos to kill?"

Kool Aid told him, "I know a place. Some of the guys said they've seen some of their cars delivering supplies to this park down by this old fire station."

Toro smiled and only said, "Bueno. Take us there."

CHAPTER 14: PRE-EMPTIVE ATTACK

Mid-September

It was about 11:00 P.M. and John had just laid down. It had been a long but boring day of working with some of the others in the base to continue putting in crops and building greenhouses in every available open space within the walls. Everybody had been working since the early morning tilling the grounds that hadn't already been made into gardens, while others helped build greenhouses. No patrols had gone out today to add to the numbers of the workers. A few days prior, groups had gone out to scavenge window panes of glass and wood scraps and other building materials from the surrounding neighborhoods. Large industrial rolls of plastic were also found in one of the stores on the west side of town. They scavenged glass from windows in abandoned houses in the nearby neighborhoods to build large greenhouses and replace sheds in backyards, using every available space and patch of dirt within the walls.

Suddenly there was a loud "BOOM" that echoed through the entire compound, shaking the windows and walls. Instantly, one of the front gate guard towers exploded. The two young county corrections officers inside were flung thirty feet in the air. They were dead even before the bone-crushing impact of their bodies on the ground. Everybody who was still awake was in shock from the explosion that seemingly came out of nowhere. A machine gun began returning fire from the tower on the opposite side of the front gate. Finally starting to snap out of it, most of those within the walls of the base began to jump to the ready, donning body armor and ballistic vests. They ran to retrieve their rifles and other weapons.

Even though the Compound was the furthest from the gate, John could hear the explosions and gunfire clearly. He jumped out of bed, threw on clothes as fast as he could, grabbed his rifle, and sprinted downstairs and out of the house, forgetting his body armor and helmet in his rush. Several other members of the Compound were also sprinting down the street toward the front gate. As they approached it, the gunfire increased.

John looked up to see Chuck with one leg propped up on the sandbags, firing his M60 down outside the gate. He was screaming something to the other young city police officer that was in the tower with him. Although Chuck's words couldn't be heard over the barrage of gunfire, the other officer had begun to frantically ring the alarm bell mounted on the tower while trying to take cover.

Another explosion rocked the front gate, bending the gate halfway open. The second tower began to topple forward outside of the walls. Chuck jumped out of the burning tower as it toppled down toward the street outside of the gates and disappeared from sight outside the wall. John turned back toward the Compound, seeing most of the crew that had still been inside were now running out. Steve was running towards him carrying John's full plate carrier and helmet. He dropped it at his feet as he ran past. Theo and Kyle passed them, running a beeline to the walls near where the towers had been. Both carried SAWs. They jumped up onto the walls and immediately started firing bursts outside.

Andrew stood on the edge of the roof of the Compound firing rounds from his AR-10. His voice came across the radio when he bumped his hand-held radio on as he secured his kit. "Ten to twenty armed men in the houses to the east. Small clumps of groups moving down the street carrying AKs and some shoulder-fired rockets. Snipers in second-story windows across the road. Keep your eyes up!"

As John finished putting on his body armor and ballistic helmet, Hoover, Old Sarge, Big Rob, and Shonna ran past in a loose four-man fireteam formation heading for the now opened gate. Steve yelled to Hoover and Old Sarge, "Go find Chuck and get him back behind the walls. We're right behind you!"

John, Steve, and Dez, now all geared up, hustled to catch up and fall in behind the group. As they neared the gates, John noticed that several other members of the base had also begun to jump up onto the walls and begin returning fire. He tried to calm himself and control his breathing as the group neared the bent and smoldering gate. He took a deep breath and exhaled slowly as the group crossed the threshold. The scene that awaited him was terrifying. As the seven crossed the threshold, suddenly there was an eruption of chaos and noise that the walls had been softening. As they exited the gate, they were caught out in the open, and the gunfire started to shift in their direction. They each dove behind the various concrete barriers out in front of the gate as the gunfire began snapping and hissing in the air around them.

Chuck was about thirty yards down from them taking cover behind a long since inoperable car parked along the curb of the street. His M60 was propped up on its bipod next to the hood of the car. He was sitting with his back leaning against the car, mopping up blood from his face with one of the sleeves of his shirt he had torn off. He didn't look too good. He was bleeding heavily from gunshot wounds around his shoulders, chest, and one of his legs. Chuck weakly gave them a thumbs up after lighting up a cigarette. The lit cigarette was limply dangling from his mouth as his chest slowly rose and fell under labored breaths. The group rushed over to him while Theo and Kyle covered them with long bursts from their machine guns from on top of the walls. John slid low behind the car as gunfire was still coming in their direction.

"Why the fuck isn't anybody else coming outside the walls to help us?" he yelled, mostly to himself. Shonna baseball slid in behind him, crawling on all fours up to Chuck and began pulling out pressure bandages and tourniquets from her plate carrier. She ignored his remark, instead focusing on giving the critical medical care to Chuck. Rob, Old Sarge, and Hoover finally made it behind the car after a bounding movement during a short break in the incoming fire.

"Fucking cowards," grumbled Old Sarge, who was replying to John's previous complaint. Hoover, who was lying flat on his back behind the vehicle, was fumbling with the handheld grenade launcher which he had worked into his chest and was loading. He said, "If someone can get out behind that M60 and lay me down some cover, I can pop out and lay a few rounds of H-E on their ass and maybe get them to back up long enough to pop some smoke and get back behind those walls."

Old Sarge was already belly-crawling to place himself behind the machine gun, first snatching another belt of ammo from Chuck's chest. Old Sarge linked the new belt onto the half-expended belt still in the gun, then rolled behind the machine gun angled out into the open at the hood of the car. Sarge quickly pulled back the side-charging handle, shouldered the machine gun, and began rapidly firing bursts down the street toward the houses where the bullets were coming from.

Hoover popped up and fired a grenade from the hand-held launcher. It landed just short of the two-story house down the block where most of the fire was originating. The grenade exploded in the front yard, throwing up a large plume of smoke and blocking the windows.

"Now's our time. Let's get him moved back!" John began to say but was drowned out by Hoover and Old Sarge both picking up and yelling, "Fuck these guys. CHARGE!"

Old Sarge slung the strap of the machine gun around his neck, picked up the M60, and began hip-firing in the direction of the plume of smoke. Hoover and Dez circled around John still crouched behind the car and bounded up the next thirty feet to the next parked car. Steve, Theo, and Kyle all joined in on the charge, running from their positions near or on top of the walls to cover the opposite side of the street as Hoover and Old Sarge.

Rob shook John's shoulder to get his attention. "Go ahead! Go kill those bastards. We'll drag Chuck back to the wall." He leaned in closer and whispered in John's ear, "I don't think he's going to going to make it, but he has a better chance the sooner we get him back to the operating room."

John nodded to Rob and grabbed Chuck's hand and squeezed. "Hang in there, brother. I love you, man. Stay strong."

Chuck weakly nodded, and the cigarette fell from his lips into the pool of blood all around him. His eyes began to slowly flutter shut.

"SHIT, SHIT, SHIT!" exclaimed Rob. He grabbed Chuck (who was about the same size and stature as him) and grunted as he flipped him onto his shoulders in an awkward half-fireman's carry. Rob slowly grunted louder as he rose to his feet, then took off at a quick jogging pace back toward the front gate of the base. Shonna slapped him on the shoulder and told him, "Go along." She picked up Rob's rifle and ran to catch up with him.

John sighed heavily as he wiped a tear form the corner of his eye. He raised his head up over the hood of the car and peeked down the street. The men and women of the Compound were pushing up the road toward the enemy and absolutely wreaking havoc. He saw Old Sarge still sending bursts from the machine gun down the street and into the second story of the occupied houses. The rest of the group continued bounding forward down the street, peeling off into houses and clearing them as they went. Hoover was continually sending grenades from the grenade launcher down the street toward a cluster of vehicles. As they pushed further and further down the street, the gang bangers shooting back at them descended into chaos. They may have had confidence in their superior numbers and firepower before, but what they weren't expecting was a counterattack mounted against them so quickly. They definitely hadn't expected a counterattack that was absolutely ferocious and ruthless. The members of the Compound were also practiced shooters, dropping the incoming marauders with much more accurate and precise fire than what was coming toward them.

As John caught up to the rest of the group, one of the houses near the end of the block was on fire after taking a direct hit from the grenade launcher. They were shooting the gang bangers as they jumped out of the windows and as some attempted to run out of the front door. The members of the Compound now stood brazenly out in the open, hosing the gang members with bursts from their weapons. The cluster of cars near the intersection began to start their engines and a few peeled off down the street in a desperate retreat.

"We need to follow them!" yelled Steve. "Let's run back and grab a few cars and catch up!"

Steve and Theo, who were two of the fastest runners, took off at a dead sprint back toward the Compound to grab a few of the vehicles. John tried to reason with them. "No, they could be regrouping or leading us back into a trap!" But he stopped as they were already too far out of earshot. He joined the rest of the group who were sweeping the immediate area and buildings, gathering up weapons and ammo, and ensuring that all of the attackers left behind were dead. He ignored the few single gunshots he heard within the houses. John no longer cared to debate the morality of executing wounded enemies.

A few minutes passed, and the Tank and Steve's truck came roaring out of the gate and down the street to them. Steve was in the lead, stopping in the street closest to them. "Chuck didn't make it... let's go and make those motherfuckers pay. I'll kill every man, woman and child I find once we find out where they're staying, I don't give a shit."

Steve had a bottle of whiskey cradled between his legs and took a long swig.

Old Sarge tossed the M60 into the bed of the truck and climbed in, mounting the machine gun to the welded mount in the bed. The old timer began pulling belts of ammo out of the storage boxes in the back. He looked at John and said, "Boy was a Marine, and I'm going to avenge his death. We'd do the same for you, son."

Hoover looked at John and nodded in agreement as he loaded a new 40mm grenade round into the tube of the launcher.

Hoover and Kyle slid into Steve's truck and they began to roll forward slowly. "With or without you, we're following them," Steve said to John.

Motioning toward a streak of spilled oil on the roadway, Hoover said, "Those cars are leaking pretty bad; they're leaving a trail for us."

Theo had jumped up into the turret of the Tank and was mounting his SAW to the mount.

Dez put a hand on John's shoulder and said, "I think we're all in agreement; everybody wants to go, baby."

John finally relented and said to the group in Steve's truck, "Okay, let's go, but we just find out where they're going. As soon as we know where they went, we've got to break contact and regroup. Make a plan."

Steve looked back at him, took another long swig of the whiskey, and passed it around. "No guarantees. Try and keep up."

Steve tore off down the street after the trail of oil and gasoline, his tires squealing. John and Dez both jumped into the Tank and sped off to catch up with them.

They followed the trail through the town and across the river, using the bridge by the firehouse from weeks earlier. They sped through the streets of downtown at breakneck speeds, moving further and further east across town. The trail turned north up toward the Junction. Potshots began ringing off their vehicles as they drove, but they continued with blind resolve, blind with rage. Driven by fury, Steve still led the way, attempting to catch up with the fleeing vehicles.

The gangbangers made an abrupt turn into the Junction neighborhood they had taken over as their temporary base of operations. The abandoned cars partially blocking the roadway didn't deter them from moving slower as they tore into the neighborhood, raising the alarm. They jumped out screaming, "TORO! The Gringos are coming. Ayúdanos!!!" Several gang members began pouring out of the nearby housing projects. Little time for words was had, as suddenly the large black SUV rammed through the improvised car blockade, throwing the abandoned vehicles aside. Most of the gang bangers out in the open barely had time to raise their weapons before they were met by a wall of fully automatic gunfire. Most were cut down into pieces by machine gun fire before reacting. Other on the opposite side of the street, a group of gang bangers who had started to shoot back at the vehicles, were disintegrated in an explosion from Hoover's grenade launcher. Within minutes, most of the resistance had subsided. After their initial "mad minute," there were no living bodies left shooting back; the shooting stopped. They also shot up the windows of all the surrounding houses in their rage, although nobody peeked their heads out or returned fire from any of the buildings. The group from the Compound spread out, looking at the men they had chased down and killed. Most appeared to be Hispanic men with gang tattoos. Some had prison ink, and others had various Latin gang symbols and clothing markings. It was an odd assortment: a mixture of Latin Kings, Saint's Disciples, Hispanic

Gangster Disciples, and even a few MS-13 markings. All members of the Hispanic criminal underworld were represented. Most of the faces didn't look familiar to Old Sarge, who was still fairly well versed in the local gang bangers and criminals.

"Looks like all out of town shitbags, son. I don't Like the looks of this..." said Old Sarge.

"And we're no closer to answering any of our questions of who has it out for us," John said, still reeling from the adrenaline dump and loss of their comrade. "And Chuck is still dead. And for what? Out of town muscle means somebody else is pulling the strings, and I'm sure as shit going to find out who and kill them myself. I'll kill everyone standing in our way to get there if I have to."

El Toro was listening from underneath the broken-out windows of the second floor of one of the nearby housing buildings. He didn't dare peek out of the window to look at gringos with the big guns. He was more scared than he had ever been in his life full of death and killing.

John looked up at the windows of the housing projects' buildings and yelled out, "We killed all your boys, pussies. Come out and face us like men!" He repeated his words in Spanish, adding a few insults peppered in. He wanted to make sure to get his point across.

Steve walked over and patted him on the shoulder. "It's over, bro. Let's get the fuck out of here before we get ambushed standing out here in the open. I want to go see to Chuck. There's nothing more we can do here. We got our point across. All the big guns are black on ammo anyways. We won't be able to win the next firefight that comes our way."

John said, "Fine. But we got one more thing to get our message across."

The rest of the group grabbed a few of the loose weapons off the ground and all quickly jumped into the vehicles and sped off back to the Compound. It was a silent ride over the rumble of their engines.

El Toro waited twenty more minutes, then stepped out of the housing complex with his remaining men. There was a steel rebar pipe sticking from the lawn. On top of the pipe was the bloody head of one of his men still dripping with blood. There was a piece of paper taped below the makeshift pike. El Toro took the handwritten note and read it out loud:

"YOU KNOW WHERE WE LIVE. WE KNOW WHERE YOU LIVE. IF WE BOTH DON'T WANT TO KILL ALL OF THE WOMEN AND CHILDREN, MEET US IN A NEUTRAL LOCATION. WINNER TAKES CONTROL OF THE WHOLE TOWN. BRING ANY OF YOUR MEN AND WEAPONS YOU WANT.
DOWNTOWN:
FARMERS MARKET SQUARE.
SATURDAY (THREE DAYS FROM NOW)
NOON
ANY EARLIER AND WE DROP A BOMB ON YOUR FAMILIES."

INTERLUDE NINE: CAGE MATCH

El Toro pulled out the satellite phone from his pocket, his hands still shaking as he pressed the buttons for the speed dial of El Jefe's number. "Patron, we have a problem...a BIG Problem down here."

"I can't even trust you with the fucking rednecks with their shotguns in the cornfields, Toro. I gave you all the tools you needed to take that town for everything it was worth, and now you're telling me you got more men killed? I'm beginning to seriously doubt my confidence in your leadership."

"Please Jefe, I'm sorry, I fucked up. But if you don't get more guys down here, we're all dead. These vaqueros are serious...and dangerous. They gave us three days to meet them in the middle of town to fight for the whole town."

"Fine...How many should I bring?"

"Bring everybody, Jefe."

El Jefe hung up the satellite phone, then dialed another number.

The leader of the Outlaws Biker Gang that had been kicked out of the city picked up. "What do you want?" the big white Neo-Nazi biker asked.

Jefe loved hearing the disdain in the biker's voice. He loved being rich and powerful in this new world. El Leon had ensured that Latinos were the superior race in this new world. El Jefe said, "I'm still paying you, but what am I getting for my money? You can't even stay in the city I paid you to work in."

The biker answered, "Look, wetback. We got chased out of town by tanks and helicopters. And from what I hear, even your guys couldn't handle it."

"Okay, enough gringo. How many men can you scrape together to come up and help us kill these army men and free up your town?"

"Maybe thirty, forty men...but that depends...what's the payout? Got to be worth the lives it's gonna cost...Set up our future..."

"It will be well worth it, gringo. One million dollars in cash and gold. A piece of all the future drug trade in the county, and absolute control of everything in town south of the river in Kankakee."

The line was quiet for a few moments. El Jefe could hear the heavy breathing from the biker pick up in pace. Then finally, an answer. "A million dollars cash? Are you...are you really fuckin serious?"

"Yes...The same offer my boss authorized me to give to the blacks too...although between you and I, since you've been in our employ before, they aren't getting half the money you are. Now, what do you say?"

"At that rate, I can get you fifty men. But we will need half the money up front."

"I can give a quarter up front. The rest you get when all of the bastards are dead. All of the spoils you can take off their dead bodies too."

"It's a deal. I never thought killin' other whites would be such good business."

"It is now. Meet in three days. In the downtown square. Just before noon."

The biker hung up the phone and leaned back in his chair. He let out a low, slow whistle and said softly to himself, "A million. Holy shit…" He yelled out to his new second in command, "Billy. Get over here!"

Once the large, balding biker made his way over to him, he said, "The wetbacks called and offered a pile of gold to do what we were going to do anyways. We hit the jackpot. Now get as many of the boys together as we can, all of the guns and bikes. And a few trailers for all of the shit we can loot. Get all the rest of the guns together, get everything. We can get out of this little shit town and back into Kankakee where we belong. We'll have a stack of gold to start a new empire for ourselves."

CHAPTER 15: INTO THE STORM
The next day

John first laid out the plans in front of the members of the Compound. He wanted to iron out the details with his trusted inner circle before bringing the orders to the remaining members. At the moment, there weren't too many friendly sentiments around the base. Strong unfriendly words had been exchanged after the county deputies and city cops hadn't left the cover of the walls of the base when Chuck fell from the tower. Many of the members of the Compound, especially the Bros, had blamed Chuck's death on the lack of help they got from their allies in those crucial first moments.

The members of the Compound sat around the kitchen table. Shonna had made a large hearty batch of chili with frozen meat from the freezer in the garage. Every member of the Compound was in attendance. Lyon had flown in by helicopter as soon as he heard word of the attack on the Compound and stayed to be a part of the planning. The. LP/OP lookout was pulled so that everyone could meet together. After the strong exchange of words about the failure of the other groups within the base, the city cops had taken the commitment to their allegiance with more vigor and took to manning the defenses and rebuilding the gate and towers. The relationship with the deputies had become extremely strained once again. They all had their doubts that they would even agree to join them in their fight against the cartel.

The members of the Compound enjoyed their hearty meals and also sipped on beers and whiskey. After they finished their meals, they all moved outside onto the back deck to relax and enjoy more drinks and cigars. They tried to keep spirits high, but the mood was still somber as John began to address them:

"I know the past few days have been really hard on most of us...And the next few days are going to be even harder. We've gotten hit hard...and taken our losses harder. In the next few days, I'm going to have to ask everyone to be ready both mentally and physically to put everything out on the line. It's literally going to be life or death. There can be no living safely while these other groups are out there. In three days' time, we are going to take the fight to them. Hit them with everything we've got.

"Colonel Lyon, first thing will be to get all the heavy weapons we can get our hands on from you guys, and any men you can spare as a backup plan. Right now, I don't think they expect us to have any link to you guys and won't be expecting your forces to fight with us. Keep your troops, your armor, and helos back, and we should only need them as a contingency plan if they roll deeper than we expected so we won't get overrun. Ideally, the only thing we might need your guys for is overwatch, containment, and maybe to sweep the battlefield clean after we kick their asses. I don't want to show all our cards up front, so if we don't need you, we won't use you."

Lyon nodded silently in agreement.

"Next, I want to set up an advance scout and set up an ambush position on the roof of the public Library building overlooking the downtown. Rockets and machine guns for plunging fire down onto the field. I want to send out a group to set up advance scouting positions and hide out gear as soon as possible, If we're gonna cheat, I'm sure they will too."

People nodded in agreement to his words, along with small comments amongst the group as he spoke.

"How many do we expect?" Lyon asked during a pause in his words.

"There's the problem. We don't know if it's gonna be thirty dudes, or three thousand. We don't know if they have small arms, or machine guns, trucks, or armor. We just know we stirred the hornet's nest and have to be ready to burn the motherfucker down."

Lyon sat and pondered the words quietly for a few moments, then said, "How many men are you putting up against them?"

He answered, "Rough math, leaving none of us at the Compound, and minimal security elements along with medical support at the rear, probably ten of us from the Compound, about twenty to twenty-five city cops, and maybe forty of the county cops and corrections guys."

Lyon answered, "Seventy to seventy-five(ish) fighting men isn't bad. Just to round it out in case they roll heavy, I'll come along with an infantry platoon to add to your number and watch your six. I'll have all my helos on standby loaded with another infantry platoon. I'll have two of the MP platoons as an outer cordon ten or so blocks out as blocking positions to the west and south across the river. I'll have a platoon of cav scouts mounted ten blocks out as ground QRF. You should be sitting pretty unless shit gets huge. We've got your back, but I can't unnecessarily put all my men's lives on the line if they don't need to, trackin'?"

He nodded in response and said, "We won't use all your people unless we absolutely have to, brother. I appreciate it."

Lyon also said, "I have a few of my own modifications to your plans for the advance scout and overwatch position. I'll let you know about it later…"

They finished their dinners and talked amongst themselves, sharing ideas and theories about the upcoming conflict. Lyon shared his plans for an advanced scout to send out onto one of the tall high rise rooftops. Lyon sipped on his glass of whiskey and said, "I can spare a couple teams of snipers, a radio guy and a forward observer. Might be good to have an overwatch on the area just in case they try and sneak in early to set up some surprises or traps."

Andrew told him, "Send them out to the highrise tomorrow as early as we can. More time to keep an eye out on the area. We'd be totally fucked if these idiots are smart enough to place IEDs and claymores."

Lyon nodded and agreed. He stood up to excuse himself to make a radio call back to the base, when Andrew also added, "Might as well give us a few heavy gun teams up on the other tower. A few 240 Bravos and a mortar team or two. No sense in trying to fight these assholes fairly. I'll go up with them the day before to set up."

Lyon nodded and said, "Works for me. I'll get the sniper teams in place tonight and fly you and the gun teams in the night before." Lyon walked out to the radio room, where he used one of the radios to send the orders back to the commanders at the National Guard base.

John readied his gear. He dressed in a simple pair of jeans and a Woodland camo BDU long-sleeved combat shirt. He didn't want to stand out on the battlefield, although he wasn't particularly concerned with what others would be wearing. The only directive he gave the others was to pack heavily armed and carry as much arms and ammo as they could manage. He buckled on his battle belt and tightened down his drop-leg holster, putting extra pistol magazines into every spare mag pouch. He loaded his 1911 and clicked it into the Safariland holster. Next, he pulled on his Multicam plate carrier. He loaded up all the mag pouches with twelve magazines for his MK-18 AR. It was heavy, but he felt the need to be able to sling as much lead as possible. He also loaded up a small assault pack with spare AR magazines and a few of the smoke and frag grenades.

Andrew was already gone as he had volunteered to lead the overwatch position on the roof of the old public library highrise, along with a few others. They would head out in advance of the main party. He'd worn a black plate carrier with multiple spare magazines for his AR-10. He'd carried his Glock in a leather pancake holster on his hip and opted to carry his assault pack with spare ammo for the .308 rifle. He had said, "When this all pops off, I'll hopefully be doing lots of shooting to look out for you." He carried a radio and a spare ammo can of loose .308 ammo.

Andrew and his crew had headed out the day before to be inserted by helicopter onto the roof of the library highrise along with a small detachment of the heavy weapons platoon of the National Guard Infantry Unit. The small detachment included a small squad of twelve soldiers, including three M240B machine guns with their ammo bearers and assistant gunners, two antivehicle specialists with shoulder fired rockets, and a squad leader with his radio. They also had two 60mm mortar teams with them. They were inserted in the middle of the night by helicopter, along with several ammo crates, rockets, mortar shells, and a small tuff box full of "treats" John had wanted to send along with food and some comfort items like a few bottles of alcohol and cigarettes for the next few days.

On top of the next tall building over, the former PNC Bank, they had a squad of scouts on sniper overwatch. A squad of three sniper/spotter teams, a squad leader and his radio operator, along with an artillery forward observer. The sniper team had been placed on the roof in advance for a few days to keep an eye out in case the gangs sent any advance scouts into the area. The scout/snipers had the unfortunate task of being dropped in on the roof and keeping a "cold camp" in the evenings, with no fires allowed so there was less chance of them being spotted.

John stepped downstairs and checked on the others. Most were already awake and had gone about starting their day. The living room was a mass jumble of gear, ammo, and equipment as they all were putting together their gear. Theo, Rob, Old Sarge, Shonna, Dez, and Kyle were cleaning their weapons and putting the last touches on their gear and bags. He stepped out on the back porch and found Steve and Hoover together. Hoover was smoking a cigar while putting magazines into his plate carrier and rearranging his MOLLE pouches. Steve was sitting in a chair, smoking a cigarette, and pouring Jack Daniels into his coffee. "Already buddy? It's only 9:00 A.M.," John said to Steve.

Hoover grabbed John's shoulder and whispered into his ear, "I don't think he ever quit from last night, brother. He's been taking Chuck's death pretty hard. But you know Steve...He's always liked to hit the bottle hard."

John said aloud, "As long as you'll be able to stand by the time we head out, I don't care."

Steve looked up at him and took a drink of his coffee, eyes red and glassy and said, "It's all good, man, I fight better when I'm pissed. Just don't stop me and the Bros when we start taking scalps for Chuck."

John nodded to Steve and Hoover and said, "Just be ready. All we gotta do is stack bodies, and you can do it however you want."

Hoover nodded and said, "Gonna be plenty of killing to go around. Let's just hope we all make it back in one piece."

John walked back Inside to check back in on the others. Rob and Shonna were buddy checking each other's gear. They were both wearing their black plate carriers with MEDIC markings and carrying their large military-style medic bags and assault packs. They were loading the back of the tank with foldable litters and spare medical equipment.

Theo was checking his radio, along with the others' hand radios to make sure they were all on the same frequency. He was dressed in his black police uniform fatigues, a black combat shirt, and his police plate carrier. He had his SAW slung on his front, and he also carried a large assault pack with his spare ammo and a military radio and whip antenna connecting to the various channels between the Compound and the National Guard. The radio pack had a headset that he wore underneath his helmet.

John told Theo, "In all this chaos, try not to lose me, alright, big guy?"

Theo nodded, gave him a thumb's up, and continued to load his gear.

The Bros were next, loading equipment into Steve's large truck. Old Sarge was standing in the bed of the truck, mounting the M-60 to the improvised turret in the bed. The rest of the truck bed was heavily weighed down with cases of the belts of ammo for the machine gun. He looked up and said, "Less walking for me. Don't need any more wear on these old hips, kiddo." with a smile. He was also wearing his police uniform and vest carrier, with his full leather duty belt.

Hoover was smoking a cigar, wearing his tan plate carrier, military boots, and fatigues, with a bandolier of 40mm grenades slung across his chest. Kyle was adding more belts of ammo for the SAW to the pouches on his vest and into his assault pack. Steve had his gear loaded into the driver's seat and was sipping on a beer looking over the other Bros and Old Sarge.

Last, Dez was loading the Tank with cases of ammo and magazines. She was wearing her police uniform and outer vest carrier, with an AR slung on the front, and her assault pack loaded onto her seat. She looked at John and put her hand on his shoulder. "Everything is gonna be alright baby."

He tried to lighten the mood. "Seems like everyone is back wearing to their police stuff. Makes it a bit easier to spot us."

Dez answered, "I think it's gonna be chaotic out there, and the more uniforms we recognize each other in, the better. I think all the other city and county cops in the base are most likely wearing their gear as well. Better to know the good guys from the bad."

A radio squawked up: "Bad News. Break. Scout bird over I-57 spotted a huge convoy of vehicles. One hundred or more vehicles. No armor, some buses and RVs. Break. You're looking at an estimated several hundred Tangos. Light arms. Birds did a strafing run on the front of the convoy and took off after taking a bunch of small arms fire. Over."

"Roger, Comanche main. Proceed with original plan. Move to original positions and pop in as needed. Out."

John lowered his radio, and let out a big sigh. "FUUUUUCK! Not good, boys."

Steve turned to him and said, "We still have the advantage of bigger arms, better position, and we're playing on our turf. We still sit low, draw them into the square, and start raining down hell on them and box 'em in."

John nodded and said, "Agreed, we wait 'til most of the vehicles in that convoy are within the square and have the overwatch hit the rear vehicles with rockets. We blow the vehicles on the routes of egress and cover the exits on the side streets. When we start shooting, I'll call to have the cordon units start converging in on the downtown and close the perimeter in. If we hit that mad minute right, there will be a lot of runners and not a lot of people shooting back. Their number superiority won't mean shit."

Steve nodded, and said, "Well…If we want this to work, we have to draw them in the exact route we want them to come in on. Sounds like the Bros and I need to go play rabbit and give that convoy something to chase. You guys better be ready and in place, because we're gonna bring them right to you and drop them right in your lap." He pulled on his plate carrier and hopped in the pickup.

Kyle and Hoover jumped in the rear seats, and Old Sarge slowly crawled into the bed of the truck. Old Sarge buckled his ballistic helmet, put on his goggles, strapped himself into the makeshift turret behind the M60, and racked the charging handle on the mounted machine gun. He gave a tap on the rear window and a thumbs up to the onlooking crowd. With that, Steve fired up the large pickup truck's engine, and the loudspeakers began blasting "Raining Blood" By Slayer. The engine began to rev, and they slowly rolled forward. The Bros all simultaneously cracked open cans of beer. Steve mouthed the Words, "KEEP UP!" and the truck sped off east down Court Street. The music could still be heard for several minutes until it faded into the distance as the truck reached the interstate.

John told the rest of the group, "Shit, I guess that means it's time to hurry up and get into position. Everybody mount up and get to the downtown square!"

Within minutes, the three groups filled out in loose columns and headed toward the downtown area, all taking different routes in case of any ambush or surprises. Their drive was uneventful, other than passing a roadblock being set up by the MPs several blocks south of the Kankakee River Bridge on the main road leading south of town. They waved and sped through, continuing onto the downtown square. The members of the Compound took up their position on the southernmost block of the downtown square, facing the large open space across the square overlooking the large street which ran down the hill just opposite them. This put the open square in between them and the large public library and PNC Bank high rises where their sniper teams lay hidden in wait. The county deputies were spread out hidden in the parking lots and houses to the east, while the city cops had set up to the west but remained visible in the SWAT-armored Bearcats and patrol SUVs.

========

As the huge convoy of cartel vehicles neared the Kankakee exit, El Jefe sat in the rear of his Range Rover, in the middle of the convoy, drinking a bottle of water. Suddenly, the vehicle stopped. El Jefe leaned forward to his driver and asked what was going on. After a few minutes, a runner came to his window.

"Jefe, there is something at the exit ramp."

"If it's another helicopter, just shoot at it until it goes away like last time, pendejo."

"No Jefe, *perdóneme*, it's one truck playing loud gringo music. It's just sitting there."

"Just shoot your way through it if there's only one fucking truck, stupid!"

The runner acknowledged the order and took off running back to the front of the stopped column of vehicles.

As the runner neared the front car to repeat the boss's orders, the world suddenly disappeared in a flash. The lead vehicle exploded from a well-placed high-explosive round. A barrage of automatic gunfire and explosions hit the lead vehicles in the convoy as the pickup truck opened fire on the convoy in a moment of chaos. The Army helicopters also returned and opened in a barrage of rockets and machine gun fire on the rest of the convoy as they took advantage of the confusion. The rockets let up, and the pickup truck did a strafing run along the front part of the convoy which was still in a state of hysteria. The pickup swung around and headed back to the exit ramp.

After the initial confusion, the convoy reorganized and began moving forward, pushing past the wreckage of mangled vehicles and burning bodies down the exit ramp and into the city. They moved forward slower than before, but once the entire convoy was off the interstate and no longer meeting resistance, they began to pick up speed toward the downtown square. As the convoy closed in on the large office buildings downtown, they saw the same pickup truck sitting in the middle of the intersection. The truck took a few more pot shots at the lead vehicles, then sped south down the hill into the main square until disappearing from view.

The convoy took off in pursuit of the truck. The convoy of cartel vehicles turned down the hill and began pouring into the empty downtown square. The square was empty aside from various cars scattered amongst the former parking lots, long since siphoned of gas and stripped of anything valuable. As the final few vehicles in the convoy filed into the square, Hoover (who had jumped off the truck and run into a hidden spot in the underground parking garage of the bank) clacked off the daisy-chain of claymore mines he had wired to the vehicles in the square and along the entrance to inlet road. The last few vehicles of the convoy were enveloped in the explosions. The twisted metal and wreckage of cars blocked any retreat for the convoy back up the hill onto the main road.

As the vehicles disappeared in the flash and boom, the other Kankakee defenders took the cue and opened fire in a mad minute ambush on the exposed and surprised convoy. The overwatch and machine gun teams opened up with the crew served weapons from the roof in a "mad minute." The mortar teams also began launching high explosive rounds onto the cartel vehicles in the square.

After several minutes of sustained gunfire and explosions, the initial chaos began to subside. The remains of the cartel convoy scurried together into a loose circle in the middle of the square. Their vehicles formed a barrier and the cartel soldiers spilled out of the vehicles into the square. While the initial foray began to subside, the cartel horde regrouped. A few members stepped out and fired rockets up at the tall office buildings where the overwatch and heavy weapons teams were.

"SHIT! They found us. They're hitting the towers!" Andrew's voice rang out over the radio net.

"Dump all the ordinance you can back onto them and get off of there. They know where you are!" came the answer from John. "Everyone else concentrate fire on anyone you see shooting RPGs!"

"Too easy!" Andrew squawked over the radio.

Mortars continued to be launched from the rooftops intermittently, but much more sporadically and much less accurately than the first wave.

"Check that mortar fire before they drop one on friendlies!" somebody yelled over the comms.

The rest of the groups on the ground then closed in and opened fire on the circle of cartel vehicles. The convoy was now enclosed on all four sides. After their initial bursts began to slow down, most of the cartel had consolidated inside the confines of the semicircle of vehicles providing them cover. There were hundreds of bodies squirting out of the buses, RVs, and cars circled around the square. Waves and waves of Hispanic gang members piled out into the open, shooting wildly in every direction. While appearing totally disorganized, they still had the advantage of superior numbers. The attackers initial panic reactions changed as more and more of the cartel foot soldiers poured out of the inner circle of vehicles and began establishing fire superiority.

"Fuck! There's hundreds of them!" Andrew yelled over the radio. "So much for fire superiority!"

John, crouched behind a car to the south reloading his Mk18, answered, "Just keep them contained to the square and keep pouring it on them!" He pulled back over the hood and fired a burst into the chest of a cartel foot soldier wildly spraying bursts from an AK-47 in their direction. He ducked back down as two more gang bangers behind him started focusing their fire on him. Bursts of automatic fire kept him pinned down beneath the motor of the car, until an engine roared past him.

A loud BRRRRRRRRRRUUUUPPP arose from the mounted M60 from Steve's truck as it crashed through the middle of the square. Old Sarge was still buckled in the makeshift turret in the back, blasting cyclic bursts into the crowds of cartel soldiers. The truck spun around when it started to catch the attention and drew incoming fire. As the truck turned around, Hoover leaned out of the passenger window and sent a 40mm grenade sailing right into the thick of the circled cartel vehicles.

"FUCK YEAHHH!" came the shouts of Steve, Hoover, and Kyle over their radios. The explosion covered their retreat as the outgoing shots slowed. "Suck on that one, ass clowns!" yelled Hoover as he sent another shot from the launcher near the southern edge of the circle of vehicles, this time popping a flume of smoke to cover their retreat back behind the lines of friendly militia from the Compound.

Taking advantage of the cartel being put back on their toes, Andrew and the machine gun teams moved over to the next tower and began raining fire back onto the mass of cartel vehicles. The tide shifted back to them as they again had the cartel pinned down and pushed back inside their limits.

"We're lookin' good! Keep it up boys!" John said over the radio. "Keep them contained inside that circle of vehicles!" John was standing over the vehicle picking off the cartel members that tried to squirt out onto the open. Theo was still in the turret of the Tank, firing bursts from his SAW, while Dez was at the other edge of the vehicle with John. The Bros had pulled the truck alongside the Compound's line of defense, allowing Old Sarge to continue shooting into the mass of cartel vehicles, while Steve, Hoover, and Kyle jumped out of the truck, joining the fight on foot.

Crouched inside the middle of the circle of Vehicles, El Jefe was consulting with his lieutenants near the entrance to his RV.

"Padron, the gringos are killing us! They shoot us every time we try and send men outside of the cars!"

El Jefe scoffed. "Pinche gringos! These fucking peasants! Call the bikers and tell them to get their fucking asses here NOW! Before we are all dead!"

El Toro pulled out his satellite phone and hit the speed dial. The line rang a few times, and then the big Nazi biker answered. "I hear the party started without us. We're still waiting south of town. The Army was nowhere to be found after you shot at the helicopters."

Toro handed the phone to El Jefe, who interrupted. "Stop your fucking yapping and get here and help us kill these fucking pieces of shit. Do what we're paying you to fucking do!"

"You got our money, wetback?" the biker asked.

"Yes, we do, all of it and even more if you fucking kill these assholes. Now get here now!"

Things were looking good, until John's radio lit up and Lyon's voice came through. "Compound Six, come in. Wolfpack, come in, over!"

John sat down behind the cover of the car and answered him, "Go for Wolfpack, Comanche Main!"

Lyon's voice answered back quicker and more frantic. "Johnny, it's not good! My outer cordon to the south just got hit hard and had to retreat. Whatever was left of them had to break contact. A huge column of bikers rode up on them and opened fire. They said there was over a hundred of them. They overwhelmed the MPs' blockade and pushed right through, heading for you guys. They'll be on you any second. We're spinning up our QRF, but we've got to go by ground. The helicopters took too much fire to keep flying. I'll be there with an Infantry Company in fifteen minutes. Just stay alive until—."

Just then, a bullet flew past them, coming from the south. The rumble of motorcycle engines was heard booming louder as the dust being raised by the horde approached them from up Schuyler Avenue. The bikers were heading toward the battle raging in the town square.

"SHIT!" John yelled, keying up the radio. "All available troops move to the south SASP. We need to set a blocking position for the incoming biker assholes!"

Lieutenant Hunter answered, "We're engaged and spread too thin to the east, Cowboy. You're on your own, kid."

"Ditto, Johnny. We don't have anybody to spare!" chimed in Lieutenant Morgan from the city police.

"Compound: Consolidate on me to the south! Set up a defensive line to repel the bikers incoming!"

John heard, "Got it!" and "Roger!" from all the members of the Compound on the ground as they made their way over to him. Dez was still crouched next to him, reloading her rifle. Steve, Hoover, and Kyle ran over to him, joining the semi-circle crouched behind the Tank. Theo and Old Sarge were still facing toward the cartel, keeping them pinned in with blasts from their machine guns. Shonna and Big Rob were dragging over a wounded city cop. Once they reached cover behind the Tank, Shonna began applying a bandage to the man's wounds.

"I guess it's just us. Hurry up and reload, guys. They're coming."

As the motorcycle engines grew louder, the shots began to ping around them. The incoming fire exploded all around them and they all dove for cover, now fighting enemies from both sides.

"We don't have enough guns for this!" Dez yelled over to him.

"We just need to hold off until Lyon gets here!"

Kyle yelled, "Fuck that! Let's bring it to 'em!" as he fired a burst at the incoming bikers, cutting down the closest incoming riders. He then ran out toward the incoming horde, firing bursts from his SAW.

Hoover launched another 40mm rocket into the path of the incoming swarm and ran out after Kyle, firing from his SIG pistol and yelling "Yippie Kiy-Yay Mother Γ—" with the tail end lost in the sound of the explosion.

Steve saw the other Bros and decided to follow their lead, pulling the pin on a smoke grenade and heaving it out in front of them as far as he could with an audible grunt. The smoke covered their advance while splitting the first several waves of bikers to either side of the plumes of smoke. This didn't help, as now the bikers split off in both directions, forming a semi-circle the block to the south. Most of the bikers dismounted their motorcycles and began moving forward on foot toward the members of the Compound who were now nearly completely surrounded.

Old Sarge continued firing the M60 toward the cartel in the town square, and Theo atop the turret in the Tank also helped contain the squirters still trying to get free of the circled vehicles in the middle of the square with short bursts from his SAW. While the two machine guns kept the cartel occupied to their backs, John, Dez, Big Rob, and Shonna turned their attention to the tons of bikers advancing on their position.

"They weren't kidding, There's a shitload!" Steve said over the radio. "We're gonna have break contact and fall back to you and consolidate again."

"No shit, Sherlock. Wasn't a very smart move in the first place, was it?" John answered.

Steve, Kyle, and Hoover bounded back the half block they had advanced earlier, covering each other's retreat to the line of wrecked cars where the others were waiting. Steve slid in behind one of the cars, catching his breath and said, "Well, this sucks…" He panted as he reloaded his rifle and adjusted his ballistic helmet.

Hoover and Kyle dove in beside them as a chorus of gunshots rang out behind them. "They're right fuckin on top of us!" Kyle yelled, reaching into his pack for another drum of ammo for his SAW. Hoover was applying a bandage to a bullet wound in his left forearm, panting heavily and wincing with pain.

Dez, Rob, and Shonna were off to the side, still firing on another group of bikers who were advancing; they were now within thirty or forty yards of them. John's rifle went empty, and while he knelt down to reload his rifle, suddenly a skinny methed-out biker jumped over the hood of the car, tackling him. The lights went out as John's head hit the ground. The next thing he knew, John was on his back, staring up at the skinny little biker. He raised a machete over his head and cackled with laughter. All this happened in seconds.

John reached for his pistol, still locked in his holster, when suddenly, with a loud snarl, his big old German Shepherd darted out and jumped at the junkie biker like a fur missile. The K-9 knocked the biker off his feet as he raised the machete.

"Get him, boy. KILL!" John yelled after catching his breath. He repeated the command in Portuguese, the language the K-9 had been trained in for attack commands when he was a puppy. The hundred-pound German Shepherd had latched onto the throat of the biker and was snarling as the biker screamed, until the arterial blood began spurting out of the guy's neck. After a few seconds, the screaming stopped, and the biker stopped flailing. He was now very much dead. The Shepherd's muzzle was covered in blood, and he was still growling and dragging the lifeless body around.

"Heel!" John told the Shepherd, again in Portuguese. The dog finally obeyed after a few loud commands from his master.

"Good boy!" the others around yelled.

Hoover was leaning up against a car, firing one of his pistols from cover. The bikers were nearly on top of them now, and they were in trouble of being overrun. Steve and Kyle were both firing their rifles rapidly at targets all around them, expending bullet after bullet and quickly reloading again and again. Kyle expended his last belt of ammo for his SAW and yelled, "FAHHHK!" He tossed the machine gun behind him and drew his Glock. He and Steve knelt nearly back to back, firing at the bikers moving in around them.

A grenade bounced off the hood of a car and landed right in the middle of their group.

"GRENADEEEE!" Kyle yelled. Everyone dove for cover. Kyle was the closest and ran to kick the grenade away from them. It exploded about fifteen feet away just off the ground. Shrapnel peppered them, but most of them had hit the ground or dove behind cover and were missed. Kyle was still standing, and some of the shrapnel from the grenade came back and peppered his outstretched left leg and foot, tearing his leg below his knee to shreds. He screamed and fell backwards, bleeding profusely.

"Kyle's HIT!" Steve yelled, crawling out from cover and making his way to him. Steve pulled out pressure bandages and a tourniquet from his IFAK first aid kit, dumping it all out next to him.

Rob and Shonna ran over, dodging the incoming gunfire and sliding in next to them. Shonna quickly began fixing on a tourniquet just above Kyle's knee and tightening it down. Kyle groaned in pain as Big Rob placed his knee on his leg to help slow the bleeding. Steve was still frantically trying to pick up the contents of his medical kit. Big Rob grabbed Steve by the shoulders and shook him to get his attention. "We got this. Get your shit together and cover our asses while we save him. He's gonna make it as long as we don't fucking die helping him. Now GET YOUR ASS BACK IN THE FIGHT!"

Steve looked down at Kyle, who nodded weakly and gave him a thumb's up. Steve said, "I'm gonna kill these motherfuckers!" and picked up his rifle. Hoover moved past him, grabbing him by the shoulder and pulling him up. Hoover still had his grenade launcher slung and was carrying an AK pistol he must have picked up off the ground somewhere. The two moved back behind cover of one of the cars and began shooting at the oncoming bikers.

John and Dez moved in next to them, firing their rifles rapidly time and time again. John had dropped his pack next to them, which was filled with AR magazines. They continued firing at the advancing bikers. They made progress, dropping several advancing gang members due to their superior marksmanship and better weapons, but they lacked numbers and their ammo supply was dwindling.

Big Rob had moved Kyle over into the bed of the Tank, and Shonna stayed with him to keep him stable in the relative safety of the armored vehicle. Big Rob returned to the rest of the group where he dropped another sack of loaded magazines. He raised his AK and began firing bursts over the hood. Rob gave a sideways glance to Steve and Hoover, and yelled, "Shonna says he's gonna be fine, boys. He might lose that leg though. A lot of tissue lost to shrapnel."

Kyle was still groaning in pain as Shonna worked to control the bleeding. In-between his groans of pain, he yelled, "Can you believe this Shit? I got blown up half a dozen times in Iraq and Afghanistan, and I'm gonna lose my fucking leg in the streets of Kankakee!"

No more words were exchanged, and they all continued firing.

The radio chimed up again, and Lyon's voice echoed, "We're almost there, boys. Hold on tight!"

They heard the roaring of the military vehicles' engines. The group cheered as they saw the column of Humvees and MRAPs emerge south over the bridge. The lead vehicles blasted through the line of parked motorcycles and the mounted machine guns belched from the turrets on top of the vehicles. The bikers were being shredded by the mounted .50 cal machine guns and scattered in every different direction. The members of the Compound cheered as the military Humvees formed a protective line around them.

Lyon hopped out of one of the lead Humvees. He wore his full military kit with his M4 slung at his front. "Sorry we're late to the party, boys, but I brought party favors!" Lyon yelled over the gunfire.

Infantrymen piled out of the Humvees and APCs and joined the fight as soon as they dismounted. The trained soldiers spread out and made a difference immediately as they continued to shoot down the running and retreating bikers. The others moved through and began to engage the cartel horde who were still pretty well dug in at the center of the square.

Lyon ran over to John and the others and said, "I think we got it from here. You guys need anything?"

Shonna yelled over, "We need a MEDEVAC for one ASAP. He's gonna lose his leg unless he's in surgery in the next half an hour. You guys got doctors, right?"

Lyon yelled over at one of his medics, "Get this man out on an ambo and MEDEVAC him to the base time now! Take two Humvees as an escort and break every speed limit sign you see!"

"Roger, sir!" the medic yelled and ran off to help move Kyle onto a litter and move him into an awaiting military ambulance. They closed the doors and the ambulance sped off toward the National Guard base.

Lyon was on the radio with his other men, ordering the outer cordons to move in tighter around the downtown area. "We can't have these squirters getting out of the containment area. The scouts left up above are telling me the cartel is still hitting the city and county sides to the east and west pretty hard. I'm trying to get a few squads around to reinforce them."

"We still got people up above?" John asked, squinting up at the smoking towers.

Andrew's voice came over the radio. "Yes, we're still alive up here; now quit clicking on your mic when you talk, jackass!"

Shots rang out from Andrew's AR-10 down onto the cartel vehicles. "It looks like between the bikers and cartel assholes, they might be down to less than a couple dozen live bodies down there.

We can keep whittling them down little by little, then move in and kill the rest of these bastards!"

"Agreed," said Lyon. "Tell my mortars to keep dropping a few more rounds on them. See if they can walk some rounds right into the middle."

Andrew answered back, "They're saying you guys have to stay back then. One city block isn't enough buffer room for them to drop H-E rounds if they gotta walk them in. Every one of these shells is danger close to your front lines."

"Alright, move the troops back and hold a steady line for a little bit so the mortars can walk in a few more rounds!"

John took a few moments to catch his breath behind the cover of the Tank. He pulled a bottle of water and took a few swigs. He dumped the rest over his head and face, tossing the empty bottle into the back of the Tank. He reloaded his plate carrier with a few fresh rifle magazines from a box in the back seat. He noticed the pool of Kyle's coagulating blood in the back bed of the SUV.

Dez walked over and grabbed the side of his thigh and squeezed. She smiled at him and said, "You holding up, big guy?" John gave a small chuckle and cracked a smile at her. "I'm thinking about where we're gonna go for our next date night. We're a totally normal couple, right?"

Dez laughed and said, "I don't think we would be a normal couple even before all this shit."

John kissed her on the cheek. Even though she was all sweaty and covered in dirt, she was still the most beautiful woman in the world to him.

The moment was interrupted by the mortars exploding on the outer circle of the cartel vehicles. Another round scored a direct hit on one of the buses further in the center of the cartel's stronghold. This sent out runners emerging in every direction from behind the circle of vehicles.

John and Dez were woken from their daydreams with the report of sniper shots from the roofs and rips from the newly relocated machine gun teams. Theo was ducked down inside the rear of the Tank reloading his SAW and pulling more bandoliers of ammo into the pouches on his plate carrier. When the firing picked back up, Theo Jumped back up into the turret of the Tank and started firing short busts at the dozens of men jumping point and running towards them.

Dez and John moved out to the rear end of the Tank and leaned out high and low, firing their rifles at the runners.

"Bad news, boys, we're all running light on ammo up here! You're gonna be losing your overwatch up here pretty soon!" yelled Andrew over the radio."

"Roger, just let us know when, then bug out. Get down from the towers and make your way around to one of the lines," John told him.

They hadn't really planned for the guns on overwatch to run dry. They hadn't been prepared for it to last this long past the initial "mad minute" and foray volley of firefight that followed. The overwatch up on top of the towers had cut the cartel off from retreating back up to the north where they had come. But they had expended the thousands of rounds they had come with. The mortars most likely had nearly run out as well.

The radios lit up again, and they heard "Gun one black on ammo!" followed shortly after by "Gun two black."

"Gun three low. Covering your team's exfil. Go now!"

~~~~~~

Crouched inside the doorway of his RV, El Jefe was giving his commands to his thirty best men—the hardened gangsters and former military members with experience in combat, including the hulking giant, El Toro. The men were loaded down with as much ammo and weapons as they could carry, including rockets and grenades.

El Jefe began, "This isn't over, amigos. We push out behind a rush of the soldiers. Fire the rockets out at every machine gun or vehicle you see. We all rush forward and overwhelm one of their vehicles, and we can get out of here. WE have the rockets and WE have the explosives, and WE have the machine guns. Now let's go!"

The men all roared in agreement and cheered. El Jefe secretly hoped none of these hardened men realized that this was a last-minute desperation push in the hopes that he and his most trusted men could break through the lines to escape. He had only hoped to cause chaos with what little fire superiority they could still muster and manage to slip out of the battle zone unnoticed, steal a car, and escape back to Chicago. Death was worse to him than defeat in this faraway city to these powerful strangers and their army.

The men charged out from their cover, spraying their bullets wildly in every direction. El Jefe had been sending his men out in small groups trying to break the lines before, but the most recent bomb dropping on top of one of the buses in the middle of the circle had alarmed him. He sent out all of the men he had alive, and they all rushed out in a mad dash.

The desperate moves worked, and the rush of nearly a hundred men running out in every direction overwhelmed the lines of these fighters surrounding them. After sending out his useless foot soldiers as meat shields, El Leon's more useful men followed, firing shoulder-mounted RPG rockets at the vehicles and fortified positions in every direction. El Leon, surrounded by his fiercest warriors, moved south toward the enemy lines. They fired rockets into the biggest vehicles, which were thrown into the air in large explosions. They charged at the enemy lines as hard and fast as they could.

THE END: A NEW BEGINNING

The burning cars littered the streets, and the air was full of the scent of gunpowder, smoke, and blood. Bodies were everywhere; some dead, some still gasping for air. Men writhed in the pools of blood and spent brass.

John came to, his head still spinning from the explosion. The volley of RPGs aimed in their direction had sent the car they'd been sheltering behind over twenty feet into the air. John had gone flying backward, bashing his head onto the concrete.

John made his way to his hands and knees, shaking his head. His eyes slowly came back into focus. He rubbed the blood and sweat out of his eyes and looked back to the north where the rocket had come from. He heard a familiar sinister cackle coming from behind the row of SUVs and low riders.

"Last chance, cabrón! Give up before you're all fuckin' dead. You think we don't got nobody else still coming? You got no one left. I already own this town, and nobody is going to stand in my motherfucking way!"

The menacing laughs continued, and bullets ricocheted around his feet and body. The gang leader was toying with him now, leading him like a cow to slaughter. John crawled closer and closer to the row of cars until he was leaning up against the large SUV that The Gang leader was behind. He pulled himself up until his back was to the wall. He panted and spit blood on himself, trying to find the strength to give what he thought would be his last words. "......Fuck...Yoooouuuuu!"

John used the last of his energy. He pulled his boot knife from his ankle and dropped down to the side of the car. He slowly and quietly crawled around the side of the large SUV, making his way around. He waited until the Gang leader began speaking again and jumped out from his blind side. He lunged at the cartel boss and plunged his knife into the side of his neck with all his remaining strength. He kept his entire body weight on top of the Gang Boss' writhing body. Bright red arterial blood gushed out like a geyser and sprayed all over John as the body underneath him continued to writhe around. The man grunted and gargled until going still a few moments later.

John waited a few moments and caught his breath. Finally, he rolled off of the dead man. He spent the next few moments in a daze. The minutes felt like hours, and he drifted in and out of consciousness. He was covered in blood, sweat, and tears. He began to think about all that had happened in the past few months. John's mind wandered, and he was jerked back to consciousness by the continued sporadic gunfire.

He was shaken awake by Dez, who was kneeling over him, bloody and battered herself. John's vision came into focus, and he saw the strong and beautiful woman over him. He turned his head to see his host of friends standing nearby. Andrew and Theo were standing to the east, still firing rounds over the cars into the distance.

The gunfire began to die down as Dez pulled John into a sitting position. John's rifle had been lost when he got tossed around in the explosion. As he looked around the immediate area for it, Dez gave him a small few slaps on the cheek as his eyes began to focus.

"Hey fucker, you still alive? We're still winning this, with or without you. Now get the fuck up!" She pulled him to his feet and handed him an AK-47 that was lying on the ground nearby. He found himself surrounded by the closest of his friends, all moving to and from cover, firing their weapons at the retreating gang members and bikers. They were making progress now, as they pushed the horde further south toward the river.

John looked to the left and right of him, seeing a mix of his militia and the National Guardsmen advancing together against the remaining of the horde's foot soldiers. They were now all actively retreating, with many outright turning their backs and running. He could see Colonel Lyon charging with his troops, still out front even though he was bloody and battered, his uniform and armor in near shreds. Carrying only a pistol, he was charging ahead of his troops and the militiamen. Lyon ordered the soldiers to keep shooting and gun all the enemies down, fleeing or not.

"No fucking surrender! Cut them down like the dogs they are!" Lyon screamed, firing his pistol and yelling at the top of his lungs. The rest of the crew from the Compound began to follow behind the advancing line, falling in amongst the mixed ragtag army. They chased the remaining fifty or so men to the banks of the Kankakee River. They caught up to the group, whose numbers were quickly dwindling as they were picked off little by little. They had them backed up to the banks of the river next to the Schuyler Bridge. They were surrounded, but many refused to give up, still shouting profanities and throwing potshots in their direction.

Eventually, they had nowhere else to go. Several of the remaining cartel members and bikers dropped their weapons and put their hands in the air. The Outlaw biker lieutenant was still holding his pistol. He refused to give up, saying, "You're going to have to fucking kill me. I'm not giving up to you, you piece of shit!"

Lyon walked up to the biker and glared at him, fire burning in his eyes. He glanced around at the other horde members, most of whom had tossed their weapons aside. Lyon whispered in his ear, "You were right to not give up. Your men are cowards and fools." Lyon raised his pistol to the biker's head and pulled the trigger. The shot rang out, and the blood and brain matter spewed all over the men close to the lieutenant. The horde members who had surrendered began to drop to their knees and a few began to cry.

Lyon grabbed the next closest man, a cartel foot soldier, who was crying and had urinated himself. The cartel foot soldier looked up at him and said, "You can't do this shit, esé. This is against the rules or some shit maaan!" Lyon punched him in the face and shouted to the remainder of the group, "Were you pieces of shit thinking about 'the rules' when you were raping the women and children, and killing all of the innocents on your path of destruction? It fucking stops here and now!" Lyon turned to the remainder of the militia and soldiers around and said, "Execute them all. Every man except one. Leave this one cartel prick alive to spread the word to Chicago. Kankakee is not to be fucked with. If they come here again, we will kill them all down to the last man, woman, or child they send. And if they do, we will go up there and burn their city to the ground!"

Lyon stepped away and had one of his men pull the cartel soldier to a nearby vehicle and push him in. The cartel soldier started the dirty old pickup truck and sped away as fast as he could, squealing the tires as it turned the corner back onto the main streets. Lyon gave the order, and his men and the militia soldiers opened up on the surrendering horde soldiers, killing them all along the banks of the river.

The Colonel wiped a bead of sweat and grime from his face and walked over to the group from the Compound. He reached out and shook his old friend's hand. "Johnny, I'm glad you were with me. And I couldn't have done it without you guys. Any other group, and none of us would have made it."

John nodded at the Colonel and gave him a big hug. He told his old friend, "Let's go home, buddy. Today is a win, and we finally have something we can be happy for."

The Colonel nodded, and they walked together back north toward downtown. They slowly regrouped, picking up stray pieces of weapons and discarded equipment lost in the battle as they went.

As they gathered their scattered personnel and equipment in the town square, Andrew and Theo came over with excited looks on their faces. They pulled John aside and said in low voices, "We found something...big. Something that might help us rebuild this town and secure our future." They took him to one of the cartel's SUVs. The rear hatch was popped open, and they gestured to a large, hard-plastic tuff box. John pulled open the lid of the box and found stacks of cash up to the top. The neat piles of hundreds, fifties, and twenties were still neatly wrapped with bands as though they had come from a bank.

"Holy shit...How much is there?" John said.

Andrew said, "Based on the number on the bands, rough count over half a million...And that's not even the best part."

John was busy exclaiming, "Half a million dollars?" softly to himself, while Andrew and Theo pulled out a smaller wooden chest that was behind the tuff box. They had already broken off the small padlock on the chest, but both grunted behind its weight. Andrew beamed as he opened the lid. The chest was filled with gold...lots of gold. Gold coins, gold bullion, and gold bars. There were also several stacks of silver coins and bars. "There has to be a couple hundred thousand dollars' worth of gold and silver in here too," Andrew said.

Theo added, "I think we just became the richest people in the entire state."

"That we know of..." John said. "Whoever had this to give, most likely has plenty more to spare. Best to keep this quiet. You two go put it in the back of the Tank and put a new lock on it. And don't tell anybody else! The only people that I trust to know about this will be the Compound members. Nobody else needs to know for now."

Theo and Andrew nodded in agreement, closed both containers, and dragged them out to stash away in their vehicle.

The group spent the next hour or so collecting their lost and discarded weapons and policing their equipment from the battleground. They also selfishly looted the vehicles that the cartel had come in. The buses and RVs that remained intact were still loaded with fuel, food, water, ammunition, and weapons. A few of the RVs were still running and in good condition, so John suggested, "We better claim these before they disappear into the wrong hands. To the victor goes the spoils, right?"

The others agreed. They had spent several thousand rounds of valuable ammo for their rifles and pistols in the battle and wanted to recoup their losses. The vehicles held nearly a hundred extra rifles, AK-47s, AR-15s, and thousands of rounds of ammo. The members of the Compound claimed these spoils quickly and quietly, not wanting to start a fight with any of the other groups over the valuable commodities.

Theo, Rob, Shonna, Old Sarge, and Hoover all consolidated this gear into the few functioning RVs and quickly removed them from the rest of the flaming wreckage. John told them to hurry back and move these vehicles back inside the inner gates of the empty lot next to the Compound.

Watching the members of the Compound leaving with some of the cartel vehicles, Lieutenant Hunter made his way over. His police vest was torn and bloody, but he still wore his dirty cowboy hat. He holstered his revolver and said, "Already looting the shit, huh, Gonzalez? You get all the good shit, as usual?"

John spun around and launched a punch with all his might, connecting squarely on Hunter's right cheek. Hunter fell back hard onto the ground, bleeding from the nose. John stood over him and said, "I've fucking HAD IT with you and your fucking mouth, Hunter. I kept you safe in my place, and all you've ever done is give me shit. You and your people didn't do a fucking thing when we first got hit, and it got Chuck killed. You didn't lift a fucking finger to help him and he's dead now. You're out. You've got one month to get your shit and get out of the Compound."

Lieutenant Hunter was taken aback and stuttered slightly as he slowly raised himself back to his feet. "What? What? What the hell?"

John cut him off. "Feel free to take whatever weapons and things you find on the ground and loot the vehicles they came in... But I'm not changing my mind, Hunter. Now get the fuck out of my face."

A few of Hunter's men came over and pulled Hunter to his feet and backed him away. This was a long time coming, and with the cartel threat seemingly gone, John was not in the mood to hide his feelings.

John made his way back over to the group gathered in the square. Dez looked at him, her eyes glowing but welling with tears. She gave him a short kiss on the cheek and grabbed his hand. "I'm glad you made it. I love you."

They walked hand in hand together back to the last few of the vehicles that were running. John grabbed her by the shoulders and told her, "I think it's finally done. At least. For now."

"This is the end of the road?" she said.

"Maybe for now," he replied, "although I'm not sure this peace lasts for long."

They heard an engine's roar and looked up into the sky. A large blue airplane flew overhead, the trails from its large wings visible streaking across the sky. They could see large white letters painted "UN" on its sides as the wings tipped. He started to stutter for words, but the words escaped him. Dez said, "If that's some kind of recon flight, we sure as hell drew a lot of attention our way. I doubt they could miss the explosions and a huge firefight from the air." They exchanged nervous looks, and he said, "Shit…That could either be a good sign…or a very bad thing."

THE END.

The heroes of "The Compound" will return again.

FROM THE AUTHOR:

I hope you enjoy my first work. If you enjoy, please share with a friend or family member. We are never alone. This book is dedicated to the men and women in uniform who fight for our country overseas, those who fight the forces of evil on our streets at home, those who fight the fires and keep our homes safe, and those who care for us in sickness and medical emergencies. To all our first responders, thank you always. This book is also for the "average joe" citizen. No matter who you are, you can also make a difference. The greatest strength of our country is all of our people.

I tried my best to keep this book apolitical. Share with your Liberal friends, your Conservative, Libertarian, or Independent friends. Regardless of your political beliefs, this story may be of some use to you. A government cannot always be relied on, but a strong individual citizenry is the strongest asset a country can have. Hold your friends and family close, treat your neighbors and communities with love and care, and keep what makes this country great together. Get involved, network, prepare, and survive.

ACKNOWLEDGEMENTS:

I'd like to take the time to thanks those of you who have encouraged me and made this possible, in no particular order, I'd like to thank:

My family: Mom and Dad, brothers Luke and Nick, and my large family (too many to name). I love you and thanks for your constant support.

Next, my literature-inclined prepper fiction editors/test readers: Kevin "Mitch" Mitchell, Brant "Andrew", and Steve Regas. Thank you for your encouragement, proofreading, editing, and ideas, and thank you for the sounding board of ideas I've been able to bounce off you.

I'd also like to thank those of you who were my friends and acquaintances who may or may not be portrayed or otherwise influenced in this book: Thanks to: the "Bros" (Steve, Kyle, Davis, and Hoover). Thanks to my favorite college roommates and Army buddies (a.k.a. the Wolfpack), Holden, Lyon, and Frazier. Thanks to my law enforcement friends, Theo, Brant, and all of the men and women serving your country in uniform, wearing the badge, and all other first responders.

ABOUT THE AUTHOR

Author BJ Garcia spent Eight years in a wide variety of Law Enforcement capacities, including Corrections, Patrol, and Investigations, having served as a Corrections Officer in a county Jail, A patrol Officer, Field Training Officer, Juvenile Officer, Officer in Charge, and Detective. During some of that time, he also spent five years as an infantryman in the Illinois Army National Guard. He now works in Corporate Business a manufacturing supervisor.

He continues to work in the private sector as a private security contractor throughout the Chicagoland area and has retained a part tine role in Law Enforcement.

When not working, he enjoys tactical training, shooting, cigars, and spending time with family.

Made in United States
North Haven, CT
24 March 2023

34490193R00163